D1278733

Written under Pen Name T.K. Welsh

Praise for *Resurrection Men*

Previously named a Junior Library Guild selection, *Publishers Weekly* called *Resurrection Men*, "A haunting tour of London's underclass during the 1830s . . . Teens will likely be both captivated by Victor's harrowing story as well as his ability to prevail in the face of harsh injustices." *VOYA* said, "Teen readers will thoroughly enjoy the hair-raising suspense in this historical thriller." *KLIATT* said, "Like M.T. Anderson's *The Astonishing Life of Octavian Nothing*, this look at sinister events in history makes the era come alive and lingers in the memory." And *School Library Journal* said, "Part historical fiction and part adventure story, the novel brings excitement to Victorian England . . . Readers will be on the edge of their seats."

Praise for *The Unresolved*

Ranked one of the Top Ten Children's Books by the *Washington Post*, THE UNRESOLVED was named an Association of Jewish Libraries *Notable Book for Teens* by the Sydney Taylor Book Award Committee, nominated for a Young Adult Library Services Association (YALSA) *Teen's Top Ten*, a *Cybils* literary award, and one of only a handful of books selected as a *Best Books for Young Adults* (BBYA), by the American Library Association (ALA). Most recently, the novel was added to *Horn Book*'s list of Recommended American Historical Fiction. *The Washington Post* said, "Welsh writes with a precision and delicacy unusual for YA fiction . . . a subtle gem (of a book)." In its starred review, *School Library Journal* said, "*The Unresolved* tells a remarkable story in a remarkable way." *Horn Book Magazine* called *The Unresolved*, "A decidedly unconventional ghost story . . . (and) a tightly wound novel." *Midwest Book Review* called the novel, "a wonderfully different kind of ghost story." And Bookslut.com said, "*The Unresolved* scores on several levels, most notably as a drama that blows apart all preconceived notions of how history can be retold."

Also by J.G. Sandom:

The Seed of Icarus (under pen name T.K. Welsh)
The Blue Men
Gospel Truths
The Hunting Club
The Publicist
The Unresolved (under pen name T.K. Welsh)
Resurrection Men (under pen name T.K. Welsh)
THE WAVE -- A John Decker Thriller
The God Machine

THE WAVE

A John Decker Thriller

J.G. Sandom

Published by:
CORNUCOPIA PRESS
Philadelphia

Printed in the United States of America
May 19, 2010

SECOND EDITION

ISBN: 1452839239
EAN-13: 978-1-452-83923-3

10 9 8 7 6 5 4 3

Acknowledgements

The following individuals not only provided me with assistance in the creation of this book, but they were – and remain – a great source of inspiration: my readers, Sylvana Joseph and James Wynbrandt; the journalist Juan Antonio Hervada, for his insights on the wars in Lebanon; Mark Douglas Thompson, whose technical expertise concerning computer systems remains unparalleled; Dr. James L. Olds, Director of the Krasnow Institute and fellow Amherst College graduate, for his broad-ranging scientific insights and knowledge of the Woods Hole Oceanographic Institute; Carl and Vanessa, in whose pool house much of *The Wave* was originally conceived and written; and my daughter, Olivia, for her patience and fortitude. To all these individuals, and to the countless others who have helped me on my way, I am forever grateful.

J. G. Sandom
May 2010

For Olivia,
who sweeps my heart away each day.

The gods visit the sins of the fathers upon the children.

EURIPIDES, *Phrixus* [fragment]

PROLOGUE

November 26 — 11:26 AM
Bimini, The Bahamas

Dr. James White had brought his wife to the Bahamas as soon as they had learned that she had cancer. Fifty-five yet spry, with short gray hair and sporting a navy one-piece bathing suit, Doris sat in a deck chair on the private beach reading yet another murder mystery. Dr. White watched her out of the corner of his eye and sighed. A great sorrow filled his heart but he only smiled when she turned and asked him, "Why don't you just get the hell out of here, James? You look bored to death."

"Not at all," he lied. He pretended to read the manuscript on his lap. It was a treatise on subduction written by one of his graduate students back at the Woods Hole Oceanographic Institute in Massachusetts. "I'm having a great time," he continued. "Want another iced tea?"

Doris scowled. "We've been married for twenty-three years, James. Don't you think I know when you're miserable? For God's sake, why don't you go for a swim? Take a walk. Hunt seashells. Go for a drive in that silly little Moke you rented. Do something! If I hear you sigh like that one more time I'm going to shoot myself before the crab gets me."

"That isn't funny, dear," he said. He dropped the manuscript on his lap.

"It wasn't meant to be." She reached out and took him by the hand. "Honestly, James. I'm fine here by myself. And if I need anything, I'll just ask Harvey." She glanced over at the muscular black man in a starched white uniform beside the swimming pool bar. "He's better looking than you ever were."

Dr. White laughed. Then he stood and stretched, looking at his wife the whole time. She was still beautiful, even after all these years. In a month or two she would be bald. After the chemotherapy. But she'd still be beautiful to him. He tried to smile, chiding himself for all the time he'd spent away from her on field trips, or lecturing at foreign universities and symposia. He'd been in the Canary Islands two months earlier, working on his book, when she had telephoned and told him to come home. They had found a lump under her left armpit. That had been the harbinger. The first sign of impending doom. The omen. "I think I'll take a drive then, head over into town," he said. "Do you want me to get you anything?"

She smiled and it occurred to him that it was this that had

made him fall in love with her, in graduate school, over twenty-five years earlier. Her smile was devastating. He could still feel his heart throb every time he saw it.

"Another bottle of rum would be nice," she said. "The dark one we had yesterday."

She was drinking like a fish, but there was little point in arguing. "Alright," he answered, as he slipped on his Hawaiian shirt and sandals. "I'll see you in an hour or so for lunch, back at the hotel. Save some lobster for me." With that he turned and trudged back up the beach.

It took him only a few minutes to dress in the bedroom of their bungalow overlooking the Atlantic. The hotel was expensive but he didn't care. Nothing mattered now but his wife's happiness and comfort. And she had grown up wealthy on Cape Cod. She was used to the finer things in life. He checked himself in the mirror – trying to ignore the distended belly, the balding head, the wrinkles around his eyes – and, with another sigh, dashed through the door.

The front seats of the Moke, a kind of open-air mini jeep, were baking hot. He started her up without a fuss and made his way along the white, shell-covered driveway of the hotel, out the main gate and into the palmary. He was glad now that he'd left Doris behind. Despite himself, her very presence made him depressed these days, and he felt guilty for a moment as he followed the twisting narrow road between the palm trees. It wasn't her fault she was sick, he told himself. Of course, the cigarettes hadn't helped; she'd been smoking since she was fifteen.

As he turned a bend and quit the palmary, the sun blasted down onto his neck and the entire east coast of the island opened up before him. It was an amazing view. The ocean glimmered to his right, gleamed and glistened, with a pale moon high in the turquoise sky. He pulled the Moke over onto the side of the road and got out.

Down the coast, he saw a chevron jutting from the water, like the naked backbone of some beached leviathan. The landscape was littered with boulders, bloated and huge, some over a thousand tons, ripped from the ocean floor and dumped unceremoniously onto the ground a hundred meters from the sea. One hundred and twenty thousand years ago, he thought. It must have been a frightful storm. Terrible in its ferocity. Relentless. As violent as the one that raged inside his heart.

He turned and stared across the shimmering Atlantic, far, far away, at the waves that crawled inexorably to shore, at the pale toenail of the crescent moon which dangled in the sky above him, the slightest paring, almost diaphanous. He knew what had launched the monumental forces that had carved these islands in the stream. It was the subject of his latest book. But despite his understanding, the sight of those great boulders and that distant chevron charged him with a sense of awe. And suddenly, from nowhere, he recalled the ending of a poem he had learned in college, years before – *Dover Beach*, by Mathew Arnold:

> Ah, love, let us be true
> To one another! for the world, which seems
> To lie before us like a land of dreams,
> So various, so beautiful, so new,
> Hath really neither joy, nor love, nor light,
> Nor certitude, nor peace, nor help for pain;
> And we are here as on a darkling plain
> Swept with confused alarms of struggle and flight,
> Where ignorant armies clash by night.

Dr. White stared across the glittering sea. Then he looked up at the sky, at the pitiless blueness of the firmament. "Dear God," he said. "What have I done?"

SECTION I

Masjid

Chapter 1
Thursday, January 6 – 4:38 PM
The Quad Cities, Iowa

John Decker, Jr., drove along I-74 in a non-descript tan van packed full of electronic equipment, across the bridge that spanned the Mississippi, from Illinois toward Bettendorf in the Quad Cities, Iowa. A Cryptanalyst Forensic Examiner with the FBI, Decker had been contacted two hours earlier and told to drive out – on the double – to a farm in the little town of New Liberty, Iowa, in order to intercept and decipher some communications. As he drove across the bridge, he stared down at the glassy Mississippi. The river moved lethargically below, wide-bellied and recalcitrant, studded with chunks of ice. It was a cold, gray day. The highway was still covered with smatterings of snow. He passed another semi carrying feed and realized that he hadn't been back to Iowa for almost fourteen months. A long time. Yet nothing had changed. Rock Island looked the same, despite the thinning of the military base. The bridge still needed painting. The river still rolled inexorably toward New Orleans. He pulled into the right lane, a dozen yards or so in front of the truck, and tried to tear his mind away. He should be happy, he told himself. It was rare he was called into the field; normally he was lashed to his desk. But he felt as though the frigid waters of the river were pulsing through his veins. Decker was going home.

As he drove along the highway, Decker tried to recall the details of the briefing he'd been given in Chicago two hours earlier. Ed McNally, leader of the local chapter of the White Apocalypse, his wife Mary, and his brother-in-law Peter Sampson were all holed up inside their ramshackle white clapboard farmhouse in New Liberty. So were the McNally's three children: Sarah, Rachael and Rebecca. Ed McNally had a long rap sheet, including arson, armed robbery and tax evasion. He and Peter Sampson had been stockpiling weapons at the McNally farm west of the Quad Cities for months. This, plus recent purchases of various chemical fertilizers that could be leveraged for bomb making, had brought the extended family to the attention of the FBI. But since both acts were legal, there was little the authorities could do.

Then, following a recent high school basketball game, Sarah McNally's boyfriend, Malcolm Burns, had gotten into a fight with the center from the predominantly African-American rival high school from Rock Island, Illinois – a kid named Evan Hudson. The facts were somewhat sketchy but witnesses later claimed that Burns had called Hudson a "nigger" in the parking lot outside the school after the game.

At first, Hudson had just ignored him. His parents were both Evangelical Christians and, summoning up a reservoir of self-restraint, he had tried to walk away. But Burns hadn't let it go. He had followed Hudson toward the bus the rival team was boarding and before the boy could get inside, had pushed him from behind, called him a "mud pussy," and kicked him when he slipped on the icy pavement to the ground. A fight ensued. Ironically, it wasn't even Hudson who responded to the assault. It was his fellow teammates. They streamed out of the bus and tore into Burns and his friends. The mêlée was brief but brutal. Several of the youths were badly injured, on both sides of the altercation. Then, just as it seemed to be winding down, Ed McNally pulled up outside the schoolyard in his battered gold Ford pickup.

McNally had come to pick up his daughter from the game. When he saw what was happening in the parking lot, saw his daughter Sarah in the midst of the thrashing arms and kicks and punches being thrown around her, he jumped out of his truck with a tire iron he kept under the front seat, and weighed into the crowd of teenagers.

It was just bad luck the coach from the rival team, a tall ex-Marine named Aaron Turner, happened to be black. He was in the midst of trying to pull the fighting boys apart when McNally struck him from behind. Turner went down, rolled, and then sprang back to his feet. He tried to reason with McNally but the man seemed absolutely deaf to his entreaties. So he had struck the farmer with a right cross that shook McNally to the core. If Turner had followed up right then, if he had taken the advantage, perhaps it would have ended at that moment. But the coach had simply raised his hands and said, "I don't want to hurt you, mister. Just take it easy."

The words only seemed to make McNally angrier. He side-stepped to the right, threw a jab and swung the tire iron at Coach Turner's head. Turner stepped back but he wasn't quite fast enough. The end of the tire iron caught him on the mouth and drove his head back with a loud *thwack*. Blood spurted from his face. Two teeth went flying. He raised his hands in self-defense but McNally swung the tire iron once again and brought it down on Turner's collarbone. It snapped like a Popsicle stick. Turner screamed as he collapsed. McNally kicked him in the face, and kept on kicking him until the combined weight of the boys from the rival high school finally managed to drag him from the bleeding man. McNally backed away. He shouted at his daughter Sarah to get back into the truck. Then he swung the tire iron threateningly at the crowd and laughed. "Fucking coons," he said. "You ain't worth my sweat." With that he turned and walked away. Everyone was in a state of shock. A few of the boys knelt down to help Coach Turner. The rest simply stared dumbfounded as McNally started up his pickup truck and drove nonchalantly out of the parking lot. He never even turned around.

The following day, at approximately 8:30 AM, two local New Liberty policemen – Sergeant Jim Crowley and Officer Alvin Cox – drove out to the McNally farm. They were there to serve McNally a warrant for assault but Mary McNally refused to let them in the farmhouse. Her husband and brother were not in, she claimed. They were in Moline, at a meeting. They wouldn't be home until late. Rather than force the issue, the local policemen decided to wait.

Eventually, about forty minutes later, McNally and Sampson were spotted driving along the country road back toward the farmhouse in McNally's battered gold Ford pickup. They slowed down when they saw the police cruiser outside the farm's main gate. But instead of pulling over when Sergeant Crowley tried to flag them down, they picked up speed and swung around a tractor lane, entering the property from the side. Then they jumped out and ran into the farmhouse, carrying what were later described as "suspicious-looking objects under their arms, possibly automatic weapons, wrapped loosely in plaid blankets."

Once again, the police approached the house, this time with their guns drawn. When they had come to within a hundred feet of the front porch, McNally appeared at the door with a shotgun in his arms. He asked them what they wanted, and they told him they were there to serve him with a warrant for his assault on Aaron Turner. McNally laughed. The police told him to put the shotgun down and, without a fuss, McNally complied. Then, as they drew closer to the house, a shot rang out from the window of the bedroom on the second floor. Sergeant Crowley went down, a bullet through his forehead. He was dead before he even hit the ground.

The second policeman, Officer Alvin Cox, retreated in a shower of bullets and barely made it back behind his car. He immediately put in a call for reinforcements. Within twenty minutes, another New Liberty police car, two state police cruisers, three local Eldridge and four Bettendorf police cars – including the Bettendorf Chief of Police, Paul "Popeye" Landry, and Sergeant Pat Higgins – had converged onto the scene. Two hours later, an FBI SWAT team had completely surrounded the farmhouse.

After three hours of fruitless negotiations, during which the police had begged McNally to send his children out from the farmhouse, they intercepted a call from McNally to a man named Jordan Fletcher, the Grand Master of the White Apocalypse, based in a small town twenty miles southwest of Sioux City. Fletcher had immediately reprimanded McNally for calling him, especially on a landline. He told him to call back on his cell phone and to use "the book." Then he hung up. The head of the FBI SWAT team, Don Morgan, had immediately called his office in Chicago and requested a device to pick up cell phone transmissions and a cryptanalyst. Within two hours, at approximately 4:20 PM, as the sun was beginning to set, John Decker Jr. left I-80 and drove up Rural Route 30 toward the McNally farm in New Liberty.

It was a strange kind of homecoming for Decker. The son of a local policeman, Decker had joined the Bettendorf Police Force himself soon after college in Chicago. But after only two years on the force, he applied to join the FBI and was accepted by the Academy in Quantico, Virginia. Following sixteen weeks of intensive training, and a stint with the Racketeering Records Analysis Unit in Washington, D.C., he had been transferred to the Bureau's office in Chicago where he worked within the Cryptanalysis Subunit, mostly on white collar crimes involving credit card fraud, money laundering, illegal gambling and a few drug cases. His superiors felt he didn't have the qualities required for a Special Agent. And besides, his abilities seemed better suited to a desk job.

As Decker approached the farmhouse, driving past the TV crews and news reporters crowded around the outer gate, Chief Landry ambled slowly down the muddy, snow-flecked road to greet him. Decker got out and they shook hands.

Just shy of six feet tall, a trifle thin but wiry, Decker had thick coal black hair, pale gray eyes dotted with blue and green specks, and the gentle features of a poet. Only a long white scar, barely visible below the hairline and sweeping along one eye, and a slight lopsidedness to his face, marred his demeanor. He had just turned thirty last December.

"It's good to see you again, John Junior," Landry said. "Happy new year."

"Happy new year, Popeye," he responded. "Sorry to hear about Crowley. He was a good cop." Popeye simply nodded. A minute later, Decker was surrounded by Alvin Cox, a dozen local New Liberty, Bettendorf, Davenport and Eldridge policemen, plus a handful of troopers from the Iowa State Patrol. Despite the somber mood, they joked with him about returning to the Quad Cities. "Look what the cat dragged in," said Sgt. Higgins. "Is this all the Bureau could spare?" Even two local state troopers, Dick and Harry Sloane – identical twins, like mirror images in their brown and light tan uniforms – swung by to say hello. It was clear they remembered Decker with fondness. Higgins handed him a steaming cup of coffee. Then Special Agent Don Morgan of the SWAT team briefed him on the situation. Within minutes, Decker was back in the surveillance van, listening to the conversation between McNally and Jordan Fletcher.

He fell into the cipher. It was always the same process, like one of those 3-D puzzles that looked like some kind of Impressionistic painting until you relaxed your eyes, stared beyond the image, and it suddenly shifted into place. His old sensei, Master Yamaguchi, had called it "Reclining in Chaos." There was no other way to describe it. Decker had possessed this skill for as long as he could remember. It was like a good ear for music, or the ability to run fast. He simply had a way with numbers and symbols, a gift for finding patterns in seemingly random data.

He took a deep breath and began, as always, with a substitution cipher, replacing true letters or numbers – plain text – with alternate characters – cipher text. He looked for patterns, series and common combinations. Nothing. Since the cipher McNally used was numeric, Decker dismissed traditional Caesar and keyword number ciphers off the bat. On the other hand, he thought, it might have been a telephone keypad cipher. But since McNally was using two-digit numbers – some of which were greater than twenty-six – he set aside this protocol as well.

It took him only a few seconds to flick through each of these contenders. After his training, and based on his innate skills, he was able to dismiss unlikely ciphers and codes virtually immediately. Also, having been brought up by his Aunt Betsy, a devout Catholic, and her husband Tom, an equally devout Episcopalian, and after his briefing on the White Apocalypse earlier, Decker believed "the book" which Fletcher had referred to in his phone call was the Bible.

In the end, Decker broke McNally's cipher in less than sixty seconds. It turned out to be a simple book code: chapter and verse, followed by a third number specifying the word in the verse McNally wanted to use in the construction of his sentences. And he discovered it just in time; the suspects were planning to make a break for it from the farmhouse through some kind of tunnel.

Decker jumped out of the van and started to make his way back toward the farmhouse, completely surrounded now by local and state police, plus the FBI SWAT team that had taken up positions with snipers around the property. As he approached, he noticed Troopers Dick and Harry Sloane – the identical twins – standing outside the main fence of the property, drinking coffee, breath steaming from their mouths. It had grown even colder in the last few minutes. The setting sun lingered in the trees across the vacant snow-flecked corn fields. A raised eyebrow of geese sliced the sky. That's when he saw the head of Peter Sampson poke out from the drainage ditch that ran along the fence line of the property, behind that clump of holly bushes, their berries livid crimson, buckshot of blood, frozen in time. He could barely make Sampson out in the blaze of spotlights the police had set up facing the house. He was only a dozen yards away from the two state troopers.

Decker ran forward. He was about to call out to the Sloane brothers when he noticed Sampson was carrying a hunting rifle. Mary McNally was right behind him, followed by the three children. He watched as Sampson crawled up out of the ditch and aimed his gun at Harry Sloane.

Without even thinking, Decker leapt into the ditch. He wrestled the rifle from Sampson's hands. Sampson was a large man, well over six feet tall, and built like a defensive guard. He swung at Decker, who danced out of the way at the last moment. Then Sampson reached for another weapon, a .357 magnum stuffed behind his belt. He drew the gun but Decker was much too fast. He jabbed his left palm up under the large man's nose, sending his head back, and shot a spear thrust deep into the jugular notch beneath his exposed chin. Sampson went down. His windpipe had collapsed, sending shards of cartilage into his throat. Within seconds he had choked to death and lay still. Mary McNally screamed and the Sloane brothers finally turned and noticed the struggle in the ditch. They ran over, their weapons drawn. Minutes later, Ed McNally crawled out of the tunnel – smoking now with tear gas – directly into the arms of the police. The stand-off was over. McNally was handcuffed and led away.

Decker was called out as a hero for saving the lives of the two Sloane brothers. But he felt badly shaken by the incident. As his old friends patted him on the back, he tried to pull away, and finally told them with a crippled smile, "Thanks but . . . too much coffee. I have to take a leak." He walked back toward the van, stepped behind it nonchalantly, bent over and threw up.

He had never killed anyone before. He hadn't been in a fight in years. He spat, wiped his mouth, and straightened up. The feeling was overwhelming. He didn't know where to put it.

Three hours later, Decker pulled up to the house of his Aunt Betsy and her husband, Tom Llewellyn, who ran a local hardware store in Davenport. They were expecting him; Betsy had been following the story of the McNally stand-off on the TV all day.

Tom ran out to greet Decker on the porch. Short and stocky, with thin gray hair combed adroitly across his shiny head, Tom wore a scarlet apron over his yellow sweater and polyester mud-brown pants. They entered the house and were immediately assaulted by the smell of home-made biscuits and roast chicken wafting from the kitchen. It was Decker's favorite meal. Tom always made it for him whenever he came home for a visit. His Aunt Betsy got up from her easy chair, dragging herself from CNN.

Thin and tall, with a handsome wrinkled face set off by snow-white hair, Aunt Betsy had the ice-blue eyes of all the Carricks. They exchanged a polite hello. "It's good to see you," she said flatly. "Happy new year, John." Despite herself, his aunt seemed genuinely relieved. They had never gotten along. Aunt Betsy had always been jealous of her sister, Decker's mother, and when both his parents had been killed, she had only reluctantly agreed to take her nephew in. Indeed, it had been Tom, her husband, who had finally pushed her to "do the Christian thing." Tom told Decker to wash up. They were going to be eating right away. The capon had been ready for an hour.

Decker went upstairs. The bathroom was at the head of the landing. He washed his hands and face, studying himself in the mirror as he dried himself off. Nothing seemed to have changed. He looked exactly like he had that morning. As he replaced the light blue hand towel and stepped out into the hall, he noticed that his old bedroom door was open, slightly ajar. He walked over and looked in.

His room hadn't changed either: the same pictures of airplanes from World War II; the same poster of Flags from Around the World; the same long distance running and martial arts trophies; the same photographs even. He stepped cautiously within. On his old desk, next to his books on Secret Codes and Differential Calculus and Hieroglyphics and The Mystery of The Labyrinth of Chartres Cathedral, there was a photograph of his parents in a walnut frame. He picked it up.

His mother, Louise Carrick, and father, John Decker Sr., were standing on the porch of their old house in Bettendorf. His father was in his uniform, one arm wrapped casually around his mother's waist. He was a small man but solidly built, with dark brown eyes and thick black hair; not unlike his own father who had once worked in the factories of north England before coming to America and settling in the farm country of eastern Iowa. His mother was almost as tall, thin and pale-skinned. She had light brown hair, tinged with red, revealing her own Irish roots. Decker could just make out the freckles on her nose. There were seventeen of them. He had scored them countless times as a child as he'd reclined against her, his head tucked safely in her lap. Before the accident. Before that drunken driver had come crashing through the night, into the other lane, and hit their old Chevy Biscayne head on as they were driving back from picking up John Jr. at a track meet in Moline. Both of his parents had died on the side of the road that night, next to that other driver. Somehow, miraculously, Decker had survived. And, after almost two months in a coma, and a year and a half in physical therapy, despite all the doctors' predictions, he had not only walked again, but run, become a Black Belt in Kung Fu at seventeen. He had thrived. At least physically.

"John?" he heard Tom call up from the first floor. "John Junior, the chicken's getting dry. Aren't you hungry?"

Decker returned the photograph to his desk. He took a final look around the room. "I'm starving," he shouted back, ducking through the door. And, strangely enough, he was.

Chapter 2
Friday, January 28 – 2:33 AM
Tel Aviv, Israel

The man stood on the balcony overlooking the tranquil sea. He held something in his arms, wrapped loosely in a carpet. Then, with a quick twist, he dropped the object from the balcony. The carpet unrolled and a woman's naked body unfurled and tumbled downward. The body landed on top of a parked car, a light blue Fiat, crushing the roof with a mighty crash, exploding the windshield. The car alarm began to wail.

Only a few feet distant, an old man walking his dog jumped back, looked up and spotted the figure on the balcony above. He immediately reached into his coat pocket, whipped out his cell phone, and punched 100 for the police.

* * *

Benjamin Seiden slept like a child. Even in repose, it was obvious he was incredibly fit, a testament to his daily workouts and ascetic diet. A handsome man, just turned forty-four, he had a wide uncompromising chin, full lips, a regal if unbalanced nose, and hair of the deepest chocolate, only recently beginning to gray along the temples.

The alarm clock rang and Seiden found himself sitting up in bed. It was 5:30 AM. Beside him, his wife Dara stirred and, with a sigh, rolled over.

Seiden slipped from the bed and padded like a cat into the bathroom. He took a cold shower, as he did each morning, letting the frigid pinpricks rinse the slumber from his skin. Within twenty minutes, he was fully dressed, wearing a pair of cotton khakis, hand-ironed the night before; a pressed white shirt; a tan Egyptian cotton tie; a pair of sturdy English walking shoes, light brown; and a brushed suede cinnamon-colored yarmulke.

Seiden made his way along the hallway. As he passed the first door on his left, he paused and poked his head in, and stared at his two daughters, Rachael and Ruth, in their beds. Ruth, the eldest at six, lay lengthways across the width of the mattress, one hand dangling down, pointing at the floor. And Rachael, his four-year-old, slept in her standard kneeling position, bottom in the air, and her little arms curled underneath her chest. Seiden wondered how she could possible find the position comfortable. She looked like a contortionist.

He stepped into the room and shook his children gently. "Time to get up, sleepyheads," he said. They moaned and came to life. "And I want you dressed and ready in ten minutes. No dilly-dallying in the bathroom." He looked pointedly at Rachael.

Seiden marched them both into the bathroom, grumbling and dragging stuffed animals. "Ten minutes," he repeated. "Ruth, help your sister with her pajamas." He hesitated for a moment longer, and then made his way back through the hallway to the kitchen.

It looked like it was going to be another beautiful day. From the kitchen, across the breakfast bar and tidy living room, he could see the open, turquoise waters of the Mediterranean shimmering beyond the sea walls. Seiden slipped an apron on and started making breakfast. The girls liked their scrambled eggs made with real milk, slightly overdone. Seiden favored yogurt and fresh honey. And Dara – she couldn't move without her Turkish coffee. A family of individualists. The New Israel. He fussed about the tiny kitchen, working efficiently, when his wife appeared at the head of the hallway wearing a light pink cotton T-shirt and a pair of boxer shorts. "Good morning," he said. "How'd you sleep?"

Dara didn't actually respond. She uttered a kind of anthropoid grunt, scratched her head, and shuffled slowly into the room. Then she yawned, and he could see her teeth flash for a moment before her thick hair fell about her face, dark as a widow's veil. "M'n'in'," she finally ushered up, squeezing a yawn.

Just then the phone rang. Dara straightened reflexively and looked up at her husband. "Don't forget you're taking the girls to school today," she said. "I have a conference at the Women's Center. You promised."

Seiden didn't respond. He simply stared at the bright red wall phone as it continued to ring, again and again.

"Aren't you going to get it?" Dara asked.

A phone call at this hour was never pleasant news. With a sigh, he picked up the receiver. "Seiden," he said.

It was Captain Hymie Rubenstein of the Tel Aviv Police. "Sorry to disturb you at this hour," he said. "Sir, I've tripped a flare."

Seiden scratched at his chin. Hymie was seldom nervous. "It's alright, Captain. Where are you?"

Captain Rubenstein gave him the address. Seiden wrote it down on a pad of paper on the kitchen counter. Dara continued to stare at him. She stood with her hip out, arms akimbo, frowning. She waited. "I'll be right there," he said, and hung up the receiver. Then he took the apron off. He walked back toward his study past his wife, unlocked his desk with the little key he kept in his pocket at all times, and pulled out his Jericho 941PS and holster. The handgun smelled of oil and polished leather. He slung it casually across his back and shoulder. He slipped on the light brown jacket which hung from his chair, and made his way back out into the hall.

Dara was standing in the kitchen. She held a cup of coffee in her hand. As he entered the living room, he turned and looked at her and shrugged a little shrug and said, "I'm sorry, Dara."

"Is it bad?" she asked, looking down at something on the floor. It was a piece of plastic, a tiny bright red Lego block. She bent down and picked it up.

"Don't know yet," he replied. Then he kissed her gently on the forehead. At six feet two inches, Seiden towered over his wife. He pressed her sleepy face between his hands. "But it's never good, is it?"

It took Seiden only thirty-five minutes to make his way to the little row of apartment buildings on the north side of Tel Aviv. At this hour, the traffic that normally snarled the seaside city streets during the day was blissfully absent. Seiden pulled up beside the building. It was a six-story white affair, typical of the apartment blocks erected north of the city over the last ten years. Anonymous and neuter. A soulless structure. The architect had designed the building so that white blocks of fossil-encrusted sandstone poked out at intermittent levels from the façade beside the balconies. While the design did something to break up the otherwise bland surface, it also afforded anyone the opportunity to scale the building quickly and efficiently. He noticed bars on many of the sliding doors leading out onto the balconies. Some enterprising tenants had even mounted razor wire on their railings, fencing off the stone protrusions.

Three policemen stood at the foot of the front steps, smoking cigarettes. They talked and laughed, ignoring the naked woman splayed out across the roof of the crumpled light blue Fiat only a meter or two away. Despite the fall, Seiden noticed, the body looked strangely intact. Her arms hung over the windshield and he could clearly see that both of her wrists were slashed. Like a suicide.

The three policemen spotted Seiden and stepped up to block his path. He flashed his identity card. The policeman closest to him gave it a cursory glance, then suddenly stepped back, dropped his cigarette to the ground, and issued a sharp salute.

Seiden saluted back. "Is Captain Rubenstein inside?"

"Apartment 2 B. Yes, sir."

Seiden stared at the policeman with a level gaze. Then he glanced down at the cigarette still burning at his feet. "As you were."

Seiden mounted the steps. As soon as he had disappeared into the lobby, the young lieutenant turned to his fellow cops and mouthed the word, "Mossad."

Seiden took the stairs instead of the elevator. He didn't like elevators. He'd always considered them a waste of electricity. Seiden couldn't understand why people invariably took the elevator even when they were only going up one flight or two. And then they paid outrageous sums to join a health club or a gym. It made no sense. He was a man who disliked tall buildings, not from vertigo or fear of fire. He simply preferred things in human dimensions.

Captain Rubenstein was waiting outside apartment 2 B. The lieutenant downstairs must have alerted him to his arrival, Seiden thought, because he stood there poised and ready. Seiden shook the Captain's hand. Rubenstein looked pale and ill at ease. His fingers were moist. Seiden had never seen him so distraught.

"Acting Chief Seiden," the Captain said, and Seiden noticed how Rubenstein found solace in the salutation. Titles were settling things. They showed you where you stood. They rooted you.

"I'm sorry I had to bother you at this hour . . ."

Seiden waved a hand and the Captain opened the door to the apartment. They were immediately assaulted by the acrid smell of smoke. Rubenstein moved ahead of him to lead the way.

Policemen and members of the Israeli Defense Forces (IDF) crowded the living room. Near the sliding glass door that opened onto the balcony, Seiden spotted a dead, middle-aged bald man tied to a chair with his back to him. Beside him, kneeling on the floor, his hands handcuffed behind him, was a skinny Arab. He was dressed in traditional Arab garb, with a grey *aba*, and the red and white *keffiyeh* headdress of the Palestinian. Two soldiers stood above the suspect, their automatic weapons trained on the back of his head.

Two young boys, no more than ten or eleven, were lashed

to another pair of chairs, perpendicular to the dead man by the windows. Seiden could see strange cuts, in the shape of Arabic script, slashed into their skin. They both appeared to be naked. It was difficult to tell. Their bodies were ribbed with glassy burn marks, gunpowder black.

Seiden turned toward Rubenstein and said, "Please have the room cleared, Captain." Then he reached into his jacket pocket and pulled out a pair of off-white latex gloves.

Rubenstein issued the order, and the soldiers and policemen filed out one by one without a word. Seiden walked over to where the Arab was kneeling on the floor. The suspect didn't look at him. He didn't even look up. He simply knelt there, facing the floor, as if in prayer. Seiden slipped on the latex gloves.

All of the victims were lined up in a row, with the middle-aged man facing the sea, and the children at right angles to him. A bloody carpet lay on the floor by the glass door leading to the balcony. Seiden approached the bodies of the boys. He touched the forehead of the nearest victim, tilting the head back. It lolled over to the side. No rigor mortis, he thought. He peered into the open mouth. The face was practically warm. He leaned over, taking a closer look at the wounds on the boy's chest and stomach: carved Arabic script; and some kind of foliation, burned into the flesh. It appeared as if each of the victims had been tortured and then set ablaze with some kind of combustible material. Probably magnesium ribbon, Seiden thought, remembering a high school science class from years before, when he had set a magnesium strip on fire, acetylene bright, spitting and smoking like a sparkler. Around their arms. Around their necks and thighs.

Captain Rubenstein was calling him. "I think you'd better take a look at this." He pointed toward a video camera set up on a tripod in a corner of the room. "He taped the entire . . . thing," he added, faltering. "Shall I play it for you?" Rubenstein rewound the tape. It was one of those Japanese models with a mini-screen that popped out to the side. It whirred like a toy.

"Not now," said Seiden. "Later. I think I can see what happened." He turned toward the sliding door. "The suspect scaled the façade of the apartment building and climbed up over the balcony. The curtains were probably drawn at the time and they didn't see him until he was in the room. By then, of course, it was too late."

Seiden walked over toward the balcony and gazed down through the sliding door at the street below, the stores and small apartment buildings just across the way, the tranquil sea . . . the naked woman lying on the broken light blue Fiat. Without turning, he added, "He probably threatened to kill the children, the two boys, unless she killed herself, sacrificed her own life for theirs." His voice was slow and steady, emotionless. "Eventually she agreed, and slit her own wrists." He turned and looked at the immolated figures in the chairs. "Then he stripped the children of their clothes and lashed them to the chairs. Once their ankles and wrists were secured, he used what appears to have been a long, sharp knife or razor blade, flaying the skin on their backs into those tiny curved strips." He shook his head. "Although he was faced the other way, I'm sure the father knew exactly what was happening to his children. Then the suspect pulled out a roll of metal ribbon and trussed the bodies up in silver coils – first the boys, and then the man – wrapping them up like . . . like presents at Hanukkah. He set them on fire, while they were still alive. You can see that from the soot in their throats. They were still breathing when their skin began to burn."

Seiden paused for a moment. "Then he took the body of the woman – wrapped in that carpet over there – and tossed her from the balcony onto the car below." He looked over at Rubenstein. He smiled a flat thin smile. "Well," he added, "am I right?"

Rubenstein nodded. He closed the side of the video camera, removed it from its tripod, and dropped it into a large clear plastic bag. "I'm sure you know what this means," he said.

Seiden walked over to the man lashed to the chair by the sliding door. Sheer white cotton curtains wafted around his body like the wings of an angel, a shroud newly thrown. They shivered on the breeze. The dead man's face looked tattooed, a mask of petrified terror. His brown eyes bulged as if the magnesium ribbon – which had been wrapped, again and again, around his neck – had constricted slowly as it burned, strangling him with fire. He had bitten his tongue off at the tip. It hung like some organic growth from his lower lip. His entire body was covered with burns, bright black, like the carapace of some gigantic beetle.

"Call in the forensics team," said Seiden. "And have the IDF take the suspect to police headquarters. I'll have a car pick him up from there."

"It's him, isn't it?" Rubenstein continued. "Isn't it, sir?" His voice was filled with awe. "Who else would . . . " He could not finish. He pointed at the boys. "This is his trademark, isn't it? This kind of writing with fire. I thought he was dead. That's what I heard. Killed by a rocket strike in Lebanon three years ago."

"Call your men please, Captain."

Rubenstein stepped forward and yanked the Arab to his feet. He was still praying. He was still mumbling underneath his breath as the soldiers returned and ushered him away.

Seiden pulled off his latex gloves, wiped his hands across his trouser legs, and glanced down at his watch. His daughters were probably on their way to school by now. Dara would be driving them, along the open and defenseless roadways of the city. And, at home, the blankets and sheets would still be warm from their small bodies, would still retain the memory of dreams.

Seiden looked over at Captain Rubenstein who hovered expectantly by the hallway. Seiden knew only too well what this trademark torture meant. The thin, rather nondescript Arab in custody was the infamous El Aqrab, one of Israel's most wanted terrorists, responsible for dozens of bombings, thousands of innocent deaths, affiliated with both Hamas and Hezbollah, leader of the Brotherhood of the Crimson Scimitar, with shadowy ties all across the Middle East and Europe, and beyond.

"He didn't even try to run," said Captain Rubenstein. "He was waiting when my men arrived, in the center of the room, just waiting like that, on his knees. It doesn't make sense, sir. Why throw her body from the balcony, alert the world? It's like he wanted to be caught. As if he's given up."

Seiden glanced once more at the two boys in the chairs, their anguished immolated faces, the script tattooed across their flesh. "No, Captain. I'm afraid he's only just begun."

Chapter 3
Friday, January 28 – 1:06 AM
La Palma, The Canary Islands

Giles Pickings pulled at the cord above him and turned on the naked light bulb overhead. Then, with a sigh, he shuffled down the narrow wooden staircase and began to rummage around in his storm cellar. After a few minutes, he found the box that he was looking for. He opened it and there it was. He pulled out the wine-colored blanket, draped it across one arm, and patted it lovingly. It had belonged to his wife, Layla. The blanket had covered up a thousand memories along the years, and they all came spilling out now as he pushed the material to his face. He could still smell her. Pickings spun about and rushed back up the stairs.

The cellar door opened up onto the side of the house overlooking the Atlantic. It was a cool and windy night on the island of La Palma. The stars glared down through inky clouds, behind the sloping shoulders of the Cumbre Vieja ridge just to the south, illuminated by a crescent moon. No wonder astronomers from all over the globe had set up domed observatories on the top of the Caldera de Taburiente National Parque, 2,400 meters above sea level. Pickings staggered around the house, buffeted by the wind that swept across the Canary Islands chain, and made his way inside.

At the center of the living room stood a Sound Leisure Beatles jukebox, half buried in a crate. Pickings draped the blanket over the veneered marine ply cabinet, the polycarbonate tube pillers, the plastic periscopes, the cartoon figurines – John, Paul, and George, and Ringo, inside their Yellow Submarine. He had purchased the jukebox in Leeds, back in the '70s. Surely, I have time for just one more, he thought. He plugged it in, turned on the jukebox, and made a selection. *Help* began to play. Listening to the music for the last time, Pickings was sad to see it go. But hard times had driven him to sell off most of his belongings. He hadn't had a choice. The Sound Leisure had fetched almost five thousand pounds. Besides, he was better off without it. The jukebox was a memory machine.

Pickings was a retired Housemaster from Wyckham College, an English boarding school in Winchester, Hampshire, England. He was fifty-six years old, with a heart-shaped face, thin gray hair and gold wire-rimmed glasses that constantly descended down his pudgy nose. An expert in Papal history, he'd been married to Layla Pickings for almost thirty years, before she had disappeared one day, never to return. Layla was Lebanese; they'd met years before in Beirut, while he was doing research on a book about the Crusades. He used to travel quite a lot in those days, going from school to school across Europe to teach, like some ancient troubadour. But now all that was finished. Pickings stumbled about the house, listening to the music. The house had once belonged to his great aunt, Jane Chilvers, who had recently passed away and left him this property between the towns of Buena Alta and Tigalate, plus a modest inheritance.

Layla had vanished before, of course. In fact, it had been a regular feature of their marriage. Every four months or so, she would simply disappear for a few days. At first Pickings had thought she'd taken a lover, but when he confronted her, she denied it. "Sometimes," she said, "I just need to be alone. It isn't about you. But with the children and your work, sometimes I need some time for me, just for myself. To be alone. To just be me." And, for some strange reason, he had believed her. He had wanted to believe her. And she'd always returned, revitalized, almost rejuvenated.

One time, at the beginning of their marriage, he had tried to follow her, but she'd spotted him with ease and they'd had a terrible row. "You have to trust me," she had said. "If you love me, just let me be." So he had given up his sleuthing. It was only for a few days anyway, at most a week, and, after a while, he found himself enjoying her departures. It gave him time to be alone as well, to work, to bond with their two children. And she always came back. Until the last time, anyway.

After a fortnight of worrying, he finally called the police. They made a half-baked effort to locate her, to no avail. Pickings ran advertisements in the local papers and in the *London Times*. He even issued a reward. But the months rolled by without a word. Layla had simply vanished. Then, a new nightmare began. The police, frustrated by the disappearance, began to ask him questions that could only be interpreted one way: They thought *he* was responsible, that *he* had murdered his own wife, and then buried her somewhere. For weeks, they kept him under surveillance. He would leave the College House and see them parked across the street. He would see them after class, or in town when he went shopping. They kept bringing him down for questioning. They grilled him for hours and hours, to no avail. He was innocent, after all, and – in the end – they'd been forced to let him go. His alibis were immaculate. He had never run afoul of the law, never been violent, never argued with Layla in public. And they could see he was an exemplary father.

Pickings winced as he remembered. It was the children who had suffered most of all. They could not understand how their mother could simply leave like that. Pickings had always made up excuses about her previous disappearances: She was visiting her sister in Paris; or friends in London; or her extensive family in Beirut. And they'd never doubted him. In the end, the mere uncertainty of it, the fact that they knew nothing, had worn the family down. They began to blame themselves. They wracked their brains trying to imagine what they'd done wrong, or what they'd said to drive her off. But, for the life of them, they could not remember anything. Even after all this time, he still couldn't.

Pickings took a walk on the verandah, wondering how he had left all that behind: the inquisitive police; the nosy neighbors; his insufferably pitying relatives; even his children. They were old enough to take care of themselves now and, despite his love for them, he found it difficult to be around them. They reminded him too much of Layla.

He sighed. Now, at last, he was untouchable, alone and safe, with the solitude he required to tend his flower garden and finish his book on Pope Pius II. Nothing ever happened on La Palma. They were in the middle of nowhere. The entire island only had eighty thousand inhabitants, and the house was nestled high along the central ridge, within a stand of tall Canary pine and tree-heather, a good way from the nearest town, and a little too close to the still-active Cumbre Vieja to entice most visitors. It had been weeks since he'd seen anyone – months, really – other than his housekeeper, Rosa. Only the occasional hiker traversing the Ruta de Los Volcanes, or some scientist studying the proximate Cumbre Vieja broke up the monotony. Like that Dr. White who had stumbled by three months before with his Jordanian friend, Dr. Hamal, the one who had heard of his dead wife's work with Palestinian relief organizations. But even they had quit the island. Dr. White's wife had fallen ill; he'd been forced to return to America in a hurry. And Dr. Hamal had left soon after. Pickings remembered the wonderful dinner they'd had in Fuencaliente, how they had come back to the house, and Dr. Hamal had played the jukebox all night long and told him how he could find a buyer on the Internet.

  Help wound down inside. Pickings looked down at the stormy sea below, the thrashing waves, the flash of moonlight on the water. For a moment he thought he saw something on the distant rocks, something moving. But it was only his imagination.

Chapter 4
Thursday, January 27 – 6:30 PM
Woods Hole, Massachusetts

Emily Swenson stood on the stage within the darkened auditorium, gilded by the halo of a lectern light. First-year students from the Woods Hole Oceanographic Institute packed the auditorium, kids who had yet to settle on a specialty. She could hear them coughing and fidgeting about in the dark. Swenson's lectures were always well attended. She was famous in certain academic circles for her presentations, their drama, her state-of-the-art graphics and California good looks. Someone had once posted a snapshot of her on the Internet – sunbathing topless on a sun-drenched beach, with a backdrop of palm trees and the glittering sea – and she would never live it down. She still got fan mail from deranged admirers whom she had never met. They forgot she came from South Dakota.

It was strange to be back in Massachusetts, to see such scenes of normalcy after all that grizzly devastation in Sri Lanka. Swenson ran through her presentation with precision, describing the events leading up to, during, and after the tsunami. It all seemed so unreal now. The slides helped to bracket the memories, to frame each experience in light and – perhaps more importantly – to block out the unwanted. She no longer smelled the distinctive stench of rotting human flesh when she awoke each morning.

"It was the morning of December Twenty-sixth," she began. "A month ago, almost to the day. The 'Queen of the Sea' train had left Colombo – Sri Lanka's capital – two minutes late, and had just pulled up at the tiny station of Telwatte just shy of 9:30 AM. The platform and cars were jammed with passengers, over a thousand, since December Twenty-sixth was a 'full moon day' – a local Buddhist holiday. Telwatte is generally a momentary stop. The conductor was waiting for the signal to turn green but – due to reports of water on the tracks down the coast – the signal never changed. This was the only harbinger of what was soon to come. Everything seemed ordinary. But deep beneath the earth," she added, "two and a half hours earlier and over a thousand miles away off the coast of Sumatra, enormous forces had strained the underlying rock. In the space of minutes, this pent-up energy was released as a 9.0 magnitude earthquake along a subduction zone in which the India plate is being thrust beneath the Burma plate. A section of the seafloor lurched upwards – as much as fifteen feet, in some places – lifting the normally flat sea surface in response.

"One of the passengers – a man named Vidu, who lost his leg in the ensuing tsunami – later described what happened on that fateful day."

She displayed a slide of Vidu. He lay in a hospital bed. His stump was wrapped with bandages. His right arm in a sling. His face was bruised and battered, lined with cuts.

"As the train idled at the station," she said, "Vidu heard a rumble, like that of a low-flying jet. A few minutes later, he saw a wall of water rushing toward the train, like a huge river. After the first wave hit, instead of climbing off the train, the water drew more people to the cars, including those who had been waiting on the platform. The water was waist high and the train seemed solid. People scrambled aboard, some handing their children up to the passengers hanging out the windows. Others climbed up onto the roofs of the various cars. For some reason, Vidu decided to leave the train; to this day, he can't say why. He picked up his two young daughters and carried them to a slab of concrete over a nearby latrine. Ten minutes or so after the first wave struck, he watched in horror as a second wave – more like a swell – rushed in from the sea and inundated the station and the train. The train, including the eighty-ton engine, was hit with such force that it was bulldozed off the tracks. The cars twisted and turned, filling with water. And Vidu and his two daughters were swept away into a nearby swamp. There, he hung in the trees, unconscious. When he awoke, he had already been attacked by saltwater crocodiles. His right leg had been ripped off just below the knee. His two daughters – six and nine years old – were nowhere to be seen. Indeed, no trace of them was ever found."

She displayed a photograph of Vidu trapped in the branches, flesh hanging in strips from his pulverized knee, crabs nibbling, the bloodstained crocodiles beneath. The audience gasped.

"He was bleeding profusely," she continued, "but he was too exhausted to move. He could barely look around. Other bodies were crucified all about him. Body parts dangled from the trees, like overripe fruit. Crabs and ravens and crocodiles crept through the underbrush, feasting on human flesh. Then he fainted once again. Were it not for the arrival of a rescue party, he would have died on the spot.

"Other villagers were not so lucky," she continued. Swenson displayed a quick series of slides of the station where the tsunami had struck the train. The first revealed the village prior to the earthquake. People were standing about beside the rust-red cars. They were smiling. They were waving. The small village of Telwatte was clearly visible nearby. It was a bright and sunny day.

The next photograph was taken from exactly the same spot, the same angle even, although – at first – it was difficult to tell. In this slide, the station of Telwatte had been obliterated. Little remained. And the railroad cars lay twisted and scattered about in great heaps.

"Like Vidu," she continued, "some of the passengers and local villagers were swept across the jungle. Many were battered to death by debris. The trees were bejeweled with sheets of corrugated iron." A series of three slides displayed the coastline. Trees were flattened, as if by a nuclear explosion.

"At least sixty people lost limbs to gangrene, or to the feral dogs and crocodiles that descended on the helpless victims. It was difficult to arrive at an accurate death count, but at least one thousand of the train passengers were killed. Less than one hundred survived. A total of six waves struck the train and village – one, as high as twenty feet. Of the few local inhabitants who knew about tsunamis, most found themselves incapable of fleeing from the coast. There was simply no place to go."

The lights in the auditorium grew brighter. Swenson could see the faces of the students clearly now. They looked horrified. Good, she thought. Most scribbled furiously in their notebooks. The scraping of pencils and pens, the chatter of keyboards: These were the most satisfying of sounds, for they marked the capture of her audience. Her tactics were working. While she hated to exploit the suffering of Vidu and the other villagers whom she had come to know and love, she realized it was necessary. She needed these students to *feel* if they were going to respond. Her discipline was desperate for additional researchers, for scientists who might one day prevent another tragedy like this one from ever happening again.

A spotlight shone upon her head and Swenson took a breath. "To understand tsunamis," she continued, "you must first distinguish them from wind-generated waves or tides. Breezes blowing across the ocean crinkle the surface into relatively short waves that create currents restricted to a rather shallow layer. While gales, hurricanes and typhoons can whip up waves of thirty meters or even higher in the open ocean, they do not move deep water. Tsunamis are never generated by the gravitational forces of the sun or moon. They're produced by earthquakes – such as in Sumatra – or, much less frequently, by volcanic eruptions, landslides, or the impact of meteors or comets."

She moved from the lectern and a QuickTime sequence filled the movie screen behind her. Blue animated waves began to heave, replaced by a 3-D cutaway of the water column down to the ocean floor. It was impressive animation, colorful and distracting. But most of the audience remained focused on Swenson.

Dressed in an off-white midi lab coat over a dark plaid skirt, she had spent a long time pinning up her hair into a kind of frumpy bun to prevent it from shimmering distractedly. She wore a pair of tortoise-shell glasses. She wore no makeup and no jewelry. But all of these well-planned counter-measures only seemed to make her more alluring.

To be intelligent and to look like this? It was a fucking outrage. This is what they were thinking. No one deserved such fortune, no matter what their previous life. Most people believed that if you were good-looking and smart, you must have some hidden failing, deep inside. And even if you didn't, not really, it meant they had to look for one, which was – in and of itself – a bit of a nuisance. And they always discovered one, even if they had to make it up. It was all about finding balance, some kind of order in their world when confronted with something that was clearly out of sync, unnatural, perhaps a genetic aberration, most certainly a statistical anomaly. Swenson saw the same thing in nature all the time. To be so fortunate meant you were already doomed. What were discrete blessings, individual gifts, together proved too much for most. Sometimes her face and figure helped; usually they were just annoying distractions. As her mother used to say, "We each carry our own cross." Research was a great place to hide.

"Tsunamis," she continued, "can attain speeds of up to 700 kilometers per hour in the central reaches of the oceans. But, despite their speed, tsunamis are generally not particularly dangerous in deep water. Most waves are less than a few meters high, although their lengths can exceed hundreds of kilometers."

Another screen popped to life, displaying a view of the Pacific Ocean from space. This morphed into an animation, charting the movement of the wave below. Then the POV collapsed, as if the satellite were falling from the sky, plummeting to the earth like Icarus, only to slow and hover a few feet from the downward side of the tsunami, revealing its low roll.

"This creates a sea-surface slope so gentle that tsunamis

usually pass unnoticed in deep water. Indeed," she said, "the Japanese word *tsu-nami* translates literally as 'harbor wave,' perhaps because a tsunami can travel undetected across oceans, then rise up unexpectedly within shallow coastal waters."

The first screen glowed with a map of the Indian Ocean. "Regardless of their origin," she said, "tsunamis evolve through three overlapping but quite separate physical processes: generation, by any force that disturbs the water column; propagation, from deeper water near the source, to shallow coastal areas; and, finally, inundation, as the waves sweep up onto dry land. Of these, the propagation phase is the best understood. Generation and inundation are much more difficult to model.

"Generation," she explained, "is the process through which a seafloor disturbance – such as a movement along a fault – reshapes the surface of the sea. When nearly all of an earthquake's energy is released in a thrust motion, as in the Sumatra quake, a large tsunami is generated. In contrast, strike-slip earthquakes, such as the one in San Francisco in 1906, are not efficient tsunami generators.

"The location of the 2004 Sumatra centroid," she continued, "defined as the location of the center of energy release, was near the Sunda trench, in relatively deep water. This generally results in an initial tsunami with larger potential energy than a tsunami whose centroid is closer to shore. Researchers use an idealized model of a quake since only the orientation of the assumed fault plane and the quake's location, magnitude and depth can be interpreted from seismic data. Other parameters, including the amount of slip, and its length and width, must be estimated. That's why initial simulations frequently underestimate inundation, sometimes by a factor of five or ten."

The second screen sparkled with numbers, spinning formulae and colorful input fields; the third with animated models of tsunamis based on the various data feeds.

"The second process," she continued, "propagation, transports seismic energy away from the earthquake through undulations of the water. Waves slow down as they travel over decreasing water depth, so that they eventually overtake one another, narrowing the distance between them in a process called shoaling."

All three screens began to display clips of different tsunami landfalls, crashing through villages and towns, in color and black-and-white, rushing up rivers and canals, sweeping the world away.

"Inundation," she concluded, "the third and final stage, is the most difficult to model. The wave height is now so large that initial linear theory fails to describe the complicated interaction between the water and the shoreline. Vertical run-up can reach tens of meters, but it typically takes only two to three meters to cause significant damage. The Indian Ocean tsunami was responsible for killing more than two hundred thousand people worldwide – from Sumatra to Somalia – although some speculate the death toll may climb higher, to as many as a quarter of a million souls."

Scenes of devastation flickered behind her: flooded fields and leveled homes; the one-legged silhouette of Vidu.

"The U.S. Geological Survey has identified sand and gravel deposits carried inland a great distance by inundation . . . "

As Swenson lectured, she drifted, thinking about her own past. Once, she too had been as fresh-faced and scrubbed and open to the world as these young students, when she'd first heard Dr. White speak at that lecture in Los Angeles. She had been at USC then, after her escape from South Dakota.

Born in a small town called Chance to Eric Swenson, a geologist, and Dolly Aalborg, part-time clerk, Emily had been precociously intelligent from the very start, skipping two grades by the time she was but ten. At twelve, she had lost her mother to lung cancer. Soon, she was working after school in the same tourist shop her mother used to manage, selling turquoise and fake Native American nick-knacks to tourists on their way to and from the Badlands. Only her swimming had kept her sane. She'd been captain of the local high school swim team, and an accomplished diver, winning a state championship at sixteen. The following year she had been accepted to USC on a scholarship where she had majored in oceanography, with a minor in geology – just like her father, with whom she was still close. On the weekends she'd worked at a local dive shop, and this too became a lifelong passion. But, even then, her beauty had worked against her.

Tall, voluptuous and blond, with robin-egg-blue eyes, few could believe she was the same person they got to know online, through her papers or academic correspondence. She looked more like a movie star. Most men were too intimidated to even ask her out, assuming, falsely, that she was destined to be busy; to the point, ironically, where she spent nearly every weekend on her own, linked to the world exclusively through her computer, forever working.

Her professors always discounted her because of her good looks. The women generally felt threatened. And the men either assumed she was a dumb blonde, or they fell in love with her. Even when it was Platonic, many ended up playing Henry Higgins to her Eliza. That's why she'd left USC, after a brief affair with one of her professors – the infamous E.J. Dubinsky, author of *This Primal Earth*, for a few brief months a best-seller on *The New York Times* non-fiction list.

She had broken it off only a week or so before a scheduled expedition – 150 kilometers east of Atlantic City – designed to study some mysterious craters suspected of being formed by gas eruptions. Despite the recent terminus of the affair, they had descended together anyway, in a three-man Deep Submergence Vehicle called the *Alvin*, and at one point, out of nowhere, Dubinsky had tried to kiss her. Then, something went wrong. They had lost power and the DSV had drifted out of control. It was only after forty-five excruciating seconds that they had finally found a fix. But not before Swenson had panicked, not before she had screamed hysterically and accused Dubinsky of disabling the craft intentionally. That had really been the end of the affair. Soon after that, she had transferred to the Woods Hole Oceanographic Institute to work with Dr. James L. White, one of the world's pre-eminent authorities on tsunamis. She rarely thought about E.J. anymore. And, since that episode aboard the *Alvin*, she had never stepped foot inside a DSV again.

"Excuse me?" someone said. Swenson looked up. A tanned, dark-haired student in the back waved his hand above his head.

"Yes?"

"Do you think it would be possible to precipitate a tsunami, by planting explosives, say, along a fault line?"

The student had a thick accent. He sounded Indian or Pakistani. It was amazing how cosmopolitan the Institute had become. "I don't believe so," she replied. "Some geologists have tried to stimulate seismic activity. You know – for oil and gas exploration. That sort of thing. But none has succeeded. At least, not to my knowledge. But you might want to ask Dr. White about that one. I know he has some pretty controversial theories on vulcan stimulation." Then she turned and looked about the crowd. They were starting to pack up. No one else had raised a hand. "Alright then," she concluded. "I notice we've reached the end of our allotted time. I'll see you all next week. Thanks for coming out so late tonight."

The students burst into applause. It had been a lecture disguised as a video game. It spoke to them in their own language, with lightning cuts, and contemporary colors and design. It pulsed and moved. And it tore at both their heads and hearts.

Swenson descended from the stage, shimmied through the usual crowd of well wishers, sycophants and Lotharios who always seemed to gather at these affairs, and made her way across the Quad to Dr. White's administrative office in the Bigelow Laboratory. She had been working there on her paper about the Indian Ocean tsunami because it was quieter than in her own shared quarters, and because – though small – the office had a spectacular view of the bay. Suddenly, someone shuffled by the door. The handle turned and Swenson was startled to see Dr. White materialize like a ghost within the brightened doorway. White had been out of the office for months, on leave, tending to his wife who was bed-ridden with cancer.

"I'm sorry," Swenson said. "Dr. White, I didn't know you were coming in." She began to gather up her papers. "I'll get out of your hair."

"Don't be silly," Dr. White said. "I'll only be a minute, Emily. I'm the one who's barging in." He glanced over at Swenson for an instant, then turned and averted her gaze. "And as I recall," he added, "I gave you permission to use my office any time you wanted to. Especially when you're working on a paper. Believe me, I know the value of solitude, and its curse."

Dr. White seemed harried and distracted. He looked exhausted. He stuffed a dozen files into a bulging leather briefcase. Swenson chalked it up to his wife's illness.

"I enjoyed your lecture, Emily," White said, after a moment. "You've come so far."

Swenson was surprised. She hadn't seen Dr. White in the audience. Normally, when he showed up, he came down to the front when it was over, mixing in with the well-wishers.

"You've become a great asset to the field," continued Dr. White. "There is nothing particularly revolutionary, nothing new about your findings, Emily, but you express them in a revolutionary way, and I guess that's what science needs today. Especially oceanography." He shook his head. "Despite the tsunami last year, our work is still under-funded compared to other fields. People have always underestimated the power of the sea. Their ships litter the sea floor. But now that we can fly – like demigods, like Angel apes – we think we're above it all. We've become too arrogant.

We whip the waves like Darius. The sea gods are not so easily dismissed. You'll see, Emily. The whole world will see." He sailed across the room, stood immediately before her, reached out and brushed a strand of golden hair behind one ear. "I may not have made much in this world – at least not financially – but I've left you a legacy of learning. I've always loved you like my daughter, you know that, Emily." He kissed her on the cheek and she suddenly realized that he'd been drinking. "Don't ever forget that."

"Don't talk that way, James," she said, stepping back. "You're acting like I'm never going to see you again."

"I'm putting Doris in a hospice," he continued. "She needs twenty-four hour care and I just can't provide that for her. After all, I can't stay on leave forever. This job may be rewarding in many ways – on an intellectual plain – but it's never made me rich. Frankly, Emily, I just don't have the money. Doris was never one to stick to a budget. She wasn't raised that way. And her inheritance is gone."

Swenson thought about her lecture. You could take all kinds of measurements of deep water, get to know something pretty well, across multiple dimensions, only to discover that you didn't know it at all. You miscalculated the inundation, the currents of the heart. "What are you going to do?" asked Swenson. Having lost her mother to cancer, she was all too familiar with the hardships of the caretaker.

"I don't know," he said. "Let this be a lesson to you. Academia is a political cesspool, with no financial return. I should have left and gone to work for some oil company years ago. Now it's too late. Look at me. I've got nothing left. I'm as dead as Doris." His voice broke. "But you," he continued, clutching at his scuffed brown leather case, "you still have a chance to get away. Get away, Emily," he stammered, leaning close to her, his brown eyes bulging, a drop of spittle on his lips, his breath unbearable.

Just then, there was a soft knock on the door. White and Swenson both looked up. The door swung open with a creak, revealing a small, Middle Eastern-looking man in the doorway. "Dr. White," he said in English as he glanced about the hall. "It is getting late."

Dr. White brushed past the desk and headed for the door. His dark companion had already disappeared. As he pressed his briefcase to his chest, White turned and said, "Don't forget what I told you. Please, Emily. Don't wait. Get away. Get away before it's too late."

SECTION II

Jami

Chapter 5
Friday, January 28 – 4:05 AM
Tel Aviv, Israel

Seiden sat in his office at Mossad headquarters, re-reviewing El Aqrab's file. After a preliminary study, no one could come up with a plausible explanation as to why the infamous terrorist had come back to Israel to kill this particular family. According to neighbors, Ariel Miller managed a furniture store. His wife was a secretary in an advertising agency. Miller was a drunk, fat and unfaithful. Harmless, really. Except for a brief stint, years before – when he'd served as a guard at Ansar II prison in Gaza, during his compulsory conscription – Miller had never done anything that would remotely connect him to Islamist terrorists. And El Aqrab had never been in prison, not even as a boy.

Perhaps it was just a random act of violence, just as the words El Aqrab burned into his victims' flesh were random snippets from the Qur'an. Or some kind of killing for hire, or for a friend who had been in prison. Seiden was mystified. One thing was clear though: El Aqrab had positioned his victims in a particular way. Miller had been facing north-northwest, directly away from Mecca, as if in a kind of anti-prayer. And the boys perpendicular to him, at right angles to the Muslim holy city.

Seiden stood up, picked up the file, and headed out the door, down the long green corridor toward the holding cells.

"Hello. My name is Saul Weinstein," he said, as he entered Interrogation Room B. It was a small cell, barely five meters long, and three and a half meters wide, with a mirror running the entire length of one wall, and a small desk by the door. In the far corner, the prisoner stood chained to the ceiling by his wrists, facing the other way. "This won't take long, perhaps an hour or two," Seiden continued. "I need to update your file. Your . . . interrogator has been delayed."

He took a DVD from the folder under his arm and slipped it into a player on the desk connected to a nearby television set. Seiden turned the screen so that it was visible to both himself and El Aqrab. Then he dropped the folder onto the desk, sat down and flipped it open. "It says here you were born Mohammed Hussein, on February Third, 1963," he began in an off-hand kind of way. "In a town called Rihane in Jezzine. It's your birthday soon.

Congratulations."

El Aqrab did not respond.

"The son of Jusef and Fatima Hussein," Seiden continued. "Your father was a . . . " He glanced down at the file, although – of course – he already knew the information intimately. " . . . part-time electrician and handyman who moved north to Beirut to work in the various stores and office buildings owned by wealthy business mogul Hanid ben Saad." He looked up at El Aqrab but the terrorist remained impassive. He did not even turn around.

"You began to work with your father," Seiden continued, "in one of Hanid ben Saad's many properties when you were just eleven. Your parents were killed by the Israeli Army in Rihane in March of '78, when we attacked PLO positions in south Lebanon. This was in retaliation for the murders of some thirty bus riders by Palestinian guerrillas. They were not alone, your parents. I believe fifteen hundred Lebanese were killed in that engagement.

"After your parents' death," Seiden continued, "you joined Imam Musa Sadr's Movement of the Deprived, Harakat al-Mahrumin, the precursor of Amal and Hezbollah. That was the same year that Musa Sadr 'disappeared' in Libya, no doubt at the hands of Colonel Khadaffi. It was around this time that you acquired the street name El Aqrab. How did you get that name?" Seiden asked. "I'm curious. You look very little like a scorpion, Mohammed."

El Aqrab turned around for the first time. He was a slight man with narrow shoulders and even narrower hips. His face was thin, almost haggard in its appearance, with high cheekbones framing a beak-like nose. He had a wispy black beard, thin as an adolescent's. In fact, he looked much younger than his forty-two years. Were it not for his eyes, large and deeply set, obsidian and glassy, he could have passed for thirty.

The terrorist grinned, lending his face a lupine quality; his canines were unnaturally large. Then he spoke for the first time. "I know you," he said in Arabic. "You were at the apartment. Your name isn't Saul Weinstein. It's Seiden. Acting Chief Seiden. What time is it?" It was a pleasant voice that served to mollify his predatory gaze.

Seiden looked at his watch. "Why?"

El Aqrab did not respond. He simply stared at Seiden.

"Almost five," said Seiden.

The terrorist nodded, smiled and turned away.

El Aqrab remembered the day that he had taken on the street name El Aqrab – the little creature of the spider, the scorpion. An Israeli commando unit had infiltrated across the Green Line to kill a particular Harakat al-Mahrumin commander. It was a sunny morning and, typical of the arrogant Zionists, they'd mounted their mission in broad daylight. After assassinating the commander in his bed, the 101 commando team was traveling back by jeep, east of the Green Line, just past the Military Hospital near the Arab University, when, without warning, they came upon two teenagers wandering across the road – Ibrahim and Jamal ben Saad. Ibrahim saw the jeep barreling down on them and pushed his older brother to the side. Just then, a rocket-propelled grenade exploded underneath the vehicle. The jeep tipped over, spilling the commandos onto the street. Two of the five Zionists were killed immediately, their bodies crushed and torn to pieces. The other three wormed their way along the street, taking heavy fire from an adjacent building and a vacant lot. Ibrahim and Jamal ben Saad were both caught in the crossfire. They threw themselves to the ground, uncertain of which way to turn. They watched as yet another of the commandos took a bullet in his chest. He somersaulted backwards, opening like a pomegranate. Then, as if from nowhere, out of a cloud of smoke, Mohammed Hussein appeared.

He walked along the smoke-filled street nonchalantly, as if he were out to buy the morning paper, his Kalashnikov stuttering in his hands. Another commando burst apart and Hussein went down, his weapon spinning like a top across the street.

Ibrahim and Jamal couldn't stand it any longer. The noise. The blood. The concussion of explosions. They leapt to their feet, completely terrified, and fled. The remaining Zionist rolled to one knee, took aim, and was about to shoot them in the back when Hussein sprang up, like a scorpion, and shot three rounds – before anyone could even breathe – into the last commando's chest. The commando looked down at his shirtfront. He pulled at the material, revealing the broken bloody ribcage underneath. A stream of blood began to fountain from his mouth. Hussein walked up to him and kicked him in the face, and he went flying backwards into the blazing jeep. His hair and clothes caught fire. He wriggled for a moment longer as he burned, and then was still.

The firefight was over. It had taken less than ninety

seconds from the initial blast. Ibrahim and Jamal ben Saad stood speechless. They looked about each other at the carnage, the shattered corpses of the 101 commando unit, at the bloody smiling face of Mohammed Hussein, and began to laugh hysterically. Hussein stepped up and ushered them away. It didn't pay to linger after a firefight. You never knew.

In the shadows, outside a tiny electronics store, as Hussein cleaned and reloaded his Kalashnikov, they introduced themselves to one another. Hussein had heard of the ben Saads. Everyone knew the wealthy business mogul, Hanid ben Saad. He was a legend in Beirut. And within half an hour they had made their way to the ben Saad villa not far from the Palais de Justice.

Hussein was overwhelmed by what he saw. He lived in the 'Ayn ar Rummanah neighborhood with three other Harakat al-Mahrumin guerrillas. His entire apartment could have fit inside the foyer of the ben Saad villa. Although it wasn't situated on the gold coast where most of Beirut's largest mansions loomed, it was impressive nonetheless. The two boys told him to sit down and wait, and then rushed off to find their father. He was in his study, just down the hall.

Still pulsing with adrenaline, Hussein was unable to sit down. Instead, he paced about the room, examining the hand-made European furniture, the Turkish carpets, the paintings of distant pastoral scenes, wheat fields and orchards, seascapes spattered with sails. After a few minutes, his curiosity got the better of him and he wandered down the hall. He passed a giant mirror on the wall, set in an ornate gilded wooden frame, and stopped to examine himself. In his ragged jeans and blood-soaked shirt, in his tattered veil, he had never felt so out of place. Not even his trusty Kalashnikov could make him feel at ease or secure in these strange opulent surroundings. He took another step and peeked between the doorframe and the door where the boys had disappeared.

Inside, he could see the boy named Ibrahim with an old man dressed in a Western suit. The old man stood behind a desk. His back was to the door. He was reaching into what appeared to be a wall safe, peeling off bills from a large stack of paper money.

"Found what you're looking for?"

Hussein spun about, ducked and trained his gun on the figure of Jamal ben Saad.

"You've heard the stories, haven't you?" continued Jamal.

"What stories?" asked Hussein.

"About the great fortune locked up in my father's safe. Just in case we have to flee."

Hussein smiled and lowered his weapon. "Are they true?"

Jamal did not respond.

"You should be glad you have such parents," Hussein continued with a laugh.

Jamal's face grew dark. "*She* is not my mother." Just then, Ibrahim returned with the reward.

A long, long time ago, thought El Aqrab. But even then there had been only three types of terrorists: first and foremost, the local street kid found in Palestine and throughout the ghettos of the Middle East, like El Aqrab himself; second, those who were radicalized by an Imam abroad, in Europe or America, who were committed to the jihad in a very personal way; and third, the indolent guilt-ridden rich, the bored, the younger brothers and cousins of the wealthy and the upper middle class – the *jinn*, who considered themselves distinct from, and above the ordinary run of people, and who reinforced their eminence through the passion of their faith.

That's what Ibrahim had been, and his older brother, Jamal. Ironically, despite their obvious differences, Jamal ben Saad and El Aqrab looked strangely alike, and this always disturbed Jamal. He was a student of architecture, it turned out. An academic. Weak and afraid. A fool. El Aqrab feared no one, and yet he was no bigger and no stronger than Jamal.

*   *   *

"You appeared to have vanished after the invasion," Seiden continued. "Was that when you first went to Kazakhstan? Perhaps you shouldn't have attacked our Ambassador in London."

El Aqrab smiled. It was an old saw. In July, 1982, the Zionists invaded Lebanon with the declared aim of routing Palestinian guerrillas. They cited as justification an attack that wounded their ambassador in London. *Operation Peace for Galilee's* ostensible goal was to push the Palestinians forty kilometers or so from the Lebanese border in order to prevent them from shelling nearby Israeli settlements. Yuri Garron headed the incursion, the same Garron, who – as Housing Minister – later reshaped the country's settlement policy, and who was now Prime

Minister. At the time, he'd been Minister of Defense, under the Likud. But Garron had had a hidden agenda. He sought not only to push the Palestinians from the border, but to alienate Lebanon from rest of the Arab states.

To accomplish his goal, Garron attempted to exploit the hatred the dominant Maronite Christians harbored against the Palestinians, whom they wanted to see driven out of Lebanon. In Garron's mind, the Maronites were natural allies. The Zionists would underpin the Maronite position; in return, the Maronites would take Lebanon out of the Arab-Israeli conflict.

But the plan failed, El Aqrab remembered with a smile. The Syrians considered Lebanon part of their sphere of influence and – once they realized what Garron was up to – they mobilized to thwart the invasion.

Garron's forces soon found themselves outside Beirut facing the Syrians and a mishmash of guerrilla factions: the pro-X Palestinians – pro-Iraq, pro-Syria, pro-Saudi, pro-Libya, etc., depending on their sponsors; the profiteering PLO; the Druze irregulars; the Morabitum; PFL; Amal; and a hundred other freelance forces. Most did not seem too serious about the struggle, more interested in holding on to their few square blocks of West Beirut than in fighting the Israelis. As soon as the Israelis broke for lunch, they would revert to killing one another instead of the Israeli Defense Forces, or slip off for a bite to eat while watching the latest World Cup soccer match.

Since the IDF didn't want to engage the Arab forces hand-to-hand inside the ghettos of the city, and since the Maronite Christians refused to do this for them, the Zionists turned to the United States. Then-President Reagan agreed to dispatch U.S. troops as part of a Multi-National Force, and by the time *Operation Peace for Galilee* was over – after the bombardments, the shelling and the air raids – more than 20,000 people lay dead.

"Of course, you never wanted a peaceful solution," Seiden said. "If you had, you wouldn't have assassinated President Gemayel."

"And, in exchange, you gave us Sabra and Shatila." El Aqrab turned and looked at Seiden. "Gemayel was an Israeli puppet. It was the Zionists who let the Christians slaughter all those people. It was Garron," he spat.

El Aqrab remembered the incident as if it had happened only yesterday. The blood. The silence and the flies. The vacant eyes.

Before Sabra and Shatila, the war had been a farce, the blackest of comedies, despite the carnage. The Zionists stationed a few tanks in the Baabda hills, which pounded the city regularly. The Israeli air force didn't start their bombing runs until well past 4:00 PM. Then they returned to base for dinner before the night shift took their place. In fact, it was a war waged mostly for the foreign press. Skirmishes not rooted in personal vendetta were fought distractedly until the cameras arrived. Then everyone took on a Rambo sensibility, posturing for the lenses, taking unprecedented risks to show off to the world. This was Phoenicia, after all. Most Lebanese were much more interested in trade, in makeshift monetary exchanges, than in political agendas.

Then, after Gemayel's assassination, Israeli troops — ringing the Palestinian refugee camps of Sabra and Shatila — had allowed revenge-seeking Maronite militiamen into the shantytowns. More than 1,500 refugees were slaughtered, including hundreds of women and children. Including babies, El Aqrab remembered. The narrow muddy lanes were choked with broken bodies, splattered with blood. Israel was widely condemned and, later, Yuri Garron was found to be "indirectly responsible" for the carnage. Indirectly responsible! "You are running out of time," said El Aqrab.

"Why? Are you planning to go somewhere?" asked Seiden. "You have an appointment, perhaps?"

"You could say that."

* * *

The UH-60L Black Hawk transport helicopter emblazoned with the Knesset seal prepared to take off in Jerusalem. More than fifteen meters in length, with a speed of 360 kilometers per hour, the Black Hawk was powered by two 1,500 horse power General Electric T700 engines that sputtered and caught as the rotors started to spin.

"What's going on?" inquired the co-pilot.

"No idea," the pilot said. "Must be urgent to get these guys up at this hour."

Just then, a door burst open in the adjacent building. Three figures huddled together for a moment by the door. Then they dashed across the tarmac and ducked inside the helicopter. The ship rose steadily. She slid across the tarmac, reached transitional lift, and lifted herself into the air at 450 feet per minute.

Chapter 6
Thursday, January 27 – 5:38 PM
Queens, New York

They had been watching the apartment in Long Island City for just shy of a week now, from a squat across the street – John Decker, Jr., recently transferred to the Joint Terrorism Task Force (JTTF) in New York, and his partner Anthony Bartolo; plus a second team made up of Special Agents Williams and Kazinski, who kept an eye on the three suspects as they commuted to and from their jobs each day. On this particular Thursday night, the second team was back at the office for a lecture on criminal financial networks by an Intel specialist named Otto Warhaftig, attached to the JTTF from the Central Intelligence Agency as part of a new, interagency Homeland Security initiative.

They knew the routines of the suspects intimately. Well . . . at least two of them. A Saudi Arabian by birth, the first was Mohammed bin Basra, a student, wanted for questioning by the FBI since the spring of 2002. The second, Ali Singh, was originally from Pakistan and worked for a local cab company. They had both been arrested once – for disorderly conduct at a mosque in Queens – but acquitted for lack of evidence.

The third suspect remained unidentified, despite many attempts to follow him over the past few days. The agents had nicknamed him "Mecca" because he always seemed to be praying, facing Mecca.

As they watched the apartment across the way, Bartolo kept up a running commentary about his fiancée, Angelina. He'd been trying to set Decker up with one of Angelina's girlfriends for the past two weeks, to no avail. A blustery Italian kid from Hell's Kitchen, Tony Bartolo was inconsolable. He was convinced that Decker needed to get laid, and Angelina's high school girlfriend, Lissy, a Boricua, was just the thing: dark and voluptuous, with a dirty reputation that Bartolo knew was well deserved. "The best blowjobs in Hell's Kitchen," he repeated. Decker just ignored him. He liked his new partner but his infinite cajoling was beginning to wear thin.

As Bartolo rambled on, he took his jacket off, his handgun and his phone, and began his endless regimen of sit-ups, push-ups and crunches. He was obsessed with his physique, vainer than any girl Decker had ever known. Yet his vanity was endearing. Bartolo was completely genuine. Indeed, he made a fetish of his self-absorption, displaying it for all to see. He was a handsome man: six feet three inches tall; thick, dark brown hair; broad-shouldered, with an iron stomach, in sharp contrast to his feminine red lips.

When Bartolo was finally finished, he rolled in one smooth movement to his feet, grabbed his jacket and raincoat and gun, and started for the door. "More coffee?" he inquired.

"Sure," said Decker. "Black. No–"

"Yeah, I know, I know," Bartolo said, slipping on his holster. "Don't get how you can drink it plain like that though. I mean, it's no espresso."

"And I don't know how you can stomach all that milk and sugar. It's a wonder you're not three hundred pounds, or more, the way you eat."

Bartolo laughed. "That's why I'm so sweet," he said, opening the door and stepping out into the hall. He caressed the raincoat draped across his arm. "And why you sleep alone at night." With that he slammed the door behind him.

Decker shook his head and returned to his surveillance. He had set up a Nikon D70 digital camera on a tripod with a telephoto lens. The suspects' apartment was on the seventh floor of a nondescript pre-war, nine-story building just across the street. It was part of a whole row of rather run-down brick apartment buildings that stretched for almost eleven blocks. Decker took photographs of Mohammed bin Basra while the suspect used his PC in the living room. He couldn't see the screen, not clearly anyway, despite the powerful lens; it was raining again. But he had seen and photographed the PC wallpaper before. It featured some kind of arabesque design and Arabic calligraphy that fascinated Decker. Indeed, curious for another perspective, a few days earlier he had even emailed copies of the images to some Islamic expert over at the CIA, who had promised to pass them on to NSA, who had . . . It was always the same, Decker thought. He likened it to skipping stones over black holes. He had yet to get a response to his email, and he doubted he ever would.

With a deep sigh, Decker zoomed in a little closer. It was difficult to read but he took some pictures anyway. As Decker photographed the PC screen, he managed to make out a few brief words in Arabic that he'd already documented in his notebook: *Pregnant she-camels.* And then, more chilling still: *When hell is stoked up.* He sketched a corner of the arabesque design. The notebook was already full of images, stray pieces of the PC wallpaper rendered over time. He flipped the pages and the images fluttered into place, coalescing like a film strip. He hesitated at the final page. In the lower right hand corner of the wallpaper was a number, clearly visible: 540,000.

Decker considered how they had first discovered the three suspects. The man on the PC, Mohammed bin Basra, had been linked to a scheme to sell stolen cigarettes tax free. Some of the profits had been funneled through bank accounts in Indonesia suspected of being connected to the Brotherhood of the Crimson Scimitar and other Islamic terrorist networks.

Originally from Saudi, bin Basra first came to the United States in 1997, when he took undergraduate courses at Hunter College in New York. His father was relatively wealthy, involved in some kind of construction business back in Saudi. A few years earlier, bin Basra senior had been suspected of being associated with Al Qa'ida; the family had given money to a charity that turned out to be a front for the terrorist network. In 1999, Mohammed was arrested with Ali Singh and a youngster named Mohammed Qashir for disorderly conduct during a disturbance at a mosque in Queens, but the charges were dropped after his family made a sizeable contribution to the mosque. In 2000, he traveled to Afghanistan where – according to suspects imprisoned at Guantanimo Bay – he turned up at an Al Qa'ida training camp. Then, in the summer of 2002, although he was now wanted for questioning by the Bureau, bin Basra somehow managed to slip across the border into Canada. From there he traveled via Russia to Kazakhstan, where he underwent further training in explosives with a man named Gulzhan Baqrah, known associate of El Aqrab, the spiritual leader of the Brotherhood of the Crimson Scimitar. This was after the U.S.-led invasion had shut down all the Afghan training camps. Henceforth his whereabouts remained a mystery, at least until the cigarette heist.

Suspect number two, Ali Singh, was born to a middle class family in Islamabad, Pakistan. Following graduation from a technical college, where he'd excelled, he worked as an electrical engineer in Islamabad from 1992 through 1995. He was discharged, but the reasons were somewhat vague. He emigrated to the U.S. in 1996. When he couldn't find work in his chosen profession, Singh got a job at the Imperial Taxi Company in Long Island City, Queens, and at a storage company in Flatbush. Not much was known about his past; his file was pretty thin. He'd been married briefly in 2000 but divorced within a year. Immigration and Naturalization Services said it was probably a marriage of convenience so that he could become a U.S. citizen. Like bin Basra, he was arrested for disorderly conduct during that incident in Queens, then released. He traveled to Germany and Russia in the spring of 2002, and to Kazakhstan later that same summer. He may have trained with Gulzhan Baqrah, but there was no hard evidence. Then he was implicated in the same black market cigarette scheme as bin Basra.

Despite their status as fugitives and their recent identification after the cigarette heist, the FBI decided not to arrest the suspects. "Sunfish lead to bass," the Special Agent in Charge intoned. Better to be patient and wait.

Ali Singh and Mecca sat together on a sofa in the living room, watching something on TV. All of a sudden, Mecca got up, said a few words, put on his coat and headed toward the door. Decker whipped out his cell phone and called Bartolo. As soon as it connected, Decker heard the phone ring – on the chair immediately behind him! He spun about. There it was, glowing. He could hear the familiar theme song from *The Godfather*. His partner had forgotten his cell.

*　*　*

Bartolo entered the Happy Day deli to the tinkle of a bell. He walked up to the counter, said hello to the Korean man behind the bulletproof glass, and ordered two coffees – one black, one light and sweet. The deli smelled of Pinesol and old mothballs. Bartolo eyed a pack of brownies on a rack. One hundred and twenty calories, he read. About six minutes on the Stairmaster. Forget it, he thought. The Korean poured the coffees, capped them with lids and stuffed them into a small brown paper bag. Bartolo paid. "Thanks," he said, and turned, and ran right into Mecca.

For a moment they stared at one another. Then Bartolo said, "Excuse me," and shuffled down the narrow aisle. Mecca stepped forward to the counter. He asked for half a pound of green tea, with scarcely an accent, as Bartolo headed for the door. Bartolo could feel the suspect staring at his back but he resisted the urge to turn. He ambled nonchalantly through the deli door. He made his way outside and risked a quick glance sideways through the window. Mecca was still staring at him. Bartolo shied away. He gazed at a silver-gray Toyota parked across the street. He strolled along the sidewalk, around the corner, and stopped to catch his breath.

*   *   *

Decker watched the men in the apartment get the call. It was Ali Singh who finally stood and answered it. He said something, turned and peered out through the window. Something was wrong. Decker picked up his infrared eavesdropper – a device that bounced a laser beam across the street and captured conversations from vibrations on the window glass – but since it was still raining, the voices were impossible to hear. Not even the noiseless PIN-Diode laser linked to a 500 mm lens could distinguish what was being said. Singh hung up the receiver. He barked something at bin Basra and then moved swiftly through the room, past the blank wall, into the bedroom where he began to pack up some belongings in a small black duffel bag. Decker swung the camera back toward the living room. Bin Basra still hovered by the personal computer. He typed furiously on the keyboard. Then he stood and made his way to the front hall. Singh joined him and they vanished.

Decker leapt to his feet, grabbed his coat, and bolted out the door.

*   *   *

At exactly the same moment, the man known only as Mecca left the deli and sauntered through an alley toward his apartment building. Bartolo spotted him as soon as he had turned the corner. The Arab glanced about, hesitated for a moment, and then ran. Bartolo gave chase. Mecca tore into the lobby of the apartment building with Bartolo close behind. The suspect ducked into an elevator. The doors closed just as Bartolo stepped into the lobby. The agent threw himself against the elevator doors but he was just too late. The doors slammed shut. Bartolo smashed his hand against the console. He spun about. After what seemed like an eternity, another elevator descended, and Bartolo got inside. The elevator doors closed soundlessly behind him, with excruciating slowness, just as Decker dashed in from the street.

Decker sprinted over to the elevators. Both were occupied, of course, ascending. He turned, searching frantically for the stairwell. There it was. In the corner. He saw the illuminated Exit sign, a livid red. He ran across the foyer, barged through the door, and started up the steps.

* * *

The elevator paused at the seventh floor and Bartolo jumped out. He checked the apartment first, then pounded up the stairs. He could hear foreign voices in the stairwell leading to the roof.

"Bartolo?" Decker shouted from below.

"The roof," Bartolo shouted back. He had already reached the top floor of the building. The door leading out onto the roof was swinging closed. Bartolo drew his gun. He stepped up to the door, kicked it open, and threw himself onto the ground outside, rolling as he fell.

The suspects were fleeing across the roof. He could see them running, rushing through the pouring rain. Bartolo spat, got to his feet and gave chase.

They made their way across the glistening rooftops in a line, leaping from one apartment building to the next, scrambling over chimneys and lawn furniture and clotheslines and giant rolls of tarpaper in the rain. Bartolo closed on Mecca, the trailing suspect. All of a sudden, the Arab leapt across a chasm between two buildings, his arms waving in the air above him as if he were holding a trapeze. He landed roughly on the next rooftop and rolled. Bartolo followed without hesitation. He ran and jumped, but slipped at the last moment on the glistening parapet. He fell just short. The lip of the next building caught him on the chest with a loud *thump,* and he felt the wind knocked out of him. Bartolo kicked and struggled but to no avail; his body slid across the parapet and he found himself dangling from the roof, his legs waving in the empty air, his muscles straining. "Decker," he cried. "Decker, help me. Help me!"

* * *

Decker appeared behind him on the other roof. "Hold on, Tony," he shouted. "Don't move."

There was a shot and Decker ducked. Mecca was firing at him. He had rolled behind a chimney and was taking potshots at him from the other roof.

Decker shielded himself behind a set of chimney pots. "Hold on, I'm coming, Tony," he shouted. "Just hold on."

Decker couldn't see Bartolo any more; he was hidden by the chimneys. Then Decker noticed Mecca on the other roof. The Arab was approaching his partner slowly through the rain.

Decker unholstered his gun – a double-action Beretta 92FS with a matte-black Bruniton finish. He aimed it at the Arab who continued to draw nearer and nearer, seemingly mindless of his obvious exposure. At first, Decker had the unreasonable feeling that he was going to pull the struggling agent to his feet. "Don't move," Decker shouted frantically. "Freeze. I said freeze!" But Mecca just ignored him. He leaned down over the parapet, as if to offer some assistance, eyeing Decker the whole time, reached out for Bartolo with his hand, and stabbed him in the back.

Decker fired.

The shot struck Mecca's knife, blasting it from his grasp and up into the air. It spiraled out of sight. Mecca ducked and rolled away behind a low brick wall.

Decker holstered his gun. He zigzagged madly across the roof, set his foot, and leapt across the wide divide. A bullet whizzed above him. He sailed and sailed and sailed, and finally hit the other roof. He pulled out his Beretta as he rolled. He aimed, but Mecca had already disappeared.

The shooting had stopped.

Then Decker saw him – tearing across the roof two buildings down, immediately behind his two companions.

"Help me," shrieked Bartolo behind him. His voice was desperate now. "John, for Christ's sake, help me!"

Decker ran back to his partner. He was about to reach down for his wrist when he saw the fingers come apart, like the splaying of a fan, and slip and disappear as Bartolo flattened out against the backdrop of the street, his arms and legs stretched out, his mouth, his eyes more pregnant with surprise and disbelief than with the terrible foreknowledge of his doom. He hit the sidewalk with a sickening *thud*, still looking up, the back of his head smashed inward like an uncooked egg, already fertilized and forming, the blood seeping out beneath him, mixing with the fallen rain.

Decker squatted there on the edge of the parapet for a long time. He could not tear his eyes away. Somewhere, a woman screamed. Finally, as the rain ran down his collar and snaked around his neck, Decker got up and shook the water from his hair. He looked up at the night sky. In the unnatural glow of the streetlights, he could see raindrops falling out of nowhere, falling like liquid string around him, tying him down.

Chapter 7
Friday, January 28 – 5:12 AM
Tel Aviv, Israel

El Aqrab sat absolutely still. Everything had been upside down after the massacres at Sabra and Shatila. Everything had been washed away . . . in a river of blood.

He had slipped home and changed and gone over to his friend Ibrahim ben Saad's house for his older brother's graduation from the Arab University. But after it was all over, but a few days hence, Ibrahim was revealed to have conspired with his wealthy father to hand over information about Syrian and Amal defense positions to the Zionists prior to the invasion, in exchange for assurances that ben Saad's real estate investments would be spared. As a result of this betrayal, the rich entrepreneur, his wife and Ibrahim had been incinerated by Amal in a car bombing. And El Aqrab had been ordered to assassinate Jamal, Ibrahim's older brother.

Jamal ben Saad had been arrested by the Israelis, and then released after only a few days. A few days! He was clearly an Israeli sympathizer too. So El Aqrab had arranged to meet him in Beirut, where he had stabbed and killed the frightened academic for his family's treachery. It had not been difficult to draw him out. Jamal had always been enamored with El Aqrab, with his reputation as a soldier, and more than a little jealous of his brother's friendship with the freedom fighter.

Throughout it all, El Aqrab remembered, Jamal had proclaimed his innocence. He'd cried and cried, invoking the name of his mother, Rabi'a, whom he had claimed was drowned by his own father. As the life drained out of him, Jamal had slipped back to his youth, describing in detail how his father had plied his mother with sleeping pills and wine, how he'd towed her out into the open water beyond the Coral Beach Hotel, until the tidal currents weakened her, and she had slipped beneath the waves. El Aqrab found it odd the kinds of things condemned men liked to talk about. Odd, but fascinating. With a spasm, Jamal had pleaded for his mother, had shrieked for her, and – looking up, his eyes clear now – had smiled and quoted the Qur'an: "'My Lord has spread the earth out like a bed for me, and heaven like a canopy.'"

* * *

"When it got too hot for you to stay in Beirut," said Seiden, "you went to Kazakhstan, to the camp of Gulzhan Baqrah. Curious that you didn't go to Afghanistan or somewhere closer. This was before the 2001 invasion. Didn't Al-Qa'ida trust you? Didn't the Taliban?"

El Aqrab did not respond.

"You studied weaponry and explosives, battlefield tactics. According to our informants, you excelled in the use of explosives. Must have made Gulzhan Baqrah proud."

Once again, El Aqrab remained impassive.

"Meanwhile," Seiden continued, "the Multinational Force returned after Lebanese President Gemayel was assassinated. In 1983, Amal's bastard offspring, Hezbollah, bombed the U.S. Marine barracks in south Beirut, killing two hundred and forty-one U.S. servicemen."

Seiden reached out and pressed a button on the DVD deck. "Here," he said. "I want to show you something." After a few seconds, an image appeared on the TV. At first, it was grainy and unclear, the picture shaking as if the person filming it had been in motion. Then the destruction of the Marine barracks was revealed.

A truck appeared at the bottom of the screen. It barreled down the narrow street, headed directly through the barricades and up into the lobby. There was a huge flash of white light as the truck exploded, sending glass and stone and body parts into the sky. The air was sucked back through the widening cavity, as if the film were being rewound. The floors began to pancake down on top of one another. The building imploded. Seiden pressed a button and the clip slipped into slow motion. A tongue of flame licked out from the shattered walls; it was the word *Allah*, in Arabic script.

"All of these ... these ... " He searched for the word. " ... atrocities astonished most of the Knesset, not to mention our U.S. allies," said Seiden, "because, until this time, you Shiites were considered the most docile, the most agreeable people in Lebanon, if not the entire Middle East. I suppose you were emboldened by the fall of the Shah in Iran. I suppose things changed forever after Sabra and Shatila." He waited for a response but El Aqrab still stared at the flickering TV screen. "The man who engineered these suicide bombings must have been a genius," he continued. "Look at the precision. Look at the perfection in planning."

El Aqrab bounced his right leg up and down. Seiden examined him. The terrorist's eyes glazed over as he slipped into another memory. "You were involved in all of these attacks," said

Seiden. "Weren't you?"

El Aqrab watched, tremulous and excited, almost orgasmic as the building tumbled to the ground. Then he stiffened, turned and said, "You're running out of time. You'd better hurry up if you want to ask me something."

"What's the hurry? You're not going anywhere."

"No," said El Aqrab. Then he grinned and added, "You are."

* * *

The UH-60L Black Hawk transport helicopter flew westward toward the sea, glistening in the morning light. It descended as it neared the coast. The engine slowed, the chopper dipped. The lights of Tel Aviv glowed like a string of pearls along the neckline of the Mediterranean. The chopper skirted the city, descended, and then hovered for a few more seconds before landing outside Mossad headquarters. The rotors slowed. The engine died. Two figures jumped out and made their way into the fortified building, careful to keep their heads down from the spinning blades.

* * *

"1990 was a tough year, wasn't it?" said Seiden with a bouquet of compassion. "The Soviet Union collapsed, bequeathing a new wave of refugees to Israel. Iraq invaded Kuwait, and was driven out. Once again, you backed the wrong horse, didn't you? Then came the intifadah."

El Aqrab found it curious, this word – *intifadah*. Intifadah meant "spasm" or "frisson" in Arabic, a rather innocuous way of describing an event that ultimately proved so deadly. They should have named the Palestinian uprising a *thawrah*, or an *inqilab* – a *revolution* or *upheaval*. But then, of course, it had been the PLO who had first coined the phrase. Caught off guard by the riots, the PLO leaders had tended to downplay them. The Palestinian community, they said, was going through a kind of convulsion, like a tremor in the earth, a small earthquake, instead of what it really was: the rising of a volcano. One day the Palestinians would finally tire of their corrupt, self-serving leadership and throw the bastards out. But who would take their place? Hamas? El-Fatah? The Brotherhood of the Crimson Scimitar? El Aqrab smiled.

"During the first Gulf war, you were involved in blowing up Kuwaiti oil wells," Seiden said. He displayed a grainy black-and-white photograph. El Aqrab was clearly visible, standing by a jeep beside a blazing oil well. "Then you vanished once again, through 1993. I presume you were back in Kazakhstan, at the camp of Gulzhan Baqrah." He threw another photograph on the table. It featured El Aqrab and Gulzhan Baqrah standing side by side. The portly Gulzhan – with a shocking white grin slitting his black beard – had his arm around El Aqrab, who was looking away, somewhat distracted.

"In July, 1993, we launched *Operation Accountability*, a week-long air, artillery and naval blitz. It was frighteningly effective. Indeed, with thousands either dead or wounded, with hundreds of thousands displaced, Prime Minister Rabin believed the Lebanese would resist, would literally rise up if Hezbollah tried to execute another operation. But only a few days after *Operation Accountability*, Hezbollah planted that booby trap at Shiheen.

"We all remember the booby trap at Shiheen," said Seiden. "In the entire history of the revolt, no booby trap had ever killed as many as twelve Israeli soldiers at one time. 'Hezbollah has beaten us,' Prime Minister Rabin was quoted as saying later. And the U.S. brokered an unwritten agreement between Israel and Hezbollah – the 1993 'Understandings,' prohibiting future attacks on civilians."

Seiden pressed the button on the DVD player. A moment later, the image of a small square filled with a dozen Israeli soldiers came into view. At first it appeared like a still. Then the soldiers began to move. They were smoking cigarettes and chatting. Other people could be seen standing around, alone or in small groups: a woman with a basket of fruit and what appeared to be a loaf of bread; a pair of men in Arab headdress; a small Palestinian girl with a checkered *keffiyeh*, no more than seven or eight, in mid-skip through the foreground. Each moved fitfully, in slow motion.

"It was you," said Seiden, "who was responsible for the booby trap at Shiheen, wasn't it?" And then the bomb exploded. "Who else would send this to us?" The flash was intense, a brilliant wave of light. Most of the soldiers simply disappeared. Two on the edge of the cluster were broken in half. The Arab men, the woman with the basket of fruit and bread, the little girl – each was picked up and blown back like a pile of autumn leaves, thrown out of frame. The calligraphy, the arabesque designs were much more intricate this time, more detailed in intensity and color. "You had come into your own," Seiden continued. "Then, once again, you vanished." He turned the image off and stared back at the papers on his desk.

"The de facto cease-fire finally broke down. There had been too many violations, too many civilian deaths. But, in reality, as you and I both know, the terms of the 'Understandings' drafted after Shiheen, drafted *because* of Shiheen, were simply . . . unenforceable."

Seiden got up for the first time. Casually, almost in slow motion – like the images on the DVD – he walked over and stood beside El Aqrab. He brought his mouth close to the terrorist's left ear. "This was the beginning of the end for Israel in Lebanon," he said. "You saw to that, didn't you? Shiheen pushed us over the edge. You knew it would. You planned it that way. You knew the conservative elements in the Knesset – the Likud and other parties – would never let it go unpunished. And so we mounted *Operation Grapes of Wrath*." He grasped El Aqrab by the nape of the neck with his right hand. He pulled his head back gently. "But without the ability to strike the civilian regions where you hid like little brown rats, and fearful now of world opinion, the 'Understandings' emasculated the IDF. You cut off our fucking balls." He let the Arab go and walked back to the desk. He sat down. He shuffled the papers in his hands. "We pulled out of Lebanon completely in May 2000. We had more pressing problems now, in Gaza and the West Bank. The new intifadah, the suicide bombings dwarfed whatever was happening in Lebanon." He laughed. It was a brittle sound, like pieces of a shattered light bulb underfoot.

"My son was nineteen the day we launched *Operation Grapes of Wrath*," said Seiden. "He was a radio operator in the Third Armored Division. He had soft brown eyes and long narrow fingers, like his mother. There was a small, chocolate-colored birthmark on his left thigh, shaped like a heart. Right here," he added, touching himself gently. "I saw it when they brought him back. It's what I used to identify him. His face was . . . gone."

El Aqrab turned his body slowly and stared at his interrogator. Seiden looked up and their eyes locked. El Aqrab was impassive. They examined each other for several seconds. Suddenly, the Arab collapsed, his body straining at the chains, his full weight now on his wrists. The sheer edge of the metal manacles cut into his skin. He continued to stare at Seiden, a strange smile playing on his lips.

"Shiheen was your finest hour, Mohammed. But since then," Seiden said, "what have you done?" His voice was light now, almost jocular. "You were involved in some collaborator assassinations in Lebanon once the IDF pulled out. Small jobs. For the money, no doubt. Bits and pieces. It must have been difficult for you to have watched the World Trade Towers collapse on Nine Eleven, when you had nothing to do with it. Now *that* was a monumental achievement, a true work of art."

El Aqrab pulled himself to his feet. He turned away. Thin rivulets of blood ran down his forearms from his wrists.

"But where were you," Seiden asked, "when the *Cole* was attacked in Yemen? Why doesn't bin Laden trust you?"

El Aqrab said nothing.

"You kept your head down during the 2002 invasion of Afghanistan. And then, most curious of all, your own people, your so-called 'friends and allies' at Hamas and Hezbollah sold you out to the Americans in exchange for a dozen mid-level *mujahadeen*. I suppose, even in the world of Islamist extremists, there is always someone at the far end of the spectrum. Even they found your brand of mayhem . . . unacceptable. Embarrassing. You were just too unpredictable, too independent, too much a force unto yourself. We destroyed the house where you were living with a rocket strike. We thought you were dead. We thought we had finally killed you. But you weren't dead, were you? You went underground. Was it because there were no more Marine barracks left to blow up in Beirut? Surely a suicide bomber killing a dozen civilians here, a half dozen there, cannot compare. Soft targets can't be as challenging. I wonder at that phrase," Seiden said off-handedly. "Don't you? *Soft targets.*" Then he tapped the table gently. "Night clubs in Bali. Hotels in Kenya. Markets in Baghdad. So many Improvised Explosive Devices, and such few casualties — in the scheme of things. In fact, what I don't understand is, why did you bother to come back at all? And for Miller! He was a nobody. And even if he had been important, why kill him personally? Why take the risk? It seems to me that you just wanted to get caught, as if you've had enough. God knows, sometimes I think I have. Soft targets," he repeated with a sigh. "Like the skin of those children you flayed with your knife and set afire. What do those Arabic messages mean, anyway?"

"Ah," said El Aqrab. "At last! Be quick now, you have lost much time."

Seiden pressed a button on the DVD deck. The recording of the murders in Tel Aviv began to play. One of the images — one of the boys on fire — was clearer than the rest. Seiden could just make out the words "Pregnant she-camels" and "Hell" in Arabic flaming on his flesh. The sound was deafening – the screams of the young boys and their helpless father, tied to his chair with his back to them, unable to even see his children as they cried out in desperate agony. It was so loud and distracting that Seiden almost missed the word El Aqrab whispered as he watched, as if the murders were a fireworks display. It was almost drowned out. Almost.

"Beautiful!"

Chapter 8
Friday, January 28 – 6:58 AM
Kazakhstan

Gulzhan Baqrah stood on the naked bluff, a thousand feet above the darkling plain. The morning sky still swirled with stars. It was teeth-chatteringly cold. Gulzhan listened patiently to the tinny voice at the other end of the satellite phone pressed against his ear. It was exactly as he'd feared. There was no doubt about it now. His most odious suspicions were confirmed.

He turned off the phone, slipped it into his vest, and wept. A rather portly man, with a low forehead, sloping shoulders and stubby legs, Gulzhan had a wide round face almost entirely covered by a thick black beard – spotted with gray – and bristling mustaches. He wiped his eyes, brushing the tears away. He had no time for tears. And then, as if on cue, a cold wind billowed across the bluff, born on the snowfields of the mountains of Kazakhstan, and blew the tears away. A young man approached from below.

"What is it?" Gulzhan said.

"Salaam," the young lieutenant answered. "It is time."

"Uhud has arrived?"

"He is just here."

Gulzhan turned his face, pitching his sorrow away. It was unseemly to appear so weak in front of his men. He was getting old, he thought. "Tell them I come."

"Yes, Gulzhan." With that, the young lieutenant disappeared.

Gulzhan stared out across the plain, now streaked with sunbeams from the gathering dawn. Uhud had finally returned. He could see him in his mind's eye. He could visualize the tall lean figure riding through the valley on his cinder stallion, hear the signal as the sentries fired off a round, feel their jubilation as they recognized the rider – slung to the side to avoid the bullet wound that still troubled his left thigh – as they recognized his handsome face. Uhud was late but this only generated more anticipation. Uhud was popular with the men. Too popular. He had come along too fast, too soon. Just back from Iraq, where he'd assisted in the bombing of the Great Mosque of Samarra in an effort to stir up sectarian violence, he would become more popular still. And now this latest news. Gulzhan was heavy with despair, weighed down by what he knew he had to do.

He looked across the bluff to the east. There was no time

to tarry. They still had a long way to drive before dying.

Gulzhan Baqrah was an Islamist fundamentalist. He had been fighting the Soviet-style autocrat – President Sergey Nazanov – for more years than he cared to remember, since the fall of the USSR. President Nazanov ruled the Newly Independent State with an iron fist, killing and maiming his political enemies through his ruthless Aristan secret police, hunting down so-called radicals, the Muslim warriors who believe in the *Ummah*, the transnational empire of Islam. Ironically, Gulzhan Baqrah had once assisted President Nazanov by kidnapping, torturing and – in some cases – killing over a dozen well-known journalists who'd spoken out against the Nazanov regime. It was alleged the Nazanov family had amassed a fortune in excess of one billion dollars squirreled away in some Swiss bank account, much of it earned by selling off bits of the country piece by piece, including vast armories of former Soviet weaponry left behind after the collapse of the Empire. Some said Nazanov had even helped facilitate the sale of nuclear technologies by his top military advisors, members of the Kazakh National Security Committee and the former KGB, renamed – inventively – the KNB: from designs and prototypes of explosive devices; to all manner of machinery, such as centrifuges used in the refinement of plutonium and uranium.

As a rule, the President's henchmen afforded Baqrah a precarious sanctuary in the desolate mountains of southeastern Kazakhstan. But whenever an opportunity arose, the government wasted little time in harassing the villagers under the guerrilla leader's care, throwing up roadblocks and tolls, taxing capriciously, mercilessly. Prominent citizens were always being fined for crimes which remained obscure even after they'd been found guilty and sentenced. Or worse, they simply disappeared, kidnapped and murdered by the Aristan police.

Gulzhan ran a camp in a small valley between two mountains northwest of the town of Taraz, a training farm for terrorists from throughout the Middle East and Africa – Afghanistan, Iraq, Pakistan, Lebanon and the Occupied Territories; Libya, Egypt, Yemen, and Somalia – made popular after the camps in Afghanistan and Iraq had been closed by the Americans. Whenever the Islamic Jihad or Hamas, whenever the Popular Front for the Liberation of Palestine or the Iraqi insurgency had a need for extra training for their swelling ranks – generally following a heavy blood-letting surrounding an Israeli or American offensive – Gulzhan was there with cots and trainers. It was lucrative work for one who'd been cast out.

As they traveled in two battered Mercedes-Benz 814 diesel trucks to their destination, Gulzhan thought about his old friend El Aqrab. They knew the risks they ran each day, but El Aqrab's arrest was still a cold awakening for Gulzhan. They had planned for it, of course, with the meticulousness with which El Aqrab drew each of his designs, years ago, the two of them, while hunting in the mountains, under the stars. If either of them were ever captured, the other would mount this mission. It was their insurance policy.

* * *

The train moved slowly through the mountain pass, chugging through the snow-flecked slopes, transporting a turbine and a shipment of highly enriched uranium (HEU) from the BN-350 fast breeder reactor at the Mangystau Atomic Energy Combine in Aktau for long-term storage at the Semipalatinsk Test Site in Kurchatov City. Inside the first car, a member of the Aristan secret police, Vladimir Petronov, was thinking about his sorry career, how everything had gone downhill since his wife had left him for another man – a schoolteacher, of all people. It wasn't fair. He'd always been a good husband, faithful and understanding. A good provider. But she had left him anyway. And all that she could tell him was that she did not love him anymore. As if, somehow, that really mattered.

As he ruminated, Petronov spotted a tall bearded man, one of the soldiers, Shafir, ambling down the aisle. There was something about him today – the way he walked, the way his eyes darted about the car. Petronov had been working this run for over a year now. He knew all of the soldiers . . . better than he knew his own wife, it appeared. Shafir was likeable enough, quiet, a bit shy. He was unmarried and a devout Muslim. His mother had died recently after a short illness.

Petronov yawned, got up from his uncomfortable wooden seat, and followed Shafir back through the car. The train was practically empty. In addition to the engineer, only a dozen soldiers guarded the shipment, and seven were dozing in the first car, waiting out the journey to Kurchatov City. Three guarded the rear car in which the HEU was stored. And then there was Shafir and

Altynbayev, the old cook.

Shafir retreated down the aisle, and vanished through the door that led into the dining car. Petronov followed, glancing down at the sleeping soldiers as he walked. They were kids mostly, barely old enough to shave. They were dressed in heavy woolen coats, pea green, drawn tightly around their bodies to ward away the cold. Petronov opened the rear door of the car and felt a frigid wind cut through him. He shuddered. The noise of the old diesel was deafening. It was amazing the train moved at all, given the condition of the engine. She had been overhauled so many times that it was fair to say none of the parts had been together very long. Like a new brigade, he thought. The pieces grated against each other. They heaved and groaned, trying to find their proper place within the jumble of machinery.

Petronov stepped into the dining car; it was really more of a baggage car with a makeshift galley in the rear. Altynbayev, the old cook, lay on the counter, a pair of dirty towels stuffed underneath his head for a pillow. He was snoring so loudly that Petronov could hear it over the groaning of the engine. His huge belly heaved and jiggled as the train climbed through the pass. Petronov looked down at him for a moment, at the stubbly beard, the bushy eyebrows, and resisted a sudden urge to heave him from the counter. This is where the men ate their meals. It was disgusting to see the old cook sleeping on this surface, with his filthy boots and grimy hair. Petronov had reported Altynbayev so many times that it hardly seemed to matter anymore. Nobody cared. Nobody gave a damn, so why should he?

He looked up and noticed Shafir only a few feet distant through the door. He was standing on the flatbed car, directly in front of the turbine, looking down at something by his feet. Then Petronov heard a dull explosion. The train rocked underneath him. He almost lost his footing for a second. He looked up and saw Shafir look back . . . and grin. The flatbed car began to pull away. Petronov cursed. He opened the rear door and almost tumbled from the train.

Shafir had blown the coupling. The last two cars were slowing down. Without even thinking, Petronov leapt across the chasm, across the glistening rails, and landed roughly on the open car.

The wind almost threw him from the train. It was blisteringly cold. Petronov turned to see the engine and the first two cars speed off, climbing through the narrow pass now at a startling speed. Then he felt a sharp blow on his back. He stumbled to his knees. Shafir was standing over him, a shovel in his hand.

The bearded soldier swung at him again, but Petronov shimmied to the side, and the shovel deflected off the surface harmlessly. Petronov kicked, connecting with Shafir's stomach. The soldier staggered backward, tripping on one of the metal cables that held the giant turbine in place. Then he went down.

Petronov leapt to his feet. He felt the wind propel him, toss him like a piece of paper across the flatbed car. He crashed against the soldier and Shafir punched him hard in the face – once, twice. Petronov punched back. Suddenly, a second explosion, much louder than the first, reverberated through the pass.

Petronov caught a vague glimpse of flames as first the engine, and then the first car and the dining car skidded from the rails. There was a mighty crash as they ground against the stone embankment.

Shafir staggered to his feet. He started running but Petronov caught him by the ankle and the bearded man went down. Petronov leapt on top of him. He pummeled his back, his neck. He grabbed him by the chin. Shafir began to crawl away but Petronov wouldn't let go. He rode him like a horse. He twisted the mighty neck, one hand around the soldier's forehead, the other clasping his beard. He pulled and pulled until he heard a brittle *snap*, and the soldier slumped to the deck.

Petronov collapsed on top of him. They had only fought for a minute or two, but he was completely exhausted. He felt his chest heave, struggle for gasps of freezing air. He pushed Shafir aside. The dead soldier's body rolled across the flatbed car, over the edge, and vanished out of sight. The car began to crawl. Without the engine, the steep grade of the mountain pass was acting like a break. Petronov sat up. He breathed a huge sigh of relief, then turned and saw another bearded man beside him standing on a rock, immediately beside the train.

The man was short and squat and held an automatic weapon in his hand. Petronov opened his mouth to shout something but the sound never made it past his lips. Before it had even formed inside his throat, a bullet had entered his mouth, passed through his neck, and blew out the back of his head. Petronov collapsed onto the flatbed car, remembering his wife, at last, remembering the blue and yellow dress she'd worn that first day he had seen her in the market square, the way she'd turned her head and looked at him, with the conception of a new world in her eyes.

Chapter 9
Thursday, January 27 – 6:18 PM
Queens, New York

Jerry Johnson, Decker's boss, was furious. He had been dragged away from Otto Warhaftig's lecture – which had been cut embarrassingly short. He'd rushed across the Fifty-ninth Street Bridge, all the way to Long Island City, without any direction from headquarters, mind you, to check out the situation personally. And he'd arrived just in time to see Bartolo being hoisted up into the Coroner's meat truck.

Special Agent in Charge (SAC) for the Joint Terrorism Task Force in New York, Johnson was the kind of boss who believed that each mistake his agents made was a personal affront to him. He had no patience for imperfection, least of all in himself. And his penchant for intolerance had only grown worse since 9/11. The stakes were higher now, he told his men. Sloppiness was a greater enemy than Al Qa'ida. It was "the enemy within."

So it came as no surprise to Decker when the SAC began to reprimand him publicly, in front of Williams and Kazinski, in front of Warhaftig too, as Bartolo's body was being lifted up into the meat truck. "What the fuck happened?" Johnson kept saying.

Decker didn't know where to begin, so he didn't. He was pondering why meat trucks were always made to look like ambulances. No hospital could ever fix their grisly occupants.

The Coroner was anxious to get going. He wanted nothing to do with Jerry Johnson. The SAC looked as though he would lash out at anyone who happened across his path. The Coroner slammed the doors of the meat truck shut, muttered something indecipherable, and scurried back into the cab. A moment later, the meat truck disappeared around the block.

He wanted to hear it all, SAC Johnson said. Every last fucking detail. And so Decker told him. When he had finished, Johnson continued to rail. "What a fucking mess, a fucking disaster. Why didn't you shoot the prick *before* he stabbed your partner? Jesus Christ. My grandmother would have handled this better. It was a simple stakeout. Mark my words, Decker, there's going to be an inquiry on this. I ought to take your gun and badge right now. Jesus fucking Christ."

Decker could feel himself grow angrier by the second. When he'd finally had enough, he said, "Well, perhaps, sir, if you hadn't ordered Williams and Kazinski to attend that lecture this evening – no disrespect, Warhaftig – this might have been avoided. We were shorthanded, sir, and now I've lost my partner and a friend . . . "

Johnson looked at Decker with a look of such penetrating venom that Decker felt the words stick in his throat. Decker had only just gotten out of the doghouse for sending those photographs of the PC wallpaper to Washington without apprising Johnson first.

Tall and thin, with pale gray eyes and even grayer hair, Jerry Johnson had a handsome, suntanned face, a black and gray mustache, well coiffed, and a polished nut-brown tonsure. His forehead was furrowed by meditation. He wore a jaunty brown tweed cashmere blend with natural shoulders, and a rust cravat in his breast pocket. His raincoat was Aquascutum. He cultivated the look of the 1960s British character actor typecast as "the Colonel," home from the Raj. But his chin was surprisingly weak. It tended to slip into the warm folds of his neck and all but disappear.

Despite his affectations, Johnson had risen through the ranks with startling speed, earning three special commendations in the last year alone. His handsome, well-shaped lips quivered as his eyes bore into Decker. He shifted from one foot to the next, glanced at Warhaftig, the Intel specialist on loan from the CIA, and bit his tongue. After a moment of unbearable silence, he looked up at the falling rain. It had grown heavier in the last few seconds. He raised the collar of his coat and started up the street. "Let's take a look at the apartment," he said over his shoulder.

Someone alerted the landlord and he let them into the apartment without a fuss. Johnson had brought along a search warrant from a local federal judge based on the tax evasion charges linked to the cigarette heist. The suspects had yet to be categorized as foreign agents under the Foreign Intelligence Surveillance Act (FISA).

The team picked their way through the apartment fastidiously, finding dozens of cell phones and hundreds of badly printed radical Islamic tracts but nothing conclusive. Williams did, however, uncover pay stubs for three men, including presumably the third suspect, Mecca.

His "real" name was Salim Moussa. He drove the night shift at the Imperial Taxi Company of Queens – the same cab company where Ali Singh worked – and labored as a handyman at a place called East Village Jukebox, on Broadway and Eleventh Street in

Manhattan. They photographed everything. Johnson still huffed and puffed. When Decker asked to examine the hard disk of the PC, the SAC denied it. The search warrant didn't permit them to scan or copy any hard disk, Johnson said. Decker noticed that a standard Windows background had replaced the PC wallpaper he'd spotted earlier. He pointed this out but Johnson was adamant; he didn't want to overstep his bounds. "Fruit from the poisoned tree," he kept on saying.

"Well, I took some photographs before," said Decker. "It was raining pretty hard but they should come out."

Warhaftig, the CIA Intel specialist, was mildly interested. "What did you see?" he asked.

Warhaftig looked like an ex-Sergeant. He was fifty, with a tough but friendly face, large brown eyes framed by a pair of wire-rimmed glasses, a nose that appeared to have been broken more than once, and a grim no-nonsense kind of mouth. But he'd grown a bit of a paunch the last few years. He was always chained to his desk, and if he did get out, it was generally to the choicest restaurant, drinking or dining with someone with expensable tastes. Veal was his principle weapon these days.

"Some kind of Arabic calligraphy," said Decker. "Bordered by an arabesque design."

"You may be some kind of genius with languages and cryptoanalytics," Johnson cut in, "some kind of wunderkid, but you've got a lot to learn about field work, Decker. This was a simple stakeout." He then told Williams and Kazinski to set up additional surveillance teams where they knew the suspects worked. "Decker," he continued, "you go back across the street and keep your eyes peeled."

"They're not coming back! With your permission, sir, I'd like to break the news to Bartolo's family. I know them."

"So do I, you may be surprised to learn. You have your orders. Try not to fuck them up this time."

And then Warhaftig said, "Sir, if you wouldn't mind. I'd like to accompany Agent Decker. Keep an eye on things."

"Good idea. Better to have someone along with some experience." With that he turned and walked away.

Decker and Warhaftig made their way back to the surveillance squat across the street. Decker ducked into the bathroom to clean up; he still had blood on his cuffs. When he returned to the window, Warhaftig was smoking a cigarette – a Camel. "Don't take it too hard," he said. "It wasn't your fault. You probably didn't have the shot. And Johnson, if you don't mind my saying so, is a bit of a blowhard. I've never heard of anyone not being sent home or to counseling after losing a partner. He's just pissed off his unit's down a man."

Decker sat down beside him and peered out through the camera at the apartment across the street. It was hauntingly empty now. Pitch black. The suspects must have turned the lights off before they left. Warhaftig said he was sorry that Decker had missed his lecture. "What do you know about El Aqrab and the Brotherhood of the Crimson Scimitar?" he asked.

"Not much," said Decker, reluctant to start yet another conversation bound to blow up in his face.

Warhaftig filled him in about the organization, and about El Aqrab himself. It was a quick synopsis from his humble birth in Lebanon. Trained in Kazakhstan with the renowned guerrilla leader Gulzhan Baqrah. Explosives expert. Implicated in a number of bombings, including the U.S. Marine barracks and U.S. embassy in Lebanon in '83. Blew up oil wells in Kuwait during the first Gulf war and was responsible for dozens of bombings in Lebanon and Israel, including the booby trap in Shiheen in '93 that murdered twelve Israeli soldiers.

Trained suicide bombers over the last decade during the intifadah, and then disappeared about three years ago, presumably killed after being targeted by an Israeli rocket strike.

But Crimson Scimitar cells continued to blow up U.S. soldiers in Iraq and in Afghanistan. The organization never died. Israeli information was uncharacteristically sketchy, especially concerning someone of El Aqrab's renown. One thing was legendary, however: Signature pyrotechnics were a featured part of each event.

"If he was killed, what's all the fuss?" asked Decker.

"Well, that's just it," Warhaftig said. "After three years, he's resurfaced. According to our sources, he's now in Israeli custody. Caught after slaughtering some family in Tel Aviv."

The two sat in silence, watching the rain fall on the window. Decker could still feel the incision of the wound in Tony's back. He could not get the image of his partner's . . . his *ex*-partner's fingers out of his head. He kept seeing them open, splay apart, and then slide across the balustrade, just out of reach. Just gone.

"Don't worry," said Warhaftig, as if reading his mind. "These things happen. I'm telling you, it wasn't your fault. Don't let Johnson get to you. It's just part of the job. Won't affect your file much."

"Look, Warhaftig, I don't need babysitting. And I'm not worried about my file."

Warhaftig stubbed his cigarette out in the saucer by his feet. "I know you're not," he said, blowing out smoke. "What I mean is, you have a solid record. That thing in Iowa, for instance."

Decker was surprised. Warhaftig had just joined the team that afternoon. "What do you know about Iowa?" he asked.

"You were born there, in Davenport," said Warhaftig, "to a policeman father – John Decker Sr. – and a librarian mother – Louise Carrick. Lost both of your parents in a car crash when you were just fifteen. Spent fourteen hours in surgery, two months in a coma, and a year-and-a-half in physical therapy. Some said you'd never walk again, but I guess you proved them wrong. Raised by your mother's older sister, Betsy, and her husband, Tom Llewellyn, in nearby Bettendorf. Your father insisted you take up martial arts since you were such a runty little kid, and you took several trophies in long-distance running and Kung Fu in high school, eventually becoming a black belt at seventeen." He laughed. "Had a growth spurt senior year, I guess. Went to College at Northwestern on a scholarship, where you majored in mathematics; minored in foreign languages. Graduated *Summa Cum Laude, Phi Beta Kappa, blah blah blah.* Did your thesis on neural network predictive modeling, whatever that is. Have a facility for finding patterns in seemingly random data. It was this skill that particularly impressed your instructors at Quantico where – after college and a two-year stint on the Bettendorf Police Force – you trained to become a Cryptanalyst Forensic Examiner with the FBI. Graduated at the top of your class. Then spent eighteen months with the Racketeering Records Analysis Unit in Washington, D.C., learning the ropes, before being transferred to Chicago."

Warhaftig paused, drifting on the river of his memory. He took a breath and said, "Had a girlfriend in college named Anne Tierney, a few love affairs in DC. Nothing too serious. A few call girls. Plus a girlfriend in Chicago named Maureen O'Donnell for about four months. Like those Irish girls. She left you when you couldn't commit. Transferred to the Joint Terrorism Task Force in New York after the McNally case in Iowa, for which you received a special commendation. Now subletting a one-bedroom in the

Village, slightly beyond your means. Don't smoke or drink, except on special occasions. Love chicken and fish, especially Sushi, but you aren't much of a red meat eater, are you, John? Read the *Journal of Cryptanalytics* religiously every Tuesday. Brought up a Democrat but you're largely apolitical. Never been in serious debt. Not much of a dresser, that's for sure. Oh, and no pets. That about sum it up?" Warhaftig smiled. "You have a facility for numbers," he added. "I'm cursed with a near photographic memory. Pick your poison."

Decker was flabbergasted at Warhaftig's breadth of knowledge. He shook his head. *Is that all I've become?* he thought. *Just a page or two in someone's file.*

"How many languages do you speak fluently? Besides Arabic, I mean," Warhaftig asked.

"Oh, did you forget that tidbit? Actually, I barely speak English fluently."

"No, seriously. How many?"

Decker scowled. "A few, I guess."

"A few!"

Decker shrugged. "Born with a good ear. My mother played piano pretty well. My dad spoke French and Italian and Spanish, in addition to English. He was a seaman once, in his teens and early twenties. Is that in the file too?"

"It is," Warhaftig said. "Must have been pretty interesting with two headstrong parents, one Catholic and one Episcopalian. But I guess you could say Episcopalian is kind of Catholic lite. Me, I'm a Jew. Not a very good one, mind you." He laughed, until he noticed his stomach wiggling. Then he frowned and said, "Still, I'd say that speaking ten languages, six fluently, is more than just 'a few.' You always this modest? What's that?" Warhaftig pointed at the floor.

Decker's notebook lay open at his feet. "Nothing," he said. "Just some sketches of that PC wallpaper."

"May I see them?"

Decker tossed the notebook over to the Intel specialist. Warhaftig began to flip through the pages slowly. "You did all these?"

Decker nodded.

"Don't get it. Why make drawings if you have photographs?"

"Sometimes you can see a pattern better when you try and replicate it, rather than just looking at it. You can see the depth. I mean . . . Okay, for example, I didn't even notice the number on the bottom right hand side until I drew the arabesque. Then I realized there was a break in the pattern."

"What number?"

"Here," said Decker, reaching out. He flipped the pages of the notebook rapidly. Once again, the illustration coalesced into a whole as the pages fanned together. "You see? The wallpaper has three obvious keys: Two lines of text, plus a number." He turned the notebook to a specific page and pointed at the image. "Those are the words, 'Pregnant She-Camels,' in Arabic. See? And here – another phrase." He flipped a few more pages. "'When Hell Is Raised Up.' I know the Arabic script is foliated. It makes it hard to read." He turned back to the beginning of the notebook. "And, finally, a number. See? 540,000. On the bottom right hand side."

"What does it mean?"

"I've no idea," said Decker. He closed the notebook. "I've examined the words using a number of techniques and ciphers. The phrases are too brief for me to figure out a source." He dropped the notebook on the floor. "And the number could be anything: A place reference or coordinate; a page, a chapter or verse; a bank account; or a time. Perhaps even a timer to something – an event."

"What does that mean?" asked Warhaftig.

"The number could represent hours or, more likely, seconds, given its size. You know: A countdown." Decker reached out for the camera. "That's the thing about illustrations. I doubt I ever would have found that number using just a camera. Pictures only deliver images two-dimensionally. Unlike illustrations, photographs are . . ." He froze. Then he glanced up, horrified. He looked at the rear panel of the camera and cursed under his breath.

"What's the matter?" asked Warhaftig.

Decker eyed Warhaftig with suspicion.

"What is it?" he repeated.

Decker flipped a switch and a panel on the camera swung open. It was empty. There was no memory stick within.

Warhaftig looked surprised. "Not your day," he said, after a moment.

"I'm sure I loaded this thing. You don't think those guys could have come back and . . ." Decker rolled to his feet and checked the apartment door. Nothing was out of place. The doorframe was clean. Nobody had tried to force it open. He walked back to the window and collapsed into his chair.

Warhaftig reached into his raincoat. He took out his cell phone and punched a number. "SAC Johnson?" he said. "It's Warhaftig."

Decker looked up in surprise. He could hear Johnson's shrill voice echo back.

"Listen," Warhaftig said, "for what it's worth, I just wanted to say that – in my opinion – you shouldn't be too hard on Decker. The way I see it, Special Agent Bartolo took it upon himself to follow those three suspects across the roof before backup had arrived. Probably would have done the same thing myself, given the circumstances, but you can hardly blame Decker." He paused, then added, "Anyone can make a mistake, sir. He didn't have the shot." He pulled the phone away from his ear as Johnson shouted back. "What I mean is," said Warhaftig, cutting him off, "I was in the field for almost fourteen years, and you'll never guess what just happened. I was leaning over, reaching for my binoculars, and – well – I knocked over your Nikon, sir. Yeah," he added, looking at Decker. "I'm afraid so. I suggest you submit a cross-charge. I'm sure the Agency insurance team will order a replacement. No, sir. Apparently nothing crucial." He winked at Decker. "Yes, a new one, sir. Of course. Alright then," he said. "Thank you, sir, for being so understanding. Yes, sir." He hung up the phone and slipped it back into his raincoat.

Decker stared at Warhaftig, feeling a strange mixture of anger and relief, fed by a renewed respect for the CIA Intel specialist, not so much for his favor as for his sheer audacity. "You shouldn't have done that," Decker said. "I didn't ask you to lie for me."

Warhaftig smiled. With one quick movement, he kicked the tripod and knocked the Nikon D70 to the floor. The camera shattered like an egg, like a broken skull on the sidewalk. "What lie?"

Chapter 10
Friday, January 28 – 5:07 AM
Tel Aviv, Israel

Seiden was interrupted by a loud knocking on the two-way mirror that ran the length of the interrogation room. He got up, walked nonchalantly to the door, and stepped outside into the hall.

The Director of the Mossad, Itzak Mandelbaum, and the Deputy Director, Chaiyim Cohen, stood in the observation room next door. They were watching the videotaped recording of the interrogation on a monitor.

"I didn't know you had a son," said Cohen. He was a slight man, with a shaved head and piercing ice-blue eyes. A small scar ran along his chin.

Seiden smiled and looked down at the monitor. "I don't," he answered simply. "Two girls."

Director Mandelbaum laughed. Seiden found the sound disturbing. It was perfectly pitched, yet hollow. It was the kind of laugh one makes after a dirty joke. He looked the Director up and down. He was a large man, in his fifties, with a wide and pleasant face topped by a shock of bright white hair. His lips were thin. His eyes were small for his face. Blue. No, hazel. No, gray. Seiden couldn't quite make out the color. They seemed to change based on the angle of his face. Then the Director smiled.

"Thank you, Acting Chief Seiden. We appreciate your efforts," he said. "You may go."

His teeth were small for his face, like those of a woman or child. "Excuse me?" Seiden said.

"We'll take over from here," Director Mandelbaum continued.

"But I'm just getting started," said Seiden. "Sir, I don't mean to be insubordinate, but–"

"Then don't be."

"Sir?" Seiden felt himself grow angry. This was *his* case. El Aqrab had been caught in Tel Aviv, in his jurisdiction.

"Acting Chief Seiden," the Director added. "It was unfortunate when Chief Stein retired so unexpectedly."

"He had a stroke, sir."

"Of course he had a stroke. Don't you think I know that?"

Seiden was thrown by the Director's sudden burst of anger.

"Be that as it may," the Director said, "we are still searching for a suitable replacement. Do not forget yourself. You are only the *acting* Chief. A temporary position." Then he smiled. "Of course, your name is one of many we're considering. It is not inconceivable that you could find yourself Chief Stein's permanent replacement. He was a remarkable man. A terrible loss. Terrible."

"He isn't dead, sir," Seiden said. "He's only paralyzed on the left side."

Deputy Director Cohen stepped forward. "Ben, what are you doing?" he said.

"Excuse me?"

"I believe the Director has made his position clear."

Seiden sighed. "I'm making progress, sir," he said. "I'm convinced the Arabic lettering, the words revealed during El Aqrab's explosions are more than random quotes from the Qur'an. I think they're messages to other members of the Brotherhood. I'd like to examine them more thoroughly."

"You have your orders," Cohen said.

Director Mandelbaum reached out and placed a hand on Seiden's shoulder. "Don't be upset, Ben," he continued. "El Aqrab is not an ordinary man. And, frankly, there have been too many leaks of late. Too many . . . " He paused for a second. " . . . indiscretions. It is a matter of great importance to the State that all evidence, every piece of information surrounding this case, all intelligence be kept in the strictest of confidence. There are things here that you do not see." He took his hand away.

"I agree, of course" said Cohen. "But before you go, Acting Chief Seiden, I'd be curious to hear what you think about our prisoner. As a trained psychologist."

Seiden stared at Mandelbaum. Both men were looking at him, waiting for his analysis. "What can I tell you?" he said. "I've only been with the suspect a few hours."

"Your first impressions then," said Cohen. "What drives him, Ben? Why is he here?"

Seiden sighed. He ran a hand back through his hair, staring through the two-way mirror at the prisoner within. "It's hard to tell. I believe he's a true believer, unmotivated by political or personal greed. A man of faith." He paused.

"Go on," said Cohen.

"But there is something else. The way he kills, the way he paints with fire and explosives. There is an aesthetic to his work, a kind of art."

"That much is obvious," the Director said. "Are you saying he kills to be an artist?"

"Yes . . . and no. His art is devastation, to be sure. He destroys with an aesthetic sensibility. I believe it's a kind of gift to Allah. Jung said that all great artists create not only for themselves and for their publics, but as an homage to God. I think this drives the expression of his work. Explosives are simply the aesthetic form he's chosen, much as an artist might choose the brush or pen or any other instrument. What drives him, and why did he return?" He shrugged. "We have yet to establish a link with Miller, or any of his family. Frankly, I wouldn't be surprised if it were just a random act of violence. There is a deep self-loathing at the heart of who he is, at the center of his animus. And it isn't just revenge, the source of hatred for so many of the Palestinians. At first I thought it was the guilt of the survivor, after the killing of his parents, or some friend. But I think there's something else." He shook his head. "He takes a pleasure in his pain. Did you see the way he threw himself against the chains when I told him of my 'son'? He revels in his own debasement, in his own torture. It's almost sexual in its expression."

"A masochist then," said Mandelbaum. "You think he's crazy?"

"Unstable, yes. But crazy?" Seiden shook his head. "No, he's not crazy. I think he's guilty. Of what, I have no idea. Perhaps he honestly regrets his actions, the deaths and suffering he's caused. His fanaticism drives him forward but that doesn't mean he fails to feel some sense of guilt for what he does. He gave himself up, after all. He wanted to be caught. And I think the Qur'anic passages he quotes are probably aimed at us as well as to his people in the field. Why else would he videotape the killings and then send them to us? It's more than just a taunting. He isn't simply trying to demonstrate his intellect. The recordings are a means for him to share his art. After all, of what value is an artist's work if only the artist views it? I don't know. I need more time. Perhaps if I could continue my interrogation . . . "

"We are out of time," said Mandelbaum. "My thanks to you, Acting Chief Seiden."

Seiden nodded. "I'm glad I could be of service," he said. Then he shook the Director's hand. His fingers felt boneless, soft as steamed asparagus.

Deputy Director Cohen followed Seiden from the room. They walked together by the holding cells toward the double doors at the end of the corridor and waited for the guard to buzz them out. When they had entered the stairwell leading up to the main floor, Cohen pulled Seiden aside and held him for a moment by the elbow. "I appreciate everything you've done, Ben," he said.

"Thank you, sir."

"Oh, and one more thing. I understand how an intelligent man might be tempted to retain some record of this event, in case he found his career . . . " He struggled for the words. "How can I put it? His career no longer moving. Stalled, if you will. Promotions elusive. But I think such a man would have to fight against this temptation."

Seiden examined the Deputy Director. He could not read his face. Cohen's light blue eyes were impenetrable and cold, the color of icebergs in an Arctic sea. "Yes, sir," Seiden said.

"Good, good," said Cohen. He shook Seiden's hand and turned away. Then he slipped back through the double doors and disappeared.

*   *   *

Mandelbaum ordered all the holding cells and corridors leading from the main entrance of the building to Interrogation Room B cleared. When the ground floor of the fortified structure looked like a ghost town, a figure left the UH-60 Black Hawk helicopter, entered the front door, and walked along the deserted corridors and stairwell to the basement. It was Yuri Garron himself, the Prime Minister. He was a huge man, tall and portly, with a round butcher's face and large, expressive brown eyes. His thin gray hair was combed casually across the glistening dome of his head. He told the Director and Deputy Director to secure the recordings of the interrogation and to vacate the observation room. He wanted to be alone, he said. They did as they were told. As soon as Cohen and Mandelbaum had disappeared, Garron entered Interrogation Room B where El Aqrab was chained to the ceiling, his back still to the door.

"It *is* you," the Prime Minister said as he finally got a good look at the prisoner. "When I heard, I couldn't believe it. After all these years." He laughed. "It's like . . . like Déjà vu, as though I've traveled back to 1987, back to that incident with the interrogator from Ansar II."

El Aqrab smiled. He knew exactly to what Garron referred. In August 1987, six Palestinians had escaped from Ansar II in Gaza. The Zionists assumed the escapees had slipped across the border into Egypt, but, subsequently, masked gunmen killed an

- 70 -

Israeli officer in a daring daylight attack. Later the IDF announced that the killers themselves had died in an exchange of gunfire with Israeli forces. Among the dead was one of the escapees. He had not fled to Egypt, as assumed, but had gone underground to await an opportunity to shoot the officer, who – it was subsequently revealed – was the chief interrogator at Ansar II. Many Palestinians were thrilled by this event. After a depressing string of setbacks, here was an incendiary morale booster. The community held a massive funeral, attended by thousands of mourners.

"Yes," said El Aqrab. "I remember."

"Why did you come back?" asked Garron. "After all this time. Surely not just to kill Miller. He was the last one, wasn't he?"

"No," said El Aqrab. "*You* are the last one." He smiled. "Tell me, Yuri. Do you still believe the Ansar escapees were responsible for the intifadah? I heard you say that once, on television."

Garron didn't respond.

"You still don't get it, do you?" El Aqrab said. "It was never about the riots. It wasn't the takeover of the government by the Likud, or your own ambitious settlement programs–"

"The Geneva Convention doesn't apply to the Territories," Garron said, interrupting him. "We're entitled to settle there. God gave us that land. And besides, within the year, we will withdraw completely from the West Bank. All the checkpoints will be opened. As promised."

"Allah has nothing to do with this. This is all about Garron. Even Rabin called the Gush Emunim and Kach, the Kahane Hay and all the other paramilitary settlers 'Jewish terrorists.'"

Garron stepped up, as if prepared to strike the prisoner.

El Aqrab smiled. "Go ahead," he said. "The truth is, Yuri, you are our greatest friend. Even though Arafat is dead, you continue to try and marginalize the PLO. And the more you marginalize the PLO, the more powerful The Brotherhood, Hamas, and Hezbollah become. You are a fool. What happens when you capitulate to the Americans and let the Palestinians have their fair and free elections? Do you think they'll vote El-Fatah once again? And if El-Fatah loses, how long before your own people consider you expendable? You have grown old and soft, Yuri, and soon you will have an accident, I'm sure." His voice was cool, clear as a mountain stream. "Old and soft," he repeated. "But what motivates a boy to strap twelve pounds of high explosives to his chest and climb across the fence to kill himself? The Qur'an says we're obliged to fight the enemies of Islam. And yet we do not do this with the support, nor the hindrance of some higher authority. No Prime Minister or President, no Mullah or Imam. The only path to self-empowerment, the only way to *be* is to defend the faith by preserving . . . no, by enlarging the boundaries of the *Ummah.* It may only be a neighborhood, a quarter or a Kasbah, but it is Muslim ground, sacred and worth defending, even unto death."

"Just answer me," Garron said. "Why did you come back? After all this time. Why?"

"I came back to for you, Yuri. For you! Don't you understand? To see your face. The explosion: It's already happening, right now, as we speak. With the cadence of glass as a liquid. The fuse has been lit. The flames are beginning to lick at your feet. Can't you feel them? I wanted to watch, to see your eyes. They are the eyes of a dead man. You are a ghost."

Garron drew nearer.

"Soon you will be a man without a party," El Aqrab said. "Disowned. Cast out. Reviled. Soon the whole world, as we know it, will be gone. And whoever is left, whoever survives will look back and blame . . . *you*. The man 'indirectly responsible' for Sabra and Shatila!" He laughed. "I came to watch your death throws, Yuri. The end of your ugly, miserable little life."

Garron struck the terrorist and this brought a smile of ghastly pleasure to El Aqrab's thin face. "Be careful," he said. "You wouldn't want anything to happen to me, Yuri, would you? Not yet. I've seen to it that – if it does – everyone will know . . . " He licked the blood off his lips. " . . . our little secret."

Garron stepped back. He raised his hand again but it simply hung there, in the air, unmoving. Then it fell back at his side. Despite his size, Garron looked small and feeble beside the terrorist.

"And then what, Yuri?" El Aqrab said. "You will come tumbling down. Control will fall back to the Labor party, the liberals, the weak. And we wouldn't want that, would we?" said El Aqrab. "When it rains, the water seller goes hungry. We have a common interest, after all, Yuri, a common enemy. It is called pity and forgiveness. It is called hope and reasonableness. Today it is embodied in the PLO's Abu Mazen. But tomorrow . . . " He laughed. "What you need is something to make the Americans veer away from peace. Something abominable. Something that will make what happened to the World Trade Towers seem like the work of children. Soon, Yuri. Soon, you will be forced to let me go. In a few days, not much more. Less than a week. You'll see. Then all will be revealed."

Chapter 11
Friday, January 28 – 8:38 AM
Kazakhstan

The blast blossomed like a fiery rose, clawed at the sky, and ripped the rear door of the railway car completely off its hinges. A moment later, as the smoke cleared, two objects sailed into the opening. There was a dull click as they hit the deck in unison, an agonizing moment – like the space between two frames within a motion picture – and the grenades exploded.

Gulzhan waited for a few more seconds before he leapt into the breach, his Kalashnikov nestled in his arms. His eyes pierced the gloomy darkness. The car was deathly still. Of the three guards, two were ragged heaps, and the other lay motionless, blood streaming from his nose and ears.

Gulzhan smiled. He motioned to his men and they began to clear the rear car of debris. Gulzhan reached into his jacket, removed a compass, and took a careful reading. When he had marked off the direction, he plucked his prayer rug from the pack that Uhud carried on his back. He spread it out across the floor. Then, grabbing a pair of crates, he began to build a makeshift *minbar*.

Uhud and the other men wired the railway car with explosives. Gulzhan watched them as they worked. Uhud moved like a dancer, lithely, with none of the mechanical precision with which the others went about their tasks. He bent over like a river reed, like a willow in the wind, picked up the charges and mounted them carefully around the base of the four walls, following the directions on the diagram in his hand. Uhud was a pleasure to watch. He always had been.

In a few minutes, Gulzhan had finished stacking up the crates. He climbed up on the second highest step, turned toward his men, and said, "In the name of Allah, Most Gracious, Ever Merciful, all that we are about to do we do in Your name." Then he quoted from the Qur'an, saying, "'Oh ye who believe, equitable retribution in the matter of the slain is prescribed for you: exact it from the freeman if he is the offender, from the slave if he is the offender, from the woman if she is the offender.'"

He paused and looked at the men about him. They stood in rapt attention. Even Uhud the Beautiful was captivated by his words. Gulzhan continued, saying, "'Allah has the Power; Allah is Most Forgiving, Ever Merciful. Allah does not forbid you to be kind and to act equitably towards those who have not fought you because of your religion, and who have not driven you forth from your homes. Surely, Allah loves those who are equitable. Allah only forbids you that you make friends with those who have fought against you because of your religion, and have driven you out of your homes and have aided others in driving you out. Whoso makes friends with them, those are the transgressors.'"

With that, Gulzhan descended from the pulpit. He smiled at Uhud, looked about the car, at the way the charges were laid out, the punctilious contour of the lines, when he glimpsed something out of the corner of his eye. He turned. The wounded soldier stirred. He inched his hand along the deck, his fingers clenched about his weapon. He was aiming it at Uhud's back.

Without a moment's pause, Gulzhan pulled out his knife — curved as a scimitar — and brought it down across the soldier's neck. The severed head flew like a soccer ball across the car, spinning and spurting blood. It came to rest at Uhud's feet. The men jumped back. Uhud raised his gun and fired into the bodies of the remaining soldiers. They jumped and rattled. They bounced in the hail of bullets as if they'd been electrocuted. Then, everything was still. Smoke lingered in the air.

Uhud looked up at Gulzhan. His eyes were wide, charged with emotion. Gulzhan just smiled and knelt down on his rug. He began to pray. Uhud stepped back. He looked down at the headless, bullet-ridden soldier. He kicked him once, with uncompromising violence, between the legs. Then he moved quickly to the rear of the car and signaled to his men to follow.

Set in a corner of the railway car was a large metallic container. Two of the men lifted the cover with difficulty. Uhud pulled out a pair of heavy leather gloves from his satchel and slipped them on. When they had removed the top of the container, one of the men handed Uhud a shiny metal cylinder, pipe-like, with a machined lid made to screw down tightly to create a seal. Uhud took off the lid. Then, with painstaking concentration, he reached into the kiln-like container with a ladle and began to remove the powdered material. Little by little, he filled the cylinder. When he was finished, he screwed the lid back on the tube and gave it to the man beside him. They handed him another cylinder, identical to the last. Once again, he reached into the container and began to fill the second cylinder. It took him only a few minutes to complete the job. He screwed the metal top back onto the tube, tightening it carefully. Then he turned toward

Gulzhan, saying, "It is done."

Gulzhan looked up from his prayers. His eyes were dreamy, distant. "Allah is merciful," he said, rolling to his feet. Uhud handed him the second cylinder. Gulzhan stared at it for a moment, turning it in his hands, and then stuffed it into his vest. He looked at his watch. They were precisely on time and this filled him with both satisfaction and pride. He smiled at his men. The operation was going like clockwork. He loved this feeling. Nothing could compare: No money; no woman; no house; no food. Nothing. This was what he lived for, when the world hummed perfectly, when everything he'd dreamed of finally came to pass. In an imperfect world, this was the closest thing to heaven. "You have done well," he said and his men puffed up with pride. Gulzhan was parsimonious with praise. Those four simple words meant more to them than their lives. He had seen to that. He had worked hard to make it so. "It is time," he said and leapt from the rear of the train.

Uhud followed him with the rest of the men. When they had gone about fifty yards down the tracks, one of the guerrillas erected a video camera on a tripod. The remainder of the men took up their positions in the rocks. In only a few minutes, everything was ready. Gulzhan gave the signal at exactly 9:00 AM, Uhud hit the switch on the transmitter, and the railway car disintegrated in a wave of light, strange pirouettes of fire, bright Arabic calligraphy and illuminated scrolls of flame. It was all being captured on tape, Gulzhan knew. Digitally imprisoned. El Aqrab would be proud.

As the smoke cleared, Gulzhan and Uhud came together, hugging like father and son. "Be careful," Gulzhan said. "I'm sure you must be tired after your journey."

"You worry too much. You're like an old woman," Uhud replied. "Everything's as it should be."

Gulzhan nodded. He stared at his lieutenant. He patted him gently on the shoulder. "As it should be. You're right," said Gulzhan. Then, without another word, he started back along the path to where they had parked the trucks.

Gulzhan climbed up into the nearest MB-814. Two of his men got in beside him. He watched as Uhud and the rest of the guerrillas mounted the second truck, another battered Mercedes Benz. "Wait," said Gulzhan. "You have the tape?"

The man beside him nodded, patting his jacket.

Uhud's truck began to crawl along the narrow track that

paralleled the snowy pass. Gulzhan watched it gradually recede. "'Lord, Thou dost comprehend all things in Thy mercy and knowledge,'" he prayed, "'so grant Thy forgiveness to those who repent and follow Thy way, and safeguard them against the punishments of hell.'" Then he turned and looked out the window. He stared at the snowy ground, the whiteness of it all, the crystalline perfection. "Allah, forgive me," he said.

* * *

Uhud's truck made its way along the circuitous road down toward the Caspian Sea. As it neared the town of Zhetybay, across an open plain, an armored car materialized from behind a stand of boulders and crashed against the old Mercedes-Benz. Uhud felt his face smash up against the windshield. A moment later, as the truck careened into a ditch, he glimpsed the soldiers in the fields around him. He pulled at the handle but the door was jammed. And then the truck tipped over and the earth rushed up to meet him.

When he awoke, Uhud was lying on the ground a dozen meters from the truck. Soldiers were streaming over the tipped MB-814, like ants around an anthill. He started to rise but someone held him down. He could taste blood in his mouth. Somehow, this reassured him. If he could taste blood, it meant he was still alive. He looked about the plain. His comrades were heaped together in a nearby ditch. Their faces were gone but he recognized them from their clothes. A great shout rose up above the ringing in his ears. The soldiers on the truck began to jump about. And then a solitary figure stood atop the cab, waving an object in his hand. It was the cylinder. Uhud could see it glinting in the sun. Suddenly a wave of nausea overcame him and Uhud threw up across his legs and thighs. Somebody laughed. He looked up. A Colonel stood above him. He was smiling. He reached down and pulled him to his feet. It was only then that Uhud realized he was bound. His hands were lashed together, behind his back. The Colonel said something. Uhud felt himself pushed roughly from behind. He started forward, stumbling. But he didn't fall. They had not bound his feet, he realized. He looked down. He could see himself walking. He could see the way each foot moved, one before the other.

The Colonel herded him along the road. When they had

reached the boulders, the Colonel kicked him and Uhud went down, onto his knees. He could not see the truck anymore. It was behind the boulders. He could not see the soldiers either. He looked up and the sun stared down at him. His face felt warm and wet. The Colonel was talking. Uhud could see that now. He was talking into some kind of field phone with a long antenna. He was saying something but the words were indistinct. Uhud couldn't make them out above the ringing in his ears. The ringing in his ears. It would not go away. And then he saw the Colonel reach down for the handgun on his hip. He pulled it out. He aimed it at Uhud's face. He smiled. He had a black mustache and coal black eyes. He was a handsome man. He held the phone out in his other hand.

"What?" said Uhud.

The Colonel kept on smiling. He pressed the gun to Uhud's face. He brought the field phone closer. The ringing was unbearably loud. The Colonel mumbled something.

"What? I cannot hear you. What do you want me to say?"

And then the Colonel laughed and mouthed the word, "Goodbye."

* * *

Gulzhan hung up his satellite phone. He looked out through the windshield at the deserted stretch of road. It seemed to unroll indefinitely across the open plain. "Uhud is dead," he said.

The two men beside him in the cab did not respond. He could feel their bodies tense up for a second but the truck didn't veer a centimeter from its path, didn't slow or pick up speed. The old Mercedes-Benz moved on relentlessly.

Gulzhan closed his eyes. With Uhud's team captured, they only had eight kilograms of Highly Enriched Uranium left – just shy of the "significant quantity" threshold as defined by the International Atomic Energy Agency. Yet enough to make a nuclear device with a one-plus kiloton yield. A very respectable bomb. El Aqrab was wise.

Chapter 12
Friday, January 28 – 2:34 PM
New York City

It had been a long, frustrating day. Decker had gone out with
Williams, Kazinski and Warhaftig just after sunrise to interview
drivers at the Imperial Taxi Company in Queens. Although
generally thankless duty, Decker had had to almost beg Kazinski to
let him tag along. Another pair of watchers had been assigned to
the squat in Long Island City. He was available, Decker had told
them. And his language skills might prove useful.

Truth was, it was meant to be a day off for Decker; he had
a number of vacation days stacked up. In fact, he should have
taken some time off during his transfer from Chicago to New York,
but the days had somehow been misplaced, along with his favorite
Nikes and that T-shirt from Key West, like so many other things in
the move from Illinois. Johnson insisted Decker take his vacation
time immediately – standard practice whenever a partner died. On
the other hand, the SAC had shuttled down to Washington, D.C.
that morning. He wouldn't be back until the following day.
Decker just wanted to help out, he told Kazinski. He just wanted
to be part of the team, to be of service. He could take his vacation
any time.

In the end, Williams and Warhaftig had felt sorry for him
and – over Kazinski's protests and better judgment – let Decker
come along. And it was a good thing too. The drivers were already
suspicious. Many of them had been interviewed by the authorities
before and they knew what to expect. They sat in the back office,
looking churlish, drinking cold coffee, trying hard not to understand
English.

After about twenty minutes of watching Kazinski stumble
through one interrogation after another, Decker got up and left the
room. What was the point? He didn't know how Williams and
Warhaftig could put up with it. Each time he tried to interject, to
translate some tidbit he thought might prove important, Kazinski
shut him down. He might as well not have come.

Decker moved out into the main garage, sat down on a
bench, and began to examine the pool. About a dozen or so men
were sitting or standing about, smoking cigarettes, checking their
cars, punching out. There appeared to be a new shift coming in. It
didn't matter where you were – from corporate boardroom to high
school cafeteria – the same set of characters always seemed to map

out each new territory, in exactly the same way. There was always a dominant male, the Alpha wolf, usually a tough but not altogether large man, in some corner, flanked by a large enforcer. Around him stood intelligence, a few omega wolves, and on the outside, the snitch, the connection to the other groups and individuals who spun about the social solar system. In this case, the snitch wore blue jeans and a cowboy shirt. He had a swarthy round face, friendly eyes and a soft rather petulant mouth.

Decker got up, strolled across the garage, and sat down right beside him. As it turned out, the snitch was also the local bookie and odds-maker, and the kind of man you went to when you wanted something organized, a union meeting or retirement party handled without incident. His name was Akbar. He was a Yemeni who spoke machine-gun Arabic with the cutting accent of the Horn of Africa. Within five minutes, Decker and he had made their way to the far corner of the garage, behind a beat-up gold Impala, where they began to talk in earnest.

How long had he been working there? asked Decker. Where did he live? How long had he been in America? Where was he from originally? This was followed by a fair amount of banter about his hometown in North Yemen, about the difficulty of making a living in America, about American movies and American women, about American food, about what he missed most about his homeland. After a few more minutes, as they sat together on a nearby bench, Decker finally brought up Ali Singh and Salim Moussa. The man stiffened. His eyes narrowed into slits and he turned away. But Decker was insistent. "You were friends with Ali Singh and Moussa when they worked here. I know you were," he said. "Perhaps you still are. It is common knowledge. Why do you deny it? Are you ashamed of them?"

The Yemeni folded his arms. Then, as if he had rehearsed this movement, he leaned against the wall of the garage and simply sat there without speaking, staring off into space.

After a full minute or two, he finally said, "We talked together, that much is true. But I didn't know them very well. Only enough to learn that they are pious men, good men, unlike so many others here who claim that they are Muslims. Yet they eat pork, and drink and copulate with whores."

"Why are you so afraid?" said Decker.

"Afraid?" The Yemeni laughed. "Why should I be afraid? The fact that you are speaking to me, right now, at this very moment, has already marked me for death. And if I am already dead, why should I be afraid? I have nothing to lose." He shook his head. "No, my friend. It is you who should be fearful. You are not dead. Not yet." Then he turned and looked away, and added in an off-hand kind of way, "What are you going to do now? Arrest me? Is that your plan?"

Decker remained impassive.

"Go ahead. Arrest me then. I will tell you nothing."

Decker shook his head. "No, I don't want to arrest you."

Akbar looked even more confused. Then he began to smile. "I did not think so. A fool could see that it would be a fruitless exercise." He grinned. "And you are clearly not a fool."

"I'm going to arrest *him*," said Decker, pointing at the Alpha wolf.

Akbar looked horrified. "Zahid Tafari! But why? What has he done?"

"Oh, I'm sure he's done something or other, somewhere along the way. First, I think I'll check with Immigration. Just in case. Then I'll see if the IRS can audit his returns – say for the last three years. Then–"

"What do you want to know?" said Akbar, looking down. It was as if all the air had been suddenly let out of him. "There is a reason why you cannot find this young Sudanese named Salim Moussa." He looked up, frowning petulantly. "For one, he is not Sudanese. His parents are, or were, but Moussa was born right here. In New York. Or, more precisely," he said, "in a town called Yonkers."

It turned out later, much to everyone's surprise, that Akbar was telling the truth. Salim Moussa had indeed been born in Yonkers to parents of Sudanese descent, had gone to local elementary schools, to the local junior high school and for two years to Yonkers High School before dropping out his junior year. Apparently, he got picked on a lot while in school. His parents were poor. His dad was a bricklayer, his mother a K-Mart cashier. He did a few odd jobs after high school, worked construction for a while during the summer months, cleaned pools and tended gardens – that sort of thing. He fell into a crew of second-story men but he never got into trouble himself. Then, just after his twenty-first birthday, when he was still living at home, he went into the city and got a job at the Imperial Taxi Company in Queens. A month later, he moved into a small apartment near Randall's Island. He kept mostly to himself. He was a quiet neighbor. He was practically invisible until, one afternoon, something happened.

He was taking a fare along First Avenue up to York and Seventy-second when this red town car, a Caddie, swept out and clipped him in the rear. His cab hooked over to the left. He struggled to straighten her out, slammed on the breaks, and pulled over, shaking. His fare, a young businessman in a charcoal suit, jumped out and dashed across the avenue into another cab. The town car that had clipped him hobbled over to the side. The impact had torn the Cadillac's bumper loose and it screeched across the macadam, showering sparks. A man climbed out of the Cadillac and looked down at the damage. He was huge, and white – a Russian, it turned out, from Brighton Beach – with a bullet-shaped head, close-cropped blond hair, a lantern jaw and washed-out light blue eyes. He wore a beautifully tailored sharkskin suit, jet-black. He said something indiscernible. He scratched the bristle on his chin. Then he approached Moussa, stepped up and slammed his palms into his chest. Moussa flew backwards onto the hood of his cab, the wind knocked out of him. He had been thrown off by the opulence of the suit. He started to protest when the palms smashed into him again. He tried to step away but the Russian towered over him. He held him down.

"You. Monkey man," he said. "You are going to fix my bumper." The Russian brought his fist back as if to strike him, but it never happened. A hand materialized from nowhere and wrapped itself around his wrist. Another man stepped up, a black man. A second cab had pulled up by the accident. Moussa recognized him. His name was Ahmed, an Imperial Taxi driver. A Sudanese, like his parents. Ahmed bent the fingers, hand and wrist of the Russian back along his arm, back and inward across the mighty shoulder, until he crumpled to his knees. "You're breaking my wrist," the giant Russian screamed. He tried to punch Ahmed with his other hand but the Sudanese stepped gingerly away.

"Get into your car," Ahmed said to Salim Moussa. "Now."

Moussa didn't argue. He jumped back into his yellow cab, started her up, and peeled out along First Avenue. In less than fifteen minutes, he had made it back across the Fifty-ninth Street Bridge to Queens.

Ahmed, it turned out, was a devout Muslim. According to Akbar, Salim Moussa and Ahmed became fast friends after that incident. Moussa started to take Arabic courses at the same mosque in Queens where bin Basra and Singh were later arrested. He learned self-defense and how to pray. He became a completely different person.

In 1999, Salim Moussa got his wish and traveled to the Sudan, his parents' birthplace, and then to Russia and a host of Newly Independent States. He returned to the United States on July 12, 2001, only a month or so before the attack on the World Trade Towers. But unlike Akbar and so many others, he had never been interviewed after 9/11. He was, after all, an American.

Akbar finished his story. He looked at Decker and said, "Is that what you wanted to hear? Is that what you were looking for?"

"Just one more thing."

"Yes?"

"Where could I find this Ahmed now? Salim Moussa's friend?"

"In Woodlawn Cemetery. It is unfortunate, but he was killed during a robbery about a week ago. It happens. It is one of the unpleasant unpredictabilities of the job."

The agents headed back across the Fifty-ninth Street Bridge into Manhattan. They drove in Kazinski's SUV south on the FDR, and made their way to Greenwich Village. The owners of East Village Jukebox – a pair of gay men from Long Island named Gerald and Ted – claimed that they couldn't remember much about Salim Moussa, except that he came and went at odd hours, as he pleased. But he was a good worker and never complained, honest and sober. He seemed painfully shy about his English, being a Sudanese. Moussa never initiated conversations and kept his political and religious views to himself. He was certainly a religious man; he prayed five times a day, and went to Mosque each Friday.

Williams asked the owners if they wouldn't mind showing him all the work orders processed over the last few months while Moussa was employed there, and they were more than happy to oblige. They still remembered 9/11. That event, and the recession which soon followed, had decimated their business. Jukeboxes were discretionary items, after all. "You don't suddenly get a feeling in your stomach at 3:00 AM to run out and pick up a couple of jukeboxes," Gerald said. "No," said Ted. "You don't do that." After about fifteen minutes, the owners finally returned, their arms laden with files. "Knock yourselves out," they said in unison and left the room.

"Now why," Williams wondered aloud, "would a boy who grew up in Yonkers be shy about his English?"

"Maybe he's ashamed of being an American," Kazinski said.

The agents spent the next few hours pouring over the work orders – mostly independent restaurants and bars, a few chains such as Hallahan's and Rock 'n Roll Planet, as well as some private residences. There were dozens and dozens of them. But, except for some shoddy bookkeeping, nothing seemed amiss.

At one point, Decker got up to take a break. His eyes were strained from the close reading. He was getting a headache. He made his way to the rear of the dealership. The place was packed with jukeboxes. Many were standard CD/DVD players, clean-lined and contemporary. A few were classic vinyl Wurlitzers, or spanking new Rock-Olas with patented SyberSonic sound, colorful plastic accents and bright multi-colored lights. Some contained water, busy with columns of bubbles or tropical fish, while others looked more like giant standing lava lamps. Decker proceeded past another office into a narrow corridor. There was a bathroom to his left. He ignored it. The corridor led to a set of stairs by a payphone. He started down, heading toward the basement.

The walls were brick here. The corridor turned, then vanished into darkness. Decker felt the wall for a light switch and flipped it on. Bright fluorescents flashed like lightning overhead, spreading along the corridor, illuminating it one section at a time. Decker made his way down the passageway, his footsteps echoing. The corridor pitched to the right, then jogged left. Finally, Decker noticed a change in temperature. It was getting warmer and his nose was suddenly assaulted by the distinctive odor of a gym – the smell of sweaty socks and sneakers, fresh mold and dank humidity. The corridor led into a narrow L-shaped basement room, a kind of changing area, with a few metal lockers propped up against the rear wall and a pair of wooden benches. There was an alcove on the far side of the room with a single shower and a torn white plastic shower curtain. Decker noticed a calendar on the wall; it was from last year, some kind of promotional piece from Wurlitzer, with a busty girl wearing antlers writhing on a snow-sprinkled, cherry-red jukebox.

Decker walked over to the lockers and inspected them one by one. Most were empty. One hid an old gray sock, another a pungent pair of sneakers. He slammed the lockers closed as he finished searching them, and the noise reverberated in the enclosed space. Somewhere upstairs someone had flipped on a jukebox. He could hear Elvis Costello lamenting. *Well it seems you've got a husband now.* He opened the last locker, peered inside. Someone

- 84 -

had left behind a dark blue windbreaker. Decker checked the pockets. Nothing. He looked behind it. Nothing. He looked down. There were a couple of sheets of paper at the bottom of the locker. He picked them up. The first was blank. So was the second. He could see where they had been torn off from the pad; each sheet was trimmed with ragged paper pigtails. But as he was about to put them back, the top sheet caught the bright reflection of the fluorescents overhead.

Decker pitched the sheet to the side, just slightly, trying to catch the light. The reflection bounced and he saw the outline clearly, the arabesque, the invisible calligraphy. Someone had written something here; or — more accurately — on the sheet immediately above it in the pad, and the indentation had come through. You could see the imprint clearly in the light.

Decker placed the paper on the bench. He took out a mechanical pencil from the pocket of his blazer and began to shade in the impression, exposing the outline underneath.

It was indeed some kind of Arabic script, but he could barely make it out: *Death Will Overtake You.* And a number: 54,000.

While similar in design, this illustration was clearly different from the one which he had spied through Moussa's window. The PC wallpaper had been less florid, less ornate.

I hear you let that little friend of mine take off your party dress. Decker folded the piece of paper and slipped it into his jacket. *Ahhhllison . . . my aim is true. My aim is true. My aim is true . . . .*

"Find anything?" Warhaftig said.

Decker almost slammed into Warhaftig as he turned the corner at the bottom of the stairs. "Not really." He started up the steps.

There was a payphone at the top of the landing, and Decker noticed someone had torn the wallpaper off at a seam. The naked concrete was spattered with phone numbers. "How about you? Any luck?" For some reason, Decker could not tear his eyes away from the wall.

"Just those work orders," Warhaftig said, huffing up the stairs behind him. "Kazinski's heading back. You coming?"

"Going uptown," said Decker.

"What for?"

"Thought I'd visit Doctor Jusef Hasan."

"That guy from Columbia?"

Decker nodded. "If anyone can help me decipher that wallpaper, it's probably him. He's an expert on Islamic culture and calligraphy. I already tried the CIA and NSA. Not a peep. They're clueless."

"He's a nut, Decker. I've seen him on the News Hour with Jim Lehrer. He's a radical extremist, always bitching about how the Patriot's Act is unconstitutional, that sort of thing. What makes you think he'll talk to you? You're the establishment, the enemy. And besides, Homeland Security considers him a risk."

Decker turned. "He'll talk to me," he said.

Chapter 13
Saturday, January 29 – 1:34 AM
Kazakhstan

The truck pulled up beside a three-story brick warehouse on the outskirts of Gurjev on the Caspian Sea. Gulzhan and his men got out and stretched their legs. As they flexed and moved about the cobblestone courtyard, three men appeared in the headlights of the truck, emerging through a corrugated iron door. They approached Gulzhan and embraced him, one by one.

The first man was small, with a narrow face and frame, interminable black eyes and ebony hair. He had the body of a gymnast, supple and muscular. He wore a pair of green fatigues and a tatty brown turtleneck sweater.

"Salaam, Ali Hammel," Gulzhan said.

"Salaam," Hammel replied. He touched his hand to his heart and kissed his fingertips.

The second man stood in stark contrast to the first. He was huge, with a large melon-like head, thick wavy black hair, and a long bushy black beard. His eyes seemed perpetually in motion, ox-like, taking in the truck, the men, the moonlight on the black canal that winked at the far end of the alley, adjacent to the warehouse. When he was satisfied that nothing was amiss, the herd safe, he hugged Gulzhan with transparent glee.

"Salaam, Auwul," said Gulzhan. He slapped him on the back. The large man grinned, his huge teeth glistening in the tangle of his beard. "It's good to see you again. You're looking fat, and happy."

The third man stepped in from the side. He had a lean and predatory look, like a jackal, a thin henna-red beard, and piercing almost amber eyes. His head was shaved. He wore a camouflage jacket that hugged his narrow waist, a pair of green parachute pants, and thick black Army boots taped up around the ankles. "Where is the other truck?" he asked.

Gulzhan glanced about. "I have bad news," he said. "Uhud is dead."

The man's eyes narrowed to the shape of almond shells. "How?" he replied.

"His truck was ambushed near Zhetybay. A' in sh'Allah." Gulzhan paused for a moment, glaring at the ground. "One of our informers called me."

"And the HEU?"

"Do not worry, Ziad," Gulzhan said, patting his vest. Then he added, "What about Kunabi?"

"On his way."

"Good, good." Gulzhan looked over at the truck. He seemed distracted for a moment, as if he were checking the pressure of the tires. Then he turned and said, "Let us sit and eat." He stretched his back, craning his neck with surprising dexterity. "It has been a long drive, and we are hungry."

The men began to file back toward the warehouse, all save Ali Hammel, who hovered for a moment in the courtyard. When everyone else had disappeared, he turned toward Gulzhan, saying, "What happened to Uhud?"

"I told you," Gulzhan said.

"Do not play games with me, Gulzhan Baqrah. I know you too well."

Gulzhan shrugged. He studied the small man next to him. "Very well," he said. "You knew him too, didn't you, Ali? I'd almost forgotten. Friends, perhaps. And I'm sure El Aqrab will want to be informed." He spat and started slowly down the alleyway that ran along the warehouse, back toward the canal. Hamel glided at his side. When they had reached the dock, Gulzhan stopped and stared up at the warehouse, blanched by the light of harbor cranes. It was a three-story brick structure with large frosted windows reinforced with chicken wire. A series of sliding doors ran almost the entire length of the ground floor facing the canal. At one end, an abandoned furnace chimney clung desperately to the side, illuminated by a streetlight.

The building had once been a manufacturing center for farm equipment – oxen plows and fencing, cisterns and windmills – before being converted into a warehouse. But following the collapse of the Soviet Union, business had fallen off. The warehouse was all but empty now. Only a clothing importer still used the facility from time to time.

Gulzhan stopped at the lip of the canal and looked down at the oily water. Pieces of plastic and paper floated on the surface. The canal ran a quarter of a mile or so along the quay before spilling out into the harbor and the Caspian Sea. It too was used infrequently these days. Most of the shipping now was handled by the container port in Gurjev's western suburb. Somewhere a seagull cawed. Gulzhan looked up. It was clouding up again. Soon it would rain.

"I'm waiting," Hammel said.

Gulzhan turned and glared down at the man beside him. "I loved him," he said. "You know that."

"Your love is legendary."

Gulzhan frowned. "I took him in when he had nothing. I fed him, Ali. I trained him. I put the clothes on his back."

"All this is known to me."

Gulzhan looked back at the canal. "Indeed," he said with a small shrug. Then he added, like an afterthought, "He was using his Swiss bank accounts to buy options, to short securities on the New York Stock Exchange."

Hammel said nothing but Gulzhan could hear him catch his breath. "It was stupid," Gulzhan continued. "It jeopardized the mission. And it cost him his life."

"You are sure of this?"

Gulzhan looked at Hammel with a mixture of horror and disbelief. He felt a spasm of revulsion in his throat. "Of course I'm sure," he said. "Do you think I wanted this? After everything I did? I loved him, like my own son. I loved him!" He could feel his coffee-colored eyes begin to water. He turned away, embarrassed. *What's happening to me?* he thought. *I'm falling apart.*

"It was written," Hammel said. Then, after a moment, he added, "I believe you, Gulzhan Baqrah. Uhud was a greedy man. Vain. Intemperate." He kicked a stone into the canal, dimpling the surface of the water. "He liked his clothes too much. His ears bristled with rings. He reminded me of a Tuareg poem, a *heinena*," he said. "*The insane son of Adam denies his death, forgets his way, loitering in darkness; his eye is full of fancy; he hears but never listens. If God looks into the mouth of he whose strident sound is empty, there will be pain. His walk is trained, his clothes refined; his neck rides stiffly on his chest; his lungs are filled with pride. The desert Djinn have gutted them within; they have no boundaries . . .* But we Algerians are not the Lebanese," he said, catching himself. He gripped Gulzhan with his eyes. "We've never had enough to miss." Then he smiled and added blithely, "You did well to have him killed, Gulzhan. El Aqrab will be pleased."

Gulzhan yanked his arm away. He stared with hatred at Hammel. "Of course he will. He's always most pleased when I'm least happy." With that he turned and walked away.

Ali Hammel followed him back along the alley to the courtyard. When they had reached the entrance to the warehouse, Gulzhan spun about and said, "I've done my job." He pointed a thick finger at the small man's chest. His great beard parted, glaring with a sudden gash of teeth. "Now make sure you do yours."

Hammel stared at him and Gulzhan felt a chill creep though his groin. Not even his hatred of the Algerian could insulate him from the feelings he felt whenever he was around Hammel. Gulzhan surrounded himself with killers. Indeed, it was his job to manufacture them, to perfect them, to help them learn or hone their skills. But there was something about the Algerian that even he found disconcerting. It was his eyes, like the eyes of those little yellow snakes he used to crush with rocks as a small boy. Gulzhan had seen Hammel in action. The Algerian had that uncanny ability to freeze his enemies before he struck, to all but hypnotize them with a glance. It was as if he didn't really kill them. He simply sucked them up into his sphere. He absorbed them into nothingness.

"With pleasure," Hammel replied, but Gulzhan knew that he was lying. Unlike men who took pleasure in their work, no matter how perverse, Ali Hammel felt neither ecstasy nor pain. He was neither proud nor humble, unmotivated by greed or political ambition, by sex or power, nor by some denial of death; of that Gulzhan was convinced. No, the Algerian felt nothing. And this was why he feared him.

The men sat around on pillows on the floor, in a corner of the warehouse, beside their MB-814s. They ate in silence, intent on their chicken and couscous, seared lamb and disks of bread. Gulzhan watched them as they fed. The Egyptian, Auwal Al-Hakim, tore at the meat from the common plate, rending the flesh with sausage-like fingers, and then stuffing large chunks into his mouth. His greasy beard was speckled with skin. His ox-like eyes rolled back and forth in his head as he chewed.

The Lebanese known only as Ziad ate more delicately. He had stationed himself by the door. Every once in a while, he would pull himself up, stretch his right leg, and glance out of the window. Then he'd sit back down again. He picked at the food like a bird, a rust-colored vulture. He selected only the meatiest morsels, snatched them up, and then eyed them once again before popping them into his mouth.

The two men who'd helped Gulzhan hijack the train sat by themselves, tucked in the corner. They felt like outsiders, he knew. They were not only unsure of the strangers around them – the stuff of legend and cartoons all at once – but more so of themselves.

They ate self-consciously, plucking off pieces and then stepping away, like bitches new to the pack.

And Ali Hammel simply sat there. He never touched the food. In fact, now that he thought about it, Gulzhan had never seen the Algerian eat anything, and they had shared many a meal together. He sat quietly watching the others, cleaning his gun – a 9-millimeter Glock 18. At one point, when most of the food had been consumed, Hammel stood up and moved about the group, pouring out sweet green tea from a brass carafe. He acted like a graceful serving boy and this made Gulzhan wonder. Hammel was no one's servant, not even El Aqrab's. He was a force unto himself.

The men leaned back upon their pillows. Gulzhan saw his opportunity and raised his glass, and quoted from *Al-Waqi'ah*, saying, "'When the Event comes to pass, the coming of which no one can avert, some it will bring low and others it will exalt. When the earth is shaken violently, and the mountains are crumbled into dust and become like motes floating in the air, you will be divided into three groups: those on the right, those on the left, and those who are foremost. They will be the honored ones, dwelling in the Gardens of Bliss.'" He drank from his glass and the men followed suit. "You will be buried in your own clothes, covered in blood," he editorialized. "You will need no threefold linen shroud, no winding cloth. You'll be *shahid* – true witnesses. 'Say not of those who are killed in the cause of Allah that they are dead; they are not dead but alive; only you perceive it not . . . Surely, to Allah we belong, and to Him shall we return.'"

He put his glass back on the floor. Suddenly, without warning, Ali Hammel stood up and ambled over to the men who had arrived with Gulzhan in the truck. They glanced up at him with consternation, then at each other. One was about to speak when he realized that his throat no longer operated. He reached a hand up, grabbed at his neck. The other man leaned forward stiffly, toward his Kalashnikov. Hammel kicked it away. It clattered harmlessly across the warehouse floor. Then the Algerian squatted down in front of the two men and stared into their eyes. They began to wheeze. They couldn't breathe. It was as if the air had been sucked out of them, first from their lungs, then from the building, then from the atmosphere itself. They began to panic. They glanced over at Gulzhan. They rolled their eyes, bloated with fear. They clenched their fists, opened their mouths as wide as they could go, and finally fell against each other in a heap. Within seconds they were still.

Ali Hammel watched them for a moment longer, tilting his head to the side, looking deep into their eyes, trying to catch the wink of their extinction. Then it finally came, and he absorbed it soundlessly. When he was satisfied, he returned to the spot where he'd been sitting earlier, and continued to clean his gun.

The rest of the men behaved as if nothing had happened. Gulzhan cleared his throat. He took another sip of tea. Then he said, "Arrangements have been made to take you across the Caspian to Rasht. From Iran you will travel westward, separately, through Iraq and into Syria. Everything has been arranged." He looked about the group. "There will be no trouble. When you reach the Mediterranean, you will journey under new directives, to different destinations."

Just then, Ziad clicked his tongue and everyone turned and stared at him. He pointed out the window. He raised a single digit, ducked and squatted down behind the corrugated iron door, drawing his gun. A moment later somebody knocked. Gulzhan wandered over nonchalantly. He peered out through the grimy window. He motioned toward Ziad to move, and opened the door.

A small bald man with glasses and a large black attaché case hesitated by the entrance. When he saw Gulzhan, he smiled and bowed. He was wearing a large black coat over a Western suit. He was pale and sported a thin dark brown mustache, trimmed close to the lip. "Gulzhan?" he said.

Gulzhan smiled and motioned for the man to enter. He stepped inside uncertainly. As soon as he saw the other men, he lifted the briefcase to his chest as if it were a shield. Then he pulled back, thought better of it, and took another step. "Salaam," he said, pitching his voice at no one in particular. His glasses twinkled in the light. "Salaam," he repeated. The men stared back at him without a word.

"Good evening," Gulzhan said. "Please, come in, Dr. Kunabi." He urged the small man forward. "Would you like something to eat, to drink?"

"No. No, thank you," Kunabi answered timidly in Kazak, the tortured Turkic dialect.

"This is Dr. Kunabi of the Kazakhstan Ministry of Nuclear Science and Technology. Dr. Kunabi, my business associates." Gulzhan waved a hand about the room.

Dr. Kunabi finally noticed the two dead men in the corner. He looked at their bulging eyes, their open mouths and backed away.

"Please, pay no attention to those . . . men."

Dr. Kunabi tried diligently not to stare at the bodies heaped together in the corner. Despite the cold, his forehead was covered with perspiration.

"Dr. Kunabi here is one of our country's foremost nuclear scientists. He is here to help us, aren't you Dr. Kunabi."

"If I can," Kunabi said.

Gulzhan took the small man by the elbow. "Of course you can. Please," he added. "Follow me."

They made their way toward a door at the opposite end of the warehouse. As they walked, Kunabi kept on turning, kept on looking back behind him at the others. He smiled at them even as Gulzhan opened the door and gently pushed him in.

The room was filled with wooden crates, most of them opened, spewing yellow straw, newspaper clippings, or snow-white Styrofoam peanuts. Instruments had been set up on a wooden table: screens and pressure pumps; two electronic devices, like two small EKG machines, linked by a pipe. Nearly everything had been unpacked, assembled. Tubing was stacked against one wall, as high as a man. Several dozen large canisters of gas were propped up in the corner. Kunabi stepped excitedly into the room.

"It is all here," Gulzhan said with pride. "You can start immediately. We have little time."

Kunabi glanced about. "Everything?" He listed the instruments he'd requested, abandoning his Kazak dialect for Russian. Most business transactions took place in Russian anyway; Kazak had been outlawed during the Soviet era. But the main reason he'd switched to Russian was because the Kazak language simply couldn't accommodate the terms. They were too technologically advanced. They had yet to be invented. Then he reverted back to Kazak, saying, "Including my money, of course."

"Of course," said Gulzhan with a laugh. "Although both you and I know you will never live to spend it."

Kunabi slumped. He glanced back at the door, hugging his attaché case.

"Do not worry, Dr. Kunabi. Your secret's safe with me. Let us speak frankly. You may be a devout Muslim, but were it not for the sacrifice you've already made for your country, you would not be here. Would you?"

Kunabi shook his head.

"I know that you are dying, Dr. Kunabi. I've known it all along. Since before our first meeting. A small exposure here. An accident there. It all adds up, does it not? And, suddenly, the world collapses. You may be a good scientist, but the safety record of the Kazakhstan Ministry of Nuclear Science and Technology has much to be desired. All this is known to me," said Gulzhan. Then he smiled and added, "As is your love for your family." He flicked a switch and the fluorescents crackled overhead.

There were four attaché cases on the table beside the instruments. Kunabi wandered over to them. Each case looked identical, covered by some kind of brushed aluminum – about a meter long, and half a meter wide. He stroked the nearest to him. He opened it and peeked inside.

The attaché case was cast into a single piece, like a computer terminal. There was a keyboard built into the lid. Within the case itself, across the lower half, was a raised area featuring several digital displays and buttons. Above the displays, on the right hand side, a bulbous protrusion – like the top half of a metal ball.

With a start, Kunabi turned toward Gulzhan Baqrah. "Why are there four cases?" he asked, suddenly on guard. He was a man used to precision instruments. "You told me there were three."

Gulzhan shrugged. "A precaution, Dr. Kunabi." He moved a step closer, smiling smoothly. "If I have learned anything over the years, it's that it always pays to have a backup plan, a redundancy. Just in case." He wrapped his arm about the scientist's small shoulders. "Don't you agree?"

Kunabi didn't respond. He simply stared at the attaché cases on the table.

"You, for example, have two children. You could have stopped at one – your daughter. After all, she is beautiful and bright, and pregnant with your first grandchild, I am told. You must be very proud." Gulzhan paused. Then he added, wagging his head, "But something told you to continue. You were driven. So you had another child – your son, Mohammed. A doctor. A pediatrician. He works not far from here, just north of Gurjev in the Children's Hospital, does he not? You are a prudent man. You see," he said, squeezing Kunabi tighter. "We have something in common. We both prepare for the contingency."

Chapter 14
Friday, January 28 – 3:15 PM
New York City

The Number One was practically deserted: only a brace of out-of-sync commuters; a scattering of women returning home from shopping; a herd of teenagers dressed in baggy jeans and puffy goose down jackets, laughing and speaking too loud. Decker leaned back in his seat. He could see his face reflected in the window across the subway car. He looked spent. Despite the familiar blazer and red tie, the navy blue overcoat, he looked like a stranger to himself. And then the glass burst into light as the train entered the One Hundred and Sixteenth Street Station, and his face was gone.

Decker picked up his gym bag and got out. As he climbed the stairs, he felt the weight of that piece of paper in his pocket. For some reason, he hadn't told Warhaftig or Kazinski about what he'd found in Salim Moussa's locker, and this troubled him. Kazinski may have acted like an asshole that morning, but no matter what they thought about each other, they were still on the same side. Decker turned and climbed another flight of stairs. He hadn't told anyone and he couldn't for the life of him say why. Perhaps because he didn't know yet if the wallpapers meant anything or not. Perhaps because he simply didn't want to raise another flag, just to have Johnson pull it down again as something silly and irrelevant, or poisoned fruit. Better to be sure first, Decker thought, but he knew that he was lying to himself. He didn't care what Johnson thought. Not really. He sighed. Truth was, he didn't play well with other people, and never had. He coveted this lead. It was a puzzle that led directly through the mind of El Aqrab. It was his, and he was going to solve it.

"Excuse me?" Decker said. "Professor Hassan? You are Dr. Jusef Hassan, right?" Decker hesitated in the open doorway. Hassan was just finishing up his office hours and a few students still milled about in the hall.

Professor Hassan looked up. He was reviewing what appeared to be a paper with some hirsute undergraduate. "May I help you?"

Decker stepped into the room, approached the desk, and plucked out his ID. "My name is Decker," he said. "Agent John Decker. I'm with the FBI."

Hassan examined the badge for several seconds. He was wearing a black four-button cashmere suit, with thin lapels, a startlingly white dress shirt, well starched around his cocoa neck, and a silk blue necktie sprinkled with scallop shells and seahorses. Decker guessed he was in his mid-fifties. His black hair was still thick and full, and slightly oiled. His dreamy brown eyes twinkled in the harsh fluorescent light through a pair of almost invisible wire-rimmed glasses. "Am I supposed to be impressed?" he said.

"Not particularly."

"Good. Because I'm not."

"I wonder if I could have a moment of your time?" Decker continued.

Hassan looked over his glasses. "To read me my rights? Or has Attorney General Oakfield forced Miranda into early retirement too?" Then he turned toward the hirsute student and said, "Let's pick this up tomorrow, Robert, after class. Okay?"

The student had climbed to his feet as soon as he saw Decker's badge. "No problem," he said, and vanished through the door.

"You're the fellow who's been hounding me," Hassan said. "On the phone."

Decker nodded.

"And why, exactly, should I help the FBI?"

Decker considered the question for a moment. Jusef Hassan was the progeny of an ancient line of Egyptian merchant bankers, who – despite a brief flirtation with Islamic Socialism in the '70s – had discovered that abandoning their appreciation for fine clothes, Western classical music and Continental food was, in the end, too great a price to pay for their political ideals. Hassan had come to the United States for four years of university . . . and ended up staying for the next thirty-five. He had married and become a U.S. citizen. In his unconstructed four-button cashmere jacket, it was clear that he wasn't one to emulate his academic peers – not these faux cosmopolitans in their ill-fitting Euro knock-offs. Dr. Jusef Hassan wasn't poor, so why did he have to dress that way? It would be hypocritical. Decker smiled to himself. "Because you're an American," he said.

"Tell that to your fellow agents, as they harass and arrest my people, as they lock them up without legal representation, as they hold them indefinitely without charge."

"Your people?" Decker smiled. "You were in New York when the towers fell, weren't you?" He pulled the sketch he'd found in Moussa's locker from his pocket and laid it gently on the professor's desk.

Hassan glanced at it momentarily and said, "Is that meant to make me feel all patriotic, all mushy and sentimental inside?"

Decker reached into his gym bag on the floor. He removed his notebook and plopped it on the desk. "But you are a naturalized citizen, are you not?" He opened the notebook casually, revealing the sketch he had made of the PC wallpaper.

"I was during Vietnam and Watergate as well," Hassan said. "And when you lied to us about WMDs in Iraq." He looked down at the notebook on his desk. Decker noticed his eyes grow wide. "There is a higher calling associated with being an American than just towing the party line, Agent Decker. Wasn't that the lesson of McCarthy? It may be considered old-fashioned, even sentimental these days, but I still believe in personal rights and freedoms." He craned his neck to get a better look at the drawing from the jukebox dealer. "So did the Founding Fathers. I wonder how they'd fare today in our political environment. Patriot's Act indeed! I'm sure they would have had their phones tapped by the current administration, and . . . where did you get these drawings?" he inquired.

"I'm sorry, but I can't tell you that."

Hassan scowled. "I'm a busy man, Agent Decker. In fact, I'm late for a meeting as it is." He stood, brushed the wrinkles from his suit, and started toward the door. A few students still lingered in the hallway.

Decker turned his notebook so that it faced Hassan. "I'm curious. What did you feel exactly when the towers fell?" he asked. The professor stopped in his tracks. "Did you know anyone who died there? Did you lose a friend, a loved one?" Decker pointed at the sketches before him. "My partner died helping me get these illustrations. I came here to ask you for your help in interpreting them. All of the official channels, our so-called Islamic experts and intelligence resources, have drawn a blank. Professor Hassan, like it or not, you're my only hope. I believe there may be other lives at stake here."

Hassan leaned forward, resting his fists on the surface of the desk. "Shall I tell you what Nine Eleven reminds me of, Agent Decker? I have a son. His name is Malik. He was on his way to school one day, not long after . . . the tragedy. Anyway, he was riding the subway and the train stopped and this gang of teenagers got on — white kids — and they saw him standing in the back. They began to make fun of him, to call him names. They said he looked like an Arab; that he was probably from Afghanistan, a member of the Taliban; that he and his kind were responsible for what had happened to the World Trade Towers; that he had no business being in America. The boys began to egg each other on. 'If you hate America so much,' one of them said as he approached Malik, 'why don't you just leave?' He said this to my son, who was born in St. Vincent's Hospital in the Village, mind you. And someone else said, 'He deserves to suffer, just like those people in the towers suffered.' That's exactly what he said. And then a third one added, and this is the best of all, 'This is what it feels like, towel head, when you know you're about to die, and there ain't nothin' you can do about it, except watch.'" Hassan shook his head. "He was only twelve," he added. "Twelve! They kicked him over and over again, until he lost consciousness. He would have probably died there too if a stranger hadn't come along and scared the boys away. So why, exactly, should I help you?"

Decker nodded, trying not to feel the car begin to slide, to spin, to feel the hit, the grim concussion as the other vehicle plowed into them again. And there had been nothing he could do. Nothing! He closed his eyes. "So that it doesn't happen again," he said in Arabic. "To Malik, or someone else's son."

"What?" Hassan took a step back. He cocked his head "What did you say?"

"I came to learn," continued Decker. His Arabic was fluent, with the trilling accent of north Egypt. He could have been born in Al Iskandariyah. "I need your help, Professor. Like your son did on that subway train, when that stranger came to his assistance."

Professor Hassan looked at Decker for several seconds. He took in the pale face, the thick black hair, the pale gray eyes that stared back with imponderable sadness. "I'm sure I'm not on your approved list of Islamic experts, Agent Decker."

Decker shrugged.

"That doesn't worry you?"

Decker shook his head. "'There will come to you a guidance from Me, then whoever follows My guidance, no fear shall come upon them.'"

"'Nor shall they grieve.'" Hassan smiled a little smile. He glanced down at the illustrations on the table. Then he closed the notebook and pushed it back across the desk. "I'm sorry, Agent Decker. But I cannot help you."

Decker held him by the elbow. "You mean you *will* not."

Hassan smiled, pulling himself free. "As you wish," he said.

Decker took out his wallet and handed the professor his card. "Please," he said. "Take it. In case you change your mind."

"I won't," Hassan replied, but he took the card anyway. "Well, unless you plan to arrest me, I do have other things to do."

"I'll walk out with you," said Decker.

"No!" snapped Hassan. "Don't bother."

Decker stepped back. He knew exactly what the professor meant. It didn't pay for a man of Hassan's reputation to be seen hobnobbing with the FBI. It would appear, well . . . unseemly to most of his constituencies. And it would certainly undermine the access he enjoyed to both the powerful throughout the Middle East, and to those who lay upon the outer fringes of the carpet of Islam – the radicals, the Fundamentalists, the pure of faith. Decker reached his hand out, adding. "Thank you, Professor."

"What for?" He looked down at Decker's hand, but he did not shake it. "You think I don't understand the threat implicit in your visit?"

"Excuse me?" Decker noticed a small crowd of students gathering by the door.

"I'm an American citizen," Hassan declared, puffing himself up. "Your veiled threats of deportation hold no currency with me. Bully me all you wish, but I will not compromise my principles. I will not turn away, or hide within the shell of my indifference."

Decker smiled. Then he spun about, he scowled and headed out the door, pushing his way through the students in the hall.

Hassan kept up his bold soliloquy. "Threaten me all you want, Agent Decker, but I know my rights. They haven't all been hijacked by the so-called 'Department of Justice.' I know tyranny when I smell it."

The door closed with a bang. Decker started back down College Walk. He had just passed Low Plaza when his phone began to vibrate on his hip. He flipped it open. It was a text message. The note read: *Reading Room 26, Avery Library*. It was not signed but Decker knew the author. He stopped and asked a pretty young female student for directions. Avery was just up those steps by Low Library – third building on the right after St. Paul's.

Reading Room 26 was empty. Even with the light turned off, Decker could tell. The air was absolutely still. But what had he expected? Then he noticed a leather-bound book on the table.

He turned on the light. It was a copy of the Qur'an. He approached the table. The Muslim holy text was opened to Al-Takwir, Sura 81. He only had to glance at it to recognize the words: *When the sun is veiled, and the stars are dimmed, and the mountains are made to move, and ten-months pregnant she-camels are discarded as a means of transportation and the wild ones are gathered together, and the rivers are diverted, and people are brought together, and when the female infant buried alive is questioned about: For what crime was she killed? And when books are spread abroad, and when heaven is laid bare, and when hell is stoked up, and when the Garden is brought nigh, then everyone will know that which He has wrought.*

Decker read the passage several times. He read the words, but while he now knew the source of the quotation, he still didn't understand its meaning. Behind each door, three more always appeared, and then nine after that.

He headed out of Avery Hall, down the steps, and back toward Broadway and the subway station. It was growing colder by the minute. A girl with a knapsack on her back approached him from the river. Probably a coed, he thought. She looked a little like Maureen, the Irish girl he'd dated in Chicago. The same wavy, reddish-brown hair. The same nose and sky blue eyes. But this girl's mouth was fuller. And she was younger too. She was wearing a long black coat with buttons that looked like they were made of bone or ivory. Decker sighed as she passed by. He watched her walk away. Then he turned and started down the steps into the subway station.

When he got back to the Village, it was almost five o'clock. Decker stopped off at a bar on Greenwich Avenue, not far from his apartment, and ordered a glass of cabernet. He drank it far too fast, trying to push the cold away, but it only made him more depressed. The case was going nowhere. Even with their APBs, they hadn't been able to locate the suspects from the apartment in Queens. Decker missed Chicago. New York seemed so much bigger, so much less manageable. He should work out, he told himself, relieve the stress, but he didn't feel like it.

Decker left the bar and suddenly resolved to go to a place about which Tony had once told him. He knew that he shouldn't, but he found himself going anyway. As he walked, he thought again about Maureen O'Donnell. She had wanted him to settle down, to give up the Bureau, and a part of him had really tried. He had loved her, in his own way. But, in the end, he simply couldn't do it. Somewhere along the road the job had become his life. He thought about Maureen's white skin, her lips, her tender heavy breasts, the soft curve of her thighs where they had come together at the top, that triangle of light he'd always spotted as she walked away from him toward the bathroom to wash up after they'd finished making love.

Decker stopped in front of a building on Twenty-third Street. He buzzed and someone let him in. It was baking inside the lobby and he could feel himself begin to sweat as he climbed the stairs. There was a door at the top of the stairs with a small peephole. He knocked. The peephole opened and he said, "Anthony Bartolo sent me." The door opened.

It was a cathouse. Young, barely dressed girls of all shapes and sizes and ethnicities were standing around by the front desk. He paid his entrance fee and ordered another glass of wine from a young Asian girl with small breasts and a heart-shaped ass. The girls kept coming up to him and, eventually, he picked one – a brunette with long straight hair. She was pale-skinned and soft and round. A little short, he thought, but decent-looking, with a pretty mouth covered in pink lipstick, and doe-like brown eyes.

She led him down the hall into a private room. It featured a simple cot with a pale blue sheet. There was only one pillow. She closed the door, told Decker to take off his clothes, and slipped into the bathroom. He could hear the water running behind the hollow wall. When she finally came out, she took her bra and panties off. She had large breasts for her frame, and two tiny dimples just above her ass. Her skin was startlingly white in the dim light. She helped him with his clothes.

"You're in good shape," she said, admiring his physique. "Are you a professional athlete or something?"

Decker smiled. "I guess you could say that."

"What's your name?"

"John."

She laughed. "I bet," she said. "Hi, John. My name is—"

He placed his hand across her mouth. He shook his head. She shrugged, plucked something from the cot, and got down on her knees before him. She took him in her mouth, staring up at him with her big brown eyes as she worked. Decker felt himself grow more and more excited, enlarging in her mouth, between those lips with the pink lipstick. She pulled back and he realized that he already had a condom on.

"You're ready," she said.

He pushed her roughly to the cot and entered her with ease. She was already wet. They fucked mechanically, methodically. He could feel his frustration, his anger rising up inside of him. After only a few minutes, he came and pulled away. She started to get up from the cot but he held her in his arms. "Not yet," he said. "Just lay here for a minute." His tone was so plaintive, so desperate and forlorn that she softened and lay back down beside him.

"It'll cost you more," she said.

He laughed bleakly. He could feel her breath on his face. It was minty fresh. He realized that she had a pockmark on one cheek, next to her ear, and a small white scar beneath her chin. For some strange reason, this made him happy. "It always does," he said.

Chapter 15
Saturday, January 29 – 9:16 AM
New York City

Seamus Gallagher sat in the Blue Moon Diner just across from the offices of WKXY-TV on Broadway and Seventy-ninth Street. He sat there every day at this time, in the same red vinyl booth, looking out the same window at the passing cars and people jostling by. His enemies and detractors – and there were many of them; of that he was most proud – claimed it was because the diner had named a sandwich after him: corned beef and tongue on rye, with mustard. Others said he liked the window booth because it increased his chances of being recognized by passersby. And then there were those who speculated it was because a Moroccan owned the diner, and Gallagher . . . well, he felt at home there.

The truth was it was sheer convenience that had brought him to the Blue Moon five years earlier when he had first moved to New York from Atlanta and joined the news team at WKXY-TV. The diner was right across the street from the studios. Not that Gallagher was lazy by disposition. He hadn't ascended through the firmament of local evening TV news, hadn't crawled his way from Boston through Duluth and Biloxi, from Atlanta to New York by shirking his responsibilities. Indeed, he had stepped on countless others, destroyed myriad careers, in order to get where he was.

Freckled, red-haired with a square-shaped face, plump and rather short, Gallagher had had to labor extra hard for his success. He wasn't just another pretty-boy-stuffed-shirt. He was a *real* reporter, a man of the streets, an old-fashioned news hound – at least, that's how he liked to see himself, and it was the image he tried desperately to project.

Two years earlier, he'd covered a story about a Hassidic Jew who'd run over a black kid in Brooklyn. The accident had sparked a series of brutal riots during which a black man stabbed a young Hassidim. The black man – it turned out – was also a devout Muslim. The story received a lot of play. Many in the Jewish community thought the piece was not only incendiary but also anti-Semitic, and Gallagher received death threats for months. But the story earned him the respect of the New York Muslim communities. Then, after 9/11, he parlayed that reputation into some interesting exclusives with various Muslim clerics throughout the tri-state area resulting in numerous awards, including a coveted Emmy for the local evening news team. He wrote a book, which did reasonably well, although the reviews were mixed at best. Gallagher didn't care. The notoriety garnered him a sizeable promotion, more money and more airtime than most with his experience. And, as a nice by-product, it had earned him his own sandwich at the Blue Moon Diner.

Gallagher finished up his cup of chicken soup and salad, and was reaching into his jacket for his wallet, when a young busboy appeared from nowhere and began to clear his table.

"Hey, I'm still eating here," he uttered with disdain.

The busboy ignored him and continued to clear the table. He was a young Arab but Gallagher didn't recognize him. He wasn't one of the owner's boys. "Are you deaf?" he said. "Can't you wait 'til I'm done?"

The busboy stared at the reporter. "Gallagher?" he said, with a thick Middle Eastern accent. "Seamus Gallagher?" He began to clean the surface of the table with a rag.

"That's right. Who are you?"

The young man didn't answer. He reached behind his apron and took out a piece of paper. Then he dropped it on the table and, without another word, moved off.

Gallagher watched him weave and wiggle through the breakfast crowd, back toward the rear of the diner. The reporter shook his head. He picked up the piece of paper. It was a hand-written note. It read: *On Friday, 28 January, a train transporting highly enriched uranium (HEU) from the BN-350 fast breeder reactor at the Mangystau Atomic Energy Combine in Aktau, Kazakhstan, for long-term storage at the Semipalatinsk Test Site in Kurchatov City, was hijacked by Gulzhan Baqrah on behalf of El Aqrab and the Brotherhood of the Crimson Scimitar. Eight kilos of HEU was stolen, enough to make a nuclear bomb with a one kiloton yield. Unless El Aqrab is released from his Zionist cell, the Brotherhood will detonate a WMD somewhere on the soil of our enemies. It is the will of Allah.*

The reporter read the note again. He could feel his pulse quicken. He looked toward the rear of the diner. The busboy had disappeared.

Gallagher got up and snaked his way through the crowd. "Hey, Omar," he said to one of the young waiters drifting by. He grabbed him by the elbow. The waiter almost dropped his plate of eggs and bacon on the floor. "Omar, what's the name of your new busboy?" Gallagher insisted.

The waiter turned, and freed himself, and laid the plate beside him on a nearby table. "What busboy?"

"The one who cleared my booth."

"Ahmed?"

"No, not Ahmed. I know Ahmed. Some other Arab kid. I think he went into the kitchen."

The waiter scanned the rear of the diner. He shook his head. "There is no other busboy. Just Ahmed, Mr. Gallagher." He inched away. "Do you want me to get him?"

It was no use. The boy had vanished. "No, it's okay. Never mind," he said.

Gallagher squeezed back to his booth, tossed a few dollars on the table, and started for the door. His heart still pounded in his chest. *This is starting out as an interesting day*, he thought. He had planned to run a follow-up on his Gentry Hall story, the senior citizens' center where a seventy-seven year old great-grandmother had been sexually molested a few weeks earlier. But now, out of the sky, out of the heavens, someone had dropped this bomb into his lap. Literally. He opened the door and stepped outside. He reached into his camel hair jacket and pulled out a pack of Marlboro Lights. He lit one up. The sidewalk buzzed with pedestrians. Cabs and vans and cars and trucks choked the streets and avenues. Gallagher looked up at the WKXY-TV studios across the way, at the offices, the stores. At the apartment buildings. *Somewhere on the soil of our enemies*. He tossed his cigarette into the street. It tasted of death. Perhaps he was getting a cold.

In the end, the story folded together with the beauty and precision of an origami bird. First, he called Jim Talon who covered the United Nations for the network. Talon had made some good contacts prior to the Second Gulf War when the International Atomic Energy Agency (IAEA) had been at the center of the search for WMDs in Iraq. Recently, IAEA Director General Dr. Mohamed El Shouhadi had called upon the United States and the other Coalition Partners to allow IAEA experts to return to Iraq in order to address what he described as a "possible radiological emergency" but, of course, the U.S. was being reticent. The Coalition didn't want to see the IAEA, nor the UN back in control. And the U.S. Administration was still smarting from the fact that no Weapons of Mass Destruction had been found. Talon promised El Shouhadi that he would play the story up, put more pressure on the Administration if he would confirm a rumor he had heard about a shipment of HEU that had allegedly been hijacked in Kazakhstan early yesterday morning. El Shouhadi was surprised. He asked Talon how he'd learned about the hijacking but Talon wouldn't answer. A confidential source, he said. Eventually, El Shouhadi confirmed the theft, but he also played it down and pointed out that the eight kilograms of HEU fell under the minimum thresholds specified by the IAEA. That's why they hadn't made it public. The amount simply wasn't large enough to cause a fuss. More than that went missing from Russian plants each month, but it generally turned up sooner or later – misplaced, mislabeled, mis-something-or-other. Thefts in excess of the thresholds were rare. Talon thanked the Director General and passed the information onto Gallagher.

Next, Gallagher called a buddy of his from journalism school named Don Abernathy who happened to work at the National Resource Defense Council. Abernathy told him the NRDC was just about to come out with a scathing attack on the IAEA and the agency's handling of its inspections in Iraq. When Gallagher pressed on, he also told him that part of the report claimed the standard minimum thresholds posted by the IAEA were ridiculously low. They were all based on dated research, ancient analyses. Modern techniques enabled the construction of WMDs from much smaller quantities of plutonium or uranium. Eight kilograms of HEU was more than enough to make a significant nuclear device, capable of generating a one-kiloton blast, or more. Gallagher thanked Abernathy, hung up and jumped online.

He combed the IAEA and NRDC sites for more data. The NRDC posted a number of articles on nuclear stockpiles located throughout the world. Gallagher cut and pasted his research, folding the story, panel by panel. Then he Googled a variety of subjects, from fission bombs to fallout. Within twenty minutes, he had gathered enough material for his piece. It was terrifying stuff, especially when you put it in a local context. He called Amanda in the animation lab. Yeah, she told him. She had time. Another fold. He emailed her the stats and started on the script.

Within forty minutes, he had pecked out a first draft on his PC and called Amanda to see how she was doing. Come on down, she told him. Take a look for yourself. He took the elevator to the third floor and watched the animation. It was crude – not all the planes were linked together yet – but still effective. Gallagher told her to add concentric circles around the map of New York City so that the viewers could see the different bands of pressure about the blast zone — from twelve pounds per square inch near the hypocenter, to five, then two, then one. No problemo, she said. He got up to leave and ran right into Ira Minsky, his producer.

"I hear you've got a hot one," Minsky said.

"Oh, hi, Ira. Just wanted to tighten it up a bit, add a few more graphics before I came to see you."

Minsky was a short fat man in his late forties, with thin receding hair and wire-rimmed glasses. He was perpetually out of breath, as if each time you saw him, he'd just finished sprinting. It was actually a mild case of asthma. Probably psychological, thought Gallagher. Minsky carried an inhaler with him everywhere he went and he squeezed it now, and took another breath, and said, "Sure you were, Seamus. What's the angle?"

Gallagher told him and Minsky took it like a body blow. "You realize this will mean another call from Homeland Security." Only two months earlier, a story Gallagher had done on the nuclear facility at Indian Point had raised the agency's ire. Gallagher had contended the plant was still vulnerable to terrorist attack, despite recent changes in security.

"Yeah, so what?"

Minsky pushed his glasses up his nose. He took another breath through his inhaler. He was sweating furiously and Gallagher took this as a good sign. "Our ratings jumped almost two points after that story," the producer said. "Mazel-tov." Then he turned and waddled off.

A few hours later, with Minsky watching from the wings, the story aired.

First there was the hijacking, confirmed by the IAEA Director General himself, Dr. Mohamed El Shouhadi. Then the contention by the NRDC that the minimum thresholds were too low, backed up by various technical experts. Then the background on Gulzhan Baqrah and El Aqrab, and the Brotherhood of the Crimson Scimitar. Some file footage of suicide attacks in Iraq and Israel. That photo of El Aqrab and Baqrah in Kuwait during the First Gulf War, with that smoking oil well in the background. And then the "closer," the colorful animation of a one-kiloton bomb exploding in Manhattan, just to give it that local angle. Amanda had really worked her magic this time. Gallagher reminded himself to take her out to dinner. No . . . lunch.

It began with an illustration of a gun-triggered fission bomb, the simplest to build. Then the explosion itself, animated on

Amanda's CGI in colorful detail. The bomb winked, blanched and bellowed, sending a shockwave like an invisible smoke ring around the island of Manhattan. The skyline collapsed. Buildings melted in a wave of flames. A great gray cloud of smoke rose up, billowing higher and higher into the sky, into that hauntingly familiar mushroom shape. Then the cloud cleared, revealing a crater at the center of Manhattan. Gallagher's VO swept in: "According to the report 'The Effects of Nuclear War' authored by the Congressional Office Of Technology Assessment, the blast generated by a one kiloton bomb would fashion a crater more than two hundred feet deep and one thousand feet in diameter, encircled by a ring of radioactive soil and debris. Nothing recognizable would remain within a half mile of the crater.

"Imagine you're a survivor, walking from the hypocenter of the blast, trying to get away from the carnage. Niney-eight percent of the people around you are dead, incinerated in the inferno. You're one of the *lucky* ones.

"By the time you reach one point seven miles from ground zero, only the strongest buildings made out of reinforced, poured concrete stand – burnt-out skeletal remains. The rest have disappeared, vaporized by a force equivalent to twelve pounds of pressure per square inch, or PSI."

Minsky beamed from behind the camera as the concentric circles gleamed.

"Virtually everything between the twelve and five PSI rings has been destroyed. The walls of all multi-story buildings – including apartment blocks – have been shredded, blown away. As you get closer to the five PSI ring, more large structures remain. But all the single-family homes have been obliterated. Only the odd foundation still reveals itself through the rubble – a ghost, an echo of some family now gone. Fifty percent of the people around you have been killed, forty percent are horribly injured. At two PSI, any single-family home not completely destroyed by the blast is heavily damaged. The windows of all the office buildings have been blown away. The contents of the upper floors – including the people who worked there – are scattered along the streets before you, like so many autumn leaves. Debris lies everywhere. Five percent of the people between the five and number two PSI rings are dead, forty-five percent seriously injured.

"And seven point four miles from the blast, at one PSI, if you make it that far before dying, you'll notice that while most of the buildings are only moderately damaged, one quarter of the population is lying in bloody heaps at your feet, the victims of flying glass and stone and concrete. Others are screaming in agony, burnt and blackened by the thermal radiation generated by the blast.

"And this, all of this, is only the beginning — just the pressure damage. Another effect will be the radioactive fallout. Immediately following the detonation, hundreds of tons of earth and debris, made radioactive by the blast, will be carried high into the atmosphere within the mushroom cloud. The material will drift downwind, and eventually fall back to earth, contaminating thousands of square miles."

The map expanded to encompass the entire eastern seaboard.

"Assuming a fifteen mile-per-hour westerly wind over a seven-day period, everyone who either lives or works within thirty miles of ground zero will be bombarded with three thousand rem. You'll be dead within a few hours. And it will be years, perhaps a decade before the levels of radioactivity in Manhattan drop low enough for the city to be considered safe for human habitation.

"If you're within ninety miles, at nine hundred rem, you'll die within two to fourteen days. At one hundred and sixty miles, or three hundred rem, you'll still suffer extensive internal injuries, including damage to nerve cells and the cells that line your digestive tract. Your white blood cell count will plummet, and your hair will fall out.

"Even if you live two hundred and fifty miles away, as far away as Boston, Massachusetts — where my mother lives — you'll still suffer a decrease in white blood cells and increase your chances of acquiring cancer. It will be two to three years before the northeastern seaboard is considered safe again by U.S. peacetime standards."

Gallagher took a deep breath. The map behind him was replaced with the photo of Baqrah and El Aqrab once more. Baqrah's smile took on a new and far more ominous intent. El Aqrab's distant stare became bone-chillingly sinister. It was as if he were looking off into the distance, through his mind's eye, at the shattered smoking shell of New York City.

Gallagher remained silent for a few more seconds. He had added that bit about his mother extemporaneously, and he felt flushed with pride. It had been a stroke of genius. Anyone looking at this rather ugly, red-haired leprechaun of a reporter would be shocked to learn that even he — as strident and gnomish as he was —

had a mother. What bathos! All were vulnerable to fallout. All, no matter how beautiful or ugly, no matter how rich or poor, smart or dumb, would die.

"Of course, it would be irresponsible for me to say that New York is definitely the target. The message this reporter received indicates the bomb's destination is 'somewhere on the soil of our enemies.' But the fact that it was delivered to me, a New York-based reporter, makes you wonder. Are we next . . . again? And can we afford to think that we are not? Seamus Gallagher reporting for WKXY-TV, New York. Back to you, Sue."

Chapter 16
Saturday, January 29 – 2:56 PM
New York City

Decker walked around The Cloisters, nestled high above the Hudson River, on a rocky promontory at the north end of Manhattan. Originally funded by John D. Rockefeller, The Cloisters had been constructed in a neo-medieval style, specifically designed to house the Metropolitan's collection of artwork from the Middle Ages. Decker's footsteps echoed through the portico. As he circled the Cuxa Cloister, with its herb and flower garden deep in winter sleep, he came upon another hall whose stone walls were festooned with tapestries.

Although he'd never seen them in person before, Decker recognized them instantly – the Unicorn Tapestries, woven in the Netherlands during the early sixteenth century, so named because they depicted the hunt for a snow-white unicorn against a backdrop of wildflowers. How strange that these wall hangings – or were they bed clothes? – had gradually mutated, over the centuries, into totems of another age. They were medieval icons now, the Mona Lisas of the 1500s. And yet, according to the plaque, the weavers were unknown. So were the owners and the reason for their use. Only a set of mysterious initials – an A and E – at the bottom of each tapestry remained to baffle scholars. He looked down at his watch. It was 3:00 PM. Time for his rendezvous.

Decker walked back to the Cuxa. Professor Hassan was sitting at the south end of the cloister, on a long black wooden bench. Decker ambled over and sat down beside him. There was no one else in the cloister, save for a guard at the far end of the portico. Although it was Saturday, the museum was practically deserted.

"I got your message," Decker said. He stared at the fallow garden at the center of the cloister, hemmed in by pilasters and walls of glass.

"Obviously. Did you bring the wallpapers?"

Decker studied Hassan. He was wearing a long black cashmere overcoat over a double-breasted midnight blue suit. His royal blue and golden tie was perfectly knotted at the neck. A pair of gold cufflinks – set with some kind of light blue stone, aquamarine or emerald – glimmered at his wrists. With a nod, Decker reached into his coat and removed the drawings. He placed them on the bench between them.

"I don't want you to misunderstand me," the Professor said. He was clearly uncomfortable. He fidgeted and said, "I'm obviously no friend of this administration, nor do I condone what the President has done in the name of Homeland Security. If there were any other way . . . " His voice trailed off. He turned and looked at Decker. His large brown eyes were red and moist, as if he had been up all night. "But after seeing that special report on WKXY-TV this morning, I really have no choice, do I? No matter what my feelings."

Decker didn't reply. Time and silence were his friends. They were all that was required to turn Hassan around. The Professor leaned over and removed a pair of books from a black briefcase at his feet. One was obviously the Qur'an. "I assume you got my message yesterday," he said.

"I did, yes. Thank you," Decker said. "Although, I must admit, I haven't had much luck in interpreting the quotation. I'm no Qur'anic scholar."

"Don't overdo it, Agent Decker. You'll only make this whole thing more distasteful for me." He opened the Muslim holy text. He lay the volume gently inbetween them. "Here, in Sura eighty-one of *Al Takwir*." The professor began to read. "'When the sun is veiled, and the stars are dimmed, and the mountains are made to move, and ten-months pregnant she-camels are discarded as a means of transportation and the wild ones are gathered together, and the rivers are diverted, and people are brought together, and when the female infant buried alive is questioned about: For what crime was she killed? And when books are spread abroad, and when heaven is laid bare, and when hell is stoked up, and when the Garden is brought nigh, then everyone will know that which He has wrought.'"

"I can read what it says, Professor. What does it mean?"

"It's a prophecy. Some believe it refers to the present age. Today, the sun *is* veiled, and pollution and city lights dim the stars. Mountains are made to move, through monumental mining practices, although some scholars think this refers to the toppling of kings – like Saddam Hussein. Real trains and other high-speed means of transportation have supplanted camel trains. I've no idea who the wild ones are. Gangs, perhaps. Terrorist groups. Your guess is as good as mine. Rivers are constantly diverted, and some believe the reference to people being 'brought together' speaks to the Internet. As far as the 'infant buried alive' is concerned, clerics speculate it refers to the practice of abortion. Even Christians are asking, 'For what crime was she killed?'"

"And books have been spread abroad," said Decker, catching on. "Through Amazon and modern digital printing presses. Heaven's been laid bare through the Hubble and other telescopes, revealing the limits of the visible universe. What about hell being stoked up?"

"Could be volcanoes, like Mount Saint Helens and Etna. But many well-respected clerics believe it refers to nuclear power and the bomb. And the Garden has been brought nigh. A few years ago, several scientists determined – leveraging the Legend of Gilgamesh, ancient place names, and the historic location of rivers and mountains – that the legend of Eden was based on a real valley in western Iran."

"I don't know, Professor. One could read almost anything into these quotes. What are they meant to prophesy?"

"The end of the world," said Hassan. "Armageddon."

Decker felt an electric chill run up his spine. He pointed at the illustrations of the wallpapers on the bench between them. "Tell me about calligraphy, about this type of arabesque design?"

"In the hierarchy of the arts, Islam accords the highest rank to calligraphy," Hassan replied, "since it's the art that embellishes the word of God. The Qur'an itself bases its authority on its being the literal word of God, dictated to the world through the mouthpiece of a messenger, the Prophet Mohammed. Qur'an literally means 'a reading.' The visible Qur'an is but a reflection of the Preserved Tablet, the supernatural archetype laid up in heaven, which is a kind of metaphor for the mind of God." The Professor paused, deep in thought. Then he added, "This principle of mirroring, of reversibility recurs throughout Islam. For example, in Islamic architecture the dome represents the vault of heaven. But in the Dome of the Rock in Jerusalem, a highly stylized Cosmological Tree spreads *downward*, upside down – the *arbor inversus*. In the same way, from each of the four corners of the earth and in Mecca itself, one always prays *towards* the Ka'aba. But once within the Ka'aba, one prays in the reverse direction; that is, *outwards*, toward any of the four walls.

"The Ka'aba is the holiest site in Islam," said Hassan. "In fact, the location was considered sacred even before Islam, but after the Muslim conquest of Mecca in 630, Muhammad destroyed the numerous pagan idols in the building. Within the courtyard of the Ka'aba are several sacred sites, including the burial place of

Abraham and the Zamzam well, which sprang up miraculously for Ishmael and his mother, Hagar. Today, there is an ablution fountain between the external and internal features of every mosque, generally located in the center of the courtyard. In Islam, water is the vehicle of purification."

Decker recollected the tapestries in the hall behind him. One featured the unicorn – before his death – dipping his horn in water, purifying a well.

Hassan picked up the second illustration, the one from Moussa's locker. He studied it for a moment before confirming what Decker had already translated: *Death Will Overtake You.* Unfortunately, said Hassan, there wasn't enough for him to guess at a source.

"And the numbers?"

The professor shook his head. "I've no idea. Wait a minute," he added. He studied the first illustration. Then he picked up the second again. "You know," he said. "This is interesting."

"What?"

"See these lines here, this kind of T-junction in both drawings?" His hand swept across the designs. "These indentations, and this round shape in the arabesque over here?"

"What about it?"

"Both of these illustrations are laid out like . . . like virtual mosques." He pointed at the illustration from the apartment in Queens. "This one looks like a *masjid*, the kind of mosque used for individual prayer." Then he pointed at the other, the one from the jukebox dealer. "But this one looks like a *musalla* or *idgah*, a community mosque. They both have *qibla* and transversal axes, but this one has a *minbar*. See?" He stabbed a finger at a small rectangular shape. "And look how open it is – a true place of *Id'*."

"Hold on a minute," said Decker. "What's a kibla and a minibar?"

Hassan laughed. "Not a minibar! A *minbar* – a pulpit." He paused to explain. "In Islam, prayer – *salat* – is conducted at four different levels. For three of these, there are distinct liturgical structures – mosques. The first mosque, the *masjid*, is said to be for Individual prayer. The prayer rug also corresponds to this level. It's used for daily worship, performed at the five liturgical hours: dawn, noon, afternoon, sunset and evening. It's not used for the Congregational or Friday prayer, nor during Community prayer. But, like all mosques, it has a *mihrab*, a niche in the center of the *qibla*. You see these lines and this concave niche?" He pointed at Decker's rough illustration.

"I'm still not following you. What's a kibla again?"

"A mosque is a building erected around a single horizontal axis, the *qibla*, which passes invisibly down the middle of the floor, and terminates eventually at the Ka'aba in Mecca. Imagine Mecca as the central point; all mosques sit at right angles to Mecca, as if Mecca is the hub of a great wheel with lines, like spokes, fanning out in a great circle. At the point where the *qibla* axis meets the far wall of a mosque – the transversal axis – an indentation is produced, a directional niche called the *mihrab*, which is the liturgical axis made visible. This is where the *imam* or prayer leader stations himself to direct the congregation in prayer."

Hassan pulled the second etching before them. "But this one is different. You see this here?" He pointed once again at the rectangle in the center. "It looks like a *minbar*, a pulpit. Of course, this mosque could be a *jami' masjid*, which is used for Congregational prayer. That's the second type, employed on Fridays. But I don't think so. It's too open and airy. I'd say it's more likely a *musalla* or *idgah*, used in the third, Community prayer. Think of it as an open prayer area with nothing but a *qibla* wall and a *mihrab*. In other words, a mosque reduced to its barest essentials. It's designed to accommodate an entire town or Community, hence the name."

"What about the fourth kind of mosque. You said there were four."

"Four types of prayer, or *salat*. But there is no liturgical structure or mosque for the fourth prayer. There couldn't be. It's meant for the *Ummah*, the entire Muslim community – worldwide. It would have to encircle the globe. The fourth prayer is reserved for the Hajj, or pilgrimage to Mecca. Unless he's sick or otherwise incapable, every Muslim is required to make the Hajj at least once in his lifetime, although pilgrimages are encouraged every year." Hassan paused for a moment, studying the second illustration. It was muddy and smudged. He looked up at Decker with a quizzical expression on his face. Then he said, "Was this traced or something, from another sheet of paper?"

Decker nodded.

The professor waited for Decker to say something but he remained impassive. "Was there something else behind the drawing?"

"What do you mean, behind?"

"Underneath. Like Palimpsest."

"Why?" asked Decker. He did not know where the Professor was going.

Then Hassan told him that one of the most basic tenets of Arabic architecture was the focus on the inside, as opposed to the outside of a building. Rarely did a façade of a Muslim building give any indication of the organization within. Indeed, hidden architecture could be considered the dominant motif of Islamic architecture.

"That's often the function of calligraphic texts," explained Hassan, "to identify the purpose of a building."

"But Western buildings use calligraphy," Decker said. "I remember a book I had when I was a kid about the Notre Dame cathedrals. Calligraphy isn't unique to Islamic architecture."

"Perhaps not. But while European architecture is created as a balanced plan, Islamic architecture shows no such characteristic. Indeed, there is a kind of dissolution of this balanced plan, its . . . " He paused for a moment, struggling for the word. " . . . *absorption* into a maze of additional structures which accumulate around the nucleus of the original design. Like crystals."

"Crystals?"

"Exactly. And like crystals, there is a basic geometrical organization to this growth. Islamic architectural drawings are executed across a grid of squares, which represent the structural modules of the plan. Simple divisions of the basic grid determine all the dimensions, such as those of the dado, the door, the doorframe, the rows of upper windows, and so on. The walls form a perfect cube, while the height of the dome corresponds to the diagonal of the generating square. This is almost universal in Islamic architecture. Proportioning is based primarily on arcs drawn from the diagonals of squares to give ratios of one to the square root of two — the 'Golden Ratio,' as Pythagoras called it."

"I've heard of that. That's *Phi*," said Decker. "It's used in Western architecture too. Like at Monticello, in Virginia. The house that Thomas Jefferson built."

"The formula was carried back by the Crusaders from the Middle East," Hassan said with a nod. "The masons who built the Gothic cathedrals of France used the same ratio. And Jefferson was a freemason. Freemasons are the intellectual and spiritual cousins of the original medieval masons."

Decker closed the book and handed it back to Hassan. The professor had been so reluctant to speak at first, and now he could scarcely contain himself. It was clear why he was legendary as an academic, and why he was so often sought after as an expert on Islam. A lifelong, ferocious advocate on behalf of the Palestinians, he made great copy, a dramatic yet incredibly well-researched and well-balanced counterpoint to the pro-Israel intellectuals he so often combated on TV. Not only was his knowledge of Middle Eastern politics considerable; not only did he serve, from time to time, as an advisor to PLO General Secretary Mahmoud Abbas himself; not only was he an architect of the American Muslim sensibility, but he was charged with passion, driven by a deep abiding interest in, and a great love for all facets of Islamic cultural history.

"The very possibility of enlarging a given structure," Hassan said, "in almost any direction by adding units of every conceivable shape and size to the original scheme, totally disregarding the form of the original structure, is a characteristic that Islamic architecture shares with no other major culture. Furthermore, the multitude of decorative treatments goes hand in hand with this non-directional plan, the tendency toward an infinite repetition of individual units – bays, arches, columns, passages, courtyards, doorways, cupolas, what have you."

He sighed and leaned against the wall. He stared at the fallow garden. "Islamic art is an art of repose, Agent Decker, intellectual more than emotional, resolving tensions by design. Patterns are limited to well-defined areas but are, at the same time, infinite – in the sense that they have unlimited possibilities of extension. Water and light are also of paramount importance since they generate additional layers of patterns, and help to transform space. It is this variety and richness of decoration, with its endless permutations, that characterizes Islamic buildings rather than their structural elements. In the Islamic context, these infinitely extensible designs have been interpreted as visual demonstrations of the singleness of God. His presence everywhere. Indeed, Islamic architecture is like the Qur'an itself. There are those who think there is little order in the sequence of the Qur'an. In truth, those who reflect upon the flow discover not one order, but a multiplicity of orders in the sequence and juxtaposition of its Sura, depending upon the character of their quest."

Professor Hassan stiffened. Decker heard voices and a group of students began to file in through a door at the far side of the cloister. He could hear French – Parisian French. Hassan began to fiddle with his briefcase. He slipped the two volumes back inside, slammed the case shut, and clambered to his feet. Decker stood beside him. "No, no, sit down," Hassan said, hissing through his teeth. "I'll contact you again," he added, moving off.

Decker watched the Professor amble slowly down the portico, gazing lackadaisically at paintings and woodcuts on the walls. The students buzzed, and swerved, and swirled around him. Then he vanished through a portico into the Late Gothic Hall.

After a few minutes, when the students had passed by, Decker circled around the other way, past the Early Gothic Hall, the Pontaut Chapter House and Langon Chapel, moving backwards through time. He made his way along a long stone corridor, down several flights of stairs, and finally exited in front of the museum.

The sky was cloudy and white. It looked like it was going to snow. He started walking back along the promontory toward his car. Decker could see the distant Hudson River far below the palisades, studded with blocks of ice, chugging lethargically along, and it brought to mind the Mississippi, Iowa and home. Or, what had once been home. The Quad Cities hadn't changed much over the last decade; yet they seemed so far away now, so alien and small – just as the tapestries remained predominantly the same; only the audience was different.

Then, out of nowhere, he remembered what Warhaftig had told him the first time they had met: *El Aqrab is no ordinary killer.*

But how a poor kid from south Lebanon, the son of a part-time electrician, could be the same man who had learned to paint with fire, to illuminate the Qur'an with incendiary pain and death, with a calligraphy of flames, Decker simply couldn't fathom. It was indeed a mystery, as inscrutable as those initials on the tapestries within.

Chapter 17
Sunday, January 30 – 6:06 AM
Damascus, Syria

The three mules of Gulzhan Baqrah arrived in Syria early Sunday morning – hungry, dusty and ground down by the road. It had taken them more than twenty-five hours of non-stop travel to make the journey from Kazakhstan to Rasht in Iran, then by land in separate cars and trucks and even, for a few hours, on horseback through the mountainous regions of northern Iraq, before finally arriving in Damascus. They traveled along separate paths to a small, non-descript apartment building just south of Al Shouhada Square, where a young man named Ghazi Khadeja greeted them. Khadeja did not know much about the operation other than the fact that the three men were important friends of Gulzhan Baqrah. The men washed up and had a hearty meal of lamb and raisins and falafel bread.

Just before noon, as the sound of the muezzins called the faithful to prayer, a man arrived at the apartment. His name was Moustapha. Tall and skinny with a scruffy thin black beard, Moustapha carried a message from Gulzhan Baqrah for each of the three mules – their instructions for the next leg of their journeys. Within an hour following the noonday prayers, the mules were packed and ready for the road, assembled in a little courtyard behind the apartment building.

Ali Hammel was the first to be collected. An old man with a patch over one eye appeared in a battered dark green Land Rover. The Algerian got in without even saying goodbye.

Five minutes later, it was Ziad's turn. A truck transporting what appeared to be chrome or manganese ore picked up the Lebanese. He nodded once toward Auwal Al-Hakim and Khadeja, and then climbed up into the cab.

Another five minutes passed and a third and final vehicle appeared. Auwal Al-Hakim watched as the black Citroen nosed its way through the alley and pulled over on the far side of the courtyard. A thin young man jumped out to help him with his case, but the giant Egyptian glanced at him with his vacant ox-like eyes, and he hesitated, stopped and backed away. Khadeja introduced the young man as Zimrilim. He would take Al-Hakim as far as the docks in Tartus. The Egyptian thanked Khadeja, picked up his silver case and knapsack, and squeezed into the front seat of the car.

*   *   *

It took Zimrilim several hours to drive the 250 kilometers north to the coastal town of Tartus, and it was dusk when they finally reached the city limits. They had barely spoken the entire journey. Zimrilim had tried to strike up conversations with Al-Hakim, on several different topics, but – in the end – he had simply given up. Al-Hakim preferred to sleep, and he snored volubly for hours until Zimrilim pulled over for the evening prayer. They stopped once more for gas before they reached the coastal plain. Zimrilim had an uncle in Tartus, and he invited the Egyptian for supper, but Al-Hakim told him it would not be wise. So they kept driving. They drove and drove until the great gray Mediterranean opened up before them in the distance, and they could drive no more.

With over 160,000 inhabitants, Tartus was Syria's second most important port town after Latakia. Zimrilim told Al-Hakim that the city had once been a charming fishing village but it had lost most of its grace over the last few years due to over-development. Even the famous Cathedral of Our Lady of Tortosa in the old city was surrounded now by modern office and apartment buildings.

Founded in antiquity, the city had originally been called Antaradus, since it was anti-Aradus, or facing the island of Aradus, a former Phoenician colony. Zimrilim pointed to the island off the coast. "The city was rebuilt in AD 346 by Emperor Constantine I," he said, "who renamed it Constantia, and it flourished during Roman and Byzantine times as a significant trading port. Eventually, Crusaders converted it into a fortress-town, successfully defending Tartus against Muslim attacks throughout the twelfth century. Even Nur Al Din took over the port city for a time before the Crusaders recaptured it and placed it under the dominion of the Templars. Tartus was the Templars' last stand on the Syrian mainland. When the city fell–"

"Did you say Nur Al Din?" interrupted Al-Hakim, as if he had just woken from a dream.

"You've heard of him?" said Zimrilim. "He was a great explorer, a conqueror and–"

"He was Egyptian. From the *Arabian Nights*," said Al-Hakim. "It would be wise for you, Zimrilim, to remember the behest he made Hasan, his son, as he was dying. 'Be overintimate with none, nor frequent any, nor be familiar with any. So shalt thou be safe from his mischief, for security lieth in seclusion of thought from the society of men, and I have heard it said by poets, *In this world there is none thou mayst count upon/To befriend thy case in nick of need/So live for thyself nursing hope of none/Such counsel I give thee now, take heed!*" The big man laughed, and looked down at his watch, and said, "How much further?"

Zimrilim glanced at the Egyptian. "Not far," he said. "Ten minutes, maybe less." Then he stared back at the road. He was young, only recently turned nineteen, but he wasn't stupid. He knew exactly what Al-Hakim was telling him.

They traveled through the narrow winding streets of the old city to the main shipping yard. As they drove along the docks, Al-Hakim noticed a number of foreign ships lit up in the harbor and Zimrilim told him that Lebanese, Egyptian and even Greek shipping companies routinely registered their bulk and cargo ships in Syria due to the country's favorable maritime regulations. Zimrilim pulled over to the side, stopped the car, and pointed toward a freighter.

It was a small ship, less than 50,000 dead weight tons, an old Handy workhorse of the dry bulk market. Al-Hakim got out at the bottom of the gangway and stretched his legs. Zimrilim remained inside the car. For some reason, the Egyptian's reference to the *Arabian Nights* had unnerved him. There was something about Al-Hakim that did not brook debate. Zimrilim waved once, slipped the Citroen into gear, and drove away.

* * *

Al-Hakim climbed the narrow gangway up onto the deck. The night watchman told him that the Chief Mate was expecting him. After a brief conversation, the Mate escorted the Egyptian to his quarters – a tiny fo'c'sle on the starboard side. There Al-Hakim remained the entire voyage south, sleeping for almost ten hours before the steward woke him early Monday morning. They would be docking in Port Said in another hour, he told the Egyptian. Time to get ready.

As soon as the freighter approached the Egyptian coast, a small launch pulled up along the starboard beam, and the harbor pilot came aboard. It was his job to help the captain navigate the local waters, and to cue up for her passage through the 192-kilometer canal – from Port Said to Port Taufik on the Red Sea. Baqrah had not lied; everything had been arranged. Once the freighter was in convoy, the launch returned to pick up the harbor pilot, and to replace him with another pilot for the passage through the canal. At last, thought Al-Hakim, as he scrambled down the rope ladder. He was almost home. He stepped aboard the launch and, half an hour later, climbed safely up onto dry land.

He was met by an Egyptian named Mashish, a placid young man who did not feel the need to chatter senselessly as Zimrilim had done. It was late morning and, despite the season, the sun was hot. Mashish drove silently along the coastal road to the Egyptian/Israeli town of Rafah. It was an uneventful journey and by the time they arrived at the border, it was well after eleven. Mashish pulled over into a narrow alleyway and stopped the car beside a nondescript white stucco house with a single desultory palm tree dozing in the front. Neither man spoke as he cut the engine and ushered Al-Hakim through the front door.

The house was situated only fifty yards or so from the Israeli border. Al-Hakim could see the barbed wire fence that marked the line between the occupied territory and Egypt through the living room window. There was a terminal a little further north. A group of Arabs was standing by the barbed wire fence, shouting and waving at another group of Arabs on the other side. No wonder they had labeled it the "calling wall." Just then, Mashish returned with a platter of fruit and a steaming pot of tea.

"You'd better eat something before we cross," he told him.

Al-Hakim did not reply. He was staring out the window. Then he asked, "What is that settlement? Over there?"

Mashish moved next to him. "Camp Canada," he said. "More than three hundred and sixty Palestinian families live there, including mine. It was built by the Zionists in '71 as a relocation camp for Rafah families left homeless by the widening of the roads in Gaza – part of Garron's Iron Fist campaign. But in 1982, when the final phase of the return of Sinai to Egypt was concluded, those in the camp were stranded on the wrong side of the border. We were told that we'd be there for just a few weeks, that the Zionists would give us land in Tel el Sultan, give us work permits. But it never happened. Although the land was allocated, it wasn't until '86 that Israel agreed upon some kind of repatriation process. Since then, only eight families have returned to Sinai. The rest are forced to renew their Egyptian tourist visas every six months. Today, unemployment in the camp hovers around seventy percent. It is a cemetery of the living." He laughed bitterly. "The Zionists could transport ten thousand *falasha*, ten thousand Ethiopian Jews, in only a few days. But for us, eight families was all that they could manage. Even when we're granted permission to immigrate, they insist we have twelve thousand U.S. dollars in construction funds. The PLO financed the first few families but, since the Gulf Wars, the money has dried up. Who has twelve thousand dollars? We barely have enough to feed our children."

"Who operates the terminal?"

"It is manned by Palestinians, but the Israeli Army is in charge. You see over there?" he added, pointing at another small settlement on the Israeli side of the fence. "That is the illegal Gush Katif Jewish settlement. Over there. By the tanks."

"I see it."

Mashish looked at his watch. "It is almost time." He moved away from the window and walked over to a corner of the room. Then he squatted on his haunches, pressed a piece of masonry in the floor, and a panel in the wall swung open. Mashish smiled and said, "They find the tunnels almost as quickly as we build them. But this one has never been used. It is brand new."

"Where does it go?" asked Al-Hakim.

"To the Palestinian Community Center, beside the Gush Katif." Mashish glanced at his watch again. "Look, now," he said.

Al-Hakim stared through the window. As he watched, a small group of boys materialized on the outskirts of Camp Canada. They began to pick up stones, and to throw them with uncanny precision over the fence at the tanks guarding a pair of bulldozers beside the Jewish settlement.

"Behold our Palestinian artillery," Mashish added with a grin.

The tanks came to life. Their turrets swung around toward the Palestinian refugee camp. Then, without warning, they opened fire with thirty-caliber machine guns. The children stood their ground. The continued to throw stones even as the sand around them exploded in puffs of dust. Al-Hakim watched with fascination. He could see tracers despite the noonday sun. Then the Israeli soldiers found their mark. A small boy, no more than eleven or twelve, picked up a stone, reeled back to throw it, when gunfire rippled through his chest and sent him sprawling to the ground. His head exploded like a firecracker. The rest of the boys dispersed in all directions.

"It is time," Mashish said. "Quickly now."

Al-Hakim followed Mashish into the opening. A narrow corridor led through the darkness to a staircase. They scrambled down wooden steps. As they moved, Al-Hakim could hear Mashish begin to cry. "Why do you weep?" he asked him. He could not see the Palestinian's face. Mashish carried a flashlight but he kept it pointed at the steps.

"It is with joy," Mashish replied. "That was my brother by the fence, the one who fell." He paused for a moment. Then he turned and said, "Now he is free."

* * *

Ben Seiden drove into the parking lot of Mossad headquarters in Tel Aviv. It was 6:00 AM on Monday and the lot was practically deserted. He parked his car and got out. It was another gorgeous day. The weather had been unusually balmy over the last few weeks, and he wondered at this as he made his way inside. Despite the recent bombings, Seiden – like so many Israelis – couldn't help feeling somewhat cheered by the recent thawing in relations between the Palestinians and Israelis. PLO General Secretary Abu Mazen and Prime Minister Garron had just returned from yet another peace conference. Ever since the Second Gulf War and the overthrow and capture of Saddam Hussein, the United States had been pressuring both sides to come to an accord. Indeed, for the first time in history, a U.S. President openly sponsored the idea of an independent Palestinian state. And while Garron continued to throw up obstacles against the Roadmap, at least there had been some movement. But, despite the good news . . . No, *because* of it, Seiden was worried that the more radical terrorist groups, such as the Brotherhood of the Crimson Scimitar, would do whatever they could to undermine the peace process. They, like the extremists on the Israeli right, were likely to become even more intransigent as hopes for peace grew stronger. And now with El Aqrab in custody, it was a virtual certainty. The fact that Gulzhan Baqrah had hijacked that trainload of HEU in Kazakhstan weighed heavily on Seiden's heart. "Somewhere on the soil of our enemies," only meant one thing to him – Israel, perhaps more than ever before, was in jeopardy. And worse, due to the power struggle between El-Fatah and Hamas, the Israeli security apparatus was being pressured *not* to clamp down on the Palestinians. At a time when such pressure was most needed. Such was the irony of peace.

Seiden entered the building, flashed his ID at Security, and made his way down the long green central corridor to his office. As he unlocked the door and stepped inside, he noticed instantly that something was amiss. The light on his desk was still on . . . and yet he had turned it off the night before. He always did. Seiden was a

- 124 -

punctilious man. He hated the idea of wasting energy. He made his way around his desk and stopped.

There. In the floor. His safe was open. He couldn't believe it. Mossad headquarters was, without doubt, the most secure location in all of Tel Aviv and yet, somehow, someone had broken in. He got onto his hands and knees and started rifling through the safe. How strange, he thought. Nothing appeared to be missing. He poured through the documents again. There was no doubt about it. Everything was there. Perhaps the thief or thieves had photographed the contents. Seiden closed the safe, fastened the door and spun the dial. Then it occurred to him. Even if nothing was missing, now someone could claim that it was.

* * *

Mashish and the Egyptian mule Al-Hakim drove along the outskirts of Beersheba, winding their way along the dusty desert road toward the old city. It had taken them several hours to make the journey from Rafah to Beersheba, but they had done so without incident. Mashish had been prepared. Despite the numerous checkpoints, despite the diligent searching of the IDF, no one had found the aluminum case that Al-Hakim had secreted in the bowels of the Renault 405.

When they had traveled a few kilometers east of the modern city, Mashish pulled over by a low stone wall and the men got out. Mashish was unhappy. It was only four o'clock but his favorite hummus joint, Bulgarit, on K.K. le Israel Street, was already closed. He was hungry, he told Al-Hakim. We will eat soon, the large Egyptian replied.

They strolled along the dusty path and Mashish told Al-Hakim about the city's past. Tel Sheva, the mound of biblical Beersheba where they now stood, was located in the northern Negev, several kilometers east of the modern city. The Arabic name of the mound, *Tell es-Sab'a*, preserved the biblical name. The ancient town was built on a low hill, on the bank of a wadi that carried floodwater during winter. The site itself was more of an administrative center than a city. It was small, about three acres in size, but it was strategically placed, for it guarded the road that ran from Transjordan to Gaza on the Mediterranean Coast, and the route proceeding from Beersheba to the Hill Country of Judah. An aquifer deep beneath the wadi ensured the year-round supply of water. It was this that had brought them to Beersheba. This and the symbolism of the town itself. From the period of David onward, Beersheba had served as the southernmost outpost of the Judean kings. Indeed, the ideal boundaries of the land of Israel were "from Dan (not far from Aval Bet Maacha, in the north) to Beersheba (in the south)," as quoted in Judges 20:1.

The men walked between two stands of olive groves and up onto the naked flinty mound itself. A large area of the site had been excavated between 1969 and 1976, revealing the remains of several settlements, including various fortified towns of the early monarchic rule of Judah, covered by remnants of smaller fortresses dating back to the Persian and Roman periods. The earliest remains were a number of rock-hewn dwellings and a twenty-meter well supplying fresh water to the first permanent unfortified settlement of the Tribe of Simon.

In the mid-tenth century BCE, the first large fortified city was established, serving as the administrative center of the southern region of the kingdom. It extended some ten dunams across the summit of the tel. This had been covered by an eighth century town, in the uppermost layer, a remarkable example of provincial city planning and indicative of the importance of Beersheba for the defense of the southern border. A sophisticated drainage system had been built beneath the streets to collect rainwater into a central channel, assuring the citizens a regular supply of water even during times of siege.

"There," said Mashish. "You see?" He pointed toward a large depression in the ground, lined with hewn stones.

Al-Hakim looked down into the circular opening. It must have been at least seven meters wide and twenty meters deep, with a narrow staircase spiraling down along the inside of the well. He started down the steps. As he descended, Al-Hakim noticed an opening at the bottom of the depression which Mashish said led into the cisterns. Moments later, they ducked into the darkened passageway.

They traveled through the tunnel for almost twenty meters before they came upon the first of the stone cisterns. Despite the flashlight Mashish carried, it was difficult to see. Al-Hakim stopped. "This is it," he said.

The cistern was exactly as Gulzhan Baqrah had described. Al-Hakim opened his aluminum case and knapsack and began to set up the equipment. After a few minutes, he turned toward Mashish and asked him for a pair of pliers. As the young man searched his satchel, Al-Hakim reached his hand into his shirt.

Then, without pausing, he grabbed Mashish by the hair, pulled his head back with a sudden jerk, and slashed his throat with one quick stroke. The boy tried to scream but the sound was trapped like a bubble in his severed voice box. He coughed and sputtered. Then, finally, he lay still. Al-Hakim felt the body wither in his grasp. Soon, he thought, Mashish would be reclining with his brother in the Gardens of Bliss. Surrounded by virgins. Anointed with oils. Free.

Chapter 18
Sunday, January 30 – 8:27 PM
Off the Coast of Gibraltar

The *El Affroun* pitched and yawed in choppy waters as the deep blue Mediterranean met the inky currents of the cold Atlantic. Leaning over the starboard rail, in the shadow of Gibraltar, the Algerian mule Hammel studied the shoreline with interest. This is where the Libyans had bought their clothes, the garments they had packed inside that suitcase bomb, which had vaporized Pan Am Flight 103 over Lockerbie in Scotland. And because of that one simple oversight, that one mistake, over a billion dollars had been handed over to the families of the infidel survivors. The Colonel had capitulated. And Abu Nidal, who had authorized the bombing, who had confessed to it at a meeting of his Fatah-Revolutionary Council, was dead – assassinated by the CIA and left to rot, to the indifferent buzzing of flies, in some Iraqi hotel room.

Ali Hammel shook his head. One little mistake; that's all it took. One loose thread and the entire tapestry unraveled. He visualized the silver briefcase in the closet of his fo'c's'le. *I must gird myself with care*, he thought. *I must check and re-check every move, the smallest of my decisions. I must be . . . perfect.*

He looked astern at the fading Mediterranean. It had been a largely uneventful journey, by fishing trawler, from Syria to Algiers. There, he had hopped this freighter bound for South America. They would put ashore at the Canary and Cape Verde Islands before landfall at Recife and Rio in Brazil. He sighed. He did not like the sea. Water was foreign to him. He had grown up in the town of Tamanrasset in Algeria, in the heart of the Sahara, and the thought of being out of sight of land, aboard this hulk of rotting wood and rusted steel, filled him with dread.

The son of a minor government official, Hammel was the descendent of Tuareg warriors of the Kel Rela, Berber tribesmen who had ruled the Sahara since the time of Herodotus. Ironically, despite the frequent tension between the indigenous Berbers and the Arabs, Hammel – like his father – became a member of the regional government, albeit as a gendarme. By the age of thirteen, he was a police informant, then a policeman at seventeen, and finally the Tam Chief of Police at twenty-six. Indeed, it had been the friction between the Arabs in the north and the Tuareg Berbers of the south that had precipitated his advancement. The officials in Algiers believed a Tuareg Chief of Police would engender greater . .

. and this was usually where they stumbled . . . "self-control amongst the local Berber population." To this day, the Tuareg called the Arabs *Les Chinois* – the Chinese – because they came from somewhere far away, and to the east. The fact that the Arab Almoravids had conquered what would eventually become Algeria back in the eleventh century didn't mean much to the Tuareg. The Berbers bore the water bag of memory. The Arabs would always be outsiders in their minds. And even though the Berber tribes were nominally Islamic, most practiced the religion with a primitive simplicity. They were animists at heart. If a spider bit, or a scorpion stung a Targui, he was made to drink a potion laced with words from the Qur'an, scribbled earnestly on a tiny scrap of paper, as if the symbols themselves would assuage the poison in his blood.

Hammel would have still been Chief of Police, to this day, if he hadn't met Fadimata – in all probability. But he had fallen in love, that most pernicious of weaknesses, ensnared by her unnatural beauty, her family and friends, seduced into a coup attempt against Abdeliza Boutenflika, the Algerian President. Fadimata's family had been the most devout of Muslims. And, despite his agnosticism at the time, Hammel had joined their fundamentalist cause with zeal. He was in love, after all, a vassal Amerid, a Harratin or slave to his own heart, more than willing to parade his loyalty and passion for the sumptuous Fadimata.

The coup failed, of course. Nearly every member of Fadimata's family had been executed, or assassinated, and Hammel had only managed to escape by venturing forth on camelback across the great erg on the track to Mali. For a time, at least, he remained in south Algeria. As an ex-gendarme, he knew the habits of the smuggler with a lover's intimacy. He knew the secret byways of the brigand, the least watched caravan routes and khans, and – most importantly – how policemen thought. For almost two years he survived as an outlaw in the desert. He became what he had hunted all his life. And, ironically, he became a true believer. Hammel found Allah in the wastes of the Sahara.

It was only when a fellow outlaw was captured and revealed Hammel's most treasured hiding places that he was forced to flee the country. If he'd had a heart to break still – after Fadimata, after watching her gunned down like that inside her tent that night as she slept – it would have shattered into a hundred million pieces as fine and weightless as the sand grains of In Salah. But he had had no choice. It was death or exile, and – to his surprise — Hammel preferred to live. After all, he had a purpose now, a raison d'être. The coup may have failed but, like Bin Laden and al-Khalayilah, like El Aqrab himself, he was committed now to something larger than his own vainglorious existence.

The Muslim world was full of Boutenflikas, corrupt false potentates and princes who went to mosque each holy Friday and denigrated the Qur'an, made hollow the Shari'a on Saturday. Islam had enemies both outside and within. And the faith to which he belonged, to which he clung, still, like a black tick on the neck of a *mehari*, required soldiers to defend her. And so he had gone to Lebanon, and met the infamous El Aqrab.

Gulzhan was right. He would become *shahid*. The story of his own, small, personal jihad was written. He would burn as brightly as one of El Aqrab's incendiary devices, bright as an atom bomb, a *Ghusl* ablution of flame, and awaken in the gardens of Heaven. Of this, Hammel was convinced. God would protect him from the tiniest mistake. Hammel accepted this without doubt, without bothering to ask how, or even why; as he accepted the *bila kayf* and all the mysteries of faith.

He stared down at the cold Atlantic, at the glassy swath the freighter cut behind her as she ploughed the waves, a path as temporary and fragile as any in the desert.

The only permanence was Allah, Hammel thought. The rest, just like these waves, just like the dunes of In Salah, like Man himself, was fleeting — a windspout in the wastes of the Sahara. When the bomb had done its work, when he was dead, it would not be these days, but only their perfection that would linger.

There was an eerie, almost palpable silence in the corridor, shattered only by the jingling of keys. Decker stood outside the metal apartment door and waited for the landlord to let him in. No one had entered the apartment since the time of the sealing. Strands of solar yellow POLICE LINE – DO NOT CROSS tape still hung across the door. Decker removed the plastic cobwebs with a single sweep of the hand. "Thanks," he said to the landlord, stepping forward. "I'll lock up when I'm finished."

He flipped on the light and made his way into the living room, past the dingy off-white nubby sofa, the wicker coffee table with the broken leg, across the well-worn carpeting, to the little wooden table with the Dell PC. He didn't waste any time. He curled into the seat like a question mark and turned on the computer.

Recent news stories had brought the theft of the HEU in Kazakhstan to the world's attention. In New York, that irrepressible hack Gallagher of WKXY-TV had done a good job scaring half the city to death. Citizen and union groups demonstrated daily outside of City Hall, and each morning saw another truckload of irate letters delivered to His Honor, Mayor Greenberg. There had been four myocardial infarctions, dozens of asthma attacks, and an elderly couple in Queens had taken their own lives in the face of the impending radioactive doom. The Manhattan DA was looking into pressing charges against Gallagher and WKXY-TV but the case was dubious at best. The First Amendment's guarantee of freedom of the press was hard to bridle even in this time of heightened vigilance.

Decker waited for the machine to boot up.

One good thing had come out of the El Aqrab Affair, as it soon came to be known: The nation's alert status had increased from Yellow to Orange. Armed with a new sense of urgency, Decker's boss, SAC Jerry Johnson, submitted a request to re-search the apartment in Queens under the provisions of the Foreign Intelligence Surveillance Act. A FISA panel of judges convened in secret and issued the search warrant. It did not have to be displayed. The raid could be done in secret, night or day. And this time, the PC hard disk was in play.

Decker linked up his portable burn unit to the computer

and copied the files from the hard disk. The process took only a few seconds. There wasn't a whole lot on the PC; he could have used a memory stick. With a loud sigh, Decker got up, packed his gear into his gym bag, and left the apartment.

As soon as he got back to FBI headquarters, Decker stopped by the Computer Lab on the third floor and downloaded a copy of the hard disk for analysis. Then he walked the four flights back to his department.

No one greeted him as he entered the bullpen. Other agents occupied the desks around him. But they were off in their own worlds, on the telephone, or with their eyes glued to their PC screens, typing reports.

Decker sat down at his desk and started pouring through his e- and snail-mail: new HR protocols; a retirement party for some guy in Accounting named Trumbel; an irritating set of questions about his expense report from SAC Johnson; a joke from Tony Bartolo . . . Decker froze. He looked at the name again: *Anthony Bartolo*. And he saw the body gradually unfurl, with that puzzled look upon his face. Decker couldn't stand it any longer. He pulled the CD burner from his gym bag and linked it to his own PC.

It took him only a few minutes to transfer the data to his Compaq and run a recovery program, unscrambling the FAT. It looked like one of the suspects – probably Mohammed bin Basra – had erased some of the files just before bolting from the apartment: a pair of .doc file letters that seemed innocuous enough; a host of Quicken files tracking an account worth thirteen thousand dollars – nothing appeared to be coded; some PDF files of speeches by an Imam in Brooklyn; and, finally, four different wallpapers, with different arabesque designs and Arabic calligraphy, which he reviewed with PhotoShop.

The first turned out to be the same design that he had seen at the apartment in Queens, the one Professor Hassan had called *masjid*, the Individual prayer. He translated the Arabic script that ran along the *qibla* and confirmed that it was from the *Al-Takwir*, Sura 81. Except that only a part of the text had been used in the design – the words, " . . . ten-month pregnant she-camels are discarded as a means of transportation . . . " and then, " . . . when hell is stoked up." He remembered what Hassan had said the phrases meant to Muslim clerics: *Real trains and other high-speed means of transportation have supplanted camel trains.* And the reference to hell: *Could be volcanoes like Mt. St. Helens and Etna. But many clerics believe it refers to nuclear power and the bomb.*

Then it hit him. Trains and bombs! The HEU stolen by Gulzhan Baqrah had been transported on a train. Could these strange quotes be harbingers of things to come, some planned but yet unexecuted crime? The date of the file was older than the theft itself – by several weeks. But what did the number 540,000 mean?

With mounting excitement, Decker examined the other wallpaper files. He had never seen the second one before. The illustration looked similar to the one he'd discovered in Moussa's locker, similar – with a *qibla* line and *minbar* – but not identical. Could it represent the second prayer Hassan had called the *jami' masjid*, used in the Congregational mosque on Fridays? He tried to translate the calligraphy but only a few words were discernable: "How many a deserted well." And then, perpendicular to the transversal axis, "Hell is the rendezvous." He couldn't make out the rest, except for another number: 205,200. The calligraphy was simply too ornate. He made a note of the translation and moved on.

The third wallpaper seemed identical to the illustration he'd found in Moussa's locker, the third prayer Hassan had referred to as *musalla* or *idgah*, the Community mosque used during the festivals of 'Id al-Fitr and 'Id al-Adha. But, once again, he could only decipher a solitary phrase, no matter how hard he tried: "Death will overtake you . . . " And the number 54,000. *I must be missing something*, he thought.

The fourth and final wallpaper was simply a collection of arabesque designs. No calligraphy, no abstract symbols broke the rhythm of the wave-like lines, the sweep of foliation, the endless repetitions. No. Wait! There. He peered more closely at the image. Those tiny curves and lines and dots – right at the center – surrounding the number 0. The words were like an island in a whirling arabesque sea. He translated them. "On the ocean like mountains." That was it. Nothing else. Just that single phrase. It was so frustrating. He needed a break.

Decker closed the files one by one. Then he stretched for a moment, started to stand and . . . stopped. He looked down at the PC screen, at the folder containing the files. Wait a minute. Something was wrong. Most wallpaper images had JPG or BMP extensions. These were all TIF files. But even more bizarre was their size. All four files were huge, ten to twenty Megs apiece. He checked the wallpaper images from his own PC. They were all in a *Wallpaper* directory in the *Web* folder under *WINNT*. But most of the JPGs were less than one hundred KB. He then converted one of the ordinary JPG wallpaper files into a TIF file. The file expanded by a factor of less than twenty. This just didn't make any sense. The TIF wallpaper files should have been around two Megs apiece, not ten to twenty. Then he remembered Professor Hassan's question: "Was there anything behind the files? Hidden architecture." Isn't that what he had called it? What better place to hide something than in plain view, on wallpaper! It reminded him of the elaborate tattoos of the *Nuestra Familia* prison gangs that he'd once been required to decipher in Chicago. They featured clandestine messages as well, a kind of epidermal, hidden architecture.

Decker right-clicked the file of the first wallpaper image, the *masjid* or Individual prayer, and tried to view it as a non-graphics file, first as a standard text file — with a TXT extension — and then as a standard ASCII file, to see if it made sense. Garbage! Indecipherable nonsense! Then he remembered that ASCII was a Western file format, designed to represent Western alphabetical characters. The equivalent for Arabic, Chinese and other non-Western languages was a UTF-8 or UTF-16 file format. He tried both and the output still didn't make sense. Given the size of the file, he stuck with the UTF-16.

Of course, the answer could have been some algorithm or formula that isolated a discrete part of the file — like ciphers used in correspondence, where only every X letter or word was important. But Decker didn't know the X. With a controlled breath, he let himself fall into the pattern, "reclining in chaos," as his *sensei* Master Yamaguchi used to say.

Decker spiraled downward through the numbers, drifted, until — as if someone were tapping him gently on the shoulder as he slept — it suddenly became clear. He remembered what Professor Hassan had said about the proportions in Arabic architecture derived from the perfect square — the "Golden Ratio," as Pythagoras had called it. The *Phi.* One to the square root of two.

Decker opened his eyes and wrote a simple program to run the ratio against the file. In this way, he could isolate which active or live points on each line contained data that could be interpreted not as image information, but as UTF-16 text data. He couldn't believe it. It still didn't make any sense. Normally, when he got this feeling and fell into a pattern, he floated up out of the depths with a solution — like snatching a coin from the bottom of a pool. He was just about to give up again when he remembered the obvious.

Arabic didn't read from left to right. He had been running the program against the scan lines from the top left to the right, and then down a line. He ran the program again, this time from the top right left, then down again, and so forth.

The Arabic fell to order. He'd been right! The formula was based on *Phi*, a constant in Islamic architecture.

He read the title of the file: *Terrorism Incident Annex*. Cold fingers clamped his heart. He read through the first paragraph. It listed a series of Signatory Agencies, from the Department of Defense (DOD) to the Federal Emergency Management Agency (FEMA).

Below the list of agencies was the Introduction: *Presidential Decision Directive 39 (PDD-39), U.S. Policy on Counterterrorism, establishes policy to reduce the Nation's vulnerability to terrorism, deter and respond to terrorism, and strengthen capabilities to detect, prevent, defeat, and manage the consequences of terrorist use of weapons of mass destruction (WMD). PDD-39 states that the United States will have the ability to respond rapidly and decisively to terrorism directed against Americans wherever it occurs, arrest or defeat the perpetrators using all appropriate instruments against the sponsoring organizations and governments, and provide recovery relief to victims, as permitted by law . . .*

He continued to scroll down through the converted file. It was approximately twenty pages long, and included detailed plans on how to evacuate New York in the event of an emergency.

Decker ran the second file through the same process. This was the smallest of the four; it popped up in a second — a sketch, an illustration, built using plain text characters. His blood congealed. He knew exactly what this was: a "gun" type nuclear device, a WMD, annotated with instructions on how to set it off.

With shaking hands, he ran the third file through the program. This was the largest of the four, just shy of twenty Megs. It seemed to take forever for the code to process, although Decker knew it was only seconds. His pulse quickened. The file began to coalesce.

It was another illustration, some kind of architectural drawing featuring structural supports and wiring. His eyes settled at the top of the PC screen. He knew this building. He saw it every day, from the corner near the subway station where he took the train to work.

The Empire State Building!

Decker processed the fourth and final file. It popped up in

a second – raw data of some kind, column after column, row after row. He scrolled up and noticed a paragraph of text, once again in Arabic. It pertained to something called the "Inundation Phase" of a tsunami. Perhaps, he thought, the kind of tidal wave created by a nuclear explosion . . . in the Empire State Building . . . on the island of Manhattan!

Decker took a slow, deep breath through his nose and let the air run down into his lungs, like rainwater falling through the downspout of his spine. He felt it settle in his stomach, collect within the reservoir of his *chi*, and then evaporate again. It rose up through his chest like some great cloud and slowly, slowly, slipped between his lips. Decker breathed again. It was a standard Kung Fu exercise. His heart rate slowed. Then he looked up and waved at Johnson and Warhaftig, who were standing less than twenty feet away in front of Johnson's office.

"Excuse me," he said. "SAC Johnson?" He ignored him. "Sir?" he said a little louder. Warhaftig glanced over but immediately turned back. They appeared to be arguing about something. "SAC Johnson, sir!" Decker said, his voice so loud now that everyone in the bullpen stopped, and turned and stared.

"What do you want?" Johnson shouted back. He was clearly annoyed.

"I think you'd better take a look at this."

Just then, the phone rang on Decker's desk. He picked up the receiver. It was the Computer Lab. They'd run a recovery program against the hard disk – as he had – but come up empty. Decker thanked the analyst and hung up.

When Warhaftig and Johnson approached his desk, he told them what he had discovered, displaying the hidden files on his computer. Warhaftig grew excited, but Johnson continued to scowl.

"Tell the Lab what you've found," he said. "And ask them to check it again. I'll be in my office."

After hearing about the technique Decker had leveraged to uncover the files, Warhaftig was even more impressed by the young cryptanalyst's abilities. Decker continued to eyeball Jerry Johnson in his office. He could clearly see the SAC behind his desk despite the tinted glass. Johnson was staring at his telephone. He was waiting for the new report.

This time they didn't call. The head of the Lab himself, Dr. Hansotia, came up to Decker's floor. He was a short fat Indian man, with gray hair and inch-thick glasses that made his eyes appear abnormally huge. He was mortified by the Lab's initial oversight but couldn't say enough about Decker. Although Johnson remained skeptical, everyone else was now convinced the clues were not only real, but potentially vital to the case. Johnson shuffled back into his office and reported the findings to his boss, Assistant Director in Charge (ADIC) of the New York office, who – in turn – reported it to the Director himself in Washington, D.C.

Half an hour later, Johnson came out of his office and began to hand out new assignments. The manpower shortage was over. Four Radiation Detection Units would henceforth be assigned to the Empire State Building. Another team would work with FEMA to see if the evacuation procedures for New York outlined in the hidden file had been made public at any time, or if the agency had experienced any loss of data from their systems in the last few months. Another six teams would continue searching for Singh, Moussa and bin Basra. And Decker was to track down the tsunami lead, despite the fact that no one thought it was particularly important. Warhaftig protested but Decker told the SAC he didn't mind. While the lead appeared off-pattern, more speculative even, Decker was intrigued. The words from the fourth wallpaper – *On the ocean like mountains* – still resonated in his head.

"See me when you get back," said Warhaftig. "I may have another assignment for you.

SECTION III

Musalla

Chapter 20
Monday, January 31 – 4:27 AM
"No Man's Land" between Lebanon and Israel

Ziad crawled along the ground, toward the barbed wire fence that marked the ingress to the no man's land between Lebanon and Israel. He pulled out a pair of wire cutters, turned over onto his back, and sliced the bottom strand. It howled as it retracted, vanishing into the night. Then he cut the second wire. When the opening was big enough, he removed the knapsack on his back, slipped it around his left foot, and worked his way under the fence. Far above him he could see stars. There was little ambient light in the Shibaa region; it was mostly farmland. The town of Aval Bet Maacha was a fair distance to the west. And there was no moon.

As he inched his way under the fence, Ziad remembered a night he had once shared with El Aqrab some years before in Kazakhstan. They had been on an evening training exercise in the mountains, and they had stopped for a bite to eat on a promontory overlooking a narrow valley. The winter sky had been full of stars – so close, so bright – and El Aqrab had told him that the ancient Romans believed the Milky Way was Juno's breast milk spilled across the heavens. Ziad had laughed at that but El Aqrab had thought the image beautiful. He was a strange man. He found beauty in the oddest things. And then he began to name the stars in the constellation of Orion: Betelgeuse, Bellatrix, Rigel, Saiph. So many of the stars, he told Ziad, had been named by Arabs, the first astronomers. So much had been brought into the world by the followers of Islam. Including nothingness.

"What does that mean?" Ziad asked.

"The Arabic number zero." El Aqrab paused and looked about. Then he continued in a whisper, as if the night itself might snatch the words away. "It was conceived in a little village in north India, carried across the tip of the Red Sea, across the Saudi peninsula on camel back, the great Sahara, and finally into Spain by the Almoravids. They carried nothingness across the wastelands, and it changed the world forever."

Ziad had never forgotten those words. They seemed to sum up El Aqrab who, in the end, was like the number zero himself: empty, yet overfilled; a water bag distended by void. Much like his protégé, Hammel.

Ziad rolled over onto his stomach. He lifted the knapsack toward his chest. He started to put it on again, when his hand touched something hard and stiff and, suddenly, that sound – like wind whistling through a wadi. Then, it stopped. A moment later, a rocket leapt into the air, and the night sky split apart with light. The trip flare hovered high above him, hanging from a tiny parachute, the smoke made visible by a brilliant luminescent glaze.

Ziad reached down for his weapon, but it was already too late. He heard the sound of machinegun fire spit somewhere just ahead, saw the ground before him gradually unravel – like a poorly sewn seam – and felt the sharp wasp sting of bullets in his shoulder, back and legs. He tried to roll away, but they had found him and there was nowhere left to roll, or run, or hide. Besides, he couldn't even move. He looked up at the sky, at the Arabian stars, and thought of nothingness.

*   *   *

IDF Captain Solomon Snow aimed his flashlight at the twisted carnage by the fence. There was little left of the guerrilla's face. He pushed at the corpse with his boot, and the body flopped onto its back. The terrorist had been lying on his knapsack. Captain Snow squatted down and opened it with care. Although it was riddled with bullets, you could never be too vigilant. If the terrorist were a Hezbollah suicide bomber, there might be some triggering mechanism within.

He peeled back the bloody flap, slowly, carefully. The light from his flashlight quivered back at him. There was something metallic inside. He held his breath and removed what appeared to be a large stainless steel attaché case. He slipped it onto the grass. The hinges had been hit. He lifted the top off delicately but it crumbled in his hands. It was some kind of electronic device, he thought, some sort of sophisticated communications or jamming instrument. He saw the bulbous protrusion on the right side of the casing and his heart came to a stop.

He knew what this was! He'd studied illustrations of nuclear devices in his early training days and, while not identical, this instrument looked similar enough to make his fingers freeze. Then, he noticed the bulbous section was cracked, almost in half. And more salient, it was empty. Impotent. Unarmed.

Captain Snow breathed a deep sigh of relief, looked up at the limpid stars, and started to pray.

Chapter 21
Monday, January 31 – 7:38 AM
The Canary Islands

On the island of Lanzarote, a hundred miles off the Moroccan coast, the Algerian mule Hammel watched as the Venieri bulldozer was hoisted by boom out of the forward hold of the freighter *El Affroun*. He had been waiting for this moment. The rest of the cargo scheduled for unloading – from generators and electronics, to razor blades and beef – had already been lowered down onto the docks over the previous hour. In most cases, the cargo was stowed in large containers and it was easy going. But the Venieri *Terne Articolate* 114 HP bulldozer was freestanding. So they had wrapped steel cables around her belly and lifted her by boom – via a pair of booms, to be precise – out of the forward hold.

Despite tight mooring lines, the ship rocked in the wind. It was almost imperceptible, but it was enough. With barely a warning, the bulldozer began to swing, to pendulum back and forth. Hammel and a host of other seamen tried to steady her with hand lines, but the Venieri pitched out of control, swung and smashed against the starboard boom, leaving a great scar on the metal plating covering the gears and winch.

Hammel's heart gave up a beat. He heaved against the hand line, pulled with all his might. The dozer shimmied back and forth a few more times, then finally settled. The winches croaked and coughed as they hoisted her higher, higher and higher and up and over the rail, and finally down onto the dock below.

As soon as the hand lines and hoisting cables were disengaged, a stevedore jumped up into the cab and started up the Venieri. Hammel watched as a plume of black smoke belched out of the exhaust pipe, and the yellow bulldozer roared away.

Captain Abdullah Shamir was standing just outside the bridge, on the starboard side, watching the activity below. Hammel lifted his right hand for an instant, as if to wipe his brow. The Captain nodded almost imperceptibly, and the Algerian turned and started toward the gangway.

Hammel waited outside the warehouse until nightfall, when the sun had disappeared behind the central volcanic slopes, and the harbor was cast into shadow. The city of Arrecife glowed to the west. Hammel could see the stone walls of the Castillo de Gabriel illuminated by spotlights only a mile or so away. A cool breeze blew in from the north and – buffeting the ancient fortress – whistled down the streets of Arrecife, capital city of Lanzarote, the easternmost isle of the Canary chain.

Hammel looked at his watch. It was almost 7:00 PM. He slipped under the wire fence, dashed across the outer perimeter, and threw himself to the ground beside the warehouse. Then, he crawled forward on his hands and knees toward the main doors. A night guard dozed outside the entrance. He was sitting in a small shack made of local palm planks with a corrugated iron roof. Hammel smiled. One of the warehouse doors was slightly open. He dashed behind the shack, slipped to the ground, and slithered through the shadows to the entrance. A moment later, he was inside.

It was a large warehouse, but Hammel spotted the Venieri bulldozer almost immediately. It was parked beside a tower of pallets near the entrance. He scanned the warehouse. The cargo was lined up in four rows, in some cases stacked almost to the ceiling on reinforced metal shelving. He checked the rows one by one. It didn't take him long to find what he was looking for.

About halfway down the second aisle, he noticed a large wooden crate scheduled to be loaded aboard the *Rêve de Chantal* in the morning. Hammel studied the label with care. When he was satisfied, he picked up a nearby crowbar and opened the lid as quietly as he could. Moments later, he spotted a wine-colored blanket and, underneath, the cartoon faces of John, Paul, George and Ringo, three plastic periscopes and a yellow submarine. This was it. He continued to expose the Sound Leisure Beatles jukebox. When he had revealed the entire cabinet, he disassembled one of the polycarbonate bubble tube pilasters on the outer edge. It was no longer filled with water and it slipped off easily, revealing a large hollow in the casing below the compact disc machine. Hammel knelt down and felt inside. Plenty of room.

He made his way back across the warehouse. There was a dramatic VF logo on one side of the yellow bulldozer; it had been manufactured by VF Venieri, Costruzione Macchine Industriali of Lugo, Italy. The bulldozer featured an articulated backhoe loader, a quick coupler, 4-in-1 shovel, a telescopic dipper stick . . . and a thermonuclear device.

Hammel removed a screwdriver from his pocket. He slipped it underneath a panel immediately below the right door. It took only a few seconds and – with a loud *pop* – the panel separated from the chassis, revealing a satchel of plastic explosives, gunpowder bladders, and an aluminum attaché case within.

Hammel looked about the warehouse. He was still alone. He snatched the satchel and attaché case, replaced the panel, and hurried back across the warehouse toward the second aisle. When he had reached the jukebox, he slipped the case into the opening. Then he mounted the plastic explosives and bladders along the inside seams, following a drawing he referred to in his hand. When he was done, he replaced the pilaster. Everything fit perfectly behind the bubble tube, invisible and safe, secure and . . .

The noise of heavy footsteps broke his reverie. Hammel swung in behind the crate. It was still open, but at least it afforded him some measure of protection; no passersby could see him. He huddled down. The footsteps drew closer. He knelt behind the jukebox. He poked behind the waistband of his pants and felt for the plastic toggles. There they were. He tugged gently and the wire began to slide out of his waistband. It snaked around his stomach, slipped out and dangled in his hand. He unfastened the extra plastic toggle and refastened it to the naked wire tip. The stranger drew near. Hammel ran his fingers around the plastic toggles and pulled the wire tight.

Nearer, nearer, and the figure shuffled into view: A large black man pushing a dolly – an African, no doubt – with thick black matted hair, a head round as a coconut, a fleshy mouth, immense flat nose and tiny eyes. He took in first the corridor, the open crate, and then the Beatles jukebox.

Ali Hammel realized he was holding his breath. He looked down at the wire in his hands, the way it shimmered in the light, so sharp, so tight. The African continued to stare at the open crate. He looked about the corridor. He seemed fitful and nervous, as if he could somehow sense Hammel behind the jukebox. Then the African passed by. He kept on walking until he stopped, all of a sudden, by another crate. He propped the dolly up against a shelf and reached down for what appeared to be a case of wine. And then another, and another. He stacked three cases onto the dolly, then started back along the corridor. Once again, he passed the open crate. But this time the African didn't stop. He simply kept on walking, turned the corner and disappeared, his footsteps gradually receding.

Hammel waited a few more minutes before he unclasped the plastic handle, clipped it to the other side of the wire, and re-threaded the garrote around his waistband. Then he began to reassemble everything: the wine-colored blanket; the frame; the planking around the crate. He made sure the label was affixed just as before. When he was done, he returned to the front of the warehouse. The guard was wide-awake now, no doubt raised by the African. Hammel got onto his hands and knees. He crawled around the little wooden hut, around the warehouse, and made a dash across the macadam perimeter, back through the outer fence.

Captain Abdullah Shamir was in his cabin when Hammel returned from the warehouse. He was relaxing, preparing to retire for the night. Hammel insisted on coming in and, after a moment's hesitation, the Captain reluctantly agreed.

"I need you to transfer me to the *Rêve de Chantal*," Hammel informed him. "She came in from Marseilles this morning."

Captain Abdullah walked over to his refrigerator and removed a Fanta. He popped the cap off using the handle of the fridge, and the orange soda fizzed and fizzled over the lip of the glass bottle. The cap rolled somewhere out of sight.

A small triumphant feeling overcame him. The Captain had been "asked" to add the mysterious Algerian to his active seamen's roster, "asked" to ship the Venieri bulldozer, and "asked" to let the Algerian go ashore in Arrecife. As a faithful Muslim, he had taken the request most seriously. Captain Abdullah knew the fate of those who refused the Algerian Islamic fundamentalists. But, now, he was more than eager to get rid of Ali Hammel.

There was something terribly unnerving about the Berber. He wasn't particularly tall. He wasn't particularly strong. He was, well . . . ordinary. Until you looked into his eyes. Then a palpable fear took hold. It was difficult to describe. His eyes were vacuous, bereft of feeling, of the compassion that made one human. Soulless, somehow.

One time, years before, Captain Abdullah had taken his nephews to the zoo outside Algiers, and they had come across a large gorilla with the same discomforting expression. The animal had looked at them with understanding, with a sentient appraisal, but somehow empty, too – a spiritual castaway.

The Chief Steward called the Algerian bewitched, a *marabout* of the shadows. Yet he went out of his way to curry favor with him, cooking him special meals, and leaving them outside the Algerian's fo'c's'le every evening after Hammel got off his watch. Ali Hammel never ate with the other men. In fact, some wondered if he ate at all, for his plates seemed no less heaped with food the following morning. All this was known to Captain Abdullah. But how to get him off the ship? "It will not be easy," he said at last.

"I didn't think it would be," Hammel replied.

The Captain took another swig of his Fanta and sat down at the table. "The only reason a man's excused from duty is in the case of illness, or personal tragedy. Then, he might transfer to another ship, like the *Rêve de Chantal*, in the hopes of reaching homeward passage. It is a courtesy, no matter what the shipping line. It's understood. But isn't the *Rêve* bound for New York?"

"It will be easier for me to find passage there," Hammel said. "Back to Algiers. What kind of illness?"

"Oh, I don't know. Appendicitis. A case of fever, perhaps, but they would see right through that; you have no temperature. No. Something else," the Captain said. "An injury. Some kind of incapacitating fall. A concussion, or a break." He shrugged. "It is unfortunate you have to leave so soon. You'd like Brazil."

Ali Hammel walked over to the Captain's refrigerator, and slipped his foot into the crack between the metal siding and the scuffed Formica counter, as if he were rooting around for something that had fallen in between.

"Everybody does," Captain Abdullah said. "The weather is beautiful this time of year. The food is wonderful, and cheap. And the women . . ."

With a smile that lingered in the Captain's head for weeks, the Algerian threw himself to the floor, across his own leg. There was a sickening *snap* as his knee popped out of place. The Captain leapt to his feet, knocking his chair over.

Hammel pushed himself slowly off the ground, using his forearms, trying to get up. He looked behind him. His right foot remained upright in the crack, while his body had turned completely over. He lay on his stomach. Pain contorted his face but he did not say a word. He did not utter a sound even as he twisted himself around, carefully, back onto his back, and removed his foot from between the refrigerator and the counter. It plopped out like a wounded fish onto the floor. The Captain looked down at the Algerian's right knee. It was already swelling. It was already bubbling in his pants.

"An injury," Hammel hissed through his front teeth, trying to control their chattering. He was going into shock. He pointed down. "Like this?"

Chapter 22
Monday, January 31 – 9:27 AM
Woods Hole, Massachusetts

It took Decker a little over four hours to make the drive from New York to Falmouth, Massachusetts, on the Bruckner to I-95, and then east along 195 toward that little spit of land called Devil's Foot, which juts out from the bottom of Cape Cod. As he approached the harbor, he noticed Martha's Vineyard lying to the south, like a pearl gray shawl across the bright Atlantic. It was a beautiful winter day, cold and crisp, blown south and east from Manitoba and Ontario, from the arctic wastelands of the north.

By the time Decker entered Falmouth it was almost noon. He traveled south along the coast road until Clearview Avenue; until he saw the mailbox leaning inbetween a pair of stunted hemlocks to the left; the number six, in bright metallic tape; and, finally, turned and snaked his way along the long black gravel driveway leading to the bay.

A rambling white Cape Cod with pale blue shutters was perched on a rocky promontory overlooking the Atlantic and Falmouth Harbor, only two hundred yards from the shoreline. The lawn in front of the house was yellowed and studded with stone. The place looked deserted.

No one answered when Decker crossed the porch and rang the doorbell. Then he noticed the door. It was slightly ajar. He poked his head in, saying, "Hello. Hello, Dr. White?" He stepped inside. Someone else was in the house. He could hear them. "Hello?" he repeated. He had a sudden premonition that he was being watched. Then he saw a young woman in the next room – reflected in a pre-Revolutionary convex mirror – look up and catch his face, and stop, and slowly turn.

"Who are you?" she said, striding toward him with conviction. "And what the hell are you doing here?"

Decker stalled at her approach. "Looking for Dr. White. Dr. James L. White? Isn't this his house?"

"Yes."

Decker stared at the woman. He waited patiently, in silence, until she added, "I'm just squatting."

Despite the bulky sweatshirt, despite the way her long blond hair was pinned up in a frumpy bun, despite her apparent aversion to any sort of makeup, the woman was absolutely stunning. She had bright, cerulean eyes, full lips, high cheekbones and the most delicate of noses. As a rule, Decker didn't find blondes particularly attractive, but he caught himself staring at her unconsciously. She had disarmed him. It was rare to see a woman who was both beautiful *and* sexy. She could have been a model. No, a movie star, or . . . "I'm sorry," he said. He took another step, stopped, looked about self-consciously, and added, "I'm here to see Dr. James L. White."

"Yeah, you said that."

She wore a pair of light blue jeans, he noticed. Very tight. And what looked like off-white Converse sneakers. "My name is Decker. John Decker, Jr. I'm with the FBI."

For a moment, the woman looked startled. Fear swept across her face, like a sudden squall at sea. Then she collected herself. "The FBI," she repeated nonchalantly. "Is something wrong?"

Decker smiled. He was used to this reaction. People often overcompensated. "No, nothing's wrong," he said. "I just have a few questions for Dr. White. Know where I might find him?"

She shook her head. Her neck was long, like that of a Balanchine dancer, and she wore a pair of tiny gold studs in her ears that twinkled as she moved. She was at least five feet ten inches, or taller – almost as tall as he was. "I'm afraid not," she said. Then she thrust her hand out. "Hi, I'm Emily Swenson. I'm afraid James – I mean, Dr. White – is on a leave of absence. I'm looking for him too."

They shook hands. Strong grip, he thought.

"His wife is sick," she continued.

"Oh, sorry to hear that. Nothing serious, I hope."

For a moment she didn't reply. Then she looked down at the floor and said, "It's cancer, I'm afraid. Terminal. What's this about?"

"I understand Dr. White is a highly respected expert on tsunamis. World-renowned," said Decker. "I have a few questions that I thought he might help me with. When I called his office, the department secretary told me I might find him here, at home, but . . ." His voice trailed off.

Swenson stared impassively at his face. Then, after a moment, she said, "That's my field of study too. Dr. White's my thesis advisor. Maybe I can help you."

Decker smiled. He reached into his jacket, pulled out a piece of paper, and handed it to her. "Do you know what this is?"

Swenson studied it for a moment. "This looks like mega-tsunami data, built from a computer model."

Decker looked confused. "Go on," he said.

"It's designed to predict a mega-tsunami's height at inundation. Where did you get this? From Dr. White?"

"I know what a tsunami is," said Decker. "A kind of tidal wave, right? But what's a mega-tsunami?"

Swenson raised an eyebrow. "Tides are moon-made, Agent Decker," she replied. "Tsunamis are earth-generated. Mega-tsunamis are formed when an entire mountain – or mountain range – collapses into the sea, usually due to seismic activity. Unlike regular tsunamis, which may be ten to fifteen meters tall and a few dozen meters long, mega-tsunamis can be hundreds, up to five hundred meters tall – or more – and hundreds of kilometers in length."

Decker did the calculation in his head. That was a wave taller than the Empire State Building. It was incredible. "I had no idea," he said.

"Most people don't," said Swenson. "And why should they? Mega-tsunamis are rare, occurring naturally every few thousand years. Here, let me show you." She motioned toward him and disappeared into another room at the far end of the living room. It appeared to be a library or study. A pair of large bay windows overlooked the open sea.

Swenson slipped behind an antique walnut desk in the far corner, and started to peck away at a PC. "This is a computer-generated simulation," she continued, not even looking up. She moved the mouse. She clicked. "It's based on a model Dr. White's been working on, the same as the one on your paper. Take a look." She swung the monitor around. Decker sat down by the desk.

The screen featured a top-down view of the Atlantic. The animated image gradually descended until it focused on a chain of islands off the coast of northwest Africa. Then, the perspective shifted. It fell to earth, swung low across the waves, like a sea bird, and approached a solitary island at a startling speed.

The island grew larger and larger until it took up the entire screen, and Decker could see volcanic peaks, smoking and spewing steam, when a rent materialized along the seaward side. The entire western flank of the island tore away. The mass of rock and stone and forest and meadow and town and road began to slither toward the sea. As the crustal layer ripped apart, the landmass picked up speed. The entire island seemed to split in half, with one side sliding with a mighty crash into the ocean.

The splash gathered momentum: a spike, then, rising higher, a bell-shaped dome, slate gray, blue, and finally frothy white. It rose and rose and rose, dwarfing the remaining peaks, still standing mist-enshrouded, still still, intact, and strangely static, perched on the footstool of the island.

The camera angle of the animation gradually ascended, drawing him higher and higher into the air, in tandem with the splash. The bell-shaped mass crowned like a flower, bloomed, then mushroomed skyward, only to turn at last, and fall back on itself. The water plunged. The dome collapsed, spreading out in all directions, rippling the surface of the ocean like the upturned edges of a giant saucer, growing ever larger by the second. The perspective kept ascending, until Decker was looking at the entire Atlantic once again, from Africa to the Americas. The wave was visible even from this vantage point above the planet's atmosphere. The eastern edge slammed up against the coast of Africa. He watched the western flank arc out across the vast expanse, like the drawing of a great bow on the surface of the sea.

"This is obviously stop-action animation," Swenson said. "A mega-tsunami of this magnitude would take between six and seven hours – at the speed of a jet plane – to sweep across the Atlantic." As she spoke, Decker watched the wave overcome the Caribbean, then Maine and Massachusetts in the north, as far south as Sao Luis and Rio in Brazil.

"Even this far from the hypocenter," Swenson continued, "the wave would be as much as twenty stories high, or higher. But it wouldn't collapse at landfall. Unlike tsunamis, mega-tsunamis don't shoal up when they encounter shallow waters. The wave would continue across the coastal plain, up river mouths, for twenty kilometers, or more."

Decker watched the water wipe away the east coast of the USA.

"Everything within the flood zone would be utterly destroyed," she added. "From Cape Breton to Key West, each town and every city. More than forty million people would perish, thirteen percent of the U.S. population. And hundreds of millions would be injured, one out of every three Americans. It would cause trillions of dollars in damage. The entire U.S. economy would be disrupted for years, if not permanently crippled."

The animation concluded and the file closed automatically. Decker stared at the folder for a moment longer. He was having a hard time digesting the scope of such a cataclysm. *The mind turns off after a few hundred deaths. Forty million is simply inconceivable, unprocessable.* He turned and looked at Swenson. She was sitting calmly behind Dr. White's desk.

"It's incredible," he said at last. "It's . . . I don't know the word. Apocalyptic. Biblical. But how likely is it that this will ever happen?"

Swenson shook her head. "I'm afraid you don't understand, Agent Decker. It's not about likelihood. It's a certainty. The only variable is time." She tapped the keyboard once again and a map of the world appeared on the screen. "A mega-tsunami occurred quite recently in Lituya Bay. It stripped timber and soil off to a height of five hundred and twenty meters above sea level. Here." She pointed to a spot in south Alaska. "Mega-tsunamis can be formed by a number of natural forces, not just by the collapse of mountain ranges. Underwater landslides, for example. Or a giant meteor or comet entering through the atmosphere and smashing into the sea. Like the one that caused the extinction of the dinosaurs. While such celestial collisions are extremely rare, landslides caused by seismic activity occur quite frequently – relatively speaking – both on land and under water.

"The Lisbon earthquake of 1755, for example, is said to have triggered a fifteen-meter wave that caused widespread destruction in Morocco, southern Spain, and as far away as Bimini in the Bahamas. Volcanic island collapses happen far less often. The last one occurred about four thousand years ago, on the island of Réunion in the Indian Ocean. Here," she added, pointing to the map. "Luckily for us there are no mountain ranges in danger of slipping into the ocean any time soon. Of course, you never know. Nature works on her own timetable. Then again, the way we're messing with the planet. With global warming and–"

"But from where," Decker insisted, "would it be likely to originate, if such an event were to occur?"

"According to Dr. White, the next mega-tsunami will originate from here." She pointed to a dot off the northwest coast of Africa. "There are seven volcanoes on La Palma in the Canary Islands. One still quite active – the Cumbre Vieja," she said.

Swenson explained the science to him, how water builds up in volcanoes within vertical sheets of permeable rubble over thousands of years, like gigantic reservoirs, held back by impermeable dykes of hardened lava. "One day, due to seismic activity," she said, "the water inside Cumbre Vieja will begin to heat, the pressure build, and the walls will come tumbling down –

like dozens of Hoover Dams colliding against each other, a line of giant dominos, five hundred billion tons collapsing into the sea. The water will move away so fast that it won't be able to flow back behind the landslide, thereby creating a large air cavity displacing far more water than the volume of the landslide itself. It will release five thousand trillion joules of kinetic energy, and create a dome of water almost one thousand meters high, and thirty to forty kilometers wide. And what goes up, of course . . . "

" . . . comes down," he finished.

She nodded. "It will rouse waves more than a hundred meters tall off the coast of Africa, fifty meters tall as far south as Brazil, and sixty meters tall off the coast of Florida and the Caribbean four thousand miles away. That's eighteen stories high." She paused for a moment, then added, "It's funny you should ask about that. James spent most of last year on La Palma working on a new book about the Cumbre Vieja. He . . . " She stopped midstream.

"Yes?"

Swenson stared at Decker, her eyes suddenly cold. Then she shook her head. "No. Nothing." She glanced down at her watch. "Wow," she said. "I didn't realize the time." She stood up from behind the desk.

"Just a minute. What were you going to say?"

Swenson hesitated, glanced out the window. "Nothing."

"Yes, you were." Decker stood up. He leaned against the desk. "Look, Ms. Swenson, you can either answer my questions here, or I can take you back to New York. It's up to you. And while I'd greatly enjoy your company on the long drive home, I feel obliged to warn you that – since Nine Eleven, when it comes to matters of national security – the government doesn't look too kindly on those who obstruct justice, wittingly or unwittingly. Have you ever actually read the Patriot's Act?"

"He's gone," she said.

"Who?"

"Dr. White!" She glanced about the room as if the scientist might suddenly appear from behind the bookcase. "It looks like he hasn't been here for days. And he'd never leave, not voluntarily. Not with his wife so sick."

"Unless he's hiding."

"From whom?"

"I don't know. Do you?" Decker stared at Swenson. She was still holding something back. He could see it in her eyes. He could sense it. "You must have some idea."

"Someone," she said. "Someone's been following me."

Decker felt a strange tingling at the back of his neck. "Who?" he said.

She shrugged. "I don't know him."

"What's he look like?"

"A foreigner. I saw him for the first time the night James disappeared. About five feet seven, or eight. Short. Dark. Dark eyes. Slim. Middle-Eastern or North African, I'd say." She shrugged and wrapped her arms about her chest, hugging herself. Decker was fascinated by the way she moved. She seemed confident and fearful all at once. Then her face completely changed, running from a kind of abstract, dull distaste to loathing, to genuine surprise. And then, finally, to horror.

"Like him," she said, pointing at the window.

Decker turned. The face that he had stared at for days, the eyes and nose and mouth of Salim Moussa were pressed against the glass. And in his hand was a gun. Decker reached for his Beretta. He turned and took a bullet in his chest.

When Decker awoke, he was handcuffed to a radiator, and Swenson was standing above him. He immediately recoiled into the snake position, and took her down in one smooth movement. With his free hand he pinned her to the floor. He wrapped his fingers around her throat. She choked and sputtered. She coughed. Then he noticed the wallet in her hand. *His* wallet. Decker loosened his grip. He brought her close to him, clenching her head in the crook of his arm. The unforgettable smell of burnt gunpowder permeated the room.

"Let go of me," she gasped.

"What were you looking for?" he said. He squeezed her tighter.

"I wanted to be sure."

"Sure? About what?"

"That you're really with the FBI."

"Who else would I be with?"

"I don't know," she gasped, relaxing, then bucking like an alligator, twisting in his grasp. He squeezed her even tighter. She stretched, and reached out for his face, trying to scratch his eyes. He pressed the soft spots immediately behind her earlobes. Swenson screamed. "I don't know," she repeated, growing still.

Her voice was laced with fear now. "I swear I don't."

Decker noticed a series of bullet holes in the front door. The shots had been fired from within. "I believe you," he said. Then he shook his wrist and said, "The key, please." He relaxed his grip slightly, just enough for her to reach into her jeans. A moment later, Decker was free. Only then did he release her.

She shimmied across the floor. "That's big of you," she said as soon as she was out of reach. She struggled to her feet. She shook the wallet in her hand. "IDs can be faked, you know."

"Then why did I let you go?"

She hesitated for a moment. "It's not a very good likeness of you," she added, tossing his wallet back.

"Did you do that?" He pointed at the door.

Swenson bent down and picked up his Beretta from behind the desk. "Oh, I get it," she said. "Because I'm a woman, I can't shoot, right?" Without looking, she pressed the release button behind the combat trigger guard. "I grew up on a ranch in South Dakota, Agent Decker." The magazine popped out in her hand. "I think I prefer the 9000 to the 92FS. Must be the polymer frame. Here." She slid the empty gun across the floor. "I was just trying to scare him off."

Decker picked up his Beretta and returned it to his Bianchi holster. "Looks like you succeeded," he said. He parted his topcoat and blazer, and slowly unbuttoned his shirt. He was wearing a Kevlar vest underneath. A flattened slug was clearly visible, buried just to the left of his heart. He picked it out and handed it to Swenson.

She stared at the shiny object in her hand with both disgust and fascination, as though it were some hideous benthic beast, freshly hauled out of the deep, potentially lethal. Then she walked over to the window – pierced by a single bullet hole – and glanced about the porch. The yard was empty. "I think he's gone," she said. "Would you like some tea?"

Decker was impressed by Swenson's calm demeanor. Most people would have been shaking like a leaf about this time. *She's got grit, this girl*, he thought, and he found himself drawn to her even more. He followed her into the kitchen. As Swenson fiddled with the kettle, he sat down at the breakfast table. He watched her fill the kettle, watched her turn and settle it upon the stove. Then she looked up, her eyes moist, indecisive, torn. Her lips were almost tremulous. She stared directly at his face and said, "Will you help me, Agent Decker?"

Decker smiled. After a few seconds, he replied, "What am I meant to say?" He shrugged his shoulders, throwing the last few words away. "You saved my life."

"I'm worried about James," she answered, riding over him. She sat down at the table. "He's been acting so strange lately. At first I thought it was because of Doris. But now . . . "

"Go on," he said. "What is it?"

"Maybe it will help. I don't know. The truth is James has got some serious financial problems. There. I said it. Doris's medical bills are huge and the health coverage at the Institute isn't what it should be, believe me. He's even started stripping his retirement accounts, his TIAA-CREF."

"Where is he now?" he asked. "With Doris?"

She shook her head. "No, that's just it. He hasn't been at the hospice to see her in days. I don't know where he is. Nobody does. He's just . . . disappeared." The kettle whistled like a train. Swenson stood up and poured the boiling water on the tea leaves. "And now this guy," she added. She handed him a steaming mug of tea. Her voice was calm but Decker could plainly see the worry in her eyes. "The man who's been following me," she said, sitting down again. "Who is he? What does he want with me?"

"I don't know." Decker took a small sip of his tea. "The fact that he came here makes me think he might be after Dr. White as well. If that's the case, maybe White's hiding someplace." Decker shrugged. He took another sip. English Breakfast. "Can you think of anywhere he might have gone, some place he likes to be when he wants to get away? A weekend cabin? Or a boat?"

Swenson shook her head. "I've looked everywhere," she said. "It's like he's vanished off the face of the earth."

"Don't worry," Decker said. "I'll make a few calls. He'll turn up." Then he stood, and stretched, and added, "Come on. I think we'd better go."

"You don't think that creep is coming back?" Swenson stood up, so close to him that he could smell the fear on her skin.

"I doubt it. Not by himself at least." He handed her his tea.

Swenson put the mugs down in the sink. She turned the water on. The faucet coughed and sputtered. Air bubble, Decker speculated. He noticed a handful of clean dishes stacked tidily in the plastic dish drain. The knives were all in one compartment. So were the spoons. So were the forks. Yet there were unwashed dishes in the sink. It looked like Dr. White had left in quite a hurry.

They walked together through the living room, back to the front door. Swenson checked to make sure it was locked behind them before turning and looking at Decker on the porch. "Well, thanks," she said. "Although I'm not exactly sure what for," she added, reaching up and massaging her neck.

"Thank you, Emily." It was the first time Decker had used her Christian name and it felt comfortable in his mouth, strangely familiar. "Here," he said, reaching into his jacket. "Take my card. If anything unusual happens, anything at all. If you feel you're in danger, or you just want to talk. My cell is with me twenty-four seven."

She examined the card, looked up at him and smiled. It was a brittle smile, still fragrant with fear. "Thanks," she said. Then she walked away.

Decker followed her with his eyes. When she had gone about ten yards, she turned, and lifted her hand, and waved a little wave.

Decker stood there for a moment longer as Swenson vanished around the corner. Her wave reverberated deep inside him like the strumming of a lone guitar. He shook his head, stepped off the porch, and shuffled back along the walkway toward his car.

It had been a long, long time since he had felt something for a woman. The other night had just been sex, a grim release, a plea for human contact. Far too long. And, as luck would have it, since he was working this case – and she was involved – there was nothing he could do about it.

Chapter 23
Tuesday, February 1 – 4: 27 AM
Kazakhstan

Gulzhan Baqrah dreamed of torture. He often dreamed of his most intimate encounters, of the battlefield at night, up close inside a ditch, with a knife against some foreign throat; or down an alley, under a new moon; or in a dark interrogation room, searching for answers. But this dream was different. Someone had accused his foremost protégé of collaborating with the Zionists. And there he was, trussed up like that by his elbows, simply hanging there from the ceiling like a side of camel meat. Gulzhan ducked his head, stepped through the narrow doorway, and descended down the concrete steps into the cell.

When he finally straightened up, he rose through dank olfactory layers of fetid rank humidity, of human feces, blood and vomit. But Gulzhan didn't care. He was staring at the prisoner, admiring his physique, the solid graceful contours of the muscles in his back.

Such a waste, he thought. Gulzhan sighed and turned and noticed a pair of rimless tires on the floor. He recognized them instantly. They were standard interrogation fare: two rubber, non-conductive footstools designed to keep the innocent inquisitor at bay, above the flooded concrete floor whenever the jumper cables were in use. This made him recollect the scent of burning human flesh, a smell that he had hated once, found nauseating – a long, long time ago – but to which Gulzhan had grown accustomed over the years, until now the sweetness brought to mind a simpler time, one of diminished ambiguity, like the aroma of freshly baked bread, or the perfume of some favorite aunt, just back from Akmola by train. *After a while, the brain adapts.*

Gulzhan stared absently at a nearby table festooned with horsewhips and leather straps, and riding crops and razor blades, scalpels and freshly sharpened knives, and copper-headed jumper cables, bright as ten-tenge pieces, newly minted, lying there neatly in rows.

He picked up a horsewhip. He flicked it once to feel its weight, and the end snapped with uncompromising certitude. The prisoner arched his back. It was a Pavlovian response. He was several yards away, on the other side of the cell.

Gulzhan flicked the long black whip behind him, letting it uncoil, relax, until with a firm flip of the wrist, the whip came up and over, and nicked an almost imperceptible nugget of raw flesh from the prisoner's naked back.

He screamed and writhed as the whip came down again, again, and again. Blood seeped out of the wounds, into tiny tributaries, rivulets of life that coursed around and down into the tight crack of his buttocks. Then it was over.

Gulzhan laid the whip back on the table, curling it into coils. He approached the prisoner. He let his fingers play along the back, along the bleeding indentations in the no-longer-perfect skin. The man winced.

"Tell me," Gulzhan said. "Is it true? If you tell me, I will end it quickly. That, I promise you. Are you working with the Zionists?"

The man's head and upper torso lolled over to the side. It was difficult to tell whether he was nodding or shaking his head. He moaned again, this time with less conviction. He was almost spent.

Gulzhan grasped him by the nape of the neck, by his short black shiny hair, and pulled. He brought his own mouth close to the prisoner's skin, breathing him in.

"Are you working with the Zionists?" he repeated. And then he shook the prisoner's head from side to side, clamping it in his short but powerful fingers, like a puppeteer testing the neck of a doll. "Do you deny it?" he said with mock surprise.

There was little point in killing him. *If* he lived. Gulzhan stared at the bloody livid welts across his back. He wondered at the dislocated shoulders, the way the figure hung there by the tendons and the nerves, without the benefit of bone or muscle. This beautiful young man had once been one of Gulzhan's best recruits. Indeed, the Kazakh leader had often looked upon him as a possible successor. The accusations were serious; this much was true. But Gulzhan knew, with an absolute conviction – unsullied by romance, by personal delusion, and grounded too by more than thirty years of grim experience at his craft – that the prisoner would remain loyal to him for the rest of his days. Something bound them now, with a greater intimacy than he had ever shared with any of his wives, or with his mistresses, or even with his closest friends.

Gulzhan leaned against the prisoner, caressed his neck and whispered, "'No one can bear the burden of another. If a heavily laden one should call another to carry his load, naught of it shall be carried by the other, even though he be a kinsman . . . Turn ye to your Lord and submit yourselves to Him before the punishment overtakes you and no one is able to help you.'"

For whom, exactly, am I praying? he thought. Gulzhan turned the prisoner around, at the same time removing a resplendent blade from behind his belt, and as he spun him, as he readied to cut the body down, the face came into view, into the light, and it was Uhud's face – his former young lieutenant. His eyes were leaching tears of blood. His erection was grotesque, unnaturally bloated, huge. Gulzhan heard a man scream. It was his own scream issued somewhere far away, as if by someone else. He screamed and screamed until the darkness fell upon him like a cloak, and Gulzhan woke inside his tent, on his own cot, his shirt soaked through with sweat, winded and paralyzed with fear.

A full minute passed before the narcotic of terror released him. Then Gulzhan swung his legs up, up and over, sat bolt upright and rubbed his salt-and-pepper beard. They were getting worse, he thought – the nightmares. He shuffled over to a writing desk at the far end of the tent. The letter was already complete. All he had to do was fold it and give it away. He looked down at the piece of paper on his desk. It read with cold, uncompromising clarity: *We demand that you release El Aqrab within twelve hours, or the Brotherhood of the Crimson Scimitar will detonate a one kiloton nuclear device in Israel.*

Chapter 24

Tuesday, February 1 – 5:17 AM
Beersheba, Israel

Specialist Gal Baror stumbled as he wound his way through the tunnel. Captain Rifkin could hear him. The boy was breathing heavily behind him, touching the stone wall with his fingertips to steady himself in the dark. It was his fourth mission with the Beersheba Bomb Disposal Unit (BBDU), and his first with Rifkin alone. Gal had only just graduated. Rifkin still remembered the moody brown eyes of his fiancée, Tor, and the solemn, studied way she had danced with her future husband at his graduation party a week earlier. Rifkin generally avoided such affairs; he didn't like to get too close to his men, at least not in the beginning. But Gal was his nephew, his sister's son, and there had been no ducking it. "Keep still," he said. "Don't touch the walls, Gal. They may be booby-trapped."

And why did everyone bestow upon their children such insipid, sexless name these days? It was as if they yearned to give their kids neutrality, or a false sense of equality between the sexes, with monikers designed to be pronounceable for international consumption. Inoculated. Pasteurized. Stripped of the burden of history. Hebrew, without being Jewish. Shir, Din, Ben, Gal, Tal, Bar. Such noncommittal monosyllables.

"Yes, Captain."

"How many times do I have to tell you? Call me David, Gal. We don't stand on ceremony in the BBDU. I don't want a sniper's bullet in my spine just because you have a compulsion to salute."

"Yes . . . David."

They came to a bend in the tunnel and Rifkin pointed his flashlight at the map in his left hand. The light illuminated his face. He was a short man in his late thirties, with a heavy frame and the sloping shoulders of a wrestler. His eyes were small, of the darkest malachite green, his eyebrows linked together at the top by a tuft of wiry brown hair. He sported a close-cropped ginger beard.

"Do you think it's true?" said Gal.

Rifkin didn't look up. He studied the map. The left branch of the tunnel connected to the well at the heart of the old tel. The right branch ran for another hundred meters or so and linked up with a series of P-style PVC sewage pipes approximately 630 millimeters in diameter.

"David?"

"What is it?" Rifkin answered tartly. He looked over at his nephew. Young Gal was corpulent and slow, clumsy on his feet. But he had a pair of the steadiest hands that Rifkin had ever seen. Of course, the boy had yet to see a friend blown up into a hundred pieces right in front of him. Not everyone got used to that.

"About the agreement. I hear they're freeing a senior member of the Brotherhood. Perhaps El Aqrab himself."

"Do you really believe Garron would ever agree to such a thing? Always with the rumors, Gal." Rifkin turned left, down toward the ancient well.

"Well, that's what they're saying."

Rifkin moved through the semi-darkness without bothering to counter. It had always been Israel's most stringent policy never to negotiate with terrorists, especially those with blood on their hands, like Gulzhan Baqrah and El Aqrab. Once you started down that path, there was no turning back. And yet, thought Rifkin, if the choice were either nuclear annihilation or letting El Aqrab go free . . . He could not let the concept linger in his head. He corralled it and drove it away. Thankfully, these were not the kinds of decisions that he was forced to make. His was a world of instantaneous results, where if you made the wrong decision, you knew it right away: either you proceeded to the next step in the process, or you were already dead. Rifkin stepped out of the tunnel and down into a circular room at the heart of the old tel.

"What now?" said Gal.

"We do as we were told. We wait."

*　*　*

Decker didn't hear about the bomb until he'd returned to the Bureau's headquarters in Manhattan from Cape Cod. By then, it was old news. Apparently, Prime Minister Garron had agreed to an exchange — two Israeli businessmen and the remains of some sixteen IDF soldiers for more than 125 Palestinian detainees, including senior members of the PLO and other terrorist organizations. While this was the public story, according to Warhaftig, the Company had it on good authority that only one prisoner was being released — none other than El Aqrab himself. The Israelis were being blackmailed. The Brotherhood of the Crimson Scimitar had placed a nuclear device within the water system of the old town of Beersheba. Exactly where, the Israelis would find out – once El Aqrab was transported safely to the Lebanese border. Only after he had been freed would he provide them with the bomb's disarming sequence. Otherwise . . .

Decker was stupefied. It seemed incredible that Garron would let a terrorist like El Aqrab go free. It just didn't make sense. Johnson disagreed. "What else can he do? Garron has to negotiate, if only to buy time," he said. "Can you imagine what an atom bomb going off in that region of the world would do? Garron has no choice. And don't forget: It isn't simply Israel at stake here. When those desert winds blow, the fallout will run right into Saudi and Iraq. I doubt we want our boys in Baghdad dying, or the Saudi oil fields contaminated just because the Prime Minister of Israel refused to let a single prisoner go free."

They debated the issue back and forth. "Perhaps he should negotiate," said Decker. "But I still can't see him doing it. He'd be sacrificing his conservative base. It's just not like Garron. And who knows if there really is a bomb?"

"Well, we'll find out soon enough," Warhaftig said. "The deadline is six AM."

"Tomorrow?"

"Six AM in Israel," said Johnson, cutting in. "Try and keep up, Decker. They're seven hours ahead of us. We have until eleven PM tonight." He glanced at his watch. "Less than half an hour now."

"Oh," Decker said. But he was already thinking of something else. He'd forgotten about the time difference. Unconsciously, almost despite his active focus on the conversation, he found his mind besieged by numbers: 540,000; 205,200; 334,800; 5,580; and 93.

If the hijacking of the train in Kazakhstan corresponds with the number 540,000; and if the second wallpaper features the number 205,200; the difference is 334,800. And 334,800 seconds from the moment of the hijacking is 5,580 minutes, or 93 hours, or six AM in Israel.

"Wait a minute," he said. "Perhaps the second wallpaper is linked to Beersheba." He explained his theory.

Johnson remained unconvinced. "You're using those numbers like statistics," he said, "massaging them to fit the scenario. You're not looking at the scenario to legitimize your numbers."

"Still, with your permission, sir," Warhaftig said. "It might be a good idea to set up communications with the field team in Beersheba. Simply as a precaution."

Johnson looked at Warhaftig with a scowl. He glanced about the room. Everyone was staring at him. "Alright," he said. "I guess it can't hurt."

*   *   *

The M113 Zelda armored personnel carrier (APC) rumbled along the narrow country road, within a stand of cypress trees that crowned the crooked hill. It was a bright blue dawn. Dew still lingered on the grasses shivering in the valley below. Only a pair of fences in perpetual race marked this bucolic place as the no man's land between Israel and Lebanon.

Inside the APC, El Aqrab sat handcuffed by a pair of plastic manacles, lashed to the rear hatch. He rose and fell on every bump, each curve, swayed back and forth, trying to spare his wrists, and peered through a narrow slit in the external armor as a team of Special Forces from the Sayerot Mat'kal materialized from nowhere. They were dressed in camouflage, with real and artificial bushes sprouting from their clothes, like scarecrows. Their faces were painted black and green. They carried high-power assault rifles, some with telescopic sights.

As the last of the commandos scurried into view, Major Ilan Ben-Ami pulled himself up and out of the APC. He dropped lightly to the grass. Although Ben-Ami was almost forty-two, he had the toned physique and raw physical demeanor of a man half his age. His friendly, heart-shaped face was boyishly handsome. His eyes were a poignant sea blue. Without a word, he motioned to the Special Forces.

El Aqrab watched the men fan out around the APC and set up a perimeter. Within seconds, the area was secure. Only then did they unfasten his manacles. They pulled him to his feet. As he emerged from the APC, El Aqrab took a long deep breath. He felt the cold air fill his lungs with an exquisite agony. It was as though he were catching the dawn, inhaling it, like a fire-eater. This was the first sunrise he had seen in days. He smiled. They pushed him from the APC and down onto the grass below.

The Major strolled back to the Zelda. One of his men handed him the mouthpiece to the radio and he said to El Aqrab, "No tricks, you hear me? Just tell them where to find the bomb. That's all. You have thirty seconds."

El Aqrab looked to the east, at the bright red tendrils of dawn dragging across the earth. He took the mouthpiece in his hand. "Are you there?" he said.

"This is Eagle," said Captain Rifkin.

"Proceed due west along the main tunnel. When you've gone approximately twenty meters, turn right up tunnel seventeen. You will notice a silver conduit above your head," said El Aqrab. "Follow it for another fifteen meters until the tunnel ends. The device is hidden behind the cistern to your left. An aluminum attaché case."

El Aqrab returned the microphone. Then he began to stretch his arms, one after the other, raising them high above his head. His shoulders were stiff; he felt a knot at the center of his back. He rolled his head and heard his neck crack. "It is a beautiful dawn, is it not, Major?" He ended the sentence with a smile.

The Major did not answer.

"Dawn is my favorite time of day," continued El Aqrab. "When everything is just beginning, so full of promise. Most people like the twilight, but it only makes me sad."

"Shut the fuck up," the Major said. "Do you think I give a shit about what you like?"

Just then the radio crackled once again. "Eagle to Raven. We're at tunnel seventeen. I can see the silver conduit. We're going in," said Rifkin.

Major Ben-Ami turned on his heels and strode away, leaving the prisoner under the watchful eye of a young corporal who stood there fingering the Zelda's 30-caliber machine gun. El Aqrab sat on the grass. It felt wet and cold in his hands. The corporal shifted the machine gun to keep the Arab in his sights. El Aqrab looked up at him, and smiled, as if posing for a snapshot. The radio crackled and the Major reappeared.

"Eagle to Raven. We have the device. Do you copy? We have the device."

"This is Raven. Is it hot?"

"That's affirmative, Raven. We have a solid reading from all counters."

"Press the red button," said El Aqrab, "on the side of the panel, just to the right and below the fuel chamber."

The Major repeated the instructions.

"I don't think that's a good idea," Captain Rifkin said.

"Why not?"

"I just don't."

El Aqrab climbed to his feet. He took a step closer to the APC. "Press it," he repeated, "or the countdown will begin automatically. Do your men *want* to die?"

"You heard him, Eagle," the Major said. He sheered the words off with clenched teeth. "Just do it. Press the button."

There was a momentary pause. Then the radio crackled once again and Captain Rifkin said, "Affirmative. The button has been pressed. Do you copy? The button has been pressed."

"We copy." The Major turned to El Aqrab. "What now?" he asked.

El Aqrab shrugged. "Now? Now, you release me."

Just then, a new sound overwhelmed the stillness of the valley. Four F16 Block 60s thundered overhead, followed trimly by six Apache helicopter gun-ships. They swept in from the south, circling the hilltop and the APC. The winter grasses billowed underneath.

"I'm afraid that won't be possible," the Major shouted above the din. "Orders," he added, looking up. The choppers were coming down. They were landing all around them. "From the Prime Minister himself. You are to accompany me back to Tel Aviv."

Major Ben-Ami pointed vaguely in El Aqrab's direction and a young commando approached him from behind, swinging another pair of plastic handcuffs in his hands.

"I don't think so," said El Aqrab in Arabic.

"What's that?" demanded the commando.

The radio coughed. "Raven, come in. Eagle to Raven."

"What is it, Eagle?" the Major said.

"The device. It's started working. It just went on, all of a sudden. It's counting down, sir. Sixty. Fifty-nine. Fifty-eight . . . "

The Major turned and glowered at El Aqrab. He towered over him. "What kind of game is this?"

"I could provide you with the disarming sequence? Would you like that?"

The Major drew his sidearm. "So help me God, I'll shoot you right here and now if anything happens, El Aqrab, believe me. What's the fucking sequence?"

"No you won't." The Arab smiled, revealing his extended canines and a network of fine wrinkles round his eyes. Laugh lines. Barely visible. "You will withdraw or the bomb will explode, and Beersheba and everyone in southern Israel will die – like that." He snapped his fingers for effect. "But if you pull back, I have instructed my associates to disarm the bomb remotely."

" . . . forty-three, forty-two . . . "

"Now go," continued El Aqrab. "Go!" he shouted. "Before it's too late."

The Major turned without a word and hopped back up onto the APC. In a moment, the entire vehicle was covered with the Sayerot Mat'kal commandos. The armor plating bristled with their camouflage. The Zelda shuddered and began to move, slowly at first, like a giant hedgehog, bumping along the road, then picking up speed. In seconds it was hurtling down the narrow country lane at more than 50 mph, between the cypress trees, powered by its brand-new turbocharged 6V53T engine.

The helicopters gradually ascended, swung round, and started south. The F16s blew overhead, away. The bold roar of their movements faded, only to be replaced by yet another engine, another helicopter, swinging in low from somewhere to the north, from Lebanon. It was painted in jungle camouflage. It hurtled down across the hill, flared for a moment, and then descended, fashioning a bowl in the winter grasses with a furious wind. A moment later it was down.

The rotors continued to spin. El Aqrab ran across the hill and dove directly into the waiting open door. Without pausing, the helicopter jumped into the air, nervous as a grasshopper. It slid across the hill, regained transitional lift, and hurtled up into the sky.

Chapter 25
Tuesday, February 1 – 5:27 AM
Beersheba, Israel

Rifkin continued to monitor the countdown as he worked. He had already removed the outer casing of the console but he could still see the LED display, the numbers flashing constantly in red. Gal Baror held the casing a few centimeters above the device as Rifkin looked beneath. A Medusa's tail of fine wires dangled from the shell. He tried to pick them out, to distinguish them in the bright halogen and LED light emanating from the Black Diamond headlamp on his head. He slipped a tiny dentist's mirror underneath. He looked about. There was the ground. Those, over there, were hot. He peeled back the plastic coating of each wire in his mind, feeling their temperature, testing them for charge against the tongue of his imagination. He followed them as they snaked around the chassis, as they seemed to come to life, wiggling like intestines, like the insides of so many of his friends and colleagues blown to smithereens. " . . . nineteen, eighteen, seventeen . . . "

Rifkin picked up a pair of wire cutters and used the dentist's mirror to separate two wires underneath the casing. "Please resist the urge to pull the casing away," he mumbled to Gal Baror. Gal eased the casing down a hair. "Thank you," Rifkin said. There were two wires, side by side, beside the flat head of the dentist's mirror. One was green. The other was blue. " . . . eleven, ten, nine . . . Are you still there, Raven?"

"Yes, we're here, Eagle One," the Major's voice responded. It echoed through the confined space of the tunnel, reverberated against the cistern. "We're with you."

" . . . six, five, four, three . . . " Captain Rifkin insinuated the wire cutters underneath the casing, the shiny metal blades around the light blue wire in the mirror, and snipped. " . . . two."

The numbers froze: 02. The digits simply sat there on the bright red LED. Motionless. Petrified. Rifkin found himself breathing. He had closed one eye unconsciously. He opened it again, very slowly. The display still read 02.

"Raven, come in. This is Eagle One. The sequence has been terminated. Do you copy?"

*   *   *

"Copy that. Congratulations, Captain." Major Ben-Ami turned

toward the driver of the APC and raised his hand. The Zelda slowed to a crawl, then stopped. "Come in Sparrow One," he said. A moment later he was connected to the pilot in the lead Apache helicopter. "This is Raven," he began. "Commence immediate retrieval." He peered out through the bulletproof window and scanned the far horizon with a pair of powerful binoculars.

El Aqrab's helicopter grew smaller by the second. In a moment it would be across the Blue Line into Lebanon. The air above the APC vibrated as the Apaches swiveled north in hot pursuit. They blazed across the hill, thundered along the valley floor. They closed the distance and although they could have fired upon the fleeing helicopter, could have incinerated her with rockets, they punched to a hard stop, flared at around a hundred feet, and hovered like a gyre of eagles above the invisible Blue Line.

"She's gone, sir. Raven, do you copy?"

"Sparrows, return to base."

"Sir?"

"Return to base," the Major repeated. "Under no circumstances are you to cross the Blue Line into Lebanon."

The Apache helicopters turned and headed south. Major Ben-Ami lowered his binoculars and watched with the naked eye as El Aqrab's helicopter faded slowly into the pale blue sky. That's when he saw the Lebanese Army gunships – five desert camouflage Apaches. They materialized from nowhere. Once again, the Major picked up his binoculars. There they were, in a flash of light. He steadied his elbows on the rim of the APC tower. El Aqrab's helicopter was hemmed in on every side. No matter how she tried to feint or dodge, she could not gain the altitude required to outrun her pursuers. It was only a matter of time. They pressed the air about her, pushing her down. El Aqrab's ship was forced to land atop another hill, beside an orange grove, less than a mile within the Lebanese border. She'd barely hit the ground when the helicopter was surrounded on all sides by the five Apache gunships. Commandos streamed out across the hill, between the fruit trees, surrounding the green chopper. Then someone pulled the door open, and dragged the pilot and co-pilot from the ship.

"Come in, Falcon. Do you copy?" Major Ben-Ami said. The radio remained silent. "Do you copy, Falcon?" he repeated. "Do you have the package?" He squinted through his binoculars. It was hard to see the pilot and co-pilot despite their crimson flight suits. They were surrounded by the Lebanese commandos. He adjusted the focus but it didn't seem to help. "Do you have the package?" he repeated. "Come in, Falcon."

"That's a negative. We do not. Just the pilot and co-pilot. I repeat. We do *not* have the package."

Major Ben-Ami hung his head. It was a ruse. El Aqrab had never boarded the green helicopter. Or, if he had, it had only been for a moment. Then he'd slipped away somehow. The Major spun about and looked back up the hill. "Go back," he shouted with frustration at the driver. "Back up the hill. Now!"

The armored vehicle turned around and charged back up the lane. A few minutes later, the APC popped out from behind the cypress trees. It shuddered to a stop. The commandos hit the ground, fanned out across the hilltop. They streamed beyond the original perimeter. They scoured every bush and tree and stone, and still they found no trace of El Aqrab. The terrorist had vanished, as suddenly as the morning dew.

"Come in, Raven," the radio crackled. "This is Eagle."

Major Ben-Ami stood almost at attention by the APC. Without even turning, he lifted a hand, snapped his fingers, and the communications officer handed him the microphone.

"This is Raven. Go ahead, Eagle."

"Sir, I've got bad news," said Captain Rifkin.

The Major ran a hand back through his close-cropped hair. He sighed and said, "Report, Eagle."

"The casing was hot, sir. We measured RADs. But now that we've had a chance to open it, well . . . it's empty, sir. There must have been some HEU inside the fuel chamber at one point. But it's no longer there. Do you copy, Raven? The device is empty."

"Copy that, Eagle. Understood. Thank you. Return to base."

Major Ben-Ami felt himself age fifteen years in the space of those three words. Return to base, he repeated to himself. His mouth felt dry as Sinai. He hung his head. *That's what will happen to me now*, he thought. *I will return to base, and never leave again . . . as long as I live.*

* * *

Warhaftig had set up a communication link with an Israeli security officer in Beersheba, some guy named Seiden, who was standing by. Acting Chief Seiden was in contact with the local Beersheba Bomb Squad in the cistern below. Decker, Warhaftig and a host of other agents were packed inside Warhaftig's office, listening to the radio transmissions on the speakerphone.

"So much for your prediction," Johnson said to Decker.

"It isn't six AM yet in Beersheba."

"No, but the bomb's already reached its designated countdown. They stopped it at 02 . . . even if it was a dud."

"He's right," Kazinski said.

"Sir, I recommend you contact Seiden and tell him to pull his men out right away," said Decker. "We only have eight minutes left."

"We've wasted enough time on this, Decker. It's late. Acting Chief Seiden, thanks for your help. This is SAC Johnson, signing off." He hit the button on the speakerphone. "Everybody out of here," he said. "I was meant to meet the AD for drinks an hour ago." He stood, shooing them away like flies. Then he put on his jacket and coat, and headed out the door.

*   *   *

Almost immediately after the SAC had disappeared into the elevator, Decker returned to Johnson's office surreptitiously, and re-established the connection with Beersheba.

Seiden was surprised to hear his voice. "I thought we'd lost you," he said.

"SAC Johnson had to go. Where are your men now?"

"They're on their way out of the well."

"Please call them, Chief Seiden. It isn't safe. They have until six AM Beersheba time."

"What are you talking about?"

"I probably shouldn't be telling you this, but we found some PC wallpapers on a suspect's personal computer here in New York. One of them featured the words, 'Pregnant She-Camels,' and 'When Hell is Stoked Up,' plus a number. That number corresponds to an event that we believe will occur at six AM Beersheba time. An event such as the detonation of a bomb."

"Did you say, 'Pregnant She-Camels'?"

"That's right. It's a quote from the Qur'an."

"I know," said Seiden. "I was there right after El Aqrab was captured."

"In Tel Aviv?"

"Yes. I saw the file."

"What file?"

"The video he made. Of the event. As he always does. I saw the way the fire burst out of those boys, the words. They are the same. 'Pregnant She-Camels.' And 'Hell.' What do they mean?"

"We don't know for sure but I believe they're somehow tied to Beersheba."

"You mean an omen?"

"Each PC wallpaper not only predicts the next event, it features a number corresponding to a specific moment in time. The first was 540,000, set when Baqrah stole that HEU in Kazakhstan. The second was 205,200. The difference is ninety-three hours. And ninety-three hours from the time Baqrah stole the HEU is six AM your time. Exactly. Which is . . . " Decker looked down at his watch. " . . . three minutes from now."

For a moment Seiden did not speak. Decker could hear him breathing on the other end. "I'm not exactly following you," he said, "but I believe you think you're right. And that's good enough for me." He shouted to someone standing by. "Contact Rifkin. Tell him he has two minutes to get the hell out of there. Now!"

*   *   *

Captain David Rifkin finished re-assembling the device with the attentive assistance of Gal Baror. It had been an agonizing day for the young recruit. He had equipped himself well, and his uncle was proud. They packed the device into a clear plastic bag and filled it with a snowy white foam that looked like shaving cream; it solidified immediately, sealing the aluminum case within. Rifkin slipped it carefully into his duffel bag. They packed up their tools and instruments, picked up their flashlights, and started back along the tunnel. That's when they got the call from Seiden. "We're on our way," said Rifkin.

They ran as quickly as they could along the darkened tunnel, when Gal misplaced his step, and reached out for support against the wall. There was a little sound, like the breaking of a twig, a gentle snap, and then a bright light filled the tunnel. Rifkin and Gal jumped back unconsciously. The light, as bright as an acetylene torch, continued to crawl along the passageway. They couldn't tear their eyes away.

"Oh, shit," said Gal. And then the world exploded. It was as if they were *inside* a firework. Talons of fire raked the air, descended from the ceiling, slashed at their bodies like phosphorescent claws. They tried to run but they were trapped. The more they struggled, the more some sort of netting settled into place around them. Their shirts burst into flames. They heard their own skin sizzling. It smelled of burning hair. They watched in horror as a line of pale green fire began to snake across their chests, began to curl from left to right, bold loops, uncompromising arcs, seductive curves, until with one last breath of flame-filled air, one final baleful moan, their lungs imploded and their horrified expressions melted off the bone.

*   *   *

There was a camera on the wall. It recorded the events dispassionately, dispatching the signal with a measured, cool efficiency through the RCA connectors, and then down into the wire on the floor. It ran along the tunnel, around the trellis which had held up the device, into a crack and down along a sleeve behind the cistern where a video recorder purred and clicked and stopped, reclining finally into sleep mode. It was exactly six AM.

Chapter 26
Tuesday, February 1 – 9:42 AM
Cairo, Egypt

The Egyptian mule Auwal Al-Hakim had not had a solid meal in days, not since Kazakhstan. His stomach growled. He cursed and curled himself into a ball, and pressed his back against the cracked stone wall of the apartment. Where was Nasir? The boy had promised to return by nine and it was almost ten o'clock. He did not trust him. He was a member of al-Jihad, not of the Brotherhood. Al-Hakim sat up, curling his arms about his knees, his frayed and ragged trouser legs, and started to rock back and forth on his haunches. There was a window in a corner of the room that overlooked the el-Hakim Mosque and, across the Sharia Ramses, the Sultan Baybars Mosque beyond.

The Mameluke General Zahir Baybars had always been a hero to Al-Hakim, ever since childhood. Baybars had been born in Mongol Russia, in the town of Kipchak, and was later sold into slavery in Damascus as a boy – at a very reasonable price, since a cataract covered his left eye. But Allah had granted him a penetrating voice, insatiable energy and ambition, and a brilliant military mind. Ruling Cairo for seventeen years, his court had been notorious for its riches.

Baybars was also responsible for rebuilding the canals, fortifications and shipyards throughout Egypt, things essential to the public works. Using both the subtlest of diplomacy as well as raw belligerence, he neutralized the crusading Christians along the Mediterranean coast. He installed the Abbasid Prince al-Mustansir as khalif at Cairo, thereby moving the Sunni religious center to Egypt, effectively gaining control of the Hajj and Mecca. A deeply religious man, Baybars even ordered all the taverns and brothels of the city closed.

But his piety failed to save him. He perished when he was fifty, the unwitting victim of his own hand. It was a fairy tale Al-Hakim's mother used to tell him before bedtime. He remembered it with fondness, with the nostalgic warmth of a soft blanket. The Sultan had intended to poison Malik Kaher, a rival prince, but – unbeknownst to him – Kaher had switched their goblets when Baybars wasn't looking. It took thirteen days for him to die an agonizing death. Baybars' sons were soon deposed and, eventually, General Qalawun was elected Sultan.

Like Baybars, Qalawun was from Kipchak. And, like the

previous Sultan, he too had been a slave. He kept the Mongols and the Christians both at bay, and made treaties with Emperor Rudolph of Hapsburg, as well as other European princes. He even continued the building programs initiated by Baybars, sponsoring both a hospital and the mosque that Al-Hakim could see outside the window, across the carpet of multi-colored rugs and tapestries that darkened the narrow passageways of the Khalili Khan.

The nearer mosque, the el-Hakim, was Auwal's namesake. El-Hakim bi-Amr Allah, literally Ruler by God's Command, was infamous in Egyptian history for his eccentric dictatorial decrees. At one point, like the Egyptian pharaohs of old, he had even declared himself divine.

Al-Hakim remembered the afternoon that he had spent with El Aqrab, wandering through this sector of the city two years earlier. Despite the fact that he was Lebanese, El Aqrab knew an inordinate amount about the mosques of Cairo, taught to him – apparently – by some childhood friend. According to El Aqrab, over its lifetime, the el-Hakim mosque had served as a prison for captive Crusaders, Napoleon's warehouse, Salah al-Din's stables, a lamp factory, and a boys elementary school under Nasser.

As they walked together south, El Aqrab pointed out features of the mosque that Al-Hakim had never noticed before, although he'd been born and raised in Cairo. The mosque was constructed of brick with stone facades and minarets, and featured an irregular rectangular plan with a rectangular central courtyard, surrounded by arcades, supported by compound piers, with a prayer hall whose arcades were similarly perched on top of compound piers. It also boasted the oldest surviving minarets in Cairo, although the tops were replaced in 1303, after an earthquake destroyed the upper tiers.

They strolled together toward the northeast corner of the mosque, and came upon the Bab al-Futuh, the Gate of Conquest, and the Northern walls. The east side of the street was lined with garlic and onion vendors. Until about 1850, this was the last slave market in Egypt, Al-Hakim told El Aqrab, trying to sound knowledgeable about his natal city. "But that was long ago, thanks be to Allah."

El Aqrab laughed. "Is that what you think?" he said. "But you are right, of course, my friend. We no longer buy and sell each other. Now, we are made slaves by the West."

Then they had headed through the Gate of Conquest, into the Northern Cemetery. Known as the City of the Dead, the cemetery was as much a city of the living as a final resting place for the deceased. Cairo's original rulers had selected this location for their tombs because it was outside the crowded metropolis, in an area that was predominantly desert. But even in early pharaonic times, the Egyptians had never thought of cemeteries as places of the dead; they were, instead, birthplaces of rejuvenation. Hence, mausoleums were exploited for personal entertainment, and guest facilities were appended to large tombs. As early as the fourteenth century, squatters took up residence in the catacombs, cohabitating with the dead. Moving through the narrow streets and alleyways, Al-Hakim noticed cenotaphs used as tables, clotheslines strung between tall headstones.

"It is good you are Egyptian," El Aqrab had told him. "There is so little distance here between the living and the dead. You're but a step away."

Auwal Al-Hakim climbed to his feet. He could hear a host of people shouting in the Khalili Khan below. And with the street noise came the scent of lamb, of barbecued baby goat, of hummus and grape leaves and freshly baked falafel. He couldn't stand it any longer. He strode across the room to the front door. He slipped his boots on, tied his laces. No matter what the risks, he thought, no matter what the dangers, he was getting something to eat.

Al-Hakim clambered down the stairs, weaved through the rushing crowd, his head down, covered with a Bedouin veil, and entered the Khalili Khan. The narrow canvas-covered passageways of the old Byzantine Bazaar were choked with gold and silver merchants, with brass and copper smiths, with hawkers of leather goods and oils and glass and water pipes and pastry shops. His stomach gurgled like a crocodile. Al-Hakim reached into his pocket for some coins. He saw a gyro vendor just across the street. He smelled the marinated meat, saw it sizzling on the spit. He pulled his hand out and the stun gun struck him just below the shoulder blade, on the right side. Al-Hakim contorted and toppled over. He continued to shake and roll across the ground, like an epileptic. A man in an *aba* over gray twill trousers kneeled beside him. A syringe was already in his hand. It entered Al-Hakim's right arm above the elbow. It hung there, like a greedy insect, for a few more seconds, then vanished and Al-Hakim just stopped. He stopped shaking. He stopped frothing at the mouth. He stopped dreaming even, as he slipped into a darkness deeper and more profoundly empty than any he had ever known.

When he awoke, Al-Hakim found himself lying on a massive wooden workbench. The outer edges of the workbench were lined with ancient swivel-base bench vises, the surface littered with wood shavings. Al-Hakim tried to sit up but his hands were lashed behind him, over his head, and a pain shot through his leg. He looked down. His left leg was pinned between two vises.

Just then, a small man with a black mustache and beard dressed in a Western suit approached the workbench from across the room. Al-Hakim hadn't noticed him before. He was 777, Al-Hakim was sure of it, a member of the Counter-Terrorist Group of the Egyptian Secret Police. Al-Hakim had seen his kind of face before.

The man leaned across the workbench and picked up a tool. It was a wood drill, hand-powered, practically antique. The man placed the pointed silver tip directly on top of Al-Hakim's left knee, the one pinned by the vises. Then he began to turn it slowly, swiveling the arm around, and around, and around as Al-Hakim watched. The material of his trouser leg wound up into the metal bit as he felt it pierce his skin. A moment later, the drill began to pull apart the flesh, then bone. Al-Hakim screamed. The pain was blinding in its intensity. He watched as blood boiled up out of the wound, as the bit kept twisting, turning up flakes of ivory-colored bone. He writhed and moaned and heaved until the pain enveloped him in a bubble of warm blood, and he drowned.

* * *

Acting Chief Seiden sat in the nondescript office, waiting. He had already been there for over an hour and his patience was beginning to wear thin. He felt distressed, on edge, prickly. In fact, he had felt that way ever since landing at Cairo International Airport in Heliopolis that afternoon. This was the land of the enemy, despite the Camp David Peace Accords. It had been since the days of the pharaohs. And, in all probability, it always would be. He crossed his legs, examined the room for the umpteenth time: the same Arabic calendar; the same Egyptian flag; the same obligatory photographs of President Ali Baruk. Why, for God's sake, Seiden thought, had they sent him? He was no diplomat, no negotiator. He writhed in his cracked plastic seat. But his experience with El

Aqrab in Tel Aviv, and his knowledge of the incident in Beersheba made him invaluable, unique, Deputy Director Cohen had insisted. He was the perfect man for the job. Besides, everyone else was busy.

The door opened, and a scruffy little man with a black mustache and beard dressed in a Western suit stepped cautiously into the room. "My apologies for keeping you waiting," he said. "My name's Aswad Talhouni." He scurried into the room, stretching out a bony hand.

Seiden stood up and shook it. Then he noticed a series of dark red spots along the Egyptian's shirtfront. "You might have washed up a little first," he said, pulling his hand away.

Talhouni looked down. "Pomegranates," he said. Then he smiled, revealing shattered brown teeth. "Sweet tooth."

"Where is he?"

The small man wagged a finger at Seiden and smiled. "A man after my own heart. Straight to the point. I like that. I'm afraid it's rare to find men who go straight to the point of anything in Egypt. Except their wives, of course." He began to cackle. "Would you like some coffee, Chief Seiden? Some tea?"

Seiden shook his head and Talhouni took a seat behind his desk. He leaned forward on his elbows, arching his fingers as if in prayer. "I'm afraid my government will not be able to release Auwal Al-Hakim into your charge, as we had hoped," he said.

"As you promised, you mean. Why not? It's either us or the Americans."

"Al-Hakim was an Egyptian national. My government doesn't look upon this matter precisely as you do. But, on a more positive note, our government is not nearly as restrictive when it comes to issues of interrogation. We are the Mecca of extraordinary rendition."

"What do you mean, *was* an Egyptian national? Be careful, Mr. Talhouni. Should I interpret the noises that I heard earlier as the screams of a dying man; should I learn that certain interrogation techniques, that specific protocols which are – how should I put it? – unorthodox are being used by my Egyptian counterparts; should I be placed into a position of foreknowledge, I would be in violation of International law, not to mention several UN Human Rights directives. Article four of the '94 Convention Against Torture obligates *all* state parties to ensure that *all* acts of torture are criminal offenses under domestic legislation."

"You have a remarkable memory, Chief Seiden. Did you

study the law?"

"Psychology, actually," said Seiden. Then he added, "You'd be surprised how useful it can be in our profession. Over time, for example, I've developed an uncanny ability to know when someone is lying." He stared at Talhouni and frowned. "You might think this a gift. It's not. It isn't always pleasant lifting off the skullcap, looking in. Where was the suspect apprehended?"

Talhouni stroked his greasy mustaches. "Not far from here," he said. "In the Khalili Khan. It is ironic, no? The Khalili market was a venue for the spice cartel controlled by the Mameluke in the Middle Ages, a monopoly which eventually encouraged the Europeans to search for new routes to the East, which prompted Columbus to discover America, without which, of course, Israel would not exist. Amusing, is it not?"

"You live in the past, Mr. Talhouni. Your whole country does."

"When the past is so much more glorious than the present, Chief Seiden, it is easy to fall out of time. But do not think me an ignorant man. I have traveled. I have been to Hangelar and Bonn. I was trained there by the German Grenzscutzgruppe Nine. I am sure you've heard—"

"Did he say anything important, before his unfortunate . . . "

" . . . demise? I'm afraid so."

"Well? Well, what did he say?"

"He believed his device was active. 'Armed and active.' Those were his very words. They all did."

"They?"

"All three of them," answered Talhouni. "Three mules dispatched by Gulzhan Baqrah. Al-Hakim, who admitted to planting the bomb in the sewers of Beersheba. A man called Ziad, shot while crossing the border from Lebanon into Israel. I'm sure you know about him."

Seiden nodded.

"And an Algerian named Ali Hammel. Only Hammel is still at large."

"Where's he going?" asked Seiden.

"Well, that's the bad news, I'm afraid. That's why Al-Hakim was being so . . . recalcitrant. He just didn't want to let it go."

"Where, Mr. Talhouni? I haven't got all day."

Talhouni sighed and looked down at the red spots on his shirt. "To New York," he answered, picking at the stains. "The

Empire State building."

Chapter 27
Tuesday, February 1 – 7:53 AM
New York City

Seamus Gallagher of WKXY-TV had only planned to drop by his office for a few minutes en route to a story in the Bronx when he noticed the little brown shipping box in the tray outside his cubicle. It looked like a videotape cassette. Gallagher hesitated for a moment, put down his cup of coffee and examined the label. Nothing. No return address. But the stamps and postmark were from Lebanon. He unwrapped the box and removed the plastic holder. As he'd suspected, it was a tape, but of what, he had no way of knowing.

Gallagher sat down behind his desk. There was no label on the box, nor on the tape itself. It was anonymous. He plopped it into his old VHS machine. Then he leaned back in his seat, pulled the lid up from his coffee cup, and took a sip. It was light and sweet, just as he liked it. He watched the TV screen. It seemed to be working but he couldn't see a thing. The screen was blank. No, black, he realized, as it came to life, as fire blossomed in a corner of the screen, crawling from right to left. Then he saw two people in the shadows, two men. One was in his forties, with sloping shoulders and a close-cropped beard. The other was a fat youth in his mid- to upper-twenties. He said something, and then more lights appeared, descending from the ceiling; they swung down in a kind of cape, a fishing net of flames.

Gallagher parked his coffee on his desk. He nuzzled closer to the TV screen. The bodies of the men were suddenly illuminated. He heard them start to scream. He watched them writhe and wiggle, even as a pale green line snaked in across their chests, bright floriated text, from right to left. Gallagher couldn't read Arabic but he knew it when he saw it. And then they simply melted, live and in color, the men, like in some cheesy horror flick. Their hair caught fire and their eyes and noses dripped like melted wax, blackened and fell away. The recording ended. The videotape went blank, then exploded into static. Gallagher hit the "rewind" button.

He watched the clip over and over again, editing it in his mind. There was only so much you could show on television. It wasn't the FCC that worried him, although Homeland Security would have a field day with this clip. It was the sponsors. Management didn't give a rat's ass about the audience – not really –

as long as it was big enough. It was the ad dollars that concerned them.

Let the chips fall where they may, he told himself. The tape was clearly the Beersheba terrorist attack. Someone was feeding him this story, was handing it to him on a platter. He didn't know who, and he didn't particularly care. It was making his career.

He examined the packing box more carefully. Something was stuck on the inside, glued to the paper. He plucked it out. It was a kind of postcard, he realized, the photo of some dome, looking up from within. He turned it over. The legend was in several languages, including English: *The muqarnas featured in the dome of the Shaykh Lutfallah Mosque, Isfahan.* It bore a postmark from Iran. He read the card. It was an invitation to some kind of event at midnight on Wednesday, the very next evening in New York. And it was signed by El Aqrab.

Gallagher put the card down on his desk. He stared down at the dome of the Iranian mosque. He looked at the ornate paneling and thought that this would probably topple Prime Minister Garron. News of his freeing El Aqrab in exchange for a fake nuclear device wouldn't go over very well in Israel. The Israeli press had recently reported that a number of PLO detainees had been released in exchange for a couple of Israeli businessmen and the remains of several soldiers — but certainly not the infamous El Aqrab. El Aqrab must have anticipated this event prior to mailing him the tape. That's why he'd sent it to an American, as opposed to an Israeli journalist. And to help cultivate suspense, no doubt, in the hearts of all New Yorkers.

What's going to happen tomorrow at midnight? he thought. Gallagher sipped his coffee, pondering. *One thing for sure: My ratings are going up.* He parked his coffee on his desk, picked up the phone, and dialed the FBI.

* * *

Long after his watch was over and most of the crew had already drifted off to sleep, the Algerian mule Hammel lingered in number two hold. The chamber had the density of a commercial garage. And it was but one of three holds, on top of one another, separated by a pair of giant metal hatches. It was dark in the hold. It was dark and cold and smelled of rotting fish. A reefer on the starboard side had sprung a leak. He'd have to report it to the Chief Mate in the morning. Hammel felt a wave of nausea hit him. He wretched and toppled over. He had been sick since early morning, ever since the *Rêve de Chantal* had steamed out of the port of Arrecife, away from Lanzarote and the Canaries, heading toward New York. Hammel was from Tamanrasset, in the heart of the Algerian Sahara. Whoever had called camels the "ships of the desert" had lied.

He was about to give up in disgust when he heard the sound of a heavy hatch creak open, then shut against the bulkhead. He struggled to his feet. The lights flicked on. It was the Gambian, Momodou. He was standing by the hatchway with a large knife in his hand. When he saw Hammel, he hesitated. Then he came forward, brandishing the knife.

Hammel leaned against the jukebox crate, nursing his knee, preparing. The Gambian drew closer. He was grinning now. Hammel could see his pink tongue dancing about in his mouth. The Gambian took another step, then two, and then – without warning, with uncanny strength and impossible agility – the Algerian was upon him. Momodou backed away but he was already too late. The knife tumbled from his hand. Hammel had wrapped an object round his neck. It whistled as it tightened, as it closed about his throat. The Algerian pulled and Momodou went down.

Hammel relieved the pressure. He did not want to kill the Gambian. It would arouse too much unwanted scrutiny, too much suspicion. He didn't want the police boarding the freighter, with all manner of questions, as soon as they docked in New York. The Gambian coughed and fell onto his stomach. He tried to crawl away but the Algerian held him in place. Hammel swung and sat upon the Gambian's back, pinning his flabby body to the floor, the garrote still wrapped about his throat. "You are an inquisitive man," he said at last.

The Gambian could not answer. He couldn't even breathe.

"But if I tell you what you want to know, I may have to kill you. You do not want that, do you? You don't want to die." He slackened the pressure and the Gambian took a breath. He coughed. He sputtered and choked. Then he took another breath. Hammel removed the wire from his neck. "I didn't think so," he said.

The Algerian stood, guarding his knee, and slipped the wire back around his waist. He leaned against the jukebox crate. The Gambian rolled onto his side, his back towards Hammel. His hands were wrapped about his throat. He was whimpering like a child.

"For if you were dead," Hammel continued, "you wouldn't be able to share in the profits from my cargo."

The Gambian rolled over. He stared at Hammel, one hand still wrapped about his throat. "What cargo?" he croaked.

"From the poppy fields of Mazar e Shariff. New York is a city of addicts, my friend. What do you care? Let them destroy themselves. I will reward you for your silence." He looked down at the Gambian with his impenetrable black eyes. He stretched his hand out with a smile. "Ten percent. Are we agreed?"

For a moment, the Gambian said nothing. Then, he smiled too. He reached for Hammel's hand and said, "Fifteen."

Chapter 28
Tuesday, February 1 – 5:47 PM
New York City

It had been another worthless day. Decker had been tracking down leads about Moussa and the other suspects since seven o'clock that morning. But no matter how promising they appeared, no matter how solid, they always disintegrated in his hands at the last moment. He felt like a rat in a maze of dead ends. He returned to the office dejected and tired. He hadn't eaten since breakfast, but he still wasn't hungry. The entire team had been working double and triple shifts since Warhaftig had briefed them about the confession of the dying Egyptian, Al-Hakim. No one had any doubts now – New York was the destination. In fact, for all they knew, the device was already in place.

As Decker got up from his desk to fetch another cup of coffee, Warhaftig approached him from the side. He took him by the elbow and inquired, nonchalantly, if he had seen the videotape from Beersheba. Decker shook his head. Just snippets on TV, he answered glumly. What Gallagher had shown on WKXY. A moment later, they were sitting in the little office that SAC Johnson had assigned Warhaftig at the beginning of the investigation. Decker watched as the CIA operative popped a tape into his VCR. He played it in slow motion.

Decker was horrified by what he saw. At first, he could barely watch the grisly scene. But then, despite himself, despite the almost palpable combustion, he found himself drawn into each detail, like a reluctant medical student concentrating on a vein instead of the whole cadaver: the way the net hung from the ceiling, crushing the soldiers up against the wall; the color of the flames, unmasking chemical composition; and then the fiery script. He had seen this amaranth of arabesque before. It matched the phrase from Moussa's notepad: *Death Will Overtake You.* But now, in living color, in active architecture, the words were even more distinct.

"What do you see?"

Decker struggled from his reverie. "What? What did you say?"

"In the flames. What do you see?" Warhaftig asked.

Decker smiled. He had been waiting for this moment. "What happened to my memory stick?" he said. "To those pictures I took of Moussa's apartment?"

"Excuse me?"

"The other wallpaper, Otto?"

Warhaftig's chin collapsed into his chest. "I'm sorry," he said. "I'm not following you."

"I bet you're not." Decker scowled. "I didn't forget to load the camera the day Bartolo died. And it wasn't Moussa or anyone else who took the memory stick, was it? You and I were the only ones inside that surveillance squat, other than Bartolo."

Warhaftig said, "I don't know what you're talking about, John. Really, I don't."

"Don't bullshit me," Decker spat. He got to his feet. He towered over the desk. "You'd seen that design before, I know you had. In the work of El Aqrab. After some other killings. Like the ones in Tel Aviv."

Warhaftig stared back at Decker with a cold, unflinching gaze. His lips were curled up in the corners. He wore a fearsome smile, well practiced and professional. Then he shrugged, the slightest movement of the shoulders, almost too subtle to be noticed. He looked back at the monitor, breaking the seal, and all the air rushed in.

Decker felt an undertow of anger ripple through him. He sat down on Warhaftig's desk, leaned in and said, "You know, one hand washes the other, as my mother used to say."

"Did she now?"

"Fuck you," said Decker. He started for the door. Then he hesitated, turned and said, "Why did El Aqrab kill Miller? What was it about the Israeli furniture salesman that linked him to the terrorist?"

"I don't know. I really don't, John."

"I'd like to get a list of all the prisoners with whom Miller had contact while he worked at Ansar II in Gaza."

"We've looked at that already. There's no connection."

"Of course there is. You just haven't found it." Decker shook his head. "And while you're at it, why don't you contact passport control in the Canary Islands? See if there's been an up-tick in tourist traffic from the Middle East, odd shipments from the Newly Independent States, any baffling thefts or murders."

"The Canaries. Why, what's up?"

"It could be nothing. Or it could mean everything."

"I'd like to help, John, I really would. But Johnson's got me running down every cab company in the city. I don't have time to—"

"You don't have time! That's a laugh. Tell you what, Otto: When you start helping me, I'll start helping you. Because if we don't start helping each other, pretty soon we won't have any time at all." With that he turned and vanished out the door.

Chapter 29
Tuesday, February 1 – 6:33 PM
New York City

Decker wandered aimlessly through the streets, past the state and city courthouses, past City Hall and southward toward the Battery. The evening was oppressively cold. He could see the condensation of his own breath in the air, suspended, ballooning under streetlights. He was still fuming, still replaying his conversation with Warhaftig when he found himself at the southernmost corner of Manhattan. He leaned against the railing and stared out across the frigid waters of the bay, at the Statue of Liberty glowing in the distance. She seemed to be carved out of a solid block of ice, blue green and absolutely still. Decker's phone began to vibrate in his pocket, making him jump. He flipped it open. It was another text message, short and sweet. It read: *Islamic Cultural Ctr, 97 - 2 & 3.*

It took Decker a good half hour to make it to the Upper East Side. The Islamic Cultural Center at Ninety-sixth and Third – with its great dome, marble walls and golden minaret – was one of the most striking buildings in a city known for its ostentatious architecture. Built at great cost, the mosque was a landmark of modern and classical design, blending two great schools of architecture.

Decker noticed they were doing some construction just east of the Cultural Center. A huge hole, mostly obstructed by graffiti-splattered plywood walls, had been carved out of the ground. Massive earth-moving machinery slaved away in the pit, bellowing like bulls, tearing at the earth. When there was so much concrete everywhere, thought Decker, it was easy to forget the soil beneath. This is what remained of Manhattan Island's gentle rolling hills, her meadows and forests and fields – a great scar in the earth, covered by Man.

The main gate leading to the mosque on Third Avenue was locked. Decker walked uptown to Ninety-seventh and noticed another entrance running along a wire fence beside the construction site. A pair of men sat by a two-wheeled *halal* stand, doling out chicken and beef, accompanied by freshly baked bread. And there he was – Professor Hassan – standing right there, alongside them, joking and laughing, biting at something in a piece of wax paper. As Decker approached, the Professor turned away, tossed the paper into a nearby garbage can, and headed toward the mosque. Decker followed. The entrance led into a narrow corridor. There was a gift shop on the right. Then the hall opened up onto a foyer. A set of double stairs led to the second floor. To his right, Decker noticed a small *masjid* studded with blue and white tile. A line of men stood praying inside, each facing the same direction. One got onto his knees. They were barefoot, Decker noticed. Their shoes and socks were stacked in little cubicles outside the entrance to the mosque.

Professor Hassan hesitated for a moment by another door. When he realized Decker was behind him, he pushed it open. It led into a kitchen with a restaurant-style range. Then the Professor disappeared through yet another door. Decker had to move quickly to keep up. He followed Hassan through the kitchen, through the next door and down along a corridor. There was a fire exit to their left. Hassan pushed it open and started to descend a set of concrete steps. Decker followed. A moment later they found themselves within another corridor, deep beneath the mosque. Hassan came to a stop by a door with the number seven stenciled on the front. He looked about. He stared at Decker for the first time. The corridor was empty. They had not seen a soul since the *masjid*. Hassan removed a key from his coat, unlocked the door and stepped inside, with Decker close behind.

The room featured a little metal cot, a washbasin and mirror, and a table. There were no windows; the room was too far underground. Books and papers were strewn across the surface of the table. There were printouts of the various wallpapers pinned to the wall, some in color, and some in black-and-white. Hassan had run a grease pencil along the Arabic, highlighting lines and punctuation marks. It was clear the professor was working on the designs recovered from the hard disk.

If anyone ever finds out I've handed over all this evidence, thought Decker, *it will mean the end of my career, such as it is.* Yet he didn't care, which rather surprised him. It was too late for that now anyway. If he succeeded, all would be forgiven. And if he failed . . . Well, it would matter even less. "What's going on?" he said.

Hassan hovered by the table, flipping through printouts, books and papers, as if searching for something in particular. "I can't add much to the first translation, the *masjid* or Individual prayer," he said. "And I'm afraid the sources of the third and fourth wallpapers still elude me. All I can make out are the same words you translated: *Death will overtake you.* And, *On the ocean like mountains.* Plus the numbers fifty-four thousand and zero. But here," he added, pulling out a printout from the pile. "I've made considerable progress on the second wallpaper." He showed him the familiar arabesque design, the curling script. He ran a fingertip along the lines. "You see," he said. "It does indeed resemble a *jami' masjid*, the prayer used on Fridays in the Congregational mosque.

"At first I was confused," he continued. "I mean I'd translated a part of it as, 'How many a deserted well and palace raised high,' which seems to be from *Al-Hajj*. But this other part," he added, pointing. "Here. You see? It didn't make any sense. Then it dawned on me. It's not an extension of the same line. It's another quote altogether? Take at look."

He handed Decker a copy of the Qur'an. He flipped it open to a specific page. "That's the first quote from *Al-Hajj*, the Pilgrimage. 'So how many a town did We destroy while it was unjust, so it was fallen down upon its roofs, and (how many) a deserted well and palace raised high.' And here's the second." He turned the pages quickly. "It's a quote from *Hijr*. It talks about Allah and Iblis — the angel who refused to genuflect to Man." He read aloud. "'I will make error appear as attractive to (people) in this life and I will lead them all astray . . . surely hell is the rendezvous for them all. It has seven gates; each gate has a portion of them allotted to it.' I've translated them but I have no idea what they mean. Iblis has nothing to do with deserted wells or palaces. I've been pulling my hair out all afternoon."

Decker studied the illustration. Unlike the first wallpaper, the calligraphy in this design didn't flow in one straight line, along the *qibla*. The two quotes from the Qur'an came together at the *mihrab*, where the *qibla* and transversal axes intersected. Indeed, two words from the two quotes were overlain — both "well" and "seven."

While Hassan struggled for logic, Decker repeated them under his breath, forging the words together as on the page. *Well and seven*, he thought, *well and seven*. And it suddenly came clear. The wells of seven. He laughed. After all this time, those years of Sunday school in Iowa had finally paid off. The wells of seven was Beersheba, the town where Abraham had made a treaty with Abimelech. "Genesis twenty-one," he said aloud. "Verse twenty-seven."

Hassan stopped fidgeting. "What?"

Decker looked up. "The wells of seven," he repeated. "It's from the Bible. Beersheba is first mentioned as the place where Hagar went—"

"After Abraham sent her away," concluded the professor. "Of course, what an idiot!" He smacked his own forehead with his palm. "I've been looking at it all day, and then you come along and . . . The wells of seven. I'll be damned. It's the same in the Qur'an. Hagar was Abraham's Egyptian-born concubine, who had a son by Abraham – Ishmael, the father of Islam – when his wife Sarah believed she was barren. Then, when Sarah eventually gave birth to Isaac – the father of the Jewish and Christian faiths – she could no longer tolerate Hagar's presence. So she demanded Abraham send the concubine away. This was the event that marked the split between the Muslim and Judeo-Christian worlds."

"I didn't know Ishmael was the father of Islam," said Decker. "I thought he and Abraham were Jews."

"The Qur'an and Bible feature many of the same characters. As does the Hebrew Torah. According to the Qur'an, Abraham wasn't a Jew. He was a deist, pure and simple. He believed in one God – call him Allah, or Yahweh, or whatever. It was only later the religions diverged."

To Muslims, Hassan continued, Jews and Christians and the followers of Islam were all "People of the Book." Indeed, the Qur'an emphasized the purity and righteousness of *every* prophet in the Bible, including Jesus Christ.

"We simply don't believe Christ was the Son of God," he said. "And this notion of the Trinity – Father, Son and Holy Spirit – is anathema to us. The *Fatihah*, with which the Qur'an begins, states clearly: *Thee alone do we worship; Thee alone do we implore for help.*"

"There is but one God," said Decker, "and Mohammed is his messenger."

"Exactly. Nor do we believe in Original Sin. In fact, the Qur'an stresses as fundamental the purity of 'the nature designed by Allah.' How could it be otherwise? Choice and free will are paramount. Faith is a matter of conscience, and conscience cannot be compelled. The Qur'an clearly states: *There shall be no compulsion in religion.* Allah calls us all."

"But the radicals, the extremists who label the United States the 'Great Satan,'" said Decker. He was confused. "This notion of Jihad. I thought . . . "

"Jihad simply means exertion," Hassan said. "Like the word Crusade, jihad can refer to anything. It doesn't necessarily mean an act of violence. You could say President Johnson's 'War on Poverty' was a Jihad. The real Jihad is the fight against everything that keeps you inward, against God, such as human passions." He sighed.

"There's also a difference between *aggressive* Jihad, which is frowned upon, and *defensive* Jihad, which is approved by the Qur'an. Even war-like examples of defensive Jihad are governed by rules. True followers, for example, are prohibited from hurting women and children, or old people, just as they're forbidden from destroying nature, such as acts of deforestation. Fighting is permitted only to repel aggression. Should the enemy be inclined to make a truce, the Qur'an says we must take advantage of it: *Whenever they kindle a fire to start a war, Allah puts it out. They strive to create disorder in the land and Allah loves not those who create disorder.* He who would seek the pleasure of Allah must not merely be just, but benevolent as well. He must render good without thought of a return, forgiving wrongs and injuries until beneficence becomes an intrinsic part of who he is. There is another term in Arabic that means Holy War. It's *harbun muqaddasatun.* But it's not in the Qur'an.

"Look," he added, "I'm a devout Muslim. You know that. You also know that I support the Palestinian cause, just like El Aqrab, with all my heart. I may be Egyptian, but the Palestinians are my brothers in the *Ummah.* I'm not an anti-Semite, but I do believe that what the conservatives have done in Israel is reprehensible, and – ironically – so do many Jews, even in Palestine. I think Garron is one of the most dangerous men on earth. Right up there with Osama Bin Laden and El Aqrab. If there is another Nine Eleven some day – Allah protect us – it will be because of Garron, because of his intransigence, his failure to resolve the tragedy of Palestine. And because of our failure to ensure he does so. One day – mark my words – if this quicksand isn't filled, if we Americans don't at least address the Palestinian problem even-handedly, the extremists throughout the Arab world will rise up like a great wave, and it will kill us all. This is what I believe, and yet I'm helping you. Why? Not because I'm American. It's not my patriotism that drives me; I think you know that. It is my Muslim faith, my sense of moral values."

Hassan smiled sadly. "There are extremists in every religion, Agent Decker. Look at those Christians who preach hatred against their fellow men, who use the Bible to justify acts of wanton cruelty. To them, to the boys who beat up Malik on that subway train, my son was simply a 'towel head.' What can you say to such people?"

Decker thought back to Ed McNally, the white supremacist from Iowa. All that he had wrought had been done in the name of Jesus Christ.

Hassan turned and spread his hands across the papers on the desk. "These drawings and illustrations," he said. "You haven't told me very much, but I'm not blind or stupid. I read the paper. I know what happened in Beersheba. In fact, I made a copy of the explosion, recorded it off the news." He pointed at a DVR and TV in the corner. "This calligraphy and design predicted it, didn't it? I don't know where you got it, or why. Frankly, I don't want to know. But it occurs to me," he continued, "if the second wallpaper predicted what was going to happen in Beersheba, the third and fourth wallpapers may be harbingers of things to come. Another Nine Eleven, or worse. Some cataclysm. If I can help in any way to stop that, it's my duty as a Muslim to try."

Decker did not respond. Instead, he crossed the reading room and began to document their findings with a thick black felt tip marker on the whiteboard on the wall.

1. **Masjid, the Individual Prayer; Daily Mosques and prayer rugs:**
   - Text: *Ten-month pregnant she-camels*; and *When hell is stoked up* (*Al-Takwir*, Sura 81)
   - Number: 540,000
   - Originally Displayed: Tel Aviv (?)
   - Harbinger of: Baqrah's hijacking of the train
   - Date/Time, forthcoming event: 9:00 AM; Friday, Jan. 28

2. **Jami' masjid, the Congregational Prayer; Congregational Mosques on Fridays:**
   - Text: *How many a deserted well* (*Al-Hajj*, Sura 22.45), and then, perpendicular to the transversal axis, *Hell is the rendezvous . . . it has seven gates* (*Hijr*, 15.35)
   - Number: 205,200
   - Originally Displayed: Train hijacking of HEU
   - Harbinger of: Incident in Beersheba
   - Date/Time, forthcoming event: 6:00 AM; Tuesday, Feb. 1

3.	Musalla or idgah, the Community Prayer; Community Mosques during the major festivals of 'Id al-Fitr – The Feast of the Breaking of the Fast – and the 'Id al-Adha – The Feast of the Sacrifice of Abraham
- Text:	*Death will overtake you (?)*
- Number:	54,000
- Originally Displayed:	Incident in Beersheba
- Harbinger of:	(?)
- Date/Time, forthcoming event:	Midnight; Wednesday, Feb. 2

4.	A collection of Arabesque designs, with an island of copy at the center; the worldwide Hajj (?)
- Text:	*On the ocean like mountains (?)*
- Number:	o
- Originally Displayed:	(?)
- Harbinger of:	(???)
- Date/Time, forthcoming event:	3:00 PM; Thursday, Feb. 3

"I don't know for certain where it started," Decker said. "Although, I'd bet it was Tel Aviv. The timing coincides. We know the first wallpaper predicted the hijacking in Kazakhstan, and the second the bombing in Beersheba." He pointed at the board. "We can also deduce from the first and second wallpapers that the numbers represent time – in seconds. Unfortunately, since we don't fully understand the third and fourth quotes, we can't know what disasters they portend. But we do know *when* they'll happen: the third event at midnight, tomorrow night, confirmed by Gallagher's postcard invitation; and the fourth, and last event, at three PM on Thursday, day after tomorrow."

"You're saying the numbers are some kind of countdown?"

"That's right. We're running out of time," said Decker. "If we don't decipher the last two images soon, we won't have a prayer of stopping them."

He walked around the desk and pressed a button on the DVR. The explosion from Beersheba came to life. Hassan stepped in beside him and they began to examine the video together, over and over again. They studied the drawing Decker had found in Moussa's locker, the *musalla* or *idgah*, the prayer of the Community mosque. And they puzzled over the fourth wallpaper with its tortured arabesque and cryptic phrase: *On the ocean like mountains*, and the ominous number o.

Professor Hassan retrieved several books on Arabic calligraphy and Islamic architecture that Decker and he consulted. One, in particular, caught Decker's eye. It was by a Dr. Jamal ben Saad of the Arab University in Beirut, an authority on Islamic architecture and design. Given the architectural context of the first two prayers, Decker tried to understand the third and fourth accordingly. But interpreting the images was tough going. Decker was convinced the third wallpaper would reveal some additional connection, no matter how oblique, to New York City. But all they could interpret were the same few words: *Death will overtake you.*

The calligraphy was written in a block-like *kufi* script, the lettering surrounded by a labyrinth of arabesque designs, twisted organic stems, splitting off and re-uniting. The entire illustration was ringed with sun wheels, female swastikas.

"The design forces the eye counterclockwise," Decker mused.

"That's pretty common," Hassan said. "Counterclockwise circumambulation is standard practice at Muslim shrines, especially at the Ka'aba, where pilgrims walk around and kiss the Black Stone seven times. And they circumambulate against the sun, so as to achieve the maximum exposure possible to *Baraka*, the invisible psychic fluid that emanates from every sacred object."

Decker's phone vibrated in his pocket. "Excuse me," he muttered, and flipped it open. "Decker," he said.

It was Emily Swenson. He heard her voice and the tension he'd been feeling all day evaporated in a second.

"I tracked down Dr. White. He's on the island of La Palma, in the Canaries," she said.

Decker wasn't surprised. "Wasn't he working on a book about the Cumbre Vieja on La Palma? That's what you said before."

"Last year," she said. "Before Doris got sick. Before she got terminal cancer. Then he came back." She sighed and he pictured her inside her office, fidgeting at her desk, her mouth, her lips right next to the receiver. "Don't you see?" she said. "Why would he leave like that? Why would he just take off? James is devoted to Doris."

"Well, perhaps he had to finish his research. Or—"

"His wife is dying, Agent Decker. He's not like you."

"What does that mean?"

"Look, it doesn't matter. It's all moot anyway. I went to see her, John. Do you hear me? I went to the hospice and she's gone."

"Gone? What do you mean? She passed away?"

"No, no," said Swenson. "God, I hope not. She's been kidnapped!"

Decker hesitated for a moment. He looked over at Hassan. Then he said, "Where are you now?"

"I'm in Manhattan, at Penn Station."

"OK," he said. "I'll meet you at your hotel."

"I don't have a hotel. I tried to call from Woods Hole, but they all seem to be booked up."

Decker closed his eyes. "Take a cab and meet me on Eighth Avenue and Fourteenth Street. Northwest corner. You can crash at my place tonight," he said. "I'll be there in less than twenty minutes." Then he hung up. He turned toward the Professor. "I'm sorry but I have to run."

Hassan nodded. "I'd better walk you out," he said.

They made their way upstairs, back through the kitchen, past the *masjid* and out onto Ninety-seventh. As soon as they hit Second Avenue, a cab swung by and Decker raised his hand. It pulled over immediately.

"I'll talk with you tomorrow," Decker said. "Call me if you come up with anything."

* * *

Hassan waved and turned away. He started across Ninety-sixth Street as Decker's cab *whooshed* by and disappeared. He stopped and looked up at the sky. Despite the ambient light, he could see stars. They seemed so far away, almost imaginary. Then they were gone, hidden by clouds. It looked like it was going to snow. He crossed the street and opened the door to a Land Rover Discovery parked in the shadows.

"Well?" said the driver. His face was hidden in the dark.

The Professor turned the collar of his coat up. "Let's just get the hell out of here," he said, and slipped inside.

The driver laughed. He shifted the car into gear and they sidled into traffic. They shivered down the street, illuminated by the streetlights as they raced cross-town. At one point, the driver attempted to switch lanes and a taxi cut him off.

"I hate this fucking town," Warhaftig said. He pressed the accelerator, and they were gone.

Chapter 30
Tuesday, February 1 – 9:14 PM
New York City

Decker unlocked the front door of his apartment and flicked on the light. Emily Swenson peered inside. Beyond the narrow corridor, immediately to the right, the hallway opened up onto a living room. There was a small cherry wood dining table in one corner beside a kind of kitchenette. Swenson closed the door behind her and Decker helped her off with her coat. There was another door at the end of the front hall that Swenson surmised must lead into the bedroom. The bathroom was to her right. "Cozy," she said.

Decker hung her coat up in the closet. A large metal bar angled up from the floor in the hallway, reinforcing the front door. "Police lock," Decker said as he spied her staring at it.

"Is that to keep people out, or in?" she said with a smile.

Decker looked surprised. He hesitated, then slipped his coat off and hung it in the closet next to hers. "Want a drink?" he asked as he moved off toward the kitchenette.

There was a large bookcase built into one wall of the apartment packed with books. Beside it, Swenson noticed a large silver steamer trunk with a CD player parked on top. At the far end of the room, between two windows facing the street, stood a small wooden desk; probably maple, she thought. It was inlaid with mother of pearl. And along the near wall ran a large green sofa, well worn and somewhat threadbare. The kitchenette was spotless. Either Decker was very clean, or he seldom ate at home.

"Or would you like some coffee?" Decker dropped the book he'd been carrying onto the dining table, and turned toward the kitchenette.

The fridge looked like an antique too, thought Swenson. "A drink would be great, thanks."

"I have some cabernet. Is that okay?"

Swenson flopped down onto the sofa and immediately began to sink into the soft foam pillows. "I'm of Norwegian stock, Agent Decker. Nothing stronger?" For the first time, she noticed that the walls were bare. There was no artwork of any kind. Not even photographs.

Decker rifled through the kitchen cabinets. "I think I have some scotch here somewhere," he said. "At least I used to."

"Scotch would be great. How long you been here?"

"Just a few weeks." Decker pulled a brand new bottle of

Dalwinnie single malt out of the cabinet, and began to remove the metal foil around the cork.

"I see you like the minimalist look. Very fashionable."

He poured out a couple of drinks into what looked like juice glasses. "I prefer to think of it as neo-landfill," he replied. "With a hint of post-modern nihilism."

Swenson laughed. He handed her a scotch. She took a sip and felt it burn her throat. "I guess you like it neat," she added, as her eyes grew misty. "Delicious."

Decker sat down on the sofa beside her. He took a sip and smiled. Then he took another sip. "This was a good idea," he said. "I mean the scotch."

Swenson looked for somewhere to put her glass down and realized that there was no coffee table. She balanced the glass in her lap. No end tables either. No TV and no PC, unless they were in the bedroom.

She took another drink, braced herself, and said, "Like I told you earlier. Doris was abducted. This morning." She put her glass down on the floor. "By three Arabic-looking men. And then a nurse said James called just two nights ago, from the Canary Islands. So I phoned the Parador Hotel in Santa Cruz. That's where he normally stays. They said he's taken a room there, but they haven't seen hide nor hair of him since he checked in. No one knows where he is. He went hiking day before yesterday, and never came back."

Decker sighed. "There's nothing you can do here, Emily," he said. "Frankly, I don't know why you came."

Swenson stood up. "What? I thought I should tell you," she said. "About Doris, I mean. And James. Excuse me, but I thought kidnapping was a federal offense," she added sarcastically.

"You could have just telephoned. You're probably just over-reacting. Why don't you go back to Woods Hole? Let me look into this. I'll call you if anything turns up."

"What are you talking about? What's wrong with you, Decker? I'm not making this shit up. Hey! Remember me? I'm Emily Swenson – the woman who saved your life."

He smiled, climbed to his feet. Then he shrugged and said, "I'm really rather busy right now, Emily. I'm not trying to be callous, but Dr. White's disappearance isn't high on my list of priorities. I don't know what happened to your friend Doris. Perhaps Dr. White wanted her moved to another facility. Happens all the time. And just because some 'Arabic-looking' men were involved doesn't mean it's a conspiracy. There are lots of perfectly normal, law-abiding Arab-Americans in this country."

Swenson peered down at the floor. Then she glanced up, wide-eyed, embarrassed. "I didn't mean to make it sound like . . . like they all look, you know . . . alike. Oh, God. You know what I mean." She picked up Decker's book from the dining table, displaying it before her. "Look at this guy," she added, pointing at the dust jacket. "Tell me he doesn't look just like that picture of El Aqrab in all the papers. They could be brothers."

Decker took the book from her hand. He studied the photograph. "A much younger brother, perhaps," he said. "And fatter too. Yeah, they look alike. That's the problem. Everyone looks alike through foreign eyes. The other. The generic enemy. The Islamic horde." He dropped the book back on the table. "Okay. I promise," he continued. "I'll look into it. On one condition, though."

"What's that?"

"That you go back to Woods Hole and let me handle it. And that you relax and drink your scotch. Okay?"

Swenson moved back toward the sofa. She plopped down on the cushions and said, "Those are two conditions." Then she reached down, picked up her glass, and took another slug of her drink.

"It's just not a good time now, Emily, that's all. I'm on a case."

"I thought *I* was your case. Don't tell me you didn't recognize that guy who shot you? Whatever," she said. "I guess that's why you don't have a coffee table."

"What?" He sat back down beside her.

"This place could use a woman's touch."

"I'm hardly ever here." Decker studied Swenson carefully, taking in each curve, each line of her face.

"What are you staring at?" she said.

"You're the most . . . Nothing." A heavy silence settled on the room. "How did you get to Woods Hole anyway?" Decker added, finally.

Swenson watched him struggle, trying to fill the space. "Born in Chance, South Dakota," she said. "Gateway to the Badlands. It's famous, you know. Doc Holiday lived there for a spell." She took another sip of scotch and the living room blushed with heat.

"Actually, my dad's a scientist too – a geologist. The ocean always seemed like such an incredible place when I was growing up. Opposites attract, I guess. We lived in a part of the country about as different from the sea as you can get. But it was an inland sea once, millions of years ago, and my dad used to bring home fossils from his digs. I guess you could say I ended up like him. Oceanography is geology in its liquid state." She laughed. "That was a joke, Decker. A sciency, nurdy kind of joke – but still a joke."

Decker smiled. "How about your mom?"

"She died of cancer when I was twelve."

"Sorry to hear that." Decker turned away. For a moment, neither of them spoke.

"I got my degree at USC," she said. "But something happened, so I came east."

"What happened?"

"You really are a cop, aren't you, Agent Decker? You go straight to the dark side."

"Actually, I'm a cryptanalyst forensic examiner. A code breaker. Most people join Homeland Security with visions of James Bond or Jack Ryan in their heads. In truth, most agents end up being more like something out of a Dilbert cartoon. You fight the bureaucracy more than the bad guys."

"I had an affair with one of my professors."

"What?"

"That's why I came east. It ended badly."

"I'm sorry."

"Don't be. I'm not." She laughed. The scotch was going to her head. "It's quite a funny story, actually. We'd ended the affair, you see, but we were scheduled to take this dive off the New Jersey coast, in a DSV called the *Alvin*. That's a Deep Submergence Vehicle, and those kinds of opportunities don't happen along every day. Anyway, we were descending and Dubinsky . . . That was the professor's name. E.J. Dubinsky."

"I think I've heard of him."

Swenson smiled. "Have you?"

"Didn't he write *This Primal Earth*? It was a best-seller."

"That's the one," she answered with a laugh. "Anyway, we were about half an hour into the dive when E.J. tried to kiss me. I pulled away and something happened to the ship. To this day, I don't know what it was. We lost power. I thought it was some kind of trick or something, a kind of ruse to scare me. E.J. was always pulling shit like that. Anyway, I guess I kind of lost it.

Haven't set foot in a DSV since. Give me the heebie-jeebies now."

"Was it on purpose?"

She shook her head. "Now, I don't think so. But at the time . . . It would have been just like her."

"Her?"

"E.J.'s a woman."

"Oh," said Decker. He looked away. "I didn't know." He took another sip of his drink.

Swenson laughed. It was completely unrestrained and genuine. It liberated her. "Don't misunderstand me, Agent Decker. I'm not gay or anything. It was just one of those things."

"What things?"

"Oh, I don't know. When you get as much male attention as I do, it was probably inevitable that I should run in the other direction at some point in my life. Am I embarrassing you?"

"No, not at all."

"Then why are you blushing? I don't know why I'm telling you all of this. I must be drunk."

"Already?" Decker stood up. He strolled over to the table and picked up the bottle of Dalwinnie. Then he walked back to Swenson and poured her another drink. "Just to be sure," he added with a grin.

"Have you no honor, Cryptanalyst Forensic Examiner Decker?"

"You've had a tough day."

"Oh, I see. It's a pity drink."

Decker poured himself another scotch and sat back on the sofa. He put the bottle on the floor beside his feet. "Are you always this combative?" he replied.

Swenson kicked her shoes off. She pulled her feet up on the sofa next to his. "Am I being combative?" She laughed and moved a little closer. She wiggled her toes. "I thought I was flirting." She took the glass of scotch from Decker's hand, and rested it on the floor. Then she leaned forward, bringing her face close, only inches away, until she could feel his breath on her lips.

"Kiss me, Agent Decker." His eyes were gray, dotted with blue and green.

Decker glanced away. He reached down for his glass and placed it inbetween them. "I don't think that's such a good idea," he said.

"Why not? What's the matter, don't you like me? Perhaps I'm not your type. What is your type, anyway?"

"That's not what I meant. It's just . . . " He hesitated. "It's just that I'm working on this case, and you're a part of it. It wouldn't be, you know – professional." Decker stood up and walked over to the CD player on his trunk. He pressed a button and the air was suddenly filled with saxophone, piano, drums and double bass.

Swenson recognized the tune. It was one hundred percent Charles Mingus, from the album *Mingus Ah Um*, but she couldn't recall the name of the track. Goodbye something.

Decker turned and, for a moment, the way the lamplight caught his face, the way it seemed to wrap around one side, to glaze his skin, he could have been some kind of Idiacanthidae, with photophores along the angle of his chin, equipped with bioluminescence.

"Why did you join the FBI?" she asked him. "I told you my tawdry tale. Ever kill anyone?"

Decker looked away. "As a matter of fact, I have. Just a few weeks ago."

"I'm sorry! I was only kidding."

"Were you? It's okay. Really. I was picking at your wounds. Besides, I've never really talked about it. Not even with that shrink the Bureau assigned me. Maybe it's time." He offered up a smile. "It's not that common, you know. I mean, not like in the movies. Believe it or not, most agents don't even discharge their weapons during their careers, at least not in the field. My dad was a cop for fifteen years and he never fired his gun." He shrugged. "I was called out to translate some telephone transmissions at a farmhouse in New Liberty, not far from where I grew up. That's where it all began."

He told her the story about McNally and the White Apocalypse. When it was over, Swenson took him by the hand and, this time, he didn't pull away. Then she reached out and ran a finger tenderly along the white scar on his brow. "Is that how you got this?"

"No, that was a traffic accident. When I was a boy."

"What happened?"

"Drunk driver. I don't remember much. Lost my memory." He paused. "Lost both my parents too."

"I'm so sorry, John," she said. "Who raised you, then?"

"My mother's sister and her husband. They took me in."

"How horrible. I know what it's like to lose a parent, but not both parents. At least you were brought up by someone who cared, not in some orphanage or something."

Decker laughed. "You have no idea."

For a long time she just stared at him. Then she reached down and took another sip of her drink. "Didn't you get along with your aunt and uncle?"

"Well enough," he said. "I like my uncle. Tom is a decent man."

"And your aunt?"

"My mother's sister wasn't too thrilled to suddenly have a child to raise. She never really liked children. At least, not like a mother should. She and Tom didn't have any of their own, and—"

"What does that mean? 'Not like a mother should.'"

"I'd rather not talk about it."

"What happened, John?"

"I said, I'd rather not talk about it."

Swenson got up from the sofa. She wandered off and stared at the books in the bookcase. He was hiding something. That much was clear. But what it was, she had no idea. Something dark. Something best left alone.

After a moment, Swenson turned, took another sip from her drink and said, "Is that why you became a code breaker?"

"What do you mean?"

"There's no logic to a car accident. No motive. No hidden pattern or agenda. No truth, even. It's just . . . random."

"What are you talking about?"

"You've spent your whole life solving puzzles, John, breaking codes. But some things – they can never be explained. They're inherently illogical, unsolvable."

"Like the randomness of a traffic accident?"

"Yeah," she said sadly. "Or love." She sat back on the sofa. She put her glass back on the floor, leaned forward and tried to kiss him.

Decker pulled away. He got up stiffly from the sofa. He looked down at his glass, then back at her and said, "Emily?"

"Yes?"

He struggled, trying to locate the right words. They seemed to float just out of reach.

"Just say it, John. What is it?"

"Would it be possible to cause a mega-tsunami?"

For a moment she hesitated. The question seemed to spin up out of nowhere. "That isn't what I thought you were going to say."

"Well, is it?"

"What do you mean, cause it? You mean set one off intentionally?"

He nodded. "You know. Like that volcano in the Canary Islands. The Cumbre Vieja."

"As long as it's quiescent, the volcano isn't dangerous." She paused. "But to cause a volcano to erupt?" She shook her head. "You'd need a hell of a lot of dynamite. Maybe with an atom bomb or something. James has some pretty crazy theories about vulcan stimulation. I guess it's possible." She laughed. "Luckily the Canary Islands aren't a nuclear power. Why do you ask?"

"Just curious," he answered. "Never mind." He smiled a feeble smile. He looked down at his watch. "It's getting late," he said, and downed his scotch. "I guess I'll sleep out here."

*   *   *

Decker lay on his old coach in the living room, reading the book Professor Hassan had given him that evening. He was particularly intrigued by a section on light and water. According to the book, the careful control of light in Islamic architecture had a mystical symbolism. Light was a symbol of divine unity. It also had two decorative functions. It modified other decorative elements, and it originated patterns. There was a subtle use of glossy floor and wall surfaces in Islamic architecture designed to catch light and throw it back over the facets of diamond-shaped ceilings which, in turn, reflected it again. *Muqarnas* – stalactite or honeycomb ornamentation, or vaulting made up of small concave segments – trapped light, refracted it. Ribbed domes appeared to rotate according to the time of day.

Decker suddenly remembered the postcard the FBI had confiscated from WKXY-TV reporter Seamus Gallagher, the one allegedly from El Aqrab himself. It had displayed *muqarnas* too, within the dome of the Shaykh Lutfallah mosque in Isfahan.

Facades, the book maintained, appeared to be lace-thin, and became transparent screens when light waves struck their stucco decorations. Mirrors, luster tiles, gilt wood, polished marble and water all shimmered, glimmered and reflected in the desert light. In this sense light – like water – contributed a dynamic quality to Islamic architectural decoration. It extended patterns, forms and designs into the fourth dimension. As the day progressed, the patterns changed, according to the angles of light and shade, like in some temporal kaleidoscope.

Decker lay the book down on the floor. He thought about waves of light and visualized Swenson sleeping only feet away, in his own bed, right through that wall, striped by the strident streetlight filtering in through his Venetian blinds – the color of her eyes, her lips, the soft shape of her breasts, the languorous curving of her hips, fecund as the plains of Iowa.

Before, when she had begged him for his help in finding Doris White, he would have given anything to have cried out, to have revealed the truth about the imminent disaster. The bomb. The Empire State. The Algerian mule – Ali Hammel! But he was under strict orders not to say or do anything that might cause a panic. It was bad enough Professor Hassan knew what he knew. "There's nothing you can do here, Emily," he'd said. "Frankly, I don't know why you came."

He could still smell her scent in the air. And it occurred to him that she was only partly right. He *had* joined the Bettendorf Police Force and the Bureau in some strange attempt to find a pattern, to solve his parents' death. They had been wrenched from him and – his entire life – he'd always blamed himself, at least subconsciously. After all, if it hadn't been for his track meet, they never would have been there on that road that night, in that precise place, as that drunk had swept across and crashed into their car. They would still be alive. And he never would have gone to live with Betsy in north Davenport, never slipped into that coma, never been crippled all those months, alone and helpless in that bed. None of it would have happened.

Perhaps that's why he relished this assignment in the field, the danger, the risk of death. The guilt lay like a stone against his heart. But he knew that it was more than that. He hadn't joined the Bureau just to decompose the randomness of his parent's death. He had joined to build a wall around his heart, to insulate himself through work – especially this work, with its odd hours and insufferable realities, its intrinsic secrecy.

The life of a special agent required a man to set himself apart from the world, from emotion, to seal the heart. On some level he had joined the Bureau so he would never have to feel again.

He reached up and turned off the light. A blanket of darkness settled on the room, enshrouding him. Once more he was invisible. He sighed, turned on his side. It had been fifteen years since the accident and, despite appearances, he was still crippled.

He still bore scars . . . and not just on his face. Perhaps he was too old to change. Perhaps he would never feel again.

As Decker fell asleep, he slipped into a dream. It began with Sampson dying once again, the white supremacist in Iowa. As Sampson choked, he turned into Bartolo, his ex-partner, spinning out of sight. Decker could see the faces of the Sloane twins, the two state troopers in their uniforms. Then, he saw the face of El Aqrab. He was looking up into the dome of a great mosque, like the dome of the Shaykh Lutfallah in Iran – the one on the postcard sent to Gallagher. Then it was Decker who was in the mosque.

He began to spin and fall against the geometric tiling until he was trapped within the pattern, half swallowed by the maelstrom. It was like quicksand, the net of a trapeze artist. And there was Betsy's face again, his mother's sister, above him as he lay there helplessly. There were her hands. Light waves reverberated. At first they shimmered through *muqarnas*, gold honeycombs of vaulting. And then the waves exploded into cavalcades of crimson, cobalt blue, light green and burnt sienna. The *muqarnas* turned to glass, became stained panels that seemed to oscillate and hum, that burned just like the fires of El Aqrab's calligraphy, the leaden muntins casting shadows on his face like scars.

Chapter 31
Wednesday, February 2 – 6:54 AM
New York City

Decker got up at his customary time to stretch, work out, and shower before heading off by subway to the office. He had left a note for Swenson on the dining table, letting her know that he had booked her on the ten o'clock shuttle back to Boston, with a connection to Hyannis near Woods Hole. He'd even reserved a car to take her from the airport to the Institute. It had cost him a small fortune but it had also given him great pleasure; more, frankly, than he'd anticipated, and this worried him.

Ever since falling asleep with Dr. Saad's book in his head, Decker felt he knew the answer. When he arrived at the office, he brought the fourth wallpaper image up on his computer screen, and printed it out. Next, he removed an X-acto knife from his top drawer. He stared down at the printout. Very carefully, with the very tip of the blade, he began to cut out each of the black spaces in the wavelike arabesque around the words: *on the ocean like mountains.* When he had finished, he folded the edges together and fastened them with tape so that it looked like a kind of lampshade. He plucked two straws out of his desk and taped them at right angles across the top of the structure for support. Where they intersected, he made a small incision. Then he picked up a pencil and stuck it in the little hole; he balanced the structure on the tip. Next, he took his desk lamp and focused it inside the shade. The object cast a shadow on the desk. Decker held his breath. He began to spin the structure counter-clockwise. At first, given the fluorescents overhead, he couldn't really see. The shadows were vague and indistinct. But then, as the wallpaper began to pick up speed, he saw the words begin to coalesce before him. Arabic text. No doubt about it. A full phrase, or a sentence. He began to translate the shadow script. Once again, it appeared to be a quote from the Qur'an.

That's when Warhaftig suddenly appeared.

Decker turned off his desk light and slipped the structure back into his drawer. "What's up?" he said, trying to look distracted. He spent a moment writing down the words he had translated.

Warhaftig dropped a stack of papers on his desk. "I believe you're looking for these," he answered flatly.

Decker scanned the documents. "What is all this?"

"What you asked for," said Warhaftig. "You were right. Apparently, there has indeed been increased traffic through the Canary Islands by Arab nationals over the last few months. More break-ins too. A construction camp was robbed of two cases of dynamite last week. And I got you that list of prisoners Miller had contact with while working at Ansar II in Gaza." Then he shook his head and said, "But, surely, John, after the confession of Al-Hakim in Egypt, after you found that picture of the Empire State Building behind the wallpaper, you gotta believe the target is New York."

Decker gawked at the documents on his desk. "I don't know what to say. Thanks, Otto."

Warhaftig smiled. "One hand washes the other."

"If you two lovebirds are finished," SAC Johnson cut in. He was approaching them down the aisle. "I want you and Warhaftig to help Novak coordinate the field teams, and to—"

"Sir, excuse me, sir," said Decker.

"What is it now?"

"I'd liked to chase down that Canary Island lead."

Johnson looked horrified. He sat back on Bartolo's desk. "You want to what?"

"I want to go to the Canary Islands."

Johnson laughed. "And I want to go to Jamaica. So what?"

"Seriously, sir. The bomb isn't going to New York. It's going to La Palma. It may already be there."

"Let me get this straight. You want to leave New York just as she faces her gravest threat? You've got to be kidding. We need you here."

"But, sir—"

"That's an order, Decker. You're staying." Then he softened and said, "Of course, if Warhaftig has a compulsion to share your theories with the CIA, he's perfectly free to do so." The SAC looked at Warhaftig and smiled. "That's the whole point of Homeland Security. Everybody working together."

Decker stood up. He gathered the papers Warhaftig had given him, as well as the translation of the shadow copy that he'd jotted down earlier. "Yes, sir. Is that all, sir?" he said.

"Yeah, that's all. Now get your skinny little ass out on the street, and get me some results." Johnson nodded toward Warhaftig. "You go with him," he said. Then he spun about and stormed off to his office.

Warhaftig looked thunderstruck. "Great," he said,

staggering to his feet. "One minute I'm the untouchable CIA guy. Then I do you a favor, and I'm on the boss's shit list. Good work," he added ruefully.

Decker smiled. "No one told you to hitch your wagon to this mule. Why's he got such a hard-on for me, anyway?"

"I don't know," Warhaftig said. "I guess he blames you for what happened to Bartolo. I don't," he added quickly. "Probably because you were forced down his throat. According to Williams, when you joined the team, Johnson couldn't promote someone else he'd promised to take care of."

"Figures," Decker said. "Come on, Pancho. Let's roll."

"Why do I have to be Pancho? Why can't I be Don Quixote? I've got the Roman nose, the distinguished features." Warhaftig displayed his profile.

"Perhaps I should call you *Pauncho*. Besides, you're shorter." Decker started toward the door.

"Well, this paunch has got to go. I'll meet you by the elevators."

When they had walked a couple of blocks from FBI headquarters, just as Warhaftig was lighting up a Camel, Decker got another message on his cell. It read: *Grand Central Terminal; Metro-North; New Haven Line; Gate 12*. He turned to Warhaftig and said, "I've got to make a stop. Grand Central Station."

They got into Warhaftig's car, a beefy Land Rover Discovery, and tore up the FDR to Twenty-third Street. Then they got off the highway and headed up Park Avenue. At Forty-second Street, Warhaftig suddenly swung right, cut down the ramp, and took a left cross-town. He skidded to a stop in front of Grand Central Station. Decker jumped out of the car and dodged into the terminal. He ran down the marble causeway, through another set of doors, and entered the massive central hall, with its majestic vaulted ceiling, pale green, outlined with constellations. The terminal was packed. He could hear footsteps echoing, reverberating through the hall. He noticed Orion, the hunter, far above, the bold sweep of his bow, like a great wave washing across the sky. He looked beyond the bold brass Information Booth. There it was. Gate twelve.

Decker dashed across the hall, weaving in and out of gray commuters. Hassan was standing by a shoeshine stand under a marble arch, reading a copy of *The New York Times*. As soon as

Decker approached, Hassan climbed up onto the stand. Decker slipped into the seat beside him. Hassan plucked at his trousers, lifting the hems up so that the polish wouldn't smudge his clothes. He continued to read his newspaper. Decker started to say something, but Hassan cut him off with a glance. "Sure, you can," the Professor said. His voice was a trifle loud. "How about Arts?" He handed Decker a section of the paper.

When they were both cocooned behind their newspapers, Decker looked over at Hassan and said, "I was just about to call you–"

"I found it," the Professor hissed.

"What?"

"The source of the third quote: *Death will overtake you*. It's from *An-Nisa*, *The Women*. The full quote is: *Wherever you are, death will overtake you, though you are in lofty towers, and if a benefit comes to them, they say: This is from Allah*. Let's face it, Agent Decker – there aren't too many towers loftier than the skyscrapers of New York."

Decker shook his head. "No, I don't believe it," he replied.

Hassan looked hurt. "I checked it several times and–"

"No, I don't mean you. I'm sure you're right. I just don't believe that whatever's planned for New York is anything more than a ruse, a non-nuclear event, a diversion from the bombing at 0. Why have a countdown if you're going to set the bomb off prematurely? It doesn't make sense. No. The fourth wallpaper. That's the key. The grand finale. The crescendo. I figured it out this morning."

"You did?"

"It's dimensional, Jusef."

"What do you mean, dimensional?"

"Picture a piece of graph paper," Decker said. "The first wallpaper featured a single line, both literally and geometrically. One axis – X. One dimension. The second featured two intersecting lines. Two axes – X and Y. Two dimensions, where the words *Well* and *Seven* coincided. The third, I'll bet, is three dimensional, either semantically or geometrically. Three axes – X, Y and Z. And the fourth, I know, is temporal. Three physical dimensions . . . over time. Just like light – the manner in which El Aqrab paints – and water – the Islamic purifying agent – contribute a dynamic quality to Islamic architectural decoration, extending forms and patterns into the fourth dimension. That's what it said in ben Saad's book, the one you loaned me."

"I was with you," the professor said, "until the fourth dimension."

Decker sighed. He looked over his newspaper and saw Warhaftig watching him from behind the Information Booth. Their eyes met and the CIA operative began to make his way across the terminal.

"I had a dream," Decker continued, "that opened up the patterns. I took an image of the fourth wallpaper, cut out the negative space, and shaped it into a kind of dome, just like the Shaykh Lutfallah Mosque in Isfahan."

"*Muqarnas.* Okay. I think I'm following you."

"I spun it counter-clockwise. It cast a shadow and all this text came spilling out: *His are the vessels with lofty sails raised high on the ocean like mountains. All that is on the earth will perish and only that will survive which is under the care of the Lord, Master of Glory and Honor.*"

Hassan dismounted the stand and paid.

"Please find me that reference, Jusef. Please. Before it's too late."

Chapter 32
Wednesday, February 2 – 8:26 AM
New York City

Decker and Warhaftig drove to Thirty-fourth Street and Fifth Avenue and found a parking spot immediately adjacent to the Empire State building. As soon as Decker stepped out of the Discovery, he felt his eyes drawn skyward by the famous New York landmark. The tower was hidden by clouds. Nothing symbolized the city more than this magnificent structure, not even the Statue of Liberty. The building had been immortalized through countless films and photographs – from *An Affair to Remember* to *Sleepless in Seattle*. Now that the World Trade Towers were gone, the Empire State building was once again the premier icon of the New York City skyline.

They approached the main entrance on Fifth, and Decker admired the huge stone eagles straddling the entrance; they were perched a good four stories up. *What have these limestone sentinels seen?* he thought, as he made his way into the lobby. He'd been to the Empire State before, of course, only a few weeks after moving to the city, and he had been amazed by the deco architecture. Now, as he and Warhaftig walked through the lobby toward the Information Desk, he was even more aware of the ornate carvings and relief work. The walls were lined with honey-colored marble. There was an etching of the building near the elevators that seemed to glow from some internal light.

Larry Dobson, Chief of ESB Security, was waiting patiently for them at the Information Desk. He was short and bald, with a wide pasty face and silver aviator glasses. "Agent Decker?" he inquired. He wore a red blazer with the logo of the landmark emblazoned on the front.

Decker and Warhaftig introduced themselves. They flashed their badges, shook Dobson's hand, and proceeded past the Information Desk toward the security checkpoint.

"We scan everybody," Dobson said. "Just like the airports." Dobson waved the agents through. Then they headed up the escalator toward the Observatory Elevators.

"There are only five entrances to the building: on Thirty-third Street, Fifth Avenue and Thirty-fourth," he said. "Most visitors use the main entrance on Fifth Avenue, or the one on Thirty-fourth Street for the handicapped. Everyone, and I mean everyone, has to pass through Security, even if they leave the building and return. That's SOP. Most people then either go to work, or to the Observatory Ticket Office on the Concourse Level. Once they buy their tickets, they take the escalators or an elevator to the second floor. It's only about 8:30, but there's already a line for the Observation Deck, even with this weather."

As they made their way along the corridor toward the Observatory Elevators, Decker noticed a series of modern paintings on the wall featuring the seven wonders of the ancient world. One in particular, the Lighthouse of Pharos, seemed to illuminate the corridor with brilliant hues of green and blue and gold. *El Aqrab would appreciate this color scheme*, thought Decker. Then he shuddered. *I'm starting to think like him. Good.*

"The construction of the Empire State Building began on January 22, 1930," Dobson continued, "and was completed in November, the same year. The framework rose at a rate of four-and-half stories per week." They stopped beside the Observatory Elevators. One of the cars arrived and a line of people began to gather near the entrance but Dobson waved them off. Then he stepped inside and motioned the agents to follow. "It took seven million man hours to complete," he added, "and came in under budget. Of course, the advent of the Great Depression halved the costs." He winked at Warhaftig. "The foundation runs fifty-five feet below the street. And it's 1,454 feet to the top of the lightning rod which, incidentally, suffers about one hundred lightning strikes per year."

The door closed and Decker could feel the car begin to rise.

"There are one hundred and three floors," continued Dobson, "with 1,860 individual steps from street level to the one hundred and second. If you don't believe me, you can count them." He laughed a thin laugh and Decker wondered how many times he'd used that same line during his career. "From the sixty-foot setback on the fifth floor, the building soars without a break up to the eighty-sixth floor."

"How many elevators?" asked Warhaftig.

"Seventy-three, including six freight elevators which run to the loading docks, operating at speeds from six hundred to fourteen hundred feet per minute. In fact, it's possible to ride from the lobby to the eightieth floor in under forty-five seconds."

"What about safety protocols?" said Decker. "You know, in case of fire or flood, or . . . "

" . . . or bomb threat," Dobson finished. He nodded gravely. "A special water system feeds four hundred fire hose connections throughout the building," he replied. "Plus, a state-of-the-art audio warning and strobe light guidance system was installed in '98. Of course, it depends on the fire. A lot of people ask me what would happen if a plane were flown into the building, like in the World Trade Towers. Few people remember that a plane actually struck the building in 1945 – a B-25, lost in the fog.

"Lieutenant Colonel William F. Smith, Jr., a decorated veteran of over one hundred combat missions, was piloting the bomber from his home in Bedford, Massachusetts to Newark, before returning to home base in South Dakota. The flight plan called for Smith to put down at LaGuardia. But Smith believed he could maneuver safely through the fog, so he asked for and received clearance to fly on to Newark airport. The last thing the air traffic controller told him was, 'At the present time, I can't see the top of the Empire State Building.'"

Dobson cackled grimly. "Apparently, neither could Smith. He thought he'd made it to the West Side when he came across the Chrysler Building. Had he kicked left, he would have been okay. Instead, he kicked the rudder right, and headed directly toward the ESB at two hundred miles per hour. Smith tried to climb, but it was already too late. At exactly 9:40 AM, the plane collided with the seventy-ninth floor.

"Luckily, the accident occurred on a Saturday, while only about fifteen hundred people were in the building, compared with the ten to fifteen thousand on an average weekday. And, luckily, the bomber was unarmed. Still, fourteen people died in the accident – eleven in the building, plus Colonel Smith and the other two occupants of the plane. An eighteen by twenty feet hole was gouged out by the bomber, and one of the plane's engines plowed through the building, emerged on the Thirty-third Street side, and crashed through the roof of a neighboring structure. The fuel tanks exploded instantaneously, shooting flames across the seventy-ninth floor in all directions. Those not severely injured had to walk down seventy flights through darkened stairwells. Many reported seeing flaming debris falling down elevator shafts.

"Unaware that the plane's other engine and part of its landing gear had dropped through one of the elevator shafts, rescue workers began to use the elevators to transport casualties to the street, one of whom was an operator named Betty Lou Oliver. She'd been blown out from behind her post up on the eightieth floor, and badly burned. After receiving first aid, they loaded her into another elevator so that they could transfer her to an ambulance below. But, as the doors closed, rescue workers heard what sounded like a gunshot. It was, in fact, the snapping of the elevator cables weakened by the crash.

Dobson grinned. "The car with Betty Lou inside – now at the seventy-fifth floor – plunged all the way to the sub-basement, a fall of over a thousand feet. Rescuers had to cut a hole in the car to get her out. Miraculously, despite a harrowing experience, Betty Lou survived. As the elevator fell, you see, the compensating cables, hanging from beneath the car, began to pile up in the pit and acted as a kind of spring, softening the impact. Also, the hatchway was high-pressure, with minimum clearance around the car. The air was literally compressed as the elevator fell, creating an air cushion in the lower portion of the shaft."

The elevator came to a sudden stop at the eightieth floor and Dobson, Decker and Warhaftig got out. "Do you always tell that story when you're in an elevator?" Warhaftig asked.

Dobson grinned. "Always."

They made their way across the hall to the Tower Elevator bank. "We're almost there," said Dobson. A few minutes later they ascended the last few stories to the Observation Deck.

It was a miserable day, wet and cloudy, yet the platform was crowded with tourists. Some gaped through telescopes, others took photographs. Decker was amazed. What could they see through all this cloud cover? Lovers hugged each other. A troupe of Boys Scouts crowded in one corner of the deck, preparing – the agents soon learned – for an urban sleep-away. Decker pulled Dobson to the side and asked him, "What about the Radiation Detection Units?"

"They're deployed throughout the building," he said. "Five teams on the ground floor, two on the second, and another four on various stories throughout the skyscraper."

"The cars look like toys," said Warhaftig. He was leaning up against the parapet. "Look, John, you can see them now. Right there. Through the fog."

"No, that's okay."

Decker stepped back. His face was pale and grim. The accident was but a few days distant. He could still see Bartolo wriggling in the air. "I think we've seen enough," he said, and started toward the door.

They headed back inside, into a vacant Tower Elevator and descended to the eightieth floor. As they waited for an Observatory Elevator to take them to street level, Decker noticed some construction going on at the far end of the corridor. "What's going on over there?" he asked.

Dobson shrugged. "Renovation. One of those Rock 'n Roll Planet restaurants," he said. "They snag the traffic on the way upstairs."

Decker began to wander slowly down the corridor. "When will it be finished?" he said.

"Another two weeks. Maybe more. You know contractors." Dobson laughed at some private joke. "They're still remodeling the kitchen." The elevator arrived. "It's here," he said.

"Just a minute," Decker said. He kept on walking down the hall. Most of the restaurant seemed to have been completed, but Decker noticed a gap in one wall, just inside the door. "What's that?" he asked.

The foreman, a huge man with a buzz cut and ham-like hands stepped forward. Dobson came over and introduced him. "This here is Sean O'Brien. Sean – Agents Decker and Warhaftig. Homeland Security." They shook hands.

"What's this gap here?" repeated Decker, pointing at the wall. He stepped across a plastic sheet laid out on the floor.

O'Brien shrugged. "Dunno," he said. He looked about and shouted to another man who was standing in the kitchen. "Hey, Keating. What's this here?" Then he turned toward Decker and said, "Keating's the restaurant manager. He'll know."

Keating said a few words to one of his assistants and eventually drew near. He was a tall man with a hatchet-thin face and wavy blond hair. "Jukebox," he said. "Should be here today, so they keep telling me. Special order."

"A jukebox?" Decker said.

"A Sound Leisure Beatles unit?" asked Warhaftig. "From the Yellow Submarine?"

"That's right. How did you know?"

Decker felt himself grow cold. "Thank you, Mr. Dobson," he said. He started toward the elevators with Warhaftig right behind. "You've been a great help. We enjoyed the tour. We'll see ourselves to the street." An elevator car arrived and the two agents stepped inside. The door closed noiselessly behind them.

"Downtown?" Warhaftig said.

The elevator gradually descended. Decker could feel it in his stomach. "East Village Jukebox," he replied. It was difficult to concentrate. He was trying to imagine what it would be like to plunge one thousand feet to the sub-basement.

Chapter 33
Wednesday, February 2 – 10:34 AM
New York City

Decker and Warhaftig tore back downtown to Park Avenue and Twelfth, just two blocks north of Grace Church. The owners of East Village Jukebox were surprised to see them again, but polite as ever. They handed over the work orders and pointed to a desk. It took Decker only a few minutes to find what they were looking for. There it was: One Sound Leisure Beatles Jukebox, Yellow Submarine. Warhaftig had been right. And it was coming in that very morning, by freighter, destined for the Rock 'n Roll Planet restaurant in the Empire State Building – eightieth floor.

Decker flipped open his cell phone and called the Coast Guard. They put him in touch immediately with the Liberian shipping line. The freighter had arrived, they confirmed. "She's unloading as we speak. The *Rêve de Chantal*. Just came in this morning from Marseilles."

Decker hung up and turned to Warhaftig "It's here," he said. "The Brooklyn shipyards." He punched the number for FBI headquarters and they patched him through to Jerry Johnson. Decker told him what they'd learned. The SAC was thrilled. This was the break that they'd been looking for, he said. The balloon was finally going up. He was deploying a Domestic Emergency Support Team (DEST) to the scene immediately. He told them to meet him at the Brooklyn shipyards, on the double. Then he hung up.

Decker and Warhaftig thanked the owners of the jukebox dealership and dashed outside. A meter maid was standing in front of Warhaftig's black Discovery. She was writing out a ticket. Warhaftig stripped it from her hand, tore it up, and leapt into the driver's seat. "I've always wanted to do that," he said as he gunned the engine. With almost exuberant joy, he shot down Broadway and skidded left on Tenth. Decker reached down for the cherry. He clipped it to the roof and a moment later the siren began to wail. Cars moved lethargically aside. Warhaftig cursed. "Move out of the fucking way," he screamed, at one point climbing the curb. Then they were on the West Side Highway, charging downtown toward the Brooklyn Bridge.

It took them over twenty agonizing minutes to make it into Brooklyn. But the traffic eased as soon as they crossed the bridge, and in another ten they were entering the shipyards. Decker could hear the cry of other sirens. A pair of blue-and-whites was already on the scene. They pulled up beside a rather nondescript brick warehouse – the office of the shipping line. Decker looked through the open doors of the warehouse and noticed Johnson and Kazinski running down the waterfront on the other side of the building. Williams and a host of uniformed policemen trailed them. A moment later, they had disappeared around the corner.

Decker and Warhaftig gave chase. They ran through the warehouse toward the river, then left along the waterfront. Williams and the policemen were disappearing into another warehouse down the dock. Decker and Warhaftig followed. As they neared the warehouse, an armored vehicle appeared just up the dock. It was the New York City Police Department's Bomb Squad. The car was followed by a dark gray van with tinted windows. NRC, most probably, thought Decker. Experts from the Office of Nuclear Security and Incident Response.

Decker and Warhaftig flashed their badges at a policeman by the warehouse armed with an M-16. He waved them through the entrance. The warehouse was crawling with police. Johnson was standing by a large metal container. The container was open. A large black man dressed in jeans and an orange goose-down parka was standing by the SAC. He was pointing at something inside.

Decker sprinted past a forklift, through the revolving crowd, and stopped just short of the cavernous entrance to the container. It was already half empty. Wooden crates were stacked up in the back, but the whole front end had been unloaded.

"It was here," said the large black man. He had the thick accent of the African.

For the first time, Johnson noticed Decker and Warhaftig. He nodded curtly at them and replied, "Just where exactly?"

"Right there," said the African, pointing at the bare container wall. "I tell you, that Ali Hammel was a crafty one. He told me he was smuggling opium, that he would offer me the hoof if I cooperated."

"Yeah, yeah, you said that," Johnson moaned. "The hoof." He began to stare at something over Decker's shoulder. "Not now," he added with frustration.

Decker followed his gaze. A pair of men dressed in white body suits with helmets approached the container carrying some kind of metal instruments. They looked like astronauts in their insulated gear. He couldn't even see their eyes through the reflective glass.

Johnson took the African by the arm. "Thank you, Mr. Marong. You've been very helpful." He began to usher him away. "Special Agent Warhaftig here will take down your particulars. I'm sure the Mayor's Office will want to contact you. I hear there's a sizeable reward, assuming we recover all the drugs."

The African perked up. Warhaftig snagged him by the elbow and began to lead him toward the warehouse door. "I knew he was a bad man from the very start," Momodou continued. "You could tell. You could just feel it."

The African hadn't even made it to the door when the men in the insulated body suits began to sweep the walls and floor of the container. Their instruments began to chirp, to click and stutter, and Decker knew immediately that they were carrying Geiger counters. One of the men began to nod. "It's hot," his helmet crackled. His voice sounded metallic, as if he were a robot, or some alien creature from another world. The entire landscape seemed surreal to Decker, as though he were on some movie set instead of at the Brooklyn docks, and he began to move away, backing up at first, and then turned to follow Warhaftig. The African was staring back at the container. He was following the actions of the two men wearing body suits.

"What are they doing?" he asked Decker.

"Checking for drugs," Warhaftig said. He pushed the African out the door.

Decker swept in from behind. The dock was crowded now with other agents and policemen. It was a sea of blue. He looked up beyond the lilting freighters. Despite the clouds, the New York skyline shimmered in the distance, just across the Hudson River. The buildings glimmered as if glazed with ice. To the north, he saw the Empire State Building. It rose above the rest, a marvelous apparition, iconic and yet real, a symbol of the pulsing hearts of millions of New Yorkers. Decker turned away and wondered, even as he drowned the thought, if this would be the last time he would see it.

Chapter 34
Wednesday, February 2 – 12:14 PM
New York City

As soon as Warhaftig had unburdened himself of the Gambian, he and Decker headed back across the Brooklyn Bridge into Manhattan. Traffic had eased slightly by this time. They were more than halfway across the bridge when Decker's phone began to vibrate in his pocket. He plucked it out. It was Hassan. The Professor started to say something but the signal kept breaking up, and Decker had a hard time hearing him. He was obviously excited.

"I thought you said we shouldn't use the phone," said Decker. "It's not secure. What? What did you say?" He could barely make him out when, suddenly, the signal cleared.

"Forget about that. There's no time," Hassan said. "I've identified the quote from the fourth wallpaper. It's from *Al-Rahman*. It says, 'He has put the two oceans in motion; they will meet. Just now there is a barrier between them; they cannot encourage one upon the other. Pearls and coral are taken out of both. His are the vessels with lofty sails raised high on the ocean like mountains. All that is on the earth will perish and only that will survive which is under the care of the Lord, Master of Glory and Honor . . . You will be afflicted with smokeless fire, and with smoke without flame, and you will not be able to help yourselves. When the heaven is rent asunder, and assumes a rosy hue like red leather . . . When the earth is shaken violently, and the mountains are crumbled into dust and become like motes floating in the air.'"

Decker felt cold fingers grab his balls. He looked up at the Empire State Building. The top was still hidden by clouds. "What do you think it means, Jusef?" he asked, almost afraid to know the answer.

Hassan said, "It's another prophecy, like the one from *Al-Takwir*, the first wallpaper you showed me. And just like in that Sura, some people say the 'vessels with lofty sails raised high' refer to future means of transportation, and the 'oceans meeting' to canals. You know: the Suez and the Panama. That sort of thing. The darker passages refer to Armageddon, the Qur'anic equivalent of the Apocrypha. The *Kahf* Sura describes it thus: 'When that day comes We shall let some of them surge against the others like waves of the ocean, and the trumpet will be blown, and We shall gather them all together. On that day We shall present hell, face to face, to the disbelievers whose eyes were veiled against My Reminder.' There's a similar reference in the *Ta Ha*. 'On that day We shall gather the sinful ones together, blue-eyed. They will commiserate with each other in low tones.' That's it. John? John, are you there?"

"Yeah, I'm here," said Decker. "Look, I'll have to call you later. And Jusef?"

"What?"

"If I were you, I'd grab your wife and kids and take a trip somewhere. Today. Somewhere out west. Just in case." He hung up and swiveled toward Warhaftig. "It's not here," he said. "Pull over."

Warhaftig looked horrified. "Excuse me?"

"I said pull over, dammit!"

They had just descended the ramp into Manhattan. Warhaftig swung over to the side of the road and parked. "What's going on?" he asked.

Decker informed him what Hassan had told him.

"I don't get it," said Warhaftig

"What do you mean, you don't get it? *The earth will shake and the mountains will crumble into dust, and become like motes floating in the air . . . The heavens will assume a rosy hue.* That's the bomb and subsequent eruption, the volcanic ash. *Lofty sails on the ocean like mountains.* The mega-tsunami. *All will perish . . . And the two oceans will meet.* What do you think will happen when that mega-tsunami hits the Panama Canal? Those dykes and locks won't mean a thing. The Atlantic and Pacific will unite."

"You don't seriously believe some thousand-year-old Qur'anic prophecy is actually going to come true?"

"Get out," said Decker.

"What?"

"I said, get out." Decker leaned across and opened the driver's side door. "Now!"

"What are you talking about? We've got to go to the Empire State."

"I don't have time to argue with you," Decker said. "Look, this is my decision. Not yours. I'm going to the airport."

"The airport! Are you nuts? You saw what happened at the dock. That jukebox is here, somewhere in the city, probably on its way to the ESB as we speak. And it's radioactive."

"I don't care," Decker said. "I'm telling you. It's just another ruse. Just like those bombs in Israel. It's El Aqrab's way of throwing us off the scent. I know it now. I'm sure."

"Just because of that quote?" said Warhaftig "It could mean anything. Those 'lofty sails' could be Manhattan skyscrapers, for all you know. And if the bomb is here, like everyone believes – everyone except you, that is – won't the collapse of all these buildings," he said, pointing at the city, "won't the explosion itself cause a tsunami?"

They continued to argue when Decker's phone began to vibrate once again. It was Jerry Johnson. The SAC was sheepish but admitted that the *Rêve de Chantal* had passed through the Canary Islands.

"That's where Hammel picked up the jukebox," Johnson said. "Only three ships were docked in Arrecife at the same time: one, en route from New York to Lisbon; the *Rêve de Chantal*, from Marseilles to New York; and one from Algiers, the *El Affroun*, en route through the Canary and Cape Verde Islands, and eventually on to Rio in Brazil. The third mule – Hammel – was Algerian. He had himself transferred to the Liberian ship in Arrecife following an injury. We're trying to pick up the Algerian captain now, but we feel confident that Arrecife is where the switch was made. You were right to call out the cavalry, Decker. I guess I owe you an apology."

"No you don't," said Decker with frustration. "I was wrong. This has all been another diversion. The bomb's in La Palma. In the Canaries, sir. I know it. I deciphered the last wallpaper. I know what it means. It's another quote from the Qur'an. 'He has put the two oceans in motion. They shall meet—'"

"Not that again," said Johnson, interrupting him. "Jesus, you're never satisfied. Look, I want you and Warhaftig back at the Empire State Building immediately, is that understood? That container you identified was hot. The NRC confirmed it. The signature was HEU, do you hear me? It was HEU, identical to the material stolen in Kazakhstan. Decker, can you hear me? Answer me, for Christ's sake."

Decker tapped the cell phone with his fingers. "Hello," he said. "Hello? You're breaking up, sir. The signal. Hello?" Then he hung up. Decker turned and looked at Warhaftig. He was shaking his head.

"I hope you know what you're doing, John. Disobeying a direct order from the SAC . . . "

"What order? I didn't hear any order. The signal dropped."

Warhaftig smiled. He unclipped his seatbelt and got out of

the car. Then he leaned back through the open door and said, "You're taking an awfully big risk, John, just on a hunch. There were three mules. Johnson's right. And two were neutralized. That leaves Hammel."

Decker slid into the driver's seat. "That's not the way I figure it. Three mules, perhaps. But El Aqrab himself makes four. Look, you guys can handle this," he said. "If I'm wrong, my absence won't be missed. But if I'm right . . . " He paused and slipped the Land Rover into gear.

Warhaftig frowned. "Be gentle with my car," he said. Then he patted Decker on the back and said, "I hope your hunch pays off, John. Or don't bother coming home."

As soon as he hit the FDR, Decker put in a call to Swenson. Her cell phone rang a good ten times before she finally picked up. "Hey, Emily," he said. "How was your flight?" He tried to sound pacific, light. He tried to sound politely interested.

"I wouldn't know," she said. "I didn't go."

"What! Why not? I thought I made it clear that—"

"I've booked myself on American Airlines flight 933 to Madrid via Miami, with a connecting flight to Santa Cruz. I'm going to the Canaries, Agent Decker. I'm going to find Dr. White. And don't try and stop me."

Decker laughed. "I'm sure I couldn't, even if I wanted to. I'm going with you."

"You're what? Do you really mean that, John?"

"What time is the flight?"

"Ten before two."

"I can just make it," he said, glancing at his watch. He had about an hour and a half. "Buy a ticket for me. I'll be there as soon as I can."

As he hung up, Decker noticed a traffic jam coalescing up ahead. One car was actually backing up along the highway, trying to get off at the previous exit. Decker craned his neck out the window. It was an accident. He could see a clot of cars a few hundred yards ahead of him and to the left. It looked like someone had plowed into the center rail. The vehicle – a metallic green Volkswagen bug – was balanced on the rail, tipped over on its back like some gigantic insect. Decker cursed. He hit the breaks. As he hiccupped through the traffic, he couldn't help rubbernecking at the twisted wreckage, the broken glass, at the rear doors of the ambulance. And suddenly he thought, *What if I'm wrong? What if I have become too close? What if Johnson is right and I'm letting my feelings for Emily cloud my judgment?*

A figure covered with a sheet was being lifted up into the ambulance. A siren wailed like a lovesick trumpet and he remembered the Qur'anic quote which Jusef had just told him: *When that day comes We shall let some of them surge against the others like waves of the ocean, and the trumpet will be blown.* He shuddered and kept driving.

Chapter 35
Wednesday, February 2 – 12:15 PM
New York City

The Gambian, Momodou Marong, stood on the dock, pointing at the freighter at his side, trying to look authoritative and calm. He was wearing a pair of jeans and his orange goose-down jacket. New York Harbor stretched behind him.

"That's it," said WKXY-TV reporter Seamus Gallagher. "Now, turn this way. No, don't smile, God dammit, Momodou. I want you to look serious. Worried. Fearful, even. Yeah, that's better."

Gallagher turned and looked back at his cameraman. "OK?" he said.

The cameraman, a slouching bear of a man with a great brown beard, gave him a thumbs-up and kept filming.

Gallagher was dressed in a black-and-white Armani herringbone, an off-white Hugo Boss dress shirt, and a golden Hermes tie. He had agonized over the outfit for twenty minutes. He took a deep breath and looked into the camera. "I'm standing beside Momodou Marong, a Gambian able-bodied seaman from the freighter, *Rêve de Chantal,* currently docked at the Brooklyn shipyards. Approximately an hour ago, Mr. Marong assisted federal agents in their search of a container unloaded from the Liberian-registered freighter earlier this morning. Tell us, in your own words, Mr. Marong, exactly what you saw."

The Gambian cleared his throat. His eyes bulged in his head and he said, "The police and FBI came to the warehouse." He pointed vaguely over his shoulder. "They looked inside the container that I showed them, the one we'd unloaded this morning. But the crate was gone. Then these astronauts came in."

"You mean federal agents dressed in protective clothing."

"Yes. They told me they were looking for drugs." Momodou laughed. "I may be a Gambian. I am proud of that. I may not be well-educated, but I am not a fool. The men in the white suits," he said. "They were carrying Geiger counters. I have seen them before, in the mines of Gambia. They were looking for something radioactive. I heard the boxes in their hands. They were clicking. And then one said, 'It's hot.'" He paused and looked into the camera. He smiled.

"Did they find what they were looking for?" asked Gallagher.

"No, it was gone. It was there before; I saw it. But now the crate is gone."

"You mean it's been unloaded? Right here? In New York City?"

"Yes."

Gallagher turned and looked back at the camera. "And what," he continued, "do you think that they were searching for? If it wasn't drugs."

The Gambian's head bobbed side to side. And then he said, "A bomb."

The camera focused in on Gallagher. He waited a few more seconds. Then he added, "A radioactive bomb." He shook his head. "This reporter has tried to obtain confirmation from the FBI but they refuse to comment. One policeman involved in the raid insisted that this was just a routine drug bust. But, if that's the case, where was the DEA? Why was the New York City Police Department's Bomb Squad here? And why technicians from the Office of Nuclear Security and Incident Response? What kinds of drugs are radioactive?

"It is well-documented that Homeland Security inspects less than five percent of all the cargo containers shipped into this country. And those are simply X-rayed, scanned to identify 'suspicious-looking' cargo. Only a fraction of that five percent is manually inspected." He shook his head once more.

"A few days ago, I reported that a Weapon of Mass Destruction might be on its way to New York City, presumably transported here at the behest of Islamist terrorist El Aqrab. Now, an anonymous source in Washington has just confirmed my gravest fears: The FBI believes a thermonuclear device has indeed been shipped to New York City, unloaded here, right here," he pointed at the dock, "in Brooklyn."

The camera pulled back, taking in the cityscape across the Hudson River.

"In the shadow of the shadows of the former World Trade Towers."

Momodou Marong climbed up the gangway. He felt deflated. The adrenaline of being on TV had come and gone. Now he was spent. Exhausted. When he reached the main deck of the freighter, he stopped and watched the TV crew climb back into the WKXY-TV van crowned with a white extendable transmitter. In truth, the Gambian had thought the Algerian was really smuggling opium or heroin, and he had hungered for a piece. Indeed, he had resolved to blackmail the Algerian. But there was something about Hammel that had frightened Momodou, and he had let it go. At least until the FBI came calling. Then he had been only too eager to show them where the container with the jukebox was – empty, of course. But to the press, to that pygmy-like reporter Seamus Gallagher, whom he had called at the request of Captain Bréton, Momodou had known that there was something wrong with the Algerian from the very start.

The Gambian walked along the port side of the freighter. He gazed astern, across the river at the cloud-capped towers of the city. In two or three hours, the *Rêve de Chantal* would put to sea again. In a day or so, he'd be scraping and painting in the glaring Caribbean sun, on his way to Caracas in Venezuela. He scratched at the cut on his neck. He smiled and closed his eyes. He couldn't wait. He had a lot of friends in Venezuela. They didn't call it the "love run" for nothing.

* * *

Gallagher finished editing the story back at WKXY-TV. *"Big Apple Atom Bomb!"* he called it. Following a quick review by Legal under producer Ira Minsky's care, the story was aired immediately, interrupting the regularly scheduled soap. It had the wrapper of a public service announcement. As soon as it had aired, Gallagher buttonholed Minsky in the hallway.

"I need a few days off," he said.

Minsky looked shocked. "What?" He couldn't believe his ears. "Are you serious?"

Gallagher nodded. "Dead serious."

"But you just broke the story. This is the opportunity of a lifetime, Seamus. It's got Emmy written all over it. You can't leave now."

"I'm leaving, Ira."

"Now wait a minute," Minsky said, puffing on his inhaler. "There may or may not be a nuclear bomb hidden somewhere in Manhattan. I need you to stay on top of things until it's found. If it exists. It's *your* story. You can't leave now. It would be totally irresponsible." He began to pant.

"I'm sorry, Ira. But I've made up my mind. What if I'm arrested?"

"We're protected by the First Amendment, Seamus. You heard Liebowitz in Legal. You're protected. This isn't someone yelling 'fire' in a cinema when there isn't one. We have real evidence that a device loaded with nuclear material was brought in here by ship."

The reporter refused to listen. He shook his head and looked away and Minsky realized that Gallagher was genuinely terrified – in all probability, of being right. Already, dozens of employees had fled the station. Soon the entire city would know. He begged Gallagher to stay, offering money, a promotion, anything, but the reporter wouldn't budge.

"Look, Ira. I need a break," Gallagher said. "I've been working like a fucking coolie on this thing. I'm going to Bermuda for a little golf and R and R. Two or three days." He shook his head. "I've had enough." Then he turned and simply walked away.

Chapter 36
Wednesday, February 2 – 11:06 PM
New York City

A pall hung over the city, muffled by snow. The wind carried no noise. Only the odd piece of garbage or newspaper billowed down the street. It was not even midnight and yet the city was practically deserted. Whoever could leave – by car, or bus, by train or plane, or on foot – had already done so. Only the occasional siren split the night, the frantic movement of emergency vehicles. Only the homeless lingered. And then an ambulance from the Cabrini Medical Center tore up the Avenue of the Americas.

Within the darkened interior, Ali Hammel leaned on the steering wheel and counted off the streets. They were almost at Twenty-ninth. Time to get ready. He barked a command in Arabic. Salim Moussa, Mohammed Qashir, bin Basra and Ali Singh began to assemble their gear.

The loading dock was on the south side of Thirty-fourth Street, near Fifth Avenue. As soon as the ambulance pulled over, Singh jumped out and spray-painted the security camera on the right side of the loading dock. He was dressed in a jet-black jogging suit and ski mask. He moved more like a shadow than a man, even through streetlights, almost unseen. He knelt down and pulled a bolt cutter from his bag. There was a loud *snap* as the heavy lock on the loading dock door fell apart. He inserted a key in the wall, turned it, and the large gray metal shutter started to rise.

Singh slithered through the darkness to another camera winking on the wall. He spray-painted the lens and ran back to the ambulance. He knocked on the rear door. It burst open, revealing Salim Moussa, bin Basra and Mohammed Qashir. They were all wearing ski masks on their heads like watch caps. They looked around the street, the loading dock, pulled the ski masks down across their faces, and followed Singh into the ill-lit loading bay. Ali Hammel remained sitting in the driver's seat, nursing his knee.

The men began to unload the jukebox from the ambulance. It was visible but fixed inside a reinforced wooden frame, lying on a gurney. With care they rolled it out across the rear lip of the ambulance and down onto the loading dock. They pushed it as gently as a pram across the bay.

Bin Basra was waiting at the elevator. He slipped a master key into the control box and unlocked the elevator door. He had already disabled the camera inside and reattached it to a digital video player the size of a large matchbox. Now, all that the security guards upstairs would see would be an endless loop of inactivity. They nudged the jukebox through the elevator door. They checked and re-checked their 9 mm Uzi fully automatic machine pistols. Each weapon shot thirty rounds in seconds. They checked their MIL-C-45010A high velocity plastic explosive, wrapped up in blocks, covered with honey-colored wax paper. It still looked somewhat powdery, but with a little kneading would plasticise and mould itself to any shape. And at only $20 a kilo, it had been the cheapest of their assets to procure. They checked their extra clips, their knives, their masks again, and closed the elevator door.

The elevator rose, ascending slowly through the narrow shaft. It seemed to take forever. The men stood absolutely still. There was no room for words inside the cab. The air would not accommodate them. The jukebox – with its dozens of CDs, hundreds of songs and thousands of notes and lyrics – sat strangely silent on the gurney. The elevator rose and rose, marking the numbers off. They winked. It was unbearably cold. They flashed. The reverse countdown decomposed. The elevator slowed. It hesitated, then stopped at the eightieth floor. The door retracted with a groan. The corridor was black.

Mohammed Qashir and Ali Singh began to push the gurney from the elevator. The first two wheels slipped with a crisp *click* over the crack, and then they heard a hissing sound and something fell onto the floor, right at their feet.

It started to shake and give off smoke. A canister. It hissed and slithered like a startled snake. Ali Singh lifted his weapon and sprayed the corridor with gunfire.

He was hit directly in the forehead. He fell but his Uzi kept on firing. Bullets lanced the walls and ceiling. Plastic shattered. Metal shrieked. Bin Basra stumbled to the floor. Mohammed Qashir coughed and sputtered as smoke began to fill the elevator. A bullet pierced his throat, and he went down. Salim Moussa tried to hide behind the jukebox. He screamed and raised his weapon and another soundless shot abandoned a small hole in his left hand, a drop of blood, and then the eyeholes of his mask seemed to explode, to pop as a bullet pierced his face, right through one temple and out the other, and he unrolled across the floor. His body shook. The elevator door began to close, then bounced against his leg. It opened and closed. It opened and closed.

Light beams transfixed the darkness. Men with night vision goggles, gas masks, body armor and small-caliber handguns appeared like cyborgs out of the dark. They approached the elevator cautiously, their weapons trained upon the lifeless occupants within. Blood started pooling, massing up, until it drained into the crack between the elevator and the floor, within the doorframe, and dribbled down the elevator shaft.

SAC Johnson appeared in a nimbus of white light. He was holding a gas mask over his face. He looked down at the bodies. Then he turned and motioned, seemingly toward nothing, at the shadows. The counter-terrorist squad checked the bodies for signs of life and pushed them roughly to the side. Then, with agonizing care, they rolled the gurney out into the hall. A figure appeared out of the shadows, wearing a reinforced body suit, breastplate and mask. The soldiers carefully removed the frame from around the jukebox. The man in the body suit knelt down, and pushed a clip, and opened the front side panel of the jukebox containing a clear plastic cylinder. The cylinder slipped out. He turned on a tiny flashlight and looked inside. Something silver twinkled back. He reached into the opening and removed an aluminum attaché case. He set it gently on the ground, studying the latches carefully. In one smooth movement, he released them and lifted the lid.

The device lay still within. It was lifeless, dead. Turned off. Or, not yet on. The man in the mask moved his gloved hand across the bulging ball of steel, and pressed a button in the console. The fuel case popped up with a click. Everyone in the corridor seemed to take a breath at once. He eased the chamber open carefully. Slowly. A small wrist Geiger counter chattered like frigid teeth. The soldiers and agents unconsciously stepped back. Some moved intentionally away.

The housing was empty. Not a trace of fuel. They were reading residual radioactivity.

Warhaftig hovered next to Jerry Johnson. He looked down at the jukebox, then back up at Johnson once again. The SAC felt his eyes burn a hole in the side of his neck. Somebody flipped a switch and the lights burst on. "Go on, say it," Johnson spat.

"Say what, sir?"

Johnson raised his shirt cuff to his mouth. "Eighty is secure," he said. "Close in on the vehicle. I repeat. Close in." Then he stepped into the elevator, adding, "Well, come on. Doesn't the Agency want to interface?"

Warhaftig followed the SAC into the elevator. He found it

difficult to keep from laughing.

As soon as they got downstairs, they slipped through an emergency exit and hovered in the shadows only a dozen yards away from the loading dock. The ambulance was still parked in front. The engine was still running, sending a white cloud of exhaust aloft into the snow-filled air.

Johnson watched as a homeless man, dressed in a dirty black jacket and torn blue jeans, staggered up the street. He approached the loading zone casually, oblivious. The vehicle's engine roared as Hammel gunned the accelerator. But the ambulance didn't move. It was in neutral still. And the stranger didn't turn. He continued to saunter over, not even looking at the ambulance. He crossed directly in front, and swung his arms, and pointed his weapon at the windshield, directly at Hammel. "Raise your hands," he screamed. "Now!"

Hammel ducked, the agent fired, and the ambulance jumped forward, pitching the man high into the air like a matador on the horns of a bull. A moment later the agent fell and struck the pavement with a nauseating *crack*, and rolled into the street. The ambulance banked right, then left, almost as if the driver were aiming at the figure rolling in the road. The vehicle bumped over him. The body wriggled for a moment, strangely inverted, and grew still. The ambulance roared on.

Johnson discharged his weapon but it appeared to have no effect. The vehicle rattled through a phalanx of policemen, by special agents, by counter terrorist SWAT teams and marksmen on the roof. Somehow, miraculously, despite the shower of lead, Hammel remained unscathed. The cab seemed reinforced. The ambulance burned west on Thirty-fourth, as a pair of police cars closed the block. They came together, nose to nose, but Ali Hammel never slowed. He charged right through the narrow gap. There was a loud crash as he struck the cars, punched them aside, and kept on going.

Johnson ran to his car with Warhaftig close behind. He started her up. With a squeal, the car peeled out into the street . . . followed by a second, a third, and then a fourth police car. Sirens wailed. Lights flashed. Within minutes, the Cabrini ambulance had made it to the West Side Highway. There was no traffic and Hammel had little trouble swinging north. The police cars hurtled close behind, their cherries flashing – bright crimson and turquoise bubbles floating through the falling snow. Their sirens howled against the night. One minute the ambulance was charging up the highway, the next it swerved against the steel divider, showering sparks. A helicopter dropped out of the sky. It struck the ambulance. Hammel continued to swerve and weave along the highway, trying to avoid the helicopter skids. Suddenly, a blazing spotlight illuminated the ambulance from above. "Pull over," a voice boomed through a loudspeaker. "Pull over now!"

Without warning, Hammel jammed on the breaks, and the ambulance slalomed on the snow. The helicopter over-shot the road. It banked and climbed. It looped around. The police cars skidded in behind. One crashed into the rear right fender of the ambulance. The ambulance was blasted up the road. It turned. It spun about. It bounced against the outer guardrail and somehow ended facing uptown once again.

The rear wheels screamed. The ambulance exploded forward, barely avoiding SAC Johnson's car, barely avoiding the guardrail as it shimmied to the left on Forty-sixth Street, then off the West Side Highway. It was heading for The Intrepid – Sea, Air and Space Museum.

The ambulance crashed through the metal gate. Sparks flew up all around it like a fireworks display. The massive light gray flank of the great aircraft carrier was suddenly illuminated. The ambulance kept going. A piece of the fencing was stuck under the axel. The ambulance kept showering sparks the entire length of the museum pier, as it paralleled the aircraft carrier, from prow to stern, as it kept churning up the night, with Hammel still at the wheel, still clutching it with all his might, until it ruptured through the wooden fence at the far end of the pier, and rose into the snowy air, and flew above the dark and inky waters of the Hudson River. It seemed to hang against the cloudy sky, against the bright face of New Jersey – with its train-set-sized high-rises – seemed to hover for a moment longer, before plunging with a mighty crash into the waves.

Police cars poured through the opening in the fence. Their engines panted in the frigid air, swept in off the river. Steam rose, illuminated by bright blues and vibrant reds. The sirens faded. The police cars came to a stop at the very lip of the pier, their headlights lancing at the waves. Agents and policemen leapt out of their vehicles, amongst them Johnson and Warhaftig. They stepped up to the water's edge. They looked out as the ambulance tipped over onto its side, illuminated by the helicopter spotlight. In seconds it had sailed a good ten yards downstream, then twenty. Then it began to slide, to slip under the water, and was gone.

Nothing remained. No sign. No marker, even. The waves rolled back upon themselves, covered in snow, erasing everything.

Chapter 37
Thursday, February 3 – 2:16 AM
Halfway across the Atlantic

The airplane shimmied through the sky, buffeted by winds. The flight attendants were having a hard time serving drinks, including the sour old crone who had spilled half a virgin Bloody Mary over Decker's shirt. Heads lolled from side to side, against innumerable headrests bobbing all about them. Decker ate another nut. And then another. He relocated his legs – once again. He stared at Emily beside him. Her eyes were closed. She was still awake; he could tell. But she was trying to sleep. *I should do the same*, he thought, but he knew it was impossible. Decker went back to reading the book by Jamal ben Saad about Islamic architecture and design. That's when he felt a jolt of recollection, like an electric current, hit him. He reached into his jacket pocket. He was still carrying that list of prisoners Warhaftig had given him, the men with whom Miller had associated back at Ansar II in Gaza. He began to scan the pages. It took him only a few seconds to confirm Warhaftig's story: El Aqrab's real name – Mohammed Hussein – wasn't on the list. But something else had caught his eye. He flipped back through the pages. There. On page sixteen. At the very bottom. The name Jamal ben Saad. He'd been arrested once, it seemed. He'd spent three days in Ansar II directly under Miller's supervision. Three days in jail was like a lifetime to some men.

Decker checked the book on Islamic architecture. The biography of the author revealed Jamal ben Saad had died in 1982, during the Israeli invasion of Lebanon – the same year El Aqrab had gone to Kazakhstan for the first time. Decker laid the photographs of El Aqrab and Jamal ben Saad beside each other on his tray. They could be brothers, he thought. Isn't that what Emily had said? He looked up and noticed her staring at the photographs. Then she glanced over at him, and caught herself, and blushed.

"Well, they do look alike," she insisted with a shrug.

"More than alike," he answered. "I agree with you. I think they're the same man."

"You do? Really? Why?"

"Well, look at the eyes. The eyes first. Then the mouth."

"No! I mean, what made you change your mind?"

Decker caught himself. "The dates are compatible," he said. "The men look strangely alike. They both share an intimate knowledge of Islamic architecture and design. It all seems too much of a coincidence. It isn't . . . natural." But Swenson was right, he thought. He didn't have anything concrete to hold onto. It was all circumstantial evidence. It was he who was acting unnaturally.

Without warning, the air phone in the seat before him started ringing. Decker stared at it, wondering if he had heard correctly. He had never heard an air phone ring before. He didn't know they did that. Then it rang again. They were about halfway through the flight and most of the passengers were asleep. The gentleman across the aisle from Swenson began to stare at him, then at the phone. Soon others turned and looked his way. Decker reached out and picked up the phone. He put it to his ear.

"You shouldn't have run," a voice said. It was Warhaftig. "I'm not your enemy," he continued.

"You haven't exactly been my friend," said Decker, staring back at his nosy neighbors. They turned away.

"Sometimes, you're better off not knowing things. For your own good, John."

"Is that the paternal crap they're teaching at Langley these days?"

"You were right, John. The bomb was a dud, another diversion, just like you predicted. New York is safe."

"All that means is that we're facing a bigger problem. If El Aqrab sets off that mega-tsunami, it won't just be New York in trouble; it'll be the whole damned world. Every financial system will go down – some temporarily, some permanently crippled. All industry on the eastern seaboard – gone. All the intellectual capital in New York, in Boston, Philly and D.C. – gone, washed literally away. Our countries oldest and most treasured universities. All of those global corporate headquarters in New York. The United Nations. Media networks. Museums and libraries too. All gone. Wiped out. Destroyed."

"Look, John," said Warhaftig. "We're all working toward the same goal, aren't we? We want to stop that bomb." He sighed. "So why operate independently, at odds? I understand why you may not trust me, but I'm asking you to anyway. Take me on faith, John. Here, let me give you something. A token. Some beads. A peace offering."

"I'm listening."

"Gulzhan Baqrah – the guy whom El Aqrab trained with in Kazakhstan – had a young lieutenant named Uhud, wanted by the Israelis in connection with several suicide bombings in the West Bank. He was also suspected of executing a half dozen bombings in

Iraq, primarily against Iraqi security forces using IEDs at M and Ms. You know: Mosques and markets. Police recruiting stations. That sort of thing."

"And?"

"According to Egyptian Intelligence, Uhud was killed in the raid that Baqrah mounted when he stole the HEU. Seems he got a little greedy."

"How so?"

"Well, after you told me about your mega-tsunami theory, I did some checking. According to Interpol, a number of bank accounts controlled by Uhud were recently used to initiate some significant stock transactions in the U.S., so-called 'Puts' on a whole series of companies. He shorted them. They only have one thing in common. I ran it through the Company computers."

"Don't tell me," Decker said. "They're all either in, or based on the East Coast."

"Bingo," said Warhaftig. "You *are* a fast study."

Decker looked at the list of prisoners from Ansar II on his tray. "Do me a favor," he said.

"What's that?"

"Run a background check on someone for me."

"Who?"

"He was on that list of prisoners you gave me. His name is Jamal ben Saad. He was some sort of adjunct professor at the Arab University in Beirut in the early '80s, an expert on Islamic architecture and design. Find out whatever you can and fax it to me at Dr. White's hotel on La Palma. It's called the Parador, in Santa Cruz. I want to know if Jamal ben Saad and El Aqrab knew each other."

"El Aqrab and his father did work for a guy named Hanid ben Saad, some wealthy real estate developer. Of course, ben Saad may be a common name. Is it important?" Warhaftig asked.

"It may be."

"You got it. By the way," Warhaftig continued, "you won't be alone on this. I sent a couple of agents along to La Palma two days ago: Nick Thompson and Colin Strand."

Decker smiled. "Otto, you surprise me," he said. "I thought you didn't have any faith."

"Never hurts to hedge your bets," Warhaftig answered blithely. "Look, I've gotta go. My station chief put in a call to Assistant Director Gammon. That may be him right now, on the other line. Director Kennick has a meeting scheduled with the

President tomorrow morning. I wish it could be earlier but, frankly, no one believes you, John."

"If the bomb's not in New York or Israel, where do they think it is? What about the missing HEU?"

"The consensus is that Gulzhan Baqrah sold it. He's a mercenary, after all. Most people think it's in Iran. The Iranians have been trying to get their hands on a nuke for years. Or in Iraq, God help us. Or hidden in some cave deep in Afghanistan." He sighed. "I mean, this whole volcano thing is a little crazy. The President's science advisors don't believe a tsunami can be manufactured. They conferred with some famous oceanographer named Dubinsky. A real star. Anyway, Dubinsky said it couldn't be done."

"Mega-tsunami," Decker said. "And I wouldn't necessarily believe what E.J. Dubinsky says. She and Emily know each other. They have a history."

"Regardless, John. Everyone thinks the crisis is over, at least temporarily. All three of El Aqrab's mules are dead. And we're getting intelligence reports that El Aqrab himself is still in Lebanon."

"He's not," said Decker. "He's on La Palma. I know he is."

"You may be right. And if you are, Thompson and Strand will find him."

Decker shook his head. "Will the Director tell the President about my theory?"

"I think he will. With any luck, we'll get permission to mobilize a team of Rangers. Be on La Palma by sunset, maybe earlier. I'm sorry, John. I wish I had better news for you."

"It's not your fault."

"Look, I've got to go. Be careful."

"Thanks, Otto," Decker said. Then Warhaftig was gone.

Decker turned and looked at Swenson. He took her by the hand. "I'm glad we have this time together," he said, trying to smile. "I've been meaning to tell you something."

She squeezed his hand back, saying, "You have? What?"

"This is just between the two of us, at least for now. You have to promise me."

"I promise. Go on, tell me."

He began to speak with her in low and measured tones, his mouth only a few inches from her ear. Voices carried unpredictably on airplanes. She slumped down in her chair, leaning further into him. He told her everything: about the suspects they'd been watching in Queens; about the wallpapers; the bombs in Israel; about Moussa and Ali Hammel; about El Aqrab and what probably awaited them on the island of La Palma.

When he was done, Swenson did not speak for a long time. She simply sat there, sipping her water directly out of the bottle.

"I'll completely understand if you want to stay in Madrid instead of flying on to Santa Cruz," continued Decker. "In fact, it's what I would advise."

"What if we're too late?" she finally offered up, in a whisper, almost at no one in particular. "What if you're right and El Aqrab is there, and he sets off that nuclear device?"

Decker shook his head. "Then the world will never be the same. There's no way to stop a mega-tsunami once it starts, right?"

Swenson looked out the window. "Not according to Newton. I don't see how. How do you dissipate five thousand trillion joules of kinetic energy? Unless . . . " Her voice trailed off.

"Unless what?"

She shook her head, continuing to stare at the glistening sea below. "No," she said. "There is no way."

SECTION IV

Hajj

Chapter 38
Thursday, February 3 – 10:05 AM
La Palma, The Canary Islands

Decker and Swenson arrived in La Palma via Madrid in the late morning. A local policeman named Juan-Antonio de la Rama met them at the airport in Santa Cruz. A willowy dark man with a drooping mustache and agreeable face, de la Rama informed them, in a thick Spanish accent, that Otto Warhaftig's fellow operatives – Thompson and Strand – would be rendezvousing with them later on that afternoon. They had been called away at the last moment.

Decker and Swenson rented a silver Citroën Saxo and followed de la Rama into Santa Cruz. With only eighteen thousand inhabitants, the city lay on the east coast of the island, on the slope of a mountain, within the amphitheater of a long-extinct volcanic crater called La Cadereta. The road from the airport skirted the sea and there were modern buildings alongside large old houses with massive covered wooden balconies jutting from their sides. Decker and Swenson were both flabbergasted by the height of the volcanic ridge that ran the length of the island, north to south. La Palma seemed to be rushing upwards toward the sky. Banana plantations, many surrounded by wind walls, covered every inch of the steep slopes.

The Parador Hotel was only a few hundred yards from the sea. It seemed oppressively dark inside the lobby; but, perhaps, that was just in contrast to the brilliant sun outside. A solitary clerk stood behind the front desk. He was no more than a boy, really, barely a teenager, and wore an ill-fitting forest green uniform with oversized epaulettes. Decker inquired politely about the missing Doctor White in Spanish but the pimply youth did little more than shrug. He was too busy sorting mail with his long fingernails. He shrugged and shrugged, and moaned about the Doctor's unpaid bill, his overbearing friends, and how – in accordance with posted policy, no matter how regrettable – they'd soon be forced to give away his room. Swenson whipped out a credit card.

Decker continued to pepper the clerk with questions as the boy ran the card. When exactly had the scientist disappeared? Had he been seen with anyone during his stay? Had he given them his own credit card, or had someone else pre-paid? The boy didn't seem to know very much until Decker handed him a twenty Euro bill. Then he perked up. He passed the credit card back to

Swenson and vanished through a small door in the back. A moment later, he returned with a large envelope and handed it to Decker.

Decker tore it open. It was the fax from Warhaftig. It had come in an hour earlier. The document featured background information on Jamal ben Saad. Apparently, the man sent to Ansar II and the author of the book on Arabic architecture were indeed one and the same. Or had been. Jamal had disappeared soon after the Israeli invasion of Lebanon in '82. According to the fax, his father – the wealthy entrepreneur Hanid ben Saad – and younger brother Ibrahim had collaborated with the Israelis; they'd handed over information about Amal and Syrian installations prior to the invasion. Hanid ben Saad, his wife and son Ibrahim were subsequently killed by Amal in a car bombing. Jamal ben Saad was later arrested by the Israelis but he only spent three days at the Ansar II prison. Then he was released. No charges were filed against him. The Mosad suspected he was killed by Amal like his father and mother and brother. No, that was wrong. Hanid ben Saad's wife, A'isha, was not Jamal's biological mother. His natural mother, Rabi'a, had drowned when he was ten – a suicide. Although no note was found, they did discover a bottle of sleeping pills inside her purse. Apparently she'd been depressed for months. The fact that Jamal had only spent three days in Ansar II undoubtedly marked him as a collaborator like his father and brother. But his body was never found. Of course, Lebanon had been in chaos in those days. A missing corpse was hardly unusual.

Swenson finished paying the bill and she and Decker headed toward the elevator. Decker wanted to examine White's room. It was on the third floor, facing the main thoroughfare. Decker pressed his ear to the door for several seconds before entering with the passkey. The room featured a queen-size bed draped with a light blue quilt, a bit tatty, somewhat stained. There was a tiny writing desk in one corner, and a dressing area. The bathroom was not very big. It did, however, include a small bath, and an even smaller shower in one corner by the sink. A pair of French doors faced the wooden terrace that ran along the length of the facade of the hotel.

Decker began to search the writing desk. His back was to the terrace, and there was no way that he could have seen the figure passing right behind him. But Swenson did.

She screamed – just as the French doors burst apart, as Decker turned and the stranger leapt onto his back. They rolled across the floor. Swenson screamed again. Decker took a right cross to his chin. Then somebody punched his stomach. There seemed to be two men now, or three. They swirled around him, held his arms. Decker dropped to the floor. He swung his right leg out and one of his attackers went down. He wore a soft blue cable-knit sweater. His hair was rather long. Decker reached out and grabbed it. He pulled, and there was the neck, and he came down on it with an elbow strike. The blow shook the stranger to the core. Decker stared about the room. Swenson was gone. She had been there a moment ago. Now she was nowhere to be seen. Another man stood on the balcony. He was looking at his friend on the floor. Decker leapt up like a predator, feeling the blood pulse in his veins, feeling his lips curl as he raced across the room.

The stranger started running down the terrace. He'd only gone about ten yards when he came to a sudden stop, jogged left, and disappeared into another room. Decker started after him. In just four steps, he was standing by the French doors where the other man had disappeared. He didn't hesitate. He leapt into the room. He rolled and locked his knees. The room was empty. The man was gone.

Decker spun about. He spied the bathroom door. It was ajar. He stared at it and felt the hair stand upright on his neck. Someone was in there. Decker could sense him. With a kind of snarl, he leapt across the room, drawing his gun, kicked the door and fired as the door sprang back. There was the sound of shattering glass. The man with the gun before him looked familiar. Too familiar. He lowered his weapon. Glass shards tumbled to the floor as the full-length mirror on the wall gave way. He'd shot himself.

Decker pulled back, just as another bullet split the doorframe by his head. He turned and fired two quick shots. They puckered the shower curtain. And then he saw the bloodstained hand.

It clasped the curtain at the top, it pulled and the curtain gradually gave way, one ring at a time. The man struck the bathroom floor with a dull *thwack*, directly on his face. There was an unnatural stillness as he bounced and settled. He was already dead. The bullets had found their mark.

Decker heard a car start. It was so loud it sounded as if it were parked in the next room. He dashed out of the bathroom, lunged toward the terrace, and there it was. An off-white two-door. A Renault. It was skidding from the lot. Even from this height, Decker could plainly see the pale outline of Emily's head framed by the window, her blonde hair waving, that terrified expression through the glass.

Decker raced back through the door, bounded downstairs, and was out in the open parking lot in seconds. He jumped into his Citroën Saxo rental. He started her up and crawled out of the lot. Eventually, as he descended a small hill, the Saxo picked up speed. He followed the narrow road. It ran outside the city, due south, and started up the mountain valley. It wound its way across a hill, then up again, beginning a harsh ascent of the volcanic walls. Decker saw the sea wink in the distance, far below.

He climbed and climbed around volcanic outpourings, round rings of magma, rotund as love handles on the mountainside. The road began to zigzag dangerously, round bends and hairpin turns, meandering, round oxbows and capricious straight-aways that gave up suddenly, only to turn again, and down, and round. That's when he saw it in the distance, the other car.

It was a Renault, after all – a Clio; some model he'd never heard of. Then it vanished around the bend. Decker stepped on the accelerator. He leaned forward toward the steering column, straining his eyes. There it was again. He pressed the accelerator to the floor until the Citroën whined. He was gaining on them. He could see Emily's hair, like spun gold, gleaming through the window. It was then he heard the motorcycles.

The first shot swept across his windshield, shattering the glass, and covering him with tiny flecks that looked like diamonds in the brilliant February light. He shook the shards out of his eyes. The wind blasted his face. He heard the sound of his own engine screaming. The wind was shockingly cold considering they were off the coast of Africa. It numbed his skin.

Decker shook his head. He ducked just as the second volley coursed across the cab. The other windows of the Saxo shattered. Now wind swept in from every side. Decker could barely see. Some of the glass had gone into his eyes. They felt like they were on fire.

The car swerved to the side and he saw the guardrail just too late.

The Saxo struck and bounced and jumped back on the road, almost instinctively. He pressed ahead at breakneck speed. For a brief moment, Decker felt invincible. He turned around just as a BMW Rockster barreled into view. A man in a bright red leather suit, holding a machine gun, angled by. He opened up on

Decker's car and the Citroën throbbed. Decker held his breath. He looked about. Miraculously, he wasn't hit. The wheels still rolled. The engine still pulsed with life.

Decker squeezed the steering wheel. He saw the distant sea below, the road diminishing. He skidded left and struck the 1150 Rockster squarely on the side. There was a thump – quite silent really, surprisingly subtle – and the motorcycle disappeared from sight behind a bush, only to reappear a moment later, spiraling skyward through the air at one hundred and twenty miles per hour. The motorcycle rolled and rolled, then finally tumbled out of sight, just as another volley tore the roof off in a burst of light.

Decker ducked. He couldn't even see the road; he drove from memory. He turned the wheel and another volley ripped the headrests into pieces. There was nothing left. Decker lifted his head and the wind scratched at his face like a cat. The top of the car was completely gone. He felt as though he were driving a jeep.

He looked to his left and saw the distant ocean twinkle. He was straddling a cliff. The water glistened several hundred feet below.

Decker turned and saw a stream of bullets traveling toward him in what appeared to be slow motion, like a swarm of bees, or a school of minnows swimming underwater. He saw the individual bullets, the single stray that tumbled suddenly, and struck him in the arm, and ripped that small filet of flesh out of his bicep with a strident *twang* – like the breaking of a violin string. Decker gritted his teeth.

He turned and saw the second motorcyclist. He was right behind him, dressed in same red leather jacket and red helmet. He was aiming his black gun.

Decker stomped on the breaks. The car squealed and slowed as he downshifted, stripping gears.

The second Rockster hit the rear of Decker's vehicle, climbed up upon the bumper, then the trunk. The rear tire of the BMW still rolled along the road, but the front was stuck now, in the back seat of the car! Decker could hear the two-spark, 1150 boxer engine roaring right behind him.

He stepped on the accelerator just as the second motorcyclist fired. Three shots tore up the dashboard. The front wheel of the Rockster suddenly broke free. It rolled back down along the Saxo's trunk, bounced on the bumper, and dropped back to the road.

The motorcyclist tried desperately to regain control. He

was almost upright when Decker applied the breaks again.

This time the motorcycle clipped the bumper, bucked like a bronco and hurled the driver up into the air, directly over Decker's car, the windshield and the hood. He landed somewhere just ahead. Decker heard the grim, telltale *thump thump* as he crushed the man against the road. He turned and saw the crimson helmet shatter like an egg, the head unraveling, unwinding from the body as he pirouetted out of sight.

Decker stepped on the accelerator. He straightened up and felt the wind assault his face. His eyes were tearing, but he could clearly see the ocean to his left, a vast expanse of blue. He was paralleling a plantation, a banana farm below, and it appeared as though he were driving on the palms themselves, across their very branches. He pulled up sharply and almost struck the dirt embankment. He saw the Clio up ahead. He was gaining on them once again. He was finally catching up. Then they turned off without warning, into the trees, and disappeared from view.

Decker skidded off the main road, straightened out, and barreled down a dirt path through the trees. Green palms and flowers blocked the sun. Bright vines, broad leaves and long tenacious grasses grasped at the wheels, smacked at the Saxo's flanks. The vegetation was so thick that Decker couldn't really see the path. He moved ahead by instinct, following the contours of the land.

The path seemed to run around the border of a grand plantation. It snaked and turned and meandered through a kind of gully. Then it simply petered out. Decker kept driving. He bulldozed his way through fronds and flowers and emerged, at last, along a small bald ridge, right at the base of the volcano.

There was the car — the two-door, off-white Renault Clio. It was parked only a dozen yards away, and it was empty.

Emily was gone.

Chapter 39
Thursday, February 3 – 12:33 PM
La Palma, The Canary Islands

Decker jumped out of the Saxo, tore across the open ground, and knelt down by the Clio. There was some kind of cavern entrance just ahead. It was large and round, and Decker suddenly realized that it was probably a lava tube, a holdover from some previous eruption. It poured out of the mountainside.

He sprinted toward the cavern. He paused for a moment just outside the entrance, painfully aware of his black silhouette against the open lava tube. He'd make an easy target, he thought. But he had no choice. He rolled across the ground. Nobody fired at him. He looked about. The lava tube was large, at least ten feet across and ten feet tall. The air was cool and somewhat moist inside. He leapt to his feet and started running down the tunnel.

It didn't take long for his eyes to adjust to the dark. Decker had only gone about twenty yards when he noticed a kind of mining car or cart up ahead. As he drew closer he realized it was just an ordinary golf cart. He climbed in. Someone or something was moving down the tunnel. He felt the dashboard with his hands, felt for a key, and turned it. A moment later the golf cart came to life. Decker flipped on the headlights and the lava tube unrolled before him, glassy and black. He touched the accelerator. The cart began to move down the path.

Decker had to concentrate to keep her steady through the tunnel. He traveled in this way for what seemed like miles when he sensed a change in the air temperature. The tunnel doglegged left, then right. He saw another cart parked up ahead. He pressed the breaks, slowed down, and took his weapon out.

The other cart looked abandoned. Decker got out and approached the vehicle with care. No, he was wrong. It wasn't empty. Two men were lying in the back. They were both dead. And then he noticed that the tunnel appeared to be blocked just up ahead, by a large boulder. It had been placed there in the center of the path on purpose.

Decker knelt down. He cocked his head. He tried to sense if anyone else was in the tunnel. But there was nothing, no one. He was alone . . . except for the two corpses in the cart. Decker checked their pockets. There. He felt a wallet. He pulled it out and held it up before him in the headlights. The CIA ID stood up just like a little flag – the photograph, the name Colin L. Strand.

And this must be Nick Thompson, Decker thought, Warhaftig's other man. He dropped the wallet in the cart. He backed away and started up the tunnel.

After only about ten yards, as he was beginning to lose visibility, he noticed a break in the stone wall. It was another tunnel, just a few feet off the ground. Decker climbed into the opening. He started to sweat. Then he realized that the temperature was rising. The lava tube had taken him due south from underneath the extinct volcano outside of Santa Cruz, all the way to the Cumbre Vieja. This volcano was still active. It was only then that he noticed the faint smell of obnoxious fumes. He held his nose. There was a light on just ahead. He pressed on through the tunnel, turned right and came upon another lava tube, much larger than the last. It led into some sort of cavern. He could see it clearly now; it was well lit. He could hear the purring of machinery.

Decker crawled forward on his hands and knees along the tunnel floor. When he reached the mouth of the lava tube, he finally got his first good look inside the cavern. It was huge. It must have been at least thirty feet high, or higher, and a couple of hundred yards in length. Roughly circular, it looked like a cathedral carved out the heart of the volcano. The ceiling was decorated with black stalactites, shiny, obsidianesque, Goth chandeliers. It was even hotter here and Decker wondered just how close he was to some still active lava tube. It felt as though he were standing in a cauldron. Somewhere, only a few yards underneath his feet, perhaps, the stone was percolating. He scanned the cave, taking in each detail.

There were two sets of lights mounted on towers across the way. They looked like concert lights. Immediately below the tower, on the left, was a kind of makeshift hut made out of packing crates and strips of black tarpaulin. Other crates and boxes were stacked around the cave. A golf cart was parked roughly in the middle. And by the tower on the other side, someone had pitched two tents. Decker crawled forward carefully. He heard voices up ahead. Despite the humming of what he guessed must be a generator, he could clearly hear the guttural sound of Arabic conversation. Decker looked up. A pair of crates blocked his view. He shimmied forward slowly, dragging his legs, and stopped.

There was a foot in front of him. It was wearing a lady's shoe. The crate shielded the remainder of the body. He turned the corner and came upon the prostrate figure of a woman. She was bald, and rather old. And she was very dead. Doris White; it had to be. There was another body next to her – a man. Who else but Dr. White? He looked just like his photographs. He looked still warm. He was holding the woman's hand, Decker noticed, even in death, and this trivial detail stung like a paper cut across his heart.

"Agent Decker," somebody said. He spun about. There was no one there. He curled into a ball behind the crates. The voice had sounded like it was coming from immediately behind him.

"Agent Decker, we know you're there. Why don't you come out and join your lady friend?"

Decker got up on his knees. He took his gun out of his holster and peeked around the crate.

Two Arabic-looking men were standing by the tents. Swenson was on her knees, in front of them. One of the men held her by the hair. He was tall and muscular, with a thick mustache. But it was the smaller man who captured Decker's gaze.

He was thin, wiry, with a narrow face. His eyes were dark, beguiling. He had a wispy black beard, thin as an adolescent's. It was El Aqrab, Decker was sure of it.

The Arab smiled a wolfish grin, stretched out his arms, and said, "Welcome to the Canary Islands, Agent Decker." He laughed. "It's good to finally meet you, after all this time. In truth, I feel like I already know you." He pointed down at Emily. "And we've already met your friend."

"Let her go," said Decker.

"I'd be happy to. Why don't you throw your weapon down and I'll release her."

"An agent never gives up his gun. That's the first rule," Decker said. "Give up your gun and you're dead. Where's the bomb?"

El Aqrab laughed. "Always the professional," he said. "Don't you care about Ms. Swenson? I was told you did."

"The only way out of here is through me."

"You really didn't know that, did you?" El Aqrab said whimsically. "But it's true. I concede that point to you. You stand between us and the only exit. That's what makes it so . . . interesting." He said something to his partner in a low voice.

The other man pulled Swenson by the hair. Then he kicked her with his knee so that she rolled onto her stomach. She tried to crawl away but he kicked her again. Her body arched and slammed against a crate. The man reached down and grabbed her by the collar of her blouse. He lifted her off the ground. There was a loud rip as the material gave way. He began to tear it from her back. She tried to move, to get away, but he grabbed her by the jeans. He ripped them down, exposing her white panties underneath. Slowly and methodically, he took her jeans off. Then he pulled her by the hair again and made her stand before him. She was crying now. She was mumbling incoherently. The man stuffed one hand into her bra. Then, with the other, he pulled the bra up, and Emily's breasts fell free, exposed and vulnerable.

Decker fired a shot above the large man's head but he didn't even move. He simply stood there, holding Emily. El Aqrab said something in Arabic that Decker couldn't hear. Decker aimed his gun. He fixed the figure in his sights. A bead of sweat dripped in his eye. He hesitated. He wiped his face with his sleeve, and suddenly withdrew.

He was afraid to shoot. He was afraid of hitting Emily.

The man pushed Emily into a nearby folding chair. He took his belt off. At first, Decker was convinced that he was going to beat her. Then he noticed he was using it to tie her hands. The man moved back behind the chair. As he looked at Decker, as he stared directly at him, he snagged her panties in his fingers and pulled them down along her long brown legs. Swenson sat there, naked, barely awake, her head tilted to the side. El Aqrab stepped up beside her.

"Give me your weapon, Agent Decker."

Decker ducked behind the crate. He couldn't bear watching. He knew exactly what was coming. He sat on the ground, his back to the crate, and pressed the barrel of his gun against his face. He closed his eyes. He could feel tears coursing down his cheeks. He cleared his throat and breathed. He breathed again. When he finally shifted back onto his knees and peeked over the crate, El Aqrab had already started wrapping Emily in tendrils of metal ribbon. Decker watched him as he worked.

He was punctilious. He was so careful, almost dainty in his movements. *I can't give up my gun,* Decker thought. *If I give up my gun, I'm dead. And if I'm dead, she's dead. I can't give up my gun. No matter what they do to her. She's just one person. There are forty million lives at stake.*

"Is it not written?" Decker shouted. "I say, is it not written? 'It is He Who hath made you His vicegerent on the earth. He hath raised you in ranks, some above others, that He may try you in the gifts He hath given you?' How then can you destroy the world, set off this mega-tsunami? Is it not unlawful to assail the environment? And the *Ahadith* say—"

"Don't speak to me of sullying the earth. The West has polluted the planet for countless generations, through your destruction of the ozone layer, through global warming. Your cars and smokestacks, your lifestyle chokes the world. A little at a time, to be sure. A decade here, a decade there. A languorous strangulation." He laughed. "What I will do will cleanse the planet of your filth. Now, give me your weapon, Agent Decker. I'm warning you for the last time. Give it to me, or your woman burns."

"Then burn her," Decker shouted back.

He started to worm his way along the ground. If he could outflank them, he might just have a chance. There was no cover to his left, but to his right . . . to his right ran a series of crates and boxes for a good ten yards, or more. If he could get around them, find more cover, he might just cut them down before they had a chance to fire back. As long as El Aqrab kept talking.

"Did you hear me? Burn her. The girl means nothing to me. Isn't that what you do, burn people? Isn't that the ultimate aesthetic of Mohammed Hussein, the infamous El Aqrab? Or should I call you Jamal ben Saad today?"

The name seemed to dangle in the air. It seemed to linger for a moment, echoing.

"What did you say?" El Aqrab's voice faltered for the first time.

"Don't you know your own name? But I guess that's always been your problem, hasn't it, Jamal? You don't know who you are. Perhaps there was so little there to begin with that you had to assume somebody else's name and background, some *real* persona, someone of substance. But you can't rent bravery, Jamal." Decker squirmed behind the first box in the line. "Tell me," he said. "What happened to you after your father and brother cooperated with the Israelis? What happened to you at Ansar II?"

"Nothing," said ben Saad. "Absolutely nothing." He laughed.

And it was only then, with that one simple response, that Decker realized what had happened. "It was *you*," he said. The truth exploded in his head. "It wasn't your father, or your brother," he continued. "It was you who cut a deal with the Israelis! And then you set them up – your own father and brother and stepmother – set them up so that Amal would kill them." Decker poked his head out from around a crate, for just a second.

El Aqrab had finished tying Emily. She was dressed from head to foot in magnesium ribbon linked to tiny bladders of explosives. The sight of her tanned skin bulging through the bright metallic sheen burned itself into his eyes.

Decker leaned his back against the crate. He tried to block it out. His heart was racing. He was sweating uncontrollably. He wiped the perspiration from his eyes with his left sleeve. Then he shouted, "It was all about revenge." Decker dropped onto his hands and knees, and started crawling forward once again. *Keep him talking. Keep him talking and you have a chance.*

El Aqrab did not respond. Decker peeked around a box. The terrorist was walking away. No, *toward* some other crate. He stopped. He bent over suddenly and picked up an object from the floor. Decker couldn't see what it was; El Aqrab's back was to him. Then the terrorist turned. He reached out and opened what appeared to be the top of a silver attaché case.

El Aqrab looked over at where Decker had been moments earlier, and reached into the case. "I'm starting the sequence, Agent Decker. Just in case. Just to let you know." Then he shouted suddenly, "Where are you, anyway?" He swiveled his body about, like some heron hunting. "I can't hear you anymore," he said. He looked directly at Decker. "You're not trying to outflank us, are you?"

The words reverberated in the air. Then he shrugged and said, "It doesn't matter. In a few minutes, it will all be over. The bomb will explode, the volcano will erupt, and the mega-tsunami will stream across the ocean to the West. And there is nothing, absolutely nothing you or anyone else can do about it. The game is over, Agent Decker, and I'm afraid you've lost."

Decker continued forward on his hands and knees. He had almost reached the end of the line of crates. If there were some scrap of cover beyond, he could outflank them. He could sneak around and take his shot.

"This is so tiresome," sighed El Aqrab.

Keep him talking. "What happened the day of your graduation?" Decker asked. "You'd finally earned your doctorate, as a young man too. Your family must have come to celebrate your triumph. Didn't they? A week later, you betrayed them."

El Aqrab strode back toward Emily. He towered over her. He ran a hand along her face. "I remember," El Aqrab said. "Yes. My graduation." He stroked Emily's cheek. "You're right. I had been looking forward to it for the longest time. My father had promised to attend, and I wanted him to see me as they gave me my diploma. I thought it would make him proud." He laughed. He began to play with a lock of Swenson's hair and, slowly but surely, the story tumbled out.

His father had come, late, he said, as always, and the old man had made that speech that no one listened to, and spent the entire evening talking with his brother, Ibrahim. Decker was right. He had set them up, all of them, and he was glad he had.

"*I* was Ishmael to Ibrahim's Isaac," he added bitterly. "*I* was the elder son. *I* should have been my father's heir, his pride. But he killed my mother, Rabi'a, because she was too strong for him, and because she was Palestinian. He hadn't minded earlier, when he was younger. No, he had loved her then. And he had used her family's money to begin his business empire. But, as he grew more and more successful, she no longer fit into the plan. She became an embarrassment to him and to his Sunni and Maronite business partners. And so he fed her full of sleeping pills and drowned her, before my very eyes, and then married that ten-dinar whore. He drove me from his heart. He deserved to die. They all did. So with the help of the Israelis, I betrayed them to Amal, only to have the Israelis betray me."

"Who betrayed you?" Decker asked. *Keep him talking.* He crawled and crawled and came upon the final crate in the long line. He peeked around it. He could see tents. He saw ben Saad and then the other man, and Swenson tied up to that chair. "Who was he, El Aqrab?"

Decker looked desperately around. But there was nowhere left to hide. The nearest cover was a good ten yards away, or more. He'd be dead before he even crossed the halfway mark. He was trapped. El Aqrab had known it all along. There was no way to outflank them. The terrorist had just been playing with him.

"Who do you think it was? Who else would the Knesset choose but the Minister of Defense."

Decker leaned his back against the crate. He looked at the gun in his hand. And then he suddenly remembered. "Garron," he whispered. "It was Garron who authorized the deal. He must have."

Jamal laughed. "I think even Yuri was a little shocked when I approached him with the proposition. It was so simple really. Together we made it appear my father and brother had collaborated with the Zionists. In exchange for information about

Syrian and Amal positions, which I was more than happy to provide, Garron promised to protect my father's properties and businesses after the invasion. Allowances would be made, he said. My father's fortune would pass on to me. A few days after we leaked the news, Amal guerrillas killed my father, my brother and my father's wife. Burned them alive in that car. That was an added bonus. But I was arrested and sent to Ansar II in Gaza. I had gone to my father's house, you see, to collect the cash he always kept there in case of a forced departure. I was making my way south through 'Ayn ar Rummanah. I planned to cross the Green Line near Ash Shiyyah where I knew the guards. And I had almost made it to the airport. Almost! I could see the airplanes on the runway just beyond Tahwitat al Ghadir when I was stopped by the IDF. The Zionists had agreed to let me go, but they betrayed me. Yuri wanted the money, you see, from my father's safe – almost two and a half million dollars. He gave it to his son to fund his next campaign for Housing Minister. Even then, he had ambitions to become Prime Minister. And then, to make things worse, I was released by Ariel Miller. After three days. Three days! I became a marked man. It appeared as if I too had collaborated with the Zionists, just like my father and brother. So I slipped back into Lebanon, where I arranged to meet Mohammed in the neighborhood of Bi'r Hasan."

Ben Saad recounted the story of how he had set up his childhood idol, Mohammed Hussein, how he had seduced the legendary El Aqrab into that bombed-out building near the sports arena.

"Mohammed had come to kill me," he continued. "And he almost did. But I told him that I hadn't known about my family's betrayal, and that the Zionists had leaked it to Amal so that my father and brother would be killed by their own people. I told him Garron had authorized my release so that I'd be killed as well. And he believed me. He believed me! He didn't want to be a puppet of the Zionists. So he put his gun down and came up to me. He hugged me in his arms and kissed me on both cheeks, and – as he looked at me and smiled – I stabbed him in the stomach. I wanted it to last, you see, because you can tell a lot about a man when you watch him die. I needed his identity."

"But how did you manage to keep it secret?" Decker asked. "All these years?"

Ben Saad described how he had gone back and killed the remainder of El Aqrab's family and friends, either directly or with the help of the Maronite militia. Then he had gone north to Kazakhstan . . . where he had almost been discovered. A man named Ali showed up one day at the camp, and he recognized Jamal. He confronted him, threatened to expose him to Gulzhan Baqrah unless he paid him off. Jamal ben Saad refused. So Ali had told the guerrilla leader, and Baqrah had tortured Jamal personally.

"They strung me up by my elbows. Then Gulzhan whipped me. He whipped me to within an inch of my life, and I confessed to everything. I wanted him to know. I had to share it with him after that, you see. And Gulzhan, to my complete surprise, to my everlasting shame, Gulzhan thought fit to let me go."

Gulzhan had sensed Jamal ben Saad's black hatred for the Zionists. And he had recognized his talent for destruction, his passion and his ruthlessness.

After his release, Jamal went up into the mountains. He told Gulzhan that he wanted to be left alone to pray. But, in reality, he planned to throw himself off a cliff. He wanted to die. Then, something happened that he hadn't counted on. Alone, in the freezing wind and snow, looking down upon the training camp, he'd had a vision.

"I saw the Archangel Gabriel," he said. "He came to me, to me, and held me in his arms, and rocked me until I cried no more. He told me what I should do, the man I should become. I was . . . reborn. I became a true *mujahadeen*. I no longer needed to play the part of El Aqrab. I *was* El Aqrab."

Ben Saad stretched and straightened up. It was strange, almost uncanny. He actually seemed to metamorphosize into another person as he reached into his robes, as he waved his arms about like a magician, and suddenly lit a match. He brought it to his face. He stared into the flame. "Your weapon, Agent Decker. This is the last time I shall ask you. Soon the entire mountain will become a mosque," he said, "with me within the *mihrab* of the Cumbre Vieja, a moveable mosque of water to purify the world. A mosque of my design to house the fourth prayer of the Hajj for the great *Ummah*, with a *qibla* running back to Mecca." He lowered the match toward Emily's face. He held it by her eye, immediately beneath a strand of the magnesium that stuck out like a fuse. "Everybody will die, including you and your woman. But, if you surrender now, at least she will not feel the agony of fire. It will be quick, I promise."

Decker stood up from behind the crate.

"Ah, there you are," said El Aqrab with a grin. "You are resourceful, aren't you, Agent Decker?" He waved his hand and the match went out. "Come closer, let me see you. That's better. Now, throw your gun down."

Decker stepped forward, his arms raised, and his pistol dangling from his fingertips. He took a few more steps. Then he stopped and slowly lowered the weapon to the floor. He kicked it over to El Aqrab. His large companion bent down and picked it up. Then he approached Decker.

"Just let her go, Jamal."

"My name isn't Jamal. Not anymore. It's El Aqrab."

"You said you'd release her."

"And you said you wouldn't give up your gun."

The other man stepped forward without warning and smacked Decker across the face. Decker buckled at the knees. His head began to ring. He was actually seeing stars. The man had hit him with his gun. Decker tried to stand but his legs were made of water.

The man grabbed him by the wrist and dragged him to the nearest crate. He handcuffed Decker's right hand around some kind of heavy machinery. Then he pulled Swenson over by the hair and attached her to the other side.

"You said you'd let her go," said Decker. His face had started to swell and it was difficult to talk.

El Aqrab approached him carrying the attaché case in his hands. He placed it on the crate, immediately beside them, only a hand's length out of reach. He turned it around so that Decker could see the bright red LED. It was counting off the sequence. There were twenty-eight minutes left. No, twenty-seven now. He stared at El Aqrab, trying to find some semblance of humanity, some touch of grace, some particle of pity in him – but there was nothing there. "You said you'd let her go," he repeated almost to himself.

El Aqrab drew near. He padded over like a cat. "I promised you she wouldn't feel the pain of fire. And she won't. Neither of you will. A nuclear explosion is probably the quickest way to die. And, therefore, the least painful." He laughed. He hovered over Decker.

"Oh, and, by the way – Salim Moussa sends his love. He told me to tell you that he still gets chills remembering your partner falling. He knew you would give up your gun. You have no heart for killing, Agent Decker. You couldn't even shoot to save your partner."

"Fuck you, you little prick. Fuck you! What a disappointment," Decker said. "The great El Aqrab." He laughed. "To destroy the world over your shattered dreams, your inconsequential ego. How fucking pathetic. This isn't about Allah or Islam, the *Ummah* or the Palestinians. It's all about Jamal. About your murdered mother. Your hunger for revenge. About Ishmael's jealousy of Isaac."

The gun came down on Decker's head. He saw a light as bright as any nuclear explosion.

Then it burnt out.

Chapter 40
Thursday, February 3 – 2:08 PM
La Palma, The Canary Islands

When Swenson came to, she was handcuffed to Decker around some piece of machinery, still half-lodged in its crate. She sat up. It felt as though someone had cleaved her forehead down the middle like a chicken breast. Then she realized she was naked, except for strand after strand of light gray metal ribbon, and the bulbous contours of what appeared to be balloons of sand, like seaweed pods. She covered herself with her hand. "Decker," she said. She tugged on the handcuffs but he still didn't stir. "Decker," she repeated more emphatically.

He was out cold. His face was puffy and red. But he was still breathing; she could see that. At least he was alive.

Swenson struggled slowly to her feet. She looked about. She tugged on the handcuffs, then tried to push the machinery with all of her might, but it wouldn't budge. That's when she noticed the aluminum attaché case, just out of reach on the crate. And then the bright red LED, the numbers counting: 25.29; 25.28; 25.27.

And it dawned on her – *the bomb!* The atom bomb, no bigger than a briefcase. It was an elegant device, scientifically speaking. A beautiful angel of death.

She sat down on the ground by the crate. Simply not seeing the numbers reassured her. "Decker," she said, "Please wake up. John? John, can you hear me? Please!"

Decker did not stir. Swenson looked about, trying to spy something that might prove useful. Nothing! They were trapped. She ran her free hand through her hair, trying to think, when she felt the hairpin. She plucked it out. She held it up against the light. It was a little bent but it would have to do. Swenson slipped it into the tiny keyhole in the cuffs, just as she had seen done a thousand times on television, and in the movies. She started to twist. The hairpin slithered out. She tried again. She worked it around in every possible direction, using different combinations and various rates of pressure. She examined it like an experiment.

After a painful three minutes, she was about to give up when – with a great sigh – she tried to rip the hairpin from the hole. *Great! Now, it's stuck,* she thought. She cursed and yanked it free. Decker rolled over. Swenson tried to catch him but he banged his face against the crate, exactly where he'd been struck with the gun.

"Oops," she said. "Sorry!" She pulled him upright once again, and slipped the hairpin back into the lock. "Decker," she said as she worked. "Decker, wake up. We've got to get out of here. John, wake up!"

He moaned. He started to move.

She let him gradually recline into her lap. She stroked his face and said, "John, if you don't wake up, we're both going to die. And I really don't want to do that."

Decker's eyes fluttered open. He stared up at Swenson and smiled. "Where am I?" he said.

"Don't you remember? We're in a cavern, at the heart of an active volcano, in the middle of the Atlantic, handcuffed to a nuclear bomb."

"Oh, right. I thought for a minute there that we were in trouble." He laughed and sat up. "That's an interesting ensemble you're wearing."

"Are you insane? You think this is funny? How hard did that guy hit you?"

Decker looked over the lip of the crate at the attaché case. They had twenty-three minutes to live. "Not hard enough," he said.

Swenson continued to fiddle with the lock.

Decker noticed her desperate prodding. "What is that?" he said. "A hairpin? That'll never work."

"Got a better idea?"

"You're right. Here, let me try."

She handed him the hairpin. He turned it first one way, and then the other. Then he tried again. And again. And again, when – out of nowhere – the patter of desperate footsteps echoed through the cave. Someone was running toward them. Decker tried to stand but the handcuffs kept him huddled over, and the sudden jerking of the chain caused Swenson to cry out. He peered over the crate. "It's him," he said.

"Who?" Swenson strained to get a better view.

"One of the men who chased us back at the hotel. I recognize him." Then Decker paused, and listened, and added in a tone of quiet desperation, "He's coming this way."

They squatted down behind the crate, both absolutely still. Swenson's thighs began to shake. She watched as a thin rivulet of blood ran past Decker's temple, down his neck, and into his shirt. The footsteps grew louder and louder as the man drew near. He was almost upon them. And then he was there, right there, beside them, towering overhead, casting a shadow over Decker, who still held the hairpin in his hand.

He was Middle Eastern. He had chocolate-brown hair and penetrating nut-brown eyes. He took in the scene at a glance, reached into his windbreaker, removed a double-action Jericho 941, and aimed it a Decker's head.

Decker and Swenson both winced and closed their eyes. They heard the shot and looked in panic at each other. The bullet had severed the chain. The cufflinks separated. They were free.

"You must be Agent Decker," said the stranger. "And Emily Swenson, of Woods Hole." He held a hand out and helped them to their feet. "Acting Chief Seiden, Mossad. Warhaftig told me you were somewhere on La Palma. I tried to link up with you at the Parador in Santa Cruz but you left in quite a hurry."

Decker pointed at the silver attaché case on the crate behind them. "Unless you also happen to be a nuclear technician," he added, "I think we should get the hell out of here."

They started running at a furious pace back toward the entrance to the cave. They made it through the tunnel, into the lava tube and stumbled across the golf cart Decker had abandoned earlier, on the way in. It was just sitting there next to that boulder in the path. The key was still in the ignition. Obviously, El Aqrab had not anticipated their release.

They jumped in, Decker floored the accelerator, and the small battery-powered engine whined. The golf cart began to move. After about twenty yards, they picked up steam, and – even with the headlights – it became difficult to see. The lave tube seemed to curl this way and that, to turn at the oddest angles, to rise and drop at will. But as fast as they were driving, the journey still seemed to take forever. At one point they passed another tunnel to the left and Decker had to stop, and try and orient himself. He hadn't noticed it before, on the way in. It joined the lava tube at a sharp angle. Without hesitating, Decker turned right and kept on driving. After another ten minutes, just as he was about to turn around and try the other tunnel, he saw a faint light up ahead, pale as a lost firefly. He hugged the steering wheel. The light seemed to be growing brighter by the second. "Do you see that?" he asked Swenson, just to be sure.

"I'm not blind."

"We're almost out," said Seiden.

They barreled through the tunnel, mindless of the bumps and curves, and suddenly the tube expanded, widened up into a cave, and they were in the open . . . and taking heavy fire. Decker jammed his foot on the breaks. The golf cart skidded and began to roll. He reached for Swenson's hand and pulled her to him, just as the cart went over. They skidded across the ground into a stand of green banana palms.

"Hold your fire," someone said.

Decker was lying on top of Swenson, covering her body. She was barely dressed, still wrapped in strands of gun-gray metal ribbon. Seiden had disappeared into the brush.

"Don't move," somebody else said. "Freeze!"

Decker looked up. A U.S. Special Forces soldier approached them through the trees. Behind him, another dozen men materialized out of the grass and jungle. They were wearing camouflage fatigues and their faces were blotched with green paint. Then he heard the helicopter. It hovered overhead – a Seahawk, and she was gradually descending, straight down on top of them! Decker covered his head.

The helicopter fell. The wind almost carried them away. Then it was down.

A soldier grabbed Decker by the arm and pulled him to his feet. Another approached Swenson. He picked her up as if she were a bag of laundry and threw her deftly through the open hatch. A second later, Decker was hoisted up into the helicopter. Then, as the landscape dropped away, Ben Seiden suddenly appeared. He was running in their shadow. He leapt into the open hatch and rolled across the deck.

The helicopter climbed. Somebody put a blanket on top of Swenson's naked form. Decker looked up to thank him when he noticed, with a start, that he was dressed in a dark gray business suit. It was Warhaftig.

The CIA operative smiled and said, "You sure go for those dramatic exits, don't you, John? I see you've met Ben Seiden."

"I'm glad to see you, Otto." Decker turned toward Seiden. "You too, Chief Seiden. You saved our lives."

"Perhaps not. How long do we have?"

Decker glanced at his watch. He shrugged and looked down through the open hatch. He could see the island of La Palma gradually receding, a green mound in a deep blue sea. He could see the various volcanoes, including the Cumbre Vieja to the south. Wet verdant mountains glistened in the sun.

"We don't."

Just then there was a thunderous roar. It was so loud, so omnipresent, that it seemed to lift the helicopter up, to flip her over for an instant. Decker rolled directly into Swenson, who rolled against Warhaftig, who rolled against Seiden and the bulkhead with a bang. Only the weight of a hundred billion tons of rock prevented them from being incinerated instantly by the nuclear explosion.

Then, the helicopter righted. She settled down. Warhaftig and Seiden pulled themselves to their feet. Decker was lying on top of Swenson. She opened her eyes and realized, looking down, that she was almost naked, exposed, her breasts pressed up against his chest. "Excuse me," she said, just as the Electro-Magnetic Pulse shot through them.

The helicopter veered to port, flipped over on her back, and began to plummet toward the earth. She fell and fell. The pilot wrestled with the stick but it was useless. The EMP had disabled every instrument on the ship. They were being sucked down by the funnel of the Cumbre Vieja, and there was nothing they could do.

Chapter 41
Thursday, February 3 – 2:59 PM
La Palma, The Canary Islands

Giles Pickings was proofreading the first draft of his *Passion of Pius II* when he felt the earth move underneath his feet.

He had just finished the manuscript the night before. It had taken him almost five years, but he was finally done. And, more importantly, he felt good about it. It was a worthy contribution to the literature. One day, perhaps, his name would be remembered. Not as a giant in the field, of course; he could not hope for that. But as a worthy squire or a page, attendant to the Hamlets of the age. A Prufrock.

He sighed. He put the manuscript aside and glanced outside the window by his writing desk. A rain had swept across the mountains in the morning and the palm trees glistened like blown glass.

That's odd, he thought. A moment earlier he'd been harassed by songbirds as he had tried to concentrate on his review. Now, they were silent as the grave.

He looked up. A cloud of daffodil-colored canaries commingled with another, and another, and yet another still when Pickings was blown backwards over his chair. A deafening explosion rocked the earth.

He landed on his back somehow, but turned the other way, with his feet propped up against the far wall. For a moment he couldn't see. Everything went blurry. Then he noticed his bookcase tipping over, right on top of him! He rolled out of the way. It shattered across the floor, sending books in all directions. The window tinkled as it cracked. No, it wasn't the window.

Pickings turned and stared wild-eyed beyond his desk. It was the wall. It was still cracking. It was being ripped apart, as if by giant hands.

*   *   *

Far, far below, in the vast subterranean reservoirs of the Cumbre Vieja, lava cascaded into steam, into water that had been accumulating for millennia in soft permeable streams. Slowly, the reservoirs began to heat, like radiator foils wrapped in impermeable stone, to roil and bubble, charged by the furious energy of the exploded bomb, nursed by the lava streams that followed. Each reservoir was several thousand meters deep, and each was stacked against another of its size for countless kilometers, like Titan tombstones. The waters boiled between these dense impenetrable towers, desperate to be free.

* * *

Pickings got up slowly. He had twisted his right knee. It felt like someone were pushing needles into him. He hobbled over to the wall. The crack had stopped expanding. The earthquake, or whatever it had been, seemed to have finally settled down. He could see his prize flower garden in the back, the birds of paradise and codeso, the colorful hibiscus. He made his way carefully toward the rear door, keeping an eye out for falling plaster. It was already strewn across the floor. The crack stretched to the ceiling.

The kitchen was a disaster. Every plate he owned, it seemed, each bowl and every glass was on the floor, smashed in a million pieces, including his most precious china. The refrigerator had fallen on its side, and milk and juice were puddling up beside it.

He crossed the floor with care, picking his feet up to avoid the shards. When he finally reached the other side, Pickings hesitated for a moment in the open doorway and gasped. He had to look twice to be sure it wasn't some sort of optical illusion, trompe l'oeil. His garden had been cut in half!

A huge hole, the size of a city bus, or larger, had opened up between his fuchsia rum runners and lavender eyes of the storm. He shuffled as fast as he could down the path. He stopped at the precipice, by the lip of the ditch, and looked down – then instantly pulled back.

He couldn't look over the edge. It was too hot! It felt like it would melt his face. The ground quivered and a vast tower of steam and stone and dust shot out of the crevasse.

Pickings was thrown backwards to the ground. The volcano was erupting! And, just as this completely terrifying thought had settled in his mind, he was assaulted with the bleak, bone-chilling certitude that he was going to die.

The ground continued to tremble violently, shaking his stunted stand of gnarled Canary Pine. His house began to groan, to wobble and finally bend and fall. Pickings ran over to his jeep. Miraculously it had been parked in front, not in the carport, beside the shattered house. He had been too lazy to walk down to his mailbox earlier that morning. He leapt into the vehicle. He turned the ignition key and the engine came to life. He put the jeep in gear and screamed out of the driveway. He turned the corner, banked. He accelerated down the straightaway. Then he breathed a deep sigh of relief, until he suddenly recalled his manuscript, the way that it had looked there on his writing desk as he had run out of the house, all stacked and neatly typed, unabashedly dense, the labor of five years, when the mountain road gave way. The tarmac started to melt. There was no way to negotiate the road. Then, there was no road.

Pickings leapt out of the jeep. He felt as if he were descending into a Pieter Bruegel mindscape, a hectare of the *Triumph of Hell.* He walked a dozen paces when the earth opened up before him, spewing steam and fire. He turned the other way. Another fissure blocked his path. It didn't matter, he thought. It was too hot to move anyway. The last thing that he thought of was his missing wife, his Layla, and his two children back in England. They were probably sitting down to tea right now. He wanted desperately to move. He wanted to reach out to them. But he couldn't do it. He couldn't do anything . . . but boil.

Chapter 42
Thursday, February 3 – 3:02 PM
La Palma, The Canary Islands

The Seahawk tumbled from the sky. The downdraft following the detonation of the bomb continued to suck the helicopter downwards toward the waiting funnel of the Cumbre Vieja. Then, without warning, the vacuum created by the shock wave filled. The instrumentation settled. The helicopter flipped, righted herself and started rising once again.

Inside the ship, Warhaftig pulled himself off Decker and struggled to his feet. "Are you alright?" he said. Seiden steadied him from behind.

Decker was still lying next to Swenson. He grabbed a nearby blanket and covered her again. Swenson sat up. She looked about. The Rangers were strapped in all around her. They were okay. She looked down, under the blanket, and began to strip away the magnesium tape still wrapped about her body. Everyone pretended not to watch.

"Excuse me," Warhaftig shouted over the din. "I have to break the news to the Director." He zigzagged forward toward the cockpit.

"And I must contact my superiors," said Seiden, following in his wake.

Decker stared out through the open helicopter hatch. The island was disappearing from view. They were headed north-northwest, toward the Azores. He looked over at Swenson. "Can I help?" he said. She was picking off the remaining metal ribbon like strands of a cocoon.

"What?" She cupped a hand behind her ear.

"Can I help?" Decker shouted, pointing.

"No thanks, I got it," she replied. Then she changed her mind. "Well, maybe you can help me with the pieces on my back."

Decker shimmied over to her. He reached his hands behind the blanket and began to pull the metal ribbon off her naked shoulders. It unraveled like dried snakeskin. "You look like a mummy in some new age horror flick," he said.

"Does that mean I'm already dead?" She turned and looked at him and smiled. He was looking at her cleavage. "Why, John Decker, Junior! You are such a boy. I had no idea. You like my outfit, huh?" She lowered the towel a little more. "Look what was sitting on your coach two nights ago," she said, "before you sent her to bed."

"I think you like to torture me, don't you?"

"Yes." She pulled the towel up, turned away. All the soldiers were staring at her.

"Emily?"

"Yes, John?"

"Before, when we were on our way to La Palma, you seemed to believe that there might be some way of stopping this. I mean, I know you said there wasn't. But you kind of hesitated. Just for a moment. I thought . . . " He tried to look away, tried to ignore the logical extension of his argument. Forty million souls, he thought, compared to one or two. "When you mentioned Newton, I thought . . . Maybe I'm wrong."

She shook her head. Her back was to him and he couldn't see her face. But he could feel the way she tightened up, the way she suddenly withdrew into herself. Then she leaned back into his arms. She lay her head on his chest. "No, you're not wrong," she said. "Maybe there is." She looked into his eyes. "For every action, there is an equal and opposite reaction."

"And for a wave?"

"A counter-wave," she said. Then she smiled. "Remember I told you about my descent into those canyons off the Jersey coast? With E.J., my professor?"

He nodded.

"Well, I was thinking. What if someone, somehow were to descend into those tunnels along the Continental Shelf? What if they planted a nuclear device, like El Aqrab did in La Palma, and set it off?"

"What if they did?"

"Well, don't you see? An explosion might precipitate eruptions of the gas trapped in the sediments beneath, initiate a massive underwater landslide. If someone were to trigger a mega-tsunami on the opposite side of the Atlantic, if we could propagate a counter-wave, traveling east – at least theoretically, and if everything worked perfectly – the two would meet and . . . "

" . . . cancel each other out. Is that it? Is that what you mean?"

"Something like that. Of course there would still be lots of damage, residual effects. But it wouldn't kill tens of millions. On the other hand, it might just make things worse."

"I doubt things could get a whole lot worse than a twenty-story wave crashing through the Eastern Seaboard. Not to mention the Caribbean, Venezuela and Brazil. Let's face it, Emily, we can't just sit here and watch the whole world go to hell. Someone will have to try."

Swenson nodded, turned away. Decker felt the labyrinth of his argument unwind.

Warhaftig stumbled down the aisle. He looked completely stunned, as if someone has just punched him in the face. "That was the President," he said. "He and his advisors all agree that there's only so much we can do in only fifteen hours. We'll do our best, of course. FEMA will supervise emergency evacuations of all the major cities on the coast. New York, thank God, is already virtually deserted. Members of Congress and the White House staff are being flown to safety as we speak. The Pentagon . . . " He shook his head. "By dawn tomorrow, more than thirty-five million Americans will be dead. Tens of thousands will die just trying to get away. If only we had listened to you sooner, John, we might have—"

"We have an idea," said Decker, interrupting him. "Well, Swenson does. A way of maybe stopping this."

Warhaftig looked shocked. "But I thought you told me—"

"A counter-wave," she said.

"A counter what?"

Swenson told him of her plan.

After a moment, Warhaftig said, "Do you really think it could work?"

"I don't know," said Swenson. "But John is right. Someone has to try."

Warhaftig walked back toward the front of the helicopter and gathered up some headsets. Seiden was standing in the cockpit chatting with his superiors. "We have a plan," Warhaftig said. He described it briefly.

"Wait a minute." Seiden tapped his microphone. "Just a moment, sir, there's been a change in strategy. I'll have to call you back."

Warhaftig carried the headsets astern. He handed them out, put one on himself, and showed them how to plug into the console.

Decker slipped his headset on. Now that it was gone, he suddenly realized how loud and irritating the noise from the blades and open hatch had been. He could hear Warhaftig's voice clear as a bell.

First, they contacted the Azores and arranged for the fastest plane available to meet them in São Miguel, some commandeered Citation X. The Spanish millionaire who owned her threatened to call the Prime Minister of Spain, but then he heard about the looming wave and changed his tune. He'd be more than happy to assist the Americans, he said. At no expense.

Swenson knew a fair amount about the islands of the Azores, having traveled there for a conference three years earlier. She informed them they were the EU's most secluded outpost, spread out across 600 kilometers of ocean, located roughly 1,500 kilometers or two hours' flying time from Lisbon. Running along a southeast to northwest axis, the islands were separated into three main clusters: the Eastern Group of São Miguel and Santa Maria; the Central Group of Terceira, Graciosa, São Jorge, Pico and Faial; and the Western Group of Flores and Corvo.

Like the Canaries, they had been formed by the eruption of volcanoes, and lay on the Mid-Atlantic Ridge, a fault line that zigzagged for some 16,000 kilometers from beneath the northern icecap southwards, turning east around the southern tip of Africa to meet with the Indian Ocean Ridge. Three plates collided underneath the ocean at the base of the Azores, or rather diverged, said Swenson, in a kind of T-shaped triple junction between Flores and Faial.

The more Decker listened to Emily, the more entranced he became — and the more uncertain. As a Midwesterner, he had never experienced earthquakes or seismic activity of any kind. The earth had always seemed a permanent place to him; indeed, uncompromising. But it wasn't fixed. Nothing was fixed. The ground swirled over molten rock, the earth twirled round the sun, the sun whirled silently around the galaxy in space.

"Decker?"

Decker looked up. Warhaftig was pointing at his headset. "Get ready."

"For what?"

"The President. I explained your plan to him. He wants to talk to you."

Decker sat up. "The President wants to talk to me?"

"To you and Emily. And Acting Chief Seiden too. Stand by. Go ahead," he said. "Mr. President, can you hear me, sir?"

"I can hear you," someone said. "Hello, Dr. Swenson. Are you there?" The voice sounded tinny and distant, and yet Decker knew it was the President. He sounded just like on TV, with the same Texas twang and nasal overtone.

"Agent Warhaftig has briefed us on the situation. I'm going to hand the phone over to one of my advisors so you can tell her exactly what we need to do. Is Special Agent Decker there?"

"Yes, sir," he said. "I can hear you, Mr. President."

Swenson grabbed Decker by the sleeve and drew him close. Their heads were almost touching.

"I just wanted to thank you two for everything you've done. Secretary Dale has been keeping me abreast of your activities, every hour, on the hour, all day long. No matter what happens, whether this plan of yours succeeds or not, you two are heroes in my book. You've both risked your lives for your country, and that's something that none of us will ever forget. That goes for you too, Chief Seiden. I understand that without your help, Special Agent Decker and Ms. Swenson wouldn't be here to accept my gratitude. This will only strengthen the alliance between our two great nations. I wish you all good luck. And God speed," he said. "Now, let me put Allegra on. Tell her exactly what she needs to do and we'll make it happen."

"OK," they heard a voice say. "Hello, Ms. Swenson, Agent Decker. This is National Security Advisor, Allegra Wheatley."

"Nice to meet you," Swenson stuttered, immediately rolling her eyes.

"Nice to meet you too, Emily. Are you okay? Don't be nervous. Just tell me what you need. We have a Navy attack-class submarine already stationed off New York."

Decker could hear Swenson sigh. He felt her hand slip into his, and squeeze. "That's not going to work," she said. "A nuclear sub's too big. The canyon passages are really narrow and unless you want the wave to end up on the coast, you'll have to plant it deep inside a fissure on the eastern flank. We're going to need a Deep Submergence Vehicle. A DSV. The nearest one's probably at WHOI. I mean the Woods Hole Oceanographic Institute, in Massachusetts. She's called the *Alvin*."

They could hear Wheatley cover up the phone and chat briefly with someone else. "That's fine, Emily," she continued. "How much does it weigh?"

"Weigh? I don't know. Ten to fifteen metric tons, I guess. In the air? Maybe more. I don't know," said Swenson nervously. "Why?"

"It will take too long for the *Alvin's* mother ship to steam down from Woods Hole. We'll have to transport it by Chinook. That's a helicopter." She was interrupted once again. Someone else seemed to be listening at the other end. "OK," she continued. "I've been told that an MH-47E Chinook can only hoist around 27,000 pounds. We're going to have to call our friends in Cuba and ask to borrow an Mi-26. It's got the hauling capacity of a Hercules."

"Are you sure the Cubans will comply?" Warhaftig said.

Wheatley did not hesitate. "Once this tsunami hits, they're going to need an awful lot of aid. Frankly, we'll be their only hope, no matter what they feel politically."

"Cuba's a long way away."

"The Mi-26 cruises at around two hundred miles per hour," said Wheatley. "If La Palma doesn't collapse for another nine or ten hours – which none of us thinks is likely – and if it then takes the wave another six plus hours to reach us, we should have enough time to fly her up to Woods Hole and hoist the *Alvin* back. Where would you like us to bring it, honey?"

"Approximately two hundred kilometers east-southeast of Atlantic City. But don't forget: we're going to need at least an hour to get down to the proper depths. And what about our cruise plan?"

Wheatley laughed. "I think they'll let it slide this time. It may be operated by WHOI, but the *Alvin*'s Navy-owned. We'll have her rendezvous with a Navy frigate. The USS *Stanfield* is off New York. And she's armed with a suitable nuclear device. The *Alvin*, Emily; is she equipped with some kind of sample tray or bucket?"

"A basket, yes."

"And how much can it carry?"

"About three hundred kilos."

"That's not going to be enough. What about manipulators?"

"Even less. Maybe a couple of hundred kilos."

"OK. Let's not worry about it now. We'll have a team of engineers rig something up in Massachusetts while they're waiting for the Mi-26. Where exactly are these blowouts on the Continental Shelf? Can you give me the coordinates?"

"Thirty-six degrees, forty-five north. Seventy-four degrees, fifty west. The Young Canyons are where we've seen the most recent faults."

As Swenson continued to relay her instructions to the President's National Security Advisor, Decker turned and looked out through the porthole at the sea below. Everything seemed completely surreal. The Atlantic was absolutely calm here. It was hard to imagine the giant wave that would soon be on their tail at the speed of a commercial jet. So much adrenaline was pumping through his veins that Decker felt giddy, almost light-headed. Swenson continued to talk with the casual tone of someone ordering up a pizza. And then the pilot suddenly cut in.

"The Azores," he said. "We'll be landing in just a few minutes. Fasten your seatbelts please."

Decker could see the islands in the distance. They rose out of the sea, mountainous and wild, ringed by white waves. He tried not to think of what they'd look like by nightfall.

Chapter 43
Friday, February 4 – 12:16 AM
La Palma, The Canary Islands

In slightly more than nine hours from the time Pickings was boiled alive, a little after midnight, a twenty-kilometer crack opened up along the Cumbre Vieja range and the island of La Palma came apart.

A titanic chunk of rock the size of Maui – five hundred billion tons – slid suddenly into the sea, creating a debris avalanche that would eventually extend sixty kilometers from La Palma.

The collapse of the volcano's western flank sent a dome of water a thousand meters into the air – three times the height of the Empire State Building – and more than forty kilometers wide in each direction. As the dome collapsed, and then rebounded, giant waves began to form and build, fueled by the great tsunami wave train, itself created as the landslide sped away below the surface of the sea.

In less than ten minutes, it was two hundred and fifty kilometers from La Palma.

As it traveled eastward and struck the shores of the Sahara, the wave grew exponentially, rising one hundred meters into the air. To the west, the wave began to flatten out, to roll toward the Americas – from Bar Harbor to Bahia – at seven hundred kilometers per hour. And to the north, it closed on the Azores.

* * *

The Seahawk helicopter landed. Swenson, Decker, Seiden and Warhaftig leapt out and ran across the tarmac to the waiting Citation X, already throbbing on the runway. The Cessna was the fastest non-military jet in the world. It would carry them at close to the speed of sound across the Atlantic, ahead of the mega-tsunami.

They boarded the plane. Emily slipped into a short black cocktail dress and heels – the only women's clothing they could find aboard. She derided Decker and Warhaftig and, desperate to cut the tension in the air, accused them of planning the wardrobe in advance. "You just wanted to see me in a miniskirt, didn't you?" she said.

They strapped themselves in and the streamlined silver ship took off like a rocket, climbing to 43,000 feet in less than half an hour. When they'd reached an altitude of 50,000 feet, the plane began to level off, cruising at around five hundred miles per hour. They were 20,000 feet above commercial traffic and the sky was absolutely clear. The ocean glimmered far below. Above, the sun looked close enough to touch.

Decker was sitting next to Swenson. He excused himself for a moment, got up and squeezed his way back between the seats towards Warhaftig, who was chatting with Seiden in the stern. "What's up?" Warhaftig asked.

He was sitting on the port side of the jet, facing Seiden and the bow, while Seiden faced the stern. Decker sat down in one of the cream-colored leather seats across the narrow aisle, directly across from Warhaftig. "I wanted to ask you something."

"What?"

Decker started to speak, then hesitated.

"What is it, John? Spit it out."

"I need to know something."

"What?"

Decker sighed. "Why did you take my memory stick, back at the surveillance squat in Queens?"

Warhaftig rolled his eyes. "Oh, that again." He laughed. "All right," he said. "If you really want to know. The Agency was aware of El Aqrab's propensity to reveal quotations at the scene of his events. When you mentioned those wallpapers, I figured they were connected somehow. But I didn't know how. And I didn't know you then either, or trust you. After all, you recruited Professor Hassan, a man with no clearance whatsoever. A man, indeed, with a vested interest – pro-Palestinian as he is – to see this mission fail."

"Professor Jusef Hassan?" said Seiden, interrupting. "From Columbia? What does *he* have to do with this?" He stared at Warhaftig.

"He helped me figure out the quotes from the Qur'an. If you were so upset about it," Decker continued, "why didn't you do something, Otto? Why didn't you tell Johnson? God knows, he always suspected something." He paused for a moment, then added, "Maybe you did tell him."

"I didn't have to," said Warhaftig. "You're right, he did suspect you of exploiting 'unofficial' resources. Why do you think he was always bitching?"

"But if you knew, how come you didn't try and stop me?"

"John, this isn't the time or place to discuss all this." He glanced forward at Seiden.

"Just answer me, Otto. I need to know."

"Alright, alright," said Warhaftig. "We were thrilled when you began to interpret those designs. None of our experts had had any success, and the Israelis — no offense, Ben — were not exactly forthcoming. We were happy to have you use Hassan . . . unofficially, since he obviously had no interest in being exposed as an FBI collaborator. Either way, Johnson won. If Hassan turned out to be useless, the SAC could let it pass, or hang you out to dry, at his discretion. On the other hand, if Hassan turned out to be effective, as the supervisor of the task force, the SAC would get the credit. Even if it got real ugly, if Hassan's participation were revealed, Johnson's strident warnings to you, his obsession about protocol and intelligence sharing would help insulate him from blame. Why do you think he was so public always in his criticism? It wasn't just because he didn't like you — which he doesn't, by the way — or because he was 'forced' to add you to the team."

Warhaftig smiled. "But in the end, John, it was *you* who elected to work with Hassan, despite the risks, and without official knowledge or approval. You were so eager to solve that puzzle, you didn't care how you did it. I didn't know if I could count on you, if you'd already been compromised by Hassan, or if you were just plain naïve. Face it, John — you're not a team player. You never have been. Some call you a loose cannon and—"

"I don't buy it," Decker said. He shook his head. "And I don't buy that story about evidence going missing."

"What's that?" said Seiden.

"I was told there was a robbery at Mossad headquarters in Tel Aviv, and that the videotape which El Aqrab made of the Miller murders had been stolen."

"Ah, I see," said Seiden. He focused on Warhaftig, a tiny smile playing on his lips. "Now I think I understand. Yes, Agent Warhaftig. Very good. *Mazel tov.*" Then he looked across the aisle at Decker, adding, "There was no robbery in Tel Aviv. Although it was certainly made to look that way."

"Jesus Christ!" Warhaftig said. He reddened visibly. "John, get back to your seat."

"You expect me to believe that?" Decker said. "One of the most wanted men in Israel, and no one bothered to make a copy of the tape that documents his latest killings? That doesn't make any sense. And even if there were only one copy, why wasn't it in some evidence locker in Jerusalem, or in the Knesset someplace, instead of in Tel Aviv?"

Decker suddenly realized he was shouting. He lowered his voice and said, "Just before he tried to kill us, El Aqrab confessed Garron had stolen money from him, cash his father kept at home in case the ben Saad family had to flee the country. A lot of cash – almost two and a half million dollars. He said Garron used it to finance his elections."

"And you believed him," Seiden said, "because, as a baby killer and murderer of women, he is such an honorable man." He looked derisively at Decker but there was something about his voice – the slightest hesitation, a faulty intonation – that undermined its authenticity.

Even Seiden's unsure, thought Decker. "He had no motive to lie. He thought I was about to die. Yes, I believed him. That's why Garron was so damned sensitive. Do you really think he'd let the only copy of that tape remain in Tel Aviv? Something doesn't add up."

Decker stood. He hovered in the narrow aisle. "No," he said. "You had a copy of that tape already, didn't you? I don't know how, but you knew about that illustration, even before I saw the wallpaper in Queens. You recognized those words. I saw your face, Otto. You probably already knew about Garron too. After everything we've been through together and you're still lying to me."

"I didn't know about Garron," Warhaftig answered testily. "But, frankly, I'm not surprised. He and his son have been under a financial cloud for years. Just because I'm a Jew doesn't mean I automatically like the man."

"What does it mean, then, Otto?"

"Don't be a fool, John. I have a job to do, and so do you. Israel is our strongest ally in the Middle East. This isn't about the Palestinians. Or the Israelis, for that matter. It's about *our* country, John. Yours and mine. Our industry and commerce. And good old American jobs. All that we are as a nation, as a people depends upon the oil and, therefore, the politico-economic security of one of the most volatile regions of the world. A world that's getting smaller, mind you, and deadlier every day. Why do you think we're in Iraq, for Christ's sake? Just because Saddam was a sadistic tyrant? Why do you think we're in Afghanistan? We have to support Israel, no matter what we think."

"I am trying to support her. Don't you get it?" Decker said. "It's time the Israelis tested the resolve of the Islamic faith. They should sue for peace. A real and lasting peace. Now that would be truly brave, instead of simply obdurate. Then, if the fundamentalists refused to cease hostilities – as prescribed by the Qur'an – they'd lose their moral authority. In front of the whole Islamic world." He shook his head. "Of all the peoples on this earth, you'd think the Israelis would understand what it means to be persecuted, to be . . . abused. It's as if they're suffering from a collective legacy of guilt, as if – as victims of abuse – they're compelled to abuse others." He paused. Then he looked down at Seiden and said, "'The sins of the father.' You're a student of psychology, aren't you? You know exactly what I'm talking about."

"Look John," said Warhaftig. "It isn't up to us to judge. We're not the politicians, thank God. I'm just trying to do my job. Sometimes it isn't a very pleasant one, but it's what I swore an oath to do."

"Oh, I get it. 'I was just following orders.' Isn't that what they said at Nuremberg?"

Warhaftig leapt to his feet. He clenched his fists. Decker puffed himself up. Seiden jumped in between them, facing Decker, a scowl darkening his face.

Then Swenson suddenly appeared. She had overheard them arguing. "Who fucking cares?" she said. "We're probably all about to die anyway."

"I care," said Decker, rising to his full height. Seiden was still a good three inches taller.

"We don't have time for this," she said. "The world's about to be destroyed and you're bickering like children. Men!" she spat. "Look at you prance. That's why this planet's so fucked up – you idiots are running things." Then she turned away and said, "I have to prepare for my descent."

"What descent?" said Decker, suddenly sobered.

"Who do you think's going to navigate the *Alvin* to set off the counter-wave? I'm the best shot we've got."

"She's right, you know," Warhaftig said.

"Shut up," said Decker. "You keep out of this. Why do you have to go? I thought you said you'd never set foot in a DSV again. Shouldn't the Navy or–"

"I know those canyons better than anyone on the East Coast," she said. "And I know the *Alvin*." She placed her hand on Decker's shoulder. "You know I'm right, John. Think about it."

The argument reached its logical conclusion. He had known it all along. He had seen this darkened terminus at the far end of the labyrinth as soon as she had mentioned Newton, and there was no amount of foliation, no plenitude of mirrors or gilded tiles that could blind him from the truth. Equal and opposite reactions.

"Then, I'm going with you," Decker said. He spoke with grim finality. "I'm not breaking up this team. Not now. Not after everything we've been through."

"I'm sure the Navy will provide me with a pilot. I don't need you, John. We probably won't . . . " She hesitated. She took him by the hand. Then she said, "We won't have time to get too far before we have to set off the device. Otherwise it won't work. The mega-tsunami will be on us."

Decker looked deep into her eyes. "You don't have a choice, Emily," he said. "It's a three-man sub. I'm paid to risk my life, as Otto here just reminded me. If you go, I go. At least that will solve his problem. Fewer people talking once this is over."

"Believe it or not, John," said Warhaftig, "I would actually enjoy seeing you two again, once this is over."

"I think the whole world will," said Seiden.

"Question is: What kind of world will it be?" said Decker. "I'm not sure it'll be much fun picking up the pieces."

"You really want to know?" Warhaftig said. He pulled a piece of paper from his jacket and handed it to Decker.

It was a damage assessment report, labeled Top Secret, an exercise in scenario planning run by DARPA and the CIA. Decker studied it carefully. It estimated damages, lives lost, infrastructure ruined. And the ripples extended worldwide. Apparently, with the annihilation of financial systems, of telecommunications and energy infrastructure, of so much industry and government and academia on the east coast, not only would the United States begin to slide into a deep depression, but *every* nation of the world would be affected.

With one third of it crippled, the global economy would eventually disintegrate. Without American funding, transnational groups would fall apart. The U.N. and NATO would flounder. Each country would be left alone to struggle in defense of its own petty national interests. Regional conflicts would expand into all-out wars. The rise of Islamic fundamentalism, accompanied by regional instability, would encourage extremist groups. The oil-producing nations of the Middle East would fall into the hands of radical Shi'i clergy, or pseudo-fundamentalists, military potentates. Oil exports would be severed, precipitating worldwide shortages.

Depression would spiral into lawlessness and blight, hopelessness to anarchy and chaos, which in turn would stimulate totalitarianism, and a whole new generation of fascists.

At the bottom of the page were the words: *Probability of Occurrence: 89%.*

Decker looked up. "We have to succeed," he said. "We have no choice."

"The sad part is," said Swenson, "we'll probably never know."

"What does that mean?"

"The shock will hit us long before the two waves come together."

Chapter 44
Friday, February 4 – 3:08 AM
Atlantic City, New Jersey

The pilot of the Citation X decided to land at the Atlantic City Airport because the runways were a lot more manageable and even longer than the runways at McGuire. It was a cold wet night in Jersey. The Hotels and Casinos on the boardwalk were deserted. News of the impending wave had already hit the media and it seemed like every resident was boarding up his house before heading west. As if it would make a difference, Decker thought.

They ran across the tarmac and transferred to another S-70B Seahawk helicopter. It lifted off immediately. They flew at breakneck speed over the grim Atlantic coast. The water was choppy and fierce, flecked with white-tops, frightening. Decker grumbled to himself. *It couldn't have been a nice night*, he lamented. *It couldn't have been starry and clear, windless and pacific.* He glanced out of his window and saw the USS *Stanfield* glowing off to port. She didn't look very big, he thought.

The helicopter banked steeply and Decker felt a hand slip over his. Swenson was sitting next to him. He looked down at her fingers. They fit perfectly around his fist. The ship descended, fell, and finally settled on the deck. Decker looked outside. It was raining hard. It was absolutely pouring. He could see two men running toward the helicopter wearing raincoats, holding hats to their heads, trying to avoid the puddles on the deck. They were carrying closed umbrellas. A moment later the door to the Seahawk opened, and a gust of ocean wind whisked through the cabin. Decker and Swenson made their way forward, joined by Warhaftig and Seiden at the door.

A young sailor held an umbrella up outside. Beside him stood an officer. His back was still in the rain, and it was getting soaked.

"This is Captain Tom Mason," said the sailor.

Warhaftig introduced himself. "And this here is Dr. Emily Swenson, Special Agent Decker of the FBI, and Ben Seiden, Israeli intelligence."

"I'm not a doctor yet," said Swenson.

"Well, practically," Warhaftig said. "We'll make it semi-official then, an honorary degree. I hear captains have extraordinary powers in these kinds of situations. Isn't that right, Captain Mason?"

"I can even marry people," Mason added with a wink. The captain was a relatively young man, in his late thirties, early forties, with a fine, well-chiseled face and pale green eyes. He tipped his hat at Swenson. "Shall we go?"

They dashed into the rain, only partially protected by the flapping black umbrellas. The wind whistled across the unprotected deck, blowing the water sideways. By the time they ducked into a hatchway, they were soaked.

Another sailor appeared and handed them some towels. The Seahawk gradually ascended. Decker watched it fly away through the open hatchway and he felt curiously alone. Now there was nowhere to go – but down, into the deep.

Swenson ran a towel across her hair. The rain had smudged her mascara. Her skin was shiny and raw. She was staring at a nearby gangway. Decker heard, then saw a pair of feet descending. A young man ambled slowly into view, smooth as a trickle of molasses.

"This here is Second Lieutenant Roger Speers," the captain said. "He's going to be piloting the *Alvin*. Volunteered."

Speers was a young man, in his late twenties, with a buzz cut, baby blue eyes, and jolly round features. "Assuming it gets here," he said laconically.

"Don't worry. It'll get here," the captain assured him.

Speers leered at Swenson. "Helluva ride in this weather."

Emily stepped back.

"Better take that off."

"What?" Swenson looked down. Her black cocktail dress clung to her skin like a wetsuit.

"Your makeup, ma'am. No makeup in the DSV."

"Yes, I know," she answered testily.

Captain Mason stepped up. "Let me show you to your cabin, Dr. Swenson. Give you a chance to freshen up a bit before your descent."

"You don't mind if I join you?" Seiden said. "I could use a change of clothes."

"Not at all," said Captain Mason.

They ambled off with Speers in tow. Decker and Warhaftig were left topside alone. "I've got some news," Warhaftig said. He stood there cleaning his glasses with his tie.

"What now?"

"El Aqrab emailed a video clip to Seamus Gallagher right before the bombing. In it, he proudly announces his intention to set off the nuclear device on La Palma and kick-start the mega-tsunami. It's been all over the Net. The Agency thinks it's real. They believe it was recorded just before the nuke went off. At least I hope so." Warhaftig shrugged. "Ironically, Gallagher's on vacation. His assistant picked it up. From the recording it appears that El Aqrab expected to die in the explosion. We haven't heard anything to the contrary."

"Don't count on it," said Decker.

All of a sudden, the giant Mi-26 appeared like a seabird off to port, thundering towards them through the halo of the deck lights, with the lumbering submersible suspended underneath by cables. Decker watched it through the open hatch. The helicopter hovered over the Navy frigate and slowly lowered the *Alvin* to the deck. Within minutes the submersible was being armed with a modified W-80 nuclear device stripped from the warhead of an 18-feet Tomahawk missile.

The entire operation took less than half an hour. Swenson and Speers and Seiden reappeared. She was dressed in a dark blue flight suit with a zipper running down the front, and a pair of solid boots. But no uniform, no matter how plain, could conceal her womanly figure. They dashed across the deck to inspect the modifications. Decker was about to join them when Warhaftig held him back, out of the rain.

"Hold on a second," he said. "I wanted to tell you something." He hesitated. "Before you go." He suddenly looked old and out of shape. He looked exhausted. "You were right, John," he said. "I knew about those murders in Tel Aviv. When you first spotted that calligraphy on the PC in Moussa's apartment, as soon as you uttered those words, I knew. We got a video clip of the killings soon after they occurred. Unofficially," he said. "I couldn't tell you. You didn't have the clearance. And your illicit meetings with Hassan made you high risk."

"I still don't," Decker said.

Warhaftig chuckled. "So court-martial me," he said.

"You have a man on the inside, don't you?" Decker said. "Within the Israeli government, in the intelligence services."

Warhaftig looked out at the DSV and nodded. "He got us a copy of the tape," he said. "But we couldn't tell you. That's why I took your pictures. But when we realized your facility, we began to feed you information bit by bit, and staged that robbery in Tel Aviv as a cover for our man. Then we recruited Hassan."

"We?"

"Yes. I was in contact with him too, but he preferred to deal with you. What I couldn't get out of you, he did. He had no choice but to cooperate. You know what we could do to him if we wanted to – detention, deportation. And, frankly, it was better for Jusef if he worked through you, rather than through more official channels. I thought you should know."

"Thanks, Otto." Decker started to leave but Warhaftig held him back.

"Good luck," Warhaftig said. He stuck his hand out.

Decker was standing in the rain. It was washing down his back. He looked down at Warhaftig's hand. Then, finally, he shook it. "Thanks for everything," he said. With that he turned and ran across the deck.

Swenson and Speers had already climbed up into the DSV. Decker could see her golden hair disappearing through the hatchway. He clambered up the narrow ladder, slipped through the hatch, and waved once more at Seiden and Warhaftig who were standing in the rain on the deck below. Then he closed the hatch, and the *Alvin* was hoisted slowly up and over the side, down into the waves.

"God help them," Seiden said as the submersible faded out of sight.

"God help us all," Warhaftig whispered back.

*   *   *

The *Rêve de Chantal* steamed slowly south, toward Venezuela. Topside, the Gambian, Momodou Marong, was fishing with a hand line, his shirt off, and a huge cigar dangling precariously from his lips.

Suddenly, he heard what sounded like distant thunder. He looked up but the sky was clear, dotted with stars. The noise grew louder. The Gambian stood up and looked across the rail to starboard. He could see whitecaps in the moonlight flowing evenly into the great bay of Bathsheba on the island of Barbados only a mile or two away. Then the freighter seemed to lurch as if she'd run aground. Marong looked back toward the shore. The sea was pulling back. It was retreating from the beach. The freighter yawed and rolled. He held on to the rail. His fishing line drew taut. He let it go and ran across the deck.

In the distance, off the port beam, Marong could see what appeared to be a great white wall of water, rising higher and higher as it approached the freighter at a frightening speed. It rose above the tallest boom, above the highest mast or funnel. It seemed to block out the entire sky, and then it was upon him, bursting his body like a great balloon against the bulwark, lifting the freighter up and over until she rolled and rolled submerged onto the island, coming to rest at last, a twisted wreck of steel and wood and dying flesh, more than a quarter of a mile inland.

Chapter 45
Friday, February 4 – 4:27 AM
The Young Canyons

The *Alvin* descended slowly into the black Atlantic. The water in the upper column was fairly turbulent but this, Speers assured them, was relatively normal. The mega-tsunami was still two hours distant.

During the descent, Swenson and Roger Speers briefed Decker on the history and capabilities of the DSV. Originally constructed in 1964, the submersible was 7.1 meters long and 3.7 meters high, with a cruising speed of approximately half a knot. Despite her age, the DSV remained a state-of-the-art submersible, thanks to a host of reconstructions and numerous improvements over the years. Constructed of 4.9 centimeters of titanium, the hull could tolerate pressures of up to 208 centimeters OD, allowing two scientists and a pilot to descend to depths of more than 4,500 meters for more than 70 hours.

Generally, a support or "mother" ship called the *Atlantis* accompanied the vessel. In this case, due to time constraints, the *USS Stanfield* was going to have to serve this role, catching the acoustic pulse the DSV emitted every three seconds through the frigate's transducer array. Everything about the voyage had been rushed and, during the descent, Speers and Swenson fretted about the compromises they'd been forced to make.

Generally, when working at maximum depths, it took about two hours for the DSV to reach the ocean floor, and another two to surface. The four hours of working time during a Day On Station (DOS) was crammed with carefully planned experiments, photography and sampling by scientists using the vessel's three twelve-inch diameter view ports, four video cameras, two hydraulic robotic arms, and a sample basket mounted on the prow. To ensure maximum productivity within this narrow timeframe, scientists spent weeks, sometimes months, preparing for a voyage before setting out to sea. A preliminary cruise plan was drawn up, including a complete dive profile, equipment requirements and descriptions (dive by dive), as well as navigation requirements.

"We haven't done any of these things," said Swenson, shaking her head. "We're basically winging it."

"We have no choice," said Decker.

Swenson frowned and looked out through her view port. Despite the quartz iodide and metal halide lights mounted on the hull, there was nothing to see as they descended slowly through the depths. "I know that," she said tightly. Then turning to Decker she added, "But I'm a scientist, John, remember? Experiments are all about the preparation. Developing a hypothesis and a way to test it."

"Either we succeed and save millions of lives, or we don't. I don't mean to be glib, but that about sums it up."

Speers chuckled to himself. "How long you guys known each other?" he said.

"None of your business," they snapped in unison.

"Not long," added Decker sheepishly.

"Just asking." Clearly Speers had hit a nerve and he turned back to the console. "The guys at WHOI did a good job with the bomb mount," he said, changing the subject. "With the sample basket gone, we should have no problem maneuvering. How big did you say those blowouts are?"

Swenson sighed. Speers had already asked this question twice before. "Some are as wide as fifteen hundred meters," she replied, "fifty deep and up to five thousand meters long."

Speers whistled. "Must have been a pretty big explosion to make that kind of hole. How were they formed?"

"Gas upwellings, in all probability, but we don't really know for sure. A couple of years ago a team from WHOI and Duke University towed a SUBSCAN — a seafloor and sub-bottom imaging system — about two thousand kilometers along the shelf. They also took some sediment core samples using a gravity core."

"Two thousand miles!" said Decker. "That's a lot of coastline."

"It wasn't linear, of course. The ship traveled back and forth over the study area in a pattern called 'mowing the lawn.' Then they built a grid of overlapping data sections to create a final image. Gas has a characteristic signal," Swenson said, "that commonly shows up as a bright, high-amplitude reflection obscuring any deeper signals. The data showed that the entire area is charged with gas, and we suspect the cracks are a system of large depressions along the edge that were formed by gas erupting through the seafloor. These layers look like the remnants of an ancient delta that reached out far beyond the current coastline during the last ice age. Sea levels were much lower then than they are today. The samples the team recovered included silty clay, sand and gravel from the bottom, and these are consistent with deltaic settings. Where these deposits are absent, the gas simply percolates harmlessly to the surface."

"So these impermeable sediments are keeping the gas from getting out," said Speers.

"That's right. But, over time, we believe pressure from the underlying gas builds up."

"Like a cork in a champagne bottle," Decker said.

"A very big bottle," Speers added ruefully. "As my daddy used to say: When you got gas, let it out."

"Some scientists," Swenson continued, ignoring him, "from both Columbia University and the Texas Institute for Geophysics speculate the rising gas might play a role in triggering collapses of the shelf. The Continental Shelf here is historically prone to landslides. An enormous slide occurred just to the south of here only sixteen to eighteen thousand years ago, at the end of the last ice age."

"So that's the plan then," Speers responded. "We plant this bomb inside one of the blowout depressions, trigger it before the other tsunami gets here, and hope it knocks a chunk off the Outer Continental Shelf. Is that it?"

"That's it," said Swenson.

"Sounds pretty straight-forward."

"It won't be. We can't just drop the bomb on the bottom and hope for the best," said Swenson. "To make sure the gas erupts – causing a landslide – and radiates a mega-tsunami in the appropriate direction, we'll have to navigate the *Alvin* as deep inside one of the dormant tunnels within the blowouts as we can."

Speers nodded. "I've made more than thirty dives in the *Alvin* over the last six years. I was on the mission when we recovered that hydrogen bomb some knucklehead dropped onto the bottom of the Mediterranean in '98. I've surveyed the *Titanic* and helped explore those deep-sea hydrothermal vents covered in tube worms. But I've never taken this DSV into a tunnel. The Submerged Operating Limits guide specifically states that *Alvin* – and I quote – 'will not be operated in such a fashion so as to pass under an object, either natural or manmade . . . *Alvin* will remain clear of wreckage, debris, or natural terrain features which have entanglement or entrapment potential.' Unquote."

"I know," said Swenson.

"Of course," continued Speers. "The manual also says, '*Alvin* will remain clear of any explosives devices which may be sighted.'" He laughed. "I guess this nuclear bomb on the prow kind of blows that one, huh?"

Decker smiled. He looked over at Swenson. She appeared pale and tense in the dim lights of the submarine. A thin sheen of perspiration glazed her forehead. He had never seen her look so nervous, not even in the arms of El Aqrab. This dive was taking its toll. "Well, to keep your certification clean, you could always navigate with a blindfold," Decker said. He laughed thinly but Swenson simply turned away and began to stare out through the view port once again.

Speers grinned back. He had a gap between his two front teeth that made him appear much younger than he was. "Look, ma. No eyes," he said.

Swenson suddenly turned and glared at them. "Why don't you save the macho crap for afterwards? The testosterone level in here is making me nauseous."

"Yes, ma'am," said Speers. Swenson looked back out through the view port. Speers glanced at Decker, rolled his eyes and shrugged. "We should be bottom-side in ten," he said. "I'm getting a blowout, CTFM."

"What's that?" Decker inquired.

"Sunwest SS300 sonar. Medium range FM. It's what we use to search and navigate the bottom. We can track negative db targets the size of a gallon gas can at six hundred feet, a zero db object like a small boulder at fifteen hundred feet, and a plus twenty-five db feature like a ridge or slope at ranges of three thousand feet or more." He pointed to a fifteen-inch TFT flat panel. Five range rings were marked on the display. "State of the art," he said. "We also use acoustic pingers from twenty to fifty kilohertz. If there's a tunnel out there, we'll see it."

As he talked, he began to fiddle with the forward center panel. Decker watched him as he held a switch marked ENABLE in the down position. Then he pushed another switch for two more seconds. The DSV lurched forward momentarily.

"What was that?" asked Decker.

"Two of our ballast weights," said Speers. "We're almost on the bottom."

Decker studied the pilot carefully. He seemed to exude confidence. He obviously knew his ship like the back of his hand. "Hey, Speers. How come you volunteered for this duty?"

Without looking up he said, "Enlisted as a SEAL ten years ago. Been in tougher spots than this one, believe me. More than twenty of us signed up for this mission. I was lucky."

"Lucky?" said Swenson. "Is that what you call it?" She

laughed bleakly.

Speers looked at her, his face absolutely serious for the first time. "I got a wife and little girl back in Virginia. I'd like to see them again, if you know what I mean."

Swenson glanced back out through the view port. Decker nodded.

All of a sudden Swenson said, "There's the bottom." She seemed excited now. She pushed her face against the Plexiglas and breathed a deep sigh of relief. "The Young Canyons." She turned toward Decker and Speers. "Listen," she said. "About what I said before . . . "

"Don't worry about it," Speers replied.

She smiled weakly. A little color seemed to be returning to her face. "I didn't mean–"

"As Pilot-in-Command," Speers interrupted, "I have the authority to terminate any dive by whatever means necessary at any time I feel a hazard to the submersible or personnel exists, without regard to mission success or completion. Unquote." He winked at Swenson. "So unless you want to go back to the surface, just forget it."

She nodded and stared back through the view port. "There," she said. "Off the starboard beam."

Speers glanced at the TFT. "I see it."

"What?" said Decker, straining at the screen. Every inch of the sphere was covered with instrumentation: buttons and dials, lights and displays. It made the cockpit of a jet look simple. "See what?" he said.

"A tunnel," Speers replied. "A little small but serviceable."

Swenson turned toward Decker. "Better buckle up," she said. "We're going in."

Speers piloted the DSV into the opening with uncanny skill and they began to inch their way along the tunnel. When they had gone about two hundred meters, the tunnel dropped out below them, and they followed it, descending another hundred meters into the shelf. Then the tunnel straightened out, running parallel to the surface for another two hundred meters or more before narrowing. Several times, the DSV bumped walls. At one point, the tunnel veered off in a jagged dogleg. Speers asked Swenson if this was far enough, but she shook her head. After a few minutes, they managed to squeeze through.

When they could go no further, Speers finally hit the switch and turned and said, "That's it. We're done. It's just too narrow."

Swenson scanned the instruments. "Ok," she said. "It'll have to do."

For a while, none of them spoke. They knew what Speers was doing at the console – trying to plant the nuclear device in the wall. He moved the instruments with care. They watched it on the monitor. The modified Tomahawk warhead appeared much bigger than El Aqrab's small briefcase bomb. It was shaped like an artillery shell. There was a tense moment as the release caught for a second, but Speers used one of the robotic arms to push the bomb away. It wobbled, started to fall, then finally settled on a shelf carved in the tunnel wall. Speers backed the ship up slightly before using the manipulator to arm the mechanism.

Then they began to back out down the tunnel. When they had gone about a hundred meters, as they were rounding the dogleg, the ship caught against the wall, and the vessel seemed to stall.

"What's happening?" said Decker. "What's going on?"

"The starboard manipulator arm is caught," said Speers. The thrusters moaned, then ground down to a halt.

"What does that mean?"

Speers shook his head. For the first time in the dive he looked worried.

Swenson sighed and said, "It means we're stuck."

Chapter 46
Friday, February 4 – 6:00 AM
Bermuda

The wave encroached upon the Caribbean. On a beautiful, manicured golf course on the island of Bermuda, Seamus Gallagher was enjoying an early-morning round at the Mid Atlantic Golf Club – ignoring every call from his office. He was only on the second hole, a grueling 471-yard par 5, and he was already in trouble. His ball had blown off to the side into the high rough overlooking the Atlantic. He scowled as he tried to get a good look at the pin. It was still pretty dark. He hated par 5s. His eyesight wasn't what it had been, he recalled nostalgically. He couldn't even see the fucking flag.

Gallagher settled into his stance, swiveled his hips and studied the ball. *Remember the wind,* he told himself. He looked back at the distant green. He wiggled his driver. Then he stared down at the ball again. As he began his swing, he was suddenly distracted by a thunderclap to the east. He sliced the ball.

"Fuck," he said. "Fuck, fuck, fuck." He threw the club down on the ground. Then he stared up at the sky as the ball curved round and tumbled toward the sea, bouncing once on the rocks below before disappearing into the surf. He turned toward his caddy, an old black man with a lime green shirt, but – luckily – the caddy seemed distracted. He hadn't seen him make a complete and utter fool of himself. The sound of thunder grew more intense.

Gallagher turned to follow the caddy's gaze and, as he did so, he noticed the tide retreating from the flats at an alarming pace. Where his ball had disappeared – only a moment before, into the surf – was now dry land. "Hey, what the . . . " he started to say when he finally noticed the wave.

It was a mile or two away. No, less. At first Gallagher thought he must be seeing things. The wave looked to be fifteen stories high. He picked up his driver. He held it against his chest. "Jesus Christ," he said, completely stupefied. He looked up at the sky. The wave was already on him. It was already there. And for some reason, his whole life didn't flash before his eyes, nor did he see his family and friends, the sacred places of his heart. All that he noticed was the divot at his feet, that patch of tattered grass. He bent down to replace it as the wave washed him away.

* * *

Speers continued to struggle with the switch panel, trying to leverage the six degrees of movement in the starboard manipulator arm: the shoulder pitch and yaw; the elbow pitch; the wrist pitch and rotation. He even tried to open and close the hand, but the *Alvin* wouldn't budge. He cursed and reached for the position feedback master/slave mechanism that controlled the port manipulator. He began to extend the arm. Decker could see the hand outside his view port gradually reach out until it was practically touching the tunnel wall. Then it stopped.

"What are you doing?" he asked.

Speers cursed again. "The port manipulator has a maximum extension of seventy-four inches. I was hoping to push us free."

"No luck?"

"It isn't long enough," said Speers. "Hold on. I've got an idea."

Speers pushed the master and the wrist began to torque. "Fully extended," the pilot continued, "the arm has a lift capacity of only one hundred and fifty pounds. But the wrist torque is rated at thirty feet over pounds, with a rotational speed of sixty-five rpm."

At first Decker didn't understand. Then he realized that Speers was trying to use the port manipulator arm to lever the starboard arm away. There was the sound of metal scraping stone. The tunnel wall began to crumble and the ship finally pulled free.

"That was fun," said Speers, looking over with a grin.

"Yeah," said Decker, smiling back. "Let's stay and do it again."

Speers whooped and laughed as they continued their ascent. Within fifteen minutes, they were back out in the open water of the blowout. But they were running out of time. If they were to detonate the bomb and intercept the mega-tsunami, they'd have to do it while still dangerously close. Without saying it, each of them knew exactly what this meant. The blast would probably kill them. It would hurl the small submersible against the Continental Shelf. Unless they could initiate a considerable amount of negative buoyancy, they'd be smashed to pieces.

"Are you ready?" Speers said, reaching for the console. He had rigged up a temporary firing switch. "We're at the point of no return." Decker looked at Swenson. She nodded and turned away.

"Go ahead," said Decker.

"Fire in the hole," said Speers and pushed the button.

At first nothing seemed to happen. Not a sound. Not a

ripple. Then a huge explosion reverberated through the ship. The shock wave from the nuclear explosion hurled them roughly through the water column. The sound caught up. Decker felt as if his ears were bursting, and the power suddenly cut off. The ship was thrust into darkness.

After a few seconds, the emergency battery-powered lights flashed on. Swenson moved over to assist Speers in the navigation of the ship. Decker felt completely helpless. "What can I do?" he said.

"Nothing," said Speers, "unless you can replace these thrusters." He slapped the console and looked up. "Three of them are fried."

Swenson turned toward Speers and said, "They're the ones mounted athwartships, in the stern, designed to turn the vessel sideways."

"Plus forward and reverse," Speers added bleakly.

"Yeah, but the thrusters amidships, the ones that enable vertical lift are still operational, right?"

"We barely have any power. Even if we could somehow generate more buoyancy, and miraculously miss the shelf, I doubt we'd have enough thrust left to make it to the surface."

"I don't like the way that sounds," said Decker. "Let's not do that."

"It's our only choice," said Swenson.

They both looked at Decker. He shrugged and tried to smile. "Fine. Let's do that then. Sounds good. Sounds like a plan."

Speers laughed and checked the SERVICE RELEASE switch on the service bus to make sure it was in the up position. Then he released the remaining ballast weights by holding the ENABLE switches in the down position, and toggling them for two seconds. The vessel shuddered. The DSV began to climb, then stalled. The current was just too strong.

Suddenly, another noise, as loud as the explosion of the bomb, perhaps louder, echoed through the craft. Decker could feel it in his bones. The ship vibrated as though they were swimming through a kettledrum.

"The shelf-edge," Swenson cried. "It's beginning to collapse."

A sound like two giant steel plates rubbing against each other reverberated through the ship. She was rocked by yet another blast. The DSV began to tumble, to freefall through the ocean depths.

"We're going to have to blow the ballast tanks," said Speers.

"We're being sucked down by the shelf."

"You can't do that," cried Swenson. "We're still below a thousand meters."

"We've got no choice. If we don't, we're going to hit the wall."

Without waiting for an answer, he checked to make sure the ballast vents were shut. Then he reached toward the lower part of the port distribution panel and began to blow the aft and forward tanks. He continued to push the switches intermittently, shooting air into the tanks. Decker couldn't feel a thing. "Nothing's happening," he shouted above the din.

Speers pointed at the computer console. "*Alvin* says it is," he cried. "That's a temperature-compensated quartz oscillator pressure transducer," he added with a smile. "Try and say that fast three times! Look out your view port. You see that Bourdon dial embedded in the housing? No, over there," he said and pointed. "That little tube on the right?"

The entire ship was vibrating. Decker glanced out of his view port and noticed an instrument just outside the Plexiglas. He had no idea how to read it, but he was comforted by the fact that it appeared to be moving. Very slowly.

Speers continued to push the VENT switch. "We're ascending but it isn't fast enough. I'll have to jettison the manipulators and the batteries."

"Don't we need the batteries?" asked Decker.

"They won't do us any good if we're in a thousand pieces on the seafloor." Speers began to fiddle with the red-bordered emergency release switches on the dump panel located at the top of the center console. First he de-energized the "A" main battery closest to *Alvin's* center of gravity by pushing the 120-volt contactor switch. Then he unfastened his safety belt. He staggered aft and port, approaching the science rack.

"What are you doing?" Swenson cried. "Sit down, for Christ's sake!"

Speers smiled. "Got to cut the safety wire." He reached into the science rack and pulled out a pair of wire cutters.

The air seemed to explode. Decker felt himself pitch sideways as the DSV rolled over and over, and the emergency lights went out. He felt his stomach rise into his throat. Unmoored, Speers hurtled against the bulkhead. He bounced like a ball inside a lottery cage as the ship tumbled out of control. Swenson screamed. It was a loud shrill sound that seemed to pierce his heart, followed by a sickening *thwack.*

The ship began to finally turn as the thrusters heaved against the torque. Decker felt a freezing liquid splash his face. The emergency lights flicked on. He looked over at Swenson. Her face was pale as snow. A thin mist of water was spraying from a hole in the hull. He looked at Speers who was curled up on the deck. His head flapped back and forth as the ship continued to right herself. His neck was clearly broken. His baby blue eyes stared blankly into space.

A moment later, the "heading hold" autopilot linked to the gyrocompass kicked in, and the vessel toggled upright. Decker looked out his view port. The DSV was descending once again.

"Emily," shouted Decker. "We're still going down!"

She glanced blankly at him, then continued to stare at Speers. A thin stream of blood was dripping from the pilot's mouth.

"What happened?" Decker asked.

"The ballast tanks. Expanding air as we ascended." Swenson shook her head. "I told him."

Decker unfastened his seatbelt, reached out for her. He cradled her in his arms. "Are you alright?" he said. "Anything broken?" He began to pat her body.

Swenson didn't answer. She didn't respond at all. She had a nasty red welt on one cheek where Speers must have struck her as he bounced about the sphere. She was in shock.

"Oh, Emily," he said. Decker pressed her against his chest. "Please, Emily, snap out of it." He started to shake her but she barely seemed to respond. "Emily, wake up! I don't know how to pilot this thing."

"I told him," she continued. Her voice was flat, robotic.

Decker continued to shake her. "We're going to die, Emily, if you don't help me. Do you hear me? I gave up my gun. For you, Emily, for you! I never thought I'd feel . . . " The words caught in his throat.

She looked up at his face but her eyes remain unfocussed. They seemed to stare right through him. Then she said, "You never thought you'd what?"

"Don't you get it?" His voice began to break. "I love you, Emily." He started to laugh. "And I haven't even kissed you yet," he said. "Listen to me! I said I fucking love you."

Swenson's eyes began to focus. She looked at Decker, a quizzical expression on her face. She put a hand around her jaw and started to move it back and forth, opening her mouth. "What did you say? Ouch! That hurts."

Decker smiled. "You heard me." Then he winced and said, "You did, didn't you? Didn't you?"

"You said you'd love to fuck me, right?" she answered with a grin. "Ouch! Don't make me smile. It hurts."

He laughed and squeezed her in his arms. "Only if we live. Now get off your ass and drive this thing."

Swenson unfastened her seatbelt and dropped into the pilot's seat. "Where are those wire cutters?" she asked, cinching the seatbelt tight around her waist.

Decker spotted them on the deck. He handed them to her.

"Strap yourself in," she said. "I don't want to lose you too."

Decker sat down and fastened his seatbelt as tight as it would go.

Swenson lifted the red cover on the emergency battery panel, cut the safety wire, placed the switch to the ON position, and flipped the switch on the dump panel. The ship lurched suddenly to port as the starboard manipulator fell away. Decker glimpsed it through the view port even though the outside lights no longer functioned. He could feel the DSV begin to rise.

Swenson flipped three other switches. The ship shuddered and the emergency lights went out. Decker was momentarily disorientated. Swenson turned on her flashlight. "The batteries," she said. "Don't worry. We don't need the co^2 scrubber anymore. There's enough oxygen in here to get us to the surface. At least I hope so."

The ship began to ascend more rapidly. "It's going to be close," she said, pointing at the computer screen. "Just one more thing to do."

She unfastened her safety belt and got down on her hands and knees. There was a small metal plate in the deck. "Hand me that T-wrench," she said. "It's over there, in the science rack. Hurry." Water sprayed across her face.

Decker unfastened his belt and brought her the wrench. "What are you doing?"

"Ever watch *Star Trek*?"

He nodded.

"You know how they sometimes separate the saucer from the thrusters? Same thing. I'm going to release the sphere from the forebody assembly. That'll make us about three thousand pounds more buoyant." She lifted the plate in the deck and removed the pin at the top of the release shaft. Then she replaced the plate and locked it in place with screws from the underside of the plate screw holes. When it was tightly secured, she inserted the T-wrench into the socket. "Okay," she said, climbing to her feet. "We're going to have to secure everything in the sphere. Once I release the forebody assembly, we're going to shoot up like a bubble toward the surface."

They began to stow their gear. Decker assumed the grisly task of lashing Speers into a seat. He had stopped bleeding. Decker closed the dead pilot's eyes and turned his head away. Then he and Swenson sat down and buckled up.

"Are you ready?" she asked him, looking over. Swenson had reassumed the pilot's chair. All her anxiety and fear seemed to have dissipated. Her face was flushed now, her eyes shiny and alert. "We have less than a minute before we hit the wall."

"I'm ready," he said.

She reached out and curled her hand around the T-wrench. "We may pass out," she said, looking up at him. Then she smiled. "And by the way," she added, "I love you too."

She pulled the T-wrench suddenly, without waiting for a response. A second later Decker heard a tearing noise as the forebody assembly tumbled free. Then the sphere shot upwards, gliding only seven meters above the new lip of the Continental Shelf.

The speed of the ascent forced the air out of his lungs. He felt as though he were in a rocket, with a one-ton weight pressed down upon his chest. His eyes stretched open, his mouth pulled down involuntarily, and suddenly the flames surrounded him again. They licked up through the tan upholstery, melting the plastic lining, engulfing the Chevy Biscayne. He was still trapped in back. He was still trapped. He reached out for the door, and suddenly he was standing on the ground, unharmed, and he was watching as the fire gradually consumed the car, his mother's face, his father's hair and ears and nose, and they were gone, and there was nothing he could do, but watch.

There was a mighty crash, an eerie high-pitched whistle as Decker's ears popped and he slipped into unconsciousness, reclining into chaos.

Chapter 47
Friday, February 4 – 6:42 AM
The Western Atlantic Ocean

The ocean rolled across herself. Black waves arose and fell, arose to meet another falling to another, falling to another still. The whitecaps skated on the surface. They heaved and lifted up and, suddenly, a mound of water bubbled up and boiled across the surface of the cold Atlantic.

A few miles off the Jersey coast, the landslide had begun. The moving mass cascaded downward, barely missing the ascending DSV. It shivered along the groaning Continental Shelf, and fell and fell and fell, ripping up sand and stone, down toward the bottomless abyss.

The water bulged, displaced by the falling landmass, began to rise and spread, to thrust the surface of the ocean skyward, a hundred meters in the air.

The mega-tsunami rolled across the sea, due east across the vast expanse. And sliding west, still rushing from La Palma, the other wave drew near.

They came together in a mighty splash that lifted spray into the clouds, a quarter of a mile above the surface of the sea. The walls of water flattened out against each other, blended and roiled into a liquid copulation, a reliquification, then bellowed with expended energy. They were one. The great wave crowned, and fell, tired of traveling. Spent. The water spread across the surface of the ocean, tickled by whitecaps. It coursed across the sea, shedding yet more kinetic energy. Then it reverberated westward once again.

The wave descended on the *Stanfield* as she turned her bow into the wall of water, as she bounced and heaved and rose up through the turbulence, and sluiced ahead unharmed. The wave passed by.

It ran ashore in Canada, then northern Maine. Almost immediately, the Boston harbor drained, then filled again, as the wave collided with the coast. It coursed along the rocky shore, rolled south-southwest, eating up trees and houses, tearing up river mouths, demolishing roads and bridges, entire seaside towns. The skeptical who had remained behind, ignoring the orders of the National Guard, were pulverized, dismembered as they tried to flee.

Within a half hour, the waters began to recede from Fire

Island and the entire eastern shoreline of Long Island. It was as if someone has pulled a giant stopper from the bottom of the sea. Then the wave came into view – two stories high.

It washed across the lowlands of Long Island. It cut a swath across both Queens and Brooklyn, swept up the Verrazano Narrows, past Staten Island, past Governor's Island and up onto the Battery. Lower Manhattan was inundated as the wave diverged along the East and Hudson Rivers. Cars bounced like corks along the empty streets of the Financial District, up Broadway past Grace Church, past Midtown, Central Park, to Harlem and beyond.

A few small buildings fell apart. Ellis Island vanished. So too the Statue of Liberty, from the legs down. Her torso, head and torch remained above the sea. As the wave finally struck the Jersey coast and drove across the land, as it funneled up the Hudson River, the Statue reappeared completely.

She shook, she seemed to stumble, but she did not fall.

Chapter 48
Friday, February 4 – 6:58 AM
The Western Atlantic Ocean

The *Alvin* bobbed to the surface some fifty kilometers off the coast in open water. It was dawn. The sun drifted on the pink horizon to the east. The vessel issued a groan for solace as she floated free.

Inside the DSV, the VHF radio cawed. "Surface Controller to *Alvin*. *Alvin*, come in please. *Alvin*, come in."

The bodies did not stir. Speers, Decker and Swenson remained within their seats, completely motionless. Lifeless.

"*Alvin*, this is Surface Controller, do you read me?" Suddenly the voice changed as Warhaftig snatched the radio. "For God's sake, Decker, are you there? Are you alright?"

Decker began to stir. His head rolled to the side. He opened his eyes and shook himself to consciousness. He reached out for the radio. "This is *Alvin*," he said groggily. "Go ahead, Surface Controller."

"Thank heavens. Is everything OK?"

Decker looked around him. Swenson was beginning to awaken. Her eyes were fluttering. Her eyelashes moved like butterflies.

"Speers didn't make it," Decker said. "But Emily and I are okay. What about the rest of the world?"

"It worked, John! Some destruction, of course, but loss of life in the States was minimal – nothing like we feared. Thanks to you two. We've had hurricanes that caused more damage. The Caribbean islands took a hit though. So did Brazil. We're about seven miles east of you. We'll be there in a few minutes to pick you up. Sorry to hear about Speers."

Decker looked over at the dead pilot. "He saved our lives, Otto. We never would have made it without him."

"Listen, I have the President on the line. He wants to congratulate you personally. You and Emily are heroes. Once Manhattan drains, I'm sure they're going to want to throw you a ticker tape parade. Can you hear me, John? John, I'm going to put the President through now. Just hold on and–"

Decker turned the radio off. He unfastened his seatbelt and helped Emily to her feet. Then he climbed up the ladder and opened the hatch. The submersible was suddenly filled with cold air. It was salty and wet and delicious. He stared out at the tranquil sea, to the east, as the sun rolled on the shimmering horizon.

The case was over, he thought. In all probability, El Aqrab was dead. The world was safe. At least for now. And suddenly he remembered what Hassan had told him with such uncanny prescience: *One day – mark my words – if this quicksand isn't filled, if we Americans don't at least address the Palestinian problem even-handedly, the extremists throughout the Arab world will rise up like a great wave, and it will kill us all.* It almost had.

Swenson climbed up and stood beside him. He glanced down at her, smiled, and took her in his arms. The dawn glowed pink and lavender and bronze as intermittent light rays played upon the surface of the waves. "Red sky in the morning," he began.

Swenson leaned a little closer. "Sailor, take warning," she said, and they folded together in a kiss.

THE END

A Note About This Book

While *THE WAVE* may be a work of fiction, the science concerning mega-tsunamis presented in this novel is very much based in fact.

As Emily Swenson says about the inevitability of the fall of the Cumbre Vieja volcano on La Palma, "I'm afraid you don't understand, Agent Decker. It's not about likelihood. It's a certainty. The only variable is time."

At some point in the future, the island will come apart and a mega-tsunami will stream across the Atlantic at the speed of a jet plane, obliterating the entire Easter Seaboard of the United States, killing more than forty million people, thirteen percent of the U.S. population. And hundreds of millions will be injured, one out of every three Americans. It will cause trillions of dollars in damage. The entire U.S. economy will be disrupted for years, if not permanently crippled.

This is not speculation. This is a fact, made more horrible when you consider these estimates are based on today's population figures and currency evaluations. It may happen in one thousand years, or it may happen tomorrow . . . but it will occur.

As our natural world is increasingly influenced by Man — through global warming, pollution and overpopulation — it is not inconceivable that someone, at some point, will intentionally disrupt our planet on a monumental scale. Indeed, one could claim global warming is a form of eco-terrorism, since most scientists are well aware of the consequences of co^2 emissions, and yet we continue to burn fossil fuels with abandon.

THE WAVE may be a work of fiction. But it is not beyond the realm of possibility.

J.G. Sandom

About the Author

Born in Chicago, raised and educated throughout Europe, and a graduate of Amherst College (where he won the Academy of American Poets Prize), J.G. Sandom founded the nation's first digital ad agency (Einstein and Sandom Interactive – EASI) in 1984, before launching an award-wining writing career.

The author has written six thrillers and mysteries including *The God Machine*, *Gospel Truths*, and *The Hunting Club*, plus three young adult novels under the pseudonym T.K. Welsh, including *The Unresolved* and *Resurrection Men*. He is currently working on a sequel to *THE WAVE* called *THE PLAGUE*.

Visit the author at www.jgsandom.com.

# # #

COMING SOON!

An excerpt from . . .

THE PLAGUE

A John Decker Thriller

Prologue

Friday, December 13

I am what I dream, what I've done, what I've seen, what I choose to remember. What I choose to forget. I choose. I . . . came home early that afternoon, around 4:00 PM, after a hard day at the office. The day that I realized. Traffic was light going north from the Farm, for a change, and I made all the lights on Dorado. Another perfect sunset, I thought, I remember, as I rolled down the window. Breathing sagebrush, I thought that the sky looked a lot like a national flag, striped with purple and orange and pink. It was hot for December.

I left the car in the driveway because my three year old daughter had built some kind of castle from boxes and blankets inside the garage. I could see her now. She was playing in the sprinkler at the edge of the yard, dressed in a neon-lime bathing suit. She laughed and looked up at me, waving. I waved back. That, I remember. I had my briefcase in one hand, with all of its secrets, and I lifted the other, and waved.

My wife was waiting for me in the kitchen. She was wearing that apron with the pair of bosc pears on the front, baking cookies or bread, but she turned toward me anyway and gave me a peck on the cheek. "How was your day?" she said, twisting back to the stove.

I told her about the Indian house crickets I'd heard chirping in the stand of Huisache trees down the street. When she didn't say anything, I went down the hall to our bedroom. I took off my jacket and tie, and I wept.

All that I'd come to believe, all that I was, and still am, came apart in my hands then – like my tie. All simply unraveled. I put my jacket back on. I needed the jacket to hide it.

I hurried outside, to the back yard, to breathe. Mr. Billings was mowing his lawn down the street. He mows it every three days, no matter what time of year. It didn't seem right for him to be mowing his lawn with all of those holiday decorations behind him. The blow-up reindeer and sled. The Santa tied to the chimney. He had bound up each bush in his garden with Christmas lights. He would have wrapped up the tumbleweeds too if he could have caught them.

I'd just reclined on a sling garden lounge chair when my wife came outside with a tray of iced tea. Under her apron, she was wearing a pair of tan stirrup pants, and a dark indigo shirt, no – iron blue, like her eyes. Her eyes.

She stood over me, smiled, and gave me a glass. I could hear the sprinkler splash-splashing, and my daughter laughing nearby. I could hear those damned Indian house crickets. I could hear Mr. Billings still mowing his lawn. Still mowing, but something was wrong. I could feel it.

I took a sip of my tea. I looked up at my wife, at her honey blond hair, her waxed eyebrows, her nose, and her perfect pink lips. I looked into her eyes. Everything was wrong.

I reached into my jacket, took my gun out and shot her – two times – in the chest.

Bang, bang.

More like two stifled sneezes than gunshots. Or the clanging of stones under water.

No one stirred. My daughter still played in the sprinkler, oblivious. And the incessant refrain of Mr. Billings's lawnmower never wavered or stilled. It droned on and on as I climbed to my feet. I stood over her, I looked down at the livid red blood pumping out of her chest, at her iron-blue, china-doll eyes.

I put the gun on the lounge chair. I stared up at the sky, and felt myself soar toward the heavens, over my rooftop and lot, higher and higher, the tract houses blending together in lines, sinuous oxbow contortions, with oases of shimmering swimming pools punctuating the desert, as the Talking Heads' Once in a Lifetime unrolled like a band of black, bitter licorice through my head.

"And you may find yourself in a beautiful house, with a beautiful wife, And you may ask yourself – well . . . how did I get here . . . And you may tell yourself, This is not my beautiful wife."

Through the clouds I rose, higher and higher.

"And you may ask yourself, am I right? Am I wrong? And you may tell yourself, My god! What have I done?"

6144509R0

Made in the USA
Lexington, KY
27 July 2010